mary malone
Never Tear Us Apart

POOLBEG
Crimson

Published 2009
by Poolbeg Press Ltd
123 Grange Hill, Baldoyle
Dublin 13, Ireland
E-mail: poolbeg@poolbeg.com

© Mary Malone 2009

The moral right of the author has been asserted.

Typesetting, layout, design © Poolbeg Press Ltd.

1 3 5 7 9 10 8 6 4 2

A catalogue record for this book is available from the British Library.

ISBN 978-1-84223-413-6

Typeset by Patricia Hope in Sabon 10.2/14
Printed by
Litografia Rosés, S.A., Spain

www.poolbeg.com

Note on the author

Mary Malone lives in Templemartin, Bandon, County Cork with her husband, Pat, and sons, David and Mark. As well as being a novelist and freelance journalist, she works in the Central Statistics Office in Cork. *Never Tear Us Apart* is her third novel. For more information, visit her website www.marymalone.ie

Acknowledgements

Being a published author is my dream come true. But without the help of others I couldn't continue living this dream.

Thank you so much to Poolbeg management and staff. I promise to keep up my end of the bargain and work my socks off! Special mention to Paula Campbell and Kieran Devlin who made my Christmas by taking a chance on me and offering me a contract. To Gaye Shortland – a magical editor with the ability to transform ugly ducklings into magnificent swans – I want to express my sincere gratitude for your insight, your time and patience. Working with you has been fantastic! Thank you so much. Huge thanks also to Niamh, Sarah and David for your commitment to *Never Tear Us Apart*. I know it's in safe hands with such a reliable team behind it.

And to my family: the best family in the world as far as I'm concerned. A huge thank-you to the three men in my life, Pat, David and Mark, who are there for me through thick and thin, reminding me I should be writing when I'm watching telly, always on hand to offer a male perspective for storylines and three willing volunteers to share in the celebrations when the opportunities arise.

Nothing gives me greater pleasure than dedicating *Never Tear Us Apart* to Mam. I'm the luckiest daughter in the world having a mother who is also a best friend. Mam promotes my writing at every given opportunity but, more than that, she's a huge part of everything I do, always on hand with wise words of wisdom.

Thanks to Barry, Miriam, Brian and Avril for their stalwart support. It's time to let everybody know I have a book out again! I know I can rely on my niece and nephew to point their aunty's book out to anyone prepared to listen.

Yet again, I have to thank my extended family and many close friends, work colleagues, neighbours and fellow writers for their support, promotional work and the fun they bring to my life!

Thanks to my cousin, Garda Ken Walsh, who painstakingly answers my questions and advises me on procedures, trusting my word that I'm not about to murder somebody and it's all in the name of fiction! And a special mention to his sons, Jack and Alex, who are my trusty Dublin book spies.

Gemma and Daragh Caulwell have also become very adept at rearranging bookshop shelves. Thank you both.

Thank you, Anita Notaro and Gráinne Fox, for invaluable professional advice.

Thanks to all the newspapers, magazines, websites and radio stations who informed the world that my books were out there. I have to give special mention to Des Breen and John Dolan in the *Evening Echo*. Your generosity is very much appreciated.

Thank you to bookshops everywhere for the warm welcome you extended when I visited. You made my journeys (near and far) very worthwhile and I look forward to seeing you again this year.

And finally, I'd like to extend a huge thank-you to my readers. A book is worth nothing unless people are prepared to delve between the pages. So thank you to everybody who reads *Never Tear Us Apart*. Please visit my website **www.marymalone.ie** and send me a message to let me know what you think.

With all my love, Mam.
This one is for you.
Thank you for a lifetime of good memories.

Prologue

IRISH INDEPENDENT – BREAKING NEWS

Discovery of Body Upgraded to Murder

The body of a woman discovered late last night when Gardaí were called to an apartment complex in a North Co Dublin suburb has been identified as that of a twenty-eight-year-old employee with Ellis Enterprise.

A postmortem investigation carried out yesterday revealed that the woman had died from head injuries. "Her death is being treated as suspicious," according to Detective Superintendent Karl Wilson who is leading the investigation.

Neighbours describe her as pleasant and polite but refrained from further comment. Detective Superintendent Wilson says the Gardaí are gathering evidence and following several lines of enquiry.

Searches by crime officers are continuing in the premises where her body was found. Her name cannot

*be released until all family members have been
notified.*

*Gardaí are looking for witnesses and would
appreciate any information in strictest confidence to
Clontarf Garda Station at 01-6664800.*

Chapter 1

Four days earlier

Sitting at her office desk on Friday afternoon, Vicky Jones found it impossible to concentrate on her work, an imaginary clock ticking loudly in her head, every passing second adding to her anxiety. She stared at the computer screen in front of her, twisting her blonde hair into a knot around her fingers, holding it tightly in place for a moment before letting it fall in soft waves to her shoulders once more. How she wished she could do the same with the concerns jiggling around in her head.

She glanced at her watch. Fintan should be home by now after the lunch-time stint at the club. She wondered about his afternoon and what he would do to pass the time. She wondered for the umpteenth time what he was hiding from her.

Her fingers itched to pick up the phone and call him.

It would be reassuring to hear his voice but she knew after that she'd want more. He could tell her anything over the phone. If he answered the land-line, he could pretend he was sitting at home alone with his feet up. And if she caught him on his mobile, he could say he was in the supermarket picking up some groceries. But she still wouldn't know for sure. She still wouldn't know if he was telling the truth.

She glanced at the door to her boss's office. How long more would the meeting last? Should she dare take a chance? She chewed on her bottom lip as she thought about it but waited a moment too long because right on cue – right when she was on the verge of making a dash from her desk, running all the way to the DART station and grabbing the first train to Malahide to hurry home and check up on Fintan – the door opened and Ariel Satlow burst out.

Her brown eyes were flashing in fury. She pulled the door shut firmly behind her and made a beeline for Vicky's desk, banging the file she was carrying down on the hardwood surface. She barely took the time to draw breath before launching into a litany of complaint.

Vicky exhaled slowly, the confines of the office stifling, Ariel's dramatic entrance overpowering. Reaching for the bottle of water on her desk, she filled her glass and took a long, refreshing drink, forgoing any notion of sneaking away and giving her full attention to her colleague instead.

"Things didn't go well with Ben then?"

Ariel shook her head, her dark hair shining under the

bright fluorescent light. "Understatement of the year! I can't get anything right around here any more." She picked up the file with both hands, banging it on the desk once more for effect. "This week is going from bad to worse!"

"I thought you two had a meeting about your accounts already this morning? Surely Ben's not still harping on about the same thing?"

"Yeah, he did speak to me earlier – just as I was getting ready to leave for that meeting with clients."

"What bad timing!"

Ariel nodded, inhaling a long deep breath through her nose before letting it escape noisily through her lips. "He wasn't one bit impressed with the work I'd handed up. I could barely concentrate on the presentation I had to give to that company afterwards!" She planted her backside on the edge of Vicky's desk.

"I can imagine."

"Nothing I send in is good enough any more. I haven't lifted my head since I got back from my meeting and he's firing accusations at me as though I'm sitting around filing my nails!" She nervously flicked imaginary dust from her fitted black skirt. "I don't have a problem taking correction, Vicky. You know that. But this? This is downright unfair."

Vicky nodded her understanding, trying to think of something to say that wouldn't sound disloyal to either party. Working as Ben's Personal Assistant had its awkward moments. Like the one she was in with Ariel now.

"He's under a lot of pressure with the tax-return deadline only a few weeks away," she ventured.

"And him being under pressure is probably my fault to begin with," the other girl deadpanned.

"But you're only human! And mistakes happen to everyone."

"But these weren't my mistakes! I know they weren't!" Ariel clasped and unclasped the delicate diamond bracelet she wore on her slim wrist. "I've hardly ever made cock-ups in my accounts before and now it's as if everything I touch turns to mush." She lowered her voice, a trace of uncertainty in her eyes as she leaned in closer to Vicky. "That's two accounts I've messed up today. Add them to the other mishaps this week and it makes five altogether! If I'm not careful, I'll be out on my ear. And I won't be able to explain why, which will look great on a job application."

Vicky chewed her lip. "And you're sure they were okay when you finished them?"

Ariel let out a long sigh, flicking absent-mindedly through the pages in her file. "I couldn't be more positive."

"So how do you explain the errors?"

She stared at the ground for a moment and shook her head. "I can't . . . When he called me in just now to go over the mistakes I'd made on the Hennessy account, I felt like such an imbecile. What if he lets me go, Vicky? What if my job is on the line?" She brought her hands to her face and groaned.

"Now you're being silly. He's always held you in the highest regard."

Ariel was one of the most popular consultants within the company, the person with the highest number of requests for repeat business. And the majority of her new accounts came to her on recommendation for a job well done.

"Huh! Not any more he doesn't!"

"As far as I know, he has a video conference with Hennessys later. Maybe that's why he's treating whatever you're working on with such urgency? He's probably under pressure to get things finished. You know what some of these companies are like. Particularly when it comes to making tax returns."

But yet again Vicky's words failed to console.

Ariel fiddled absent-mindedly with the diamond studs in her ears and stared into the distance, catching a glimpse of the DART as it sped along in a blur of green. "No. Ben doesn't yield under duress. And the clients rely on us to keep an eye on deadlines, not the other way around! No. The only person Ben has issue with at the moment is me. He's like a dog with a bone."

"I hope it's not me you're gossiping about, girls!" Marcus, one of the other consultants, wagged a finger as he approached them, strolling in the direction of the tiny cafeteria, an empty coffee cup in his hand.

"You wish!" Ariel turned to face him, laughing with him when he shrugged and smiled, his warm green eyes twinkling.

"Don't worry, Marcus. We've got much more exciting things to discuss!" Vicky called after him and then turned back to Ariel. "What were we saying? Oh, yes. A dog with a bone. Not very friendly then, I take it?"

"Definitely not. More like the leading husky pulling a heavily laden sleigh!" Ariel let out a long sigh.

Vicky smirked, visualising a team of huskies with her boss barking orders from the front. "Let's hope his bark is worse than his bite then!"

"I won't be taking any chances. At the rate he's checking my work he'd be better off actually doing it himself. He might trust me enough to look over the figures before they're returned to the client." She picked up the file and hugged it to her chest. "I was this close, Vicky," she made a gesture with her index finger and thumb, "to pressing delete on the set of accounts he had open on his desktop. If he's going to treat me like a child, why shouldn't I act like one!"

She delivered her last sentence as more of a statement than a question, glancing behind her towards Ben's office, opening her mouth wide and letting out a silent scream.

Vicky watched her closely, noticing her flushed cheeks and exasperated expression. She also recognised the hurt and confusion in her eyes.

"It's not like you to let things get you down. You're usually so . . ."

"Usually so what? Calm? Measured?"

Vicky pushed her chair slightly back from her desk. "So in control. I was going to say you're usually so in control."

"But I'm not in control. I can't understand what's happened and none of the others are getting the gruelling he's giving me. Then again, they're all men! I'm the only female on the team." She shrugged indifferently as if she had already given up the race.

"You're not suggesting Ben is sexist, are you?"

Ariel inhaled a slow, deep breath. "It's not something I've noticed before but it has to be more than a coincidence that he's singling me out. What do you think? Could there be a grain of truth in it? Have you ever noticed a chauvinistic side to him?"

"That's a fairly loaded accusation, Ariel." And, after all, the errors in the accounts *did* exist, she thought. Her fingers flew across her keyboard as she clicked on her electronic scheduler and added a reminder entry to the tasks column, her eyes focusing on the screen in front of her. "You're sure you haven't anything else bothering you? Anything distracting you?" She stopped typing and looked up again, assessing the girl sitting at the edge of her desk.

Ariel shook her head. "No. Nothing's distracting me. That's not it." She dropped her gaze to the floor once more.

"Pressure of work?" Vicky prompted.

But she met with another cul-de-sac.

"If anything, I work better under pressure."

"Put it behind you is my advice then."

But Ariel wasn't quite ready to let go. "The only solution I can come up with is that the place must be haunted." She smiled. "Little gremlins living in our computers, dancing around the files when we're not at our desks. Can you imagine them?"

"Do you think they'd show their faces if we asked them nicely?"

Ariel giggled at the absurdity of their conversation "Unlikely," she conceded. "I'd better get back to work or Ben will be shouting for figures." She ran her fingers through her black shoulder-length hair, sweeping it back from her pretty face, then jumped up from the desk in haste at the sound of Ben's door opening.

"Ariel, why are you still here? And was that my name I heard?"

She swung around to face him. "Oh, er, yes, Ben. I'm just discussing some files with Vicky, telling her I needed to get them back to you as soon as possible." Her voice was unsteady, her tone guarded, as if she was waiting for him to fire yet another accusation in her direction.

"Since when did you need Vicky's advice to get things done?"

A deep red blush began in the hollow of Ariel's throat, creeping along her slim neck and into her cheeks, embarrassment spreading all over her face. "Vicky's helping me tidy up a few correspondence lists," she improvised. "That's all."

"I thought I told you I needed that file straight away. You're not going to get it done standing gossiping to Vicky! Prioritise, Ariel. The correspondence can wait. What about deadlines? Do they mean anything to you any more?" He put his hands in his trouser pockets and stood a couple of feet away from her as he waited for her to respond, the deep-etched lines around his eyes a trademark of his fifty-five years, his broad shoulders and lean physique a testament to regular visits to the swimming pool.

"Yes, of course they do. I'm always working with deadlines in mind."

Dropping her head for the briefest of seconds, Ariel

8

took a few steps away from Vicky's desk. But then she stopped and turned to face Ben again, straightening her posture and pulling herself up to her full five feet, seven inches – five feet, eight and a half including the heels she was wearing.

"If I have to stay up all night, I will sort this mess out. I will get to the bottom of it, Ben," she promised. "Those mistakes weren't my doing." She moved swiftly towards her office, shutting the door quietly behind her.

Once inside the door, Ariel leaned against it, closed her eyes and waited for her heart rate to return to normal.

Chapter 2

Ariel's departure left Vicky feeling uncomfortable in Ben's company. She'd seldom seen him lose his temper outside the confines of a private office. And only then when he was under serious pressure.

"Is there anything I can do to help?" she asked him in an attempt to fill the lengthening pause that had settled between them.

He raised an eyebrow, a hint of a smile playing around his lips. "Unless you've acquired a maths or financial degree overnight, I don't think there's very much you can do."

"No degrees here, I'm afraid,' she answered, shaking her head and smiling wryly, relieved to see that he was no longer wearing the 'beware' expression he'd had on for a large part of the day. She liked her boss but had learned to stay out of his way when things weren't running smoothly, also knowing that a cup of strong coffee was the quickest route to help him take the sting out of a bad day.

"I'm beginning to think you have the best degree of all under your belt," he said with a smile. "The degree of life, learned at the school of life. Sometimes I think it's worth more than all the certificates in the world. And it's free!"

Vicky nodded. She didn't agree with his philosophy that life's experiences came free of charge. There were times she regretted not trying for a more conventional qualification. But she wasn't about to tell him about the earlier years of her life. There were some things best left untold. Best left in the past.

"I was just going to make a coffee," she told him. "You look as though you could do with one."

Ben rubbed a hand over his early-afternoon shadow. "Go on then. I've a feeling I'll be stuck here for hours tonight and a few shots of espresso might help keep me awake."

"You work too many hours, Ben."

"Sometimes," he agreed. "But if I'm going to get all the files on my desk checked thoroughly and returned to the various companies by the deadline, I'll have to stay late. It's so unusual . . ." he began but then stopped abruptly. "I'd better call Jenny and let her know I'll miss dinner. Again!" He cast his eyes upward at the prospect of her scolding. "If I don't get things under control here soon, I won't have a home to go to!"

She wasn't sure if he was joking or not but the frustration in his voice left her in little doubt that his patience was wearing thin. "Let me get that espresso for you. I'm sure everything will be sorted out soon and we'll all be back on track."

"I wish I had your confidence, Vicky, but it's been one thing after another this week. I thought we were going to lose the McSweeney account when Revenue sent their auditors in." He scratched his head, his brow wrinkling in concentration. "You did send them that voucher and hamper I suggested?"

"Absolutely. I sent it by courier straight away, as well as a complimentary Spa hotel break for the G Hotel in Galway."

"Good thinking," Ben approved. "That might keep them happy for a while and hopefully prevent them from withdrawing their business any time soon."

"You know you have a group meeting with the consultants at half four?" she reminded him.

"Oh God, have I?" he groaned. "I didn't notice that on my calendar. I've been so preoccupied!"

"I'm not surprised with all that's going on, Ben. Anyway, if you didn't forget things every now and again, there'd be no need for me to sit outside your door!"

He leaned an elbow on the filing cabinet near Vicky's desk, checking the time on his watch and thinking aloud as he planned the rest of his day. "That means I've only got a couple of hours to get through another mountain of paperwork for the items on the agenda. And after the way the morning has gone, it might be time to add a few new items to that list. This meeting is well timed as it turns out and gives me the chance to shuffle things up a bit."

She raised an eyebrow but didn't pry. She'd find out soon enough what Ben's new strategies were. "I've made a start on a few things for you. The overall quarterly results are already compiled. It should speed things up a bit for you at least. I can email them to you and you can take a look before the meeting."

"Thanks, Vicky. You're a lifesaver. Pity others wouldn't take a leaf from your book." And with that parting comment, he turned on his heel and returned to his office.

After she'd emailed the file, she made her way to the tiny office kitchen and made Ben a double espresso, bringing it through to him on a tray with his favourite salted crackers. "Anything else I can get you?"

"No, this is perfect. Thanks. And that file you sent on?"

"Yes?" She hoped she hadn't made a mess of it.

"Excellent work," he affirmed.

"Glad to help."

"It'll save me hours of prep work. Make sure you remind me of that when we're discussing your end-of-year bonus!" He peered at her over the rim of his glasses, watching for her reaction to his comment as he picked up a cracker and bit into it.

"I'll make a note of it," she said.

Maintaining professionalism was a pet love of Ben's and if she'd learnt anything in the ten years she'd worked as his Personal Assistant, it was to remain calm and exercise controlled reactions . . . a characteristic that had recently come in very useful in many other aspects of her life.

Excusing herself, she returned to her desk and put the finishing touches to an invitation list she was working on. Ben had organised an event manager to plan a publicity evening as part of a marketing strategy to attract new business, an evening she hoped would bring a lot more to the company than trays of empty wineglasses and partly chewed nibbles. The invitations had been delivered that morning, landing on Vicky's desk with unspoken instructions to make sure they were sent out to all relevant parties. For some reason, Ben preferred to keep control of guest lists in-house. It didn't make a lot of sense to Vicky, not when the freelance event manager was already including the task in her pricing specification!

Snipping the light string with a scissors, she undid the packaging, slipped a single invitation from the waxen brown paper and read it with interest. The event was being held on Fintan's birthday: Thursday December 8th, less than one week away. That was the first coincidence. And the second was the venue: The Deerpark Hotel in Howth, the hotel she'd once sworn she would never set foot in again. The hotel where they had celebrated their wedding.

Chapter 3

An hour later Ariel finished what she was working on and thumped the desk with her fist. Wincing from the sharp pain burning her skin, she knew without doubt that she was awake, wide awake at that. Ben wouldn't be able to accuse her at a later date – as he'd already suggested that morning – that she'd been sleeping on the job. The account she'd finished revising made perfect sense. At least it did now. She didn't trust the figures to remain like that, didn't trust that something wouldn't reach into the heart of the file and juggle the details around like balls in a lottery drum. She tapped against the page with a red pen. She'd found nothing, not a single mistake or typo. Everything balanced. All the entries were exactly where they should be. If only Ben would accept a hard copy! But he didn't believe in paper trails, forever going on about saving the environment and working with a green ethos. She had no explanation for what happened earlier, no explanation for the stupid – another bang of her fist – irresponsible – yet another bang of her fist – errors.

She twirled around in her chair, staring through the huge window at the magnificent view beyond. It was one of those incredibly beautiful winter days, one of those days when it was difficult to stay miserable for very long, one of those days when she usually found a reason to smile. All traces of the harsh early morning frost were long thawed, the bright sun glistening in the clear sky. Such natural beauty never failed to capture her attention, never failed to slow her heartbeat and make her stop for a moment to appreciate what was all around her. But today was different. Today, the sight of Howth Head failed to relieve the feeling of unease that had wrapped itself tightly around her, the growing feeling of suspicion, the gnawing belief that her files were being tampered with.

She stood up from her chair, rubbing the side of her hand as she moved towards the window. Banging the surface of the desk had hurt. Hurt a lot. But not nearly as much as the dressing-down she'd received from Ben.

Taking correction had never been an issue for Ariel. She relished being shown how, took delight in a challenge and learning something new. But being repeatedly corrected for something she hadn't done, for something she couldn't understand, left a bitter aftertaste in her mouth. She was dreading the consultants' meeting. What a disaster that it has to be on today of all days, she thought, coming to a stop in front of the large world map she had pinned to the wall the first week she'd started working there.

She stood still and stared, her eyes scanning from east to west, north to south, the large expanse of blue sea bringing a smile to her face as she recalled the luxurious cruise she'd enjoyed with Roger less than six months before. "What I wouldn't give to be on the other side of the world now!" she sighed, running a finger along the waxen canvas, an array of memories blurring and overlapping as she allowed her touch to pause at some of the spots she'd visited, savouring the experiences she'd enjoyed at various stages of her life, both pre-Roger and during-Roger. The experiences she'd enjoyed before she'd lost her entitlement to leave the country. Before she'd been instructed to surrender her passport.

Giving a quick glance at the time, she realised she was late for the meeting. She needed to hurry. She turned off her computer and left the room.

Fintan Jones was putting a call through to Malahide Credit Union to check on the status of his loan application. He wiped beads of perspiration from his brow as he waited for the outcome, wondering how at twenty-eight years of age, in his first six months of marriage, he had landed himself in such a mess. He leaned against the doorframe and looked out into the back garden, his brown hair standing in tufts on his head, his dark eyes clouded with concern.

"What repayments have they suggested?" he asked, when the Credit Union official came back on the line and told him his application had been granted with conditions. He didn't ask her to explain the conditions. Whether he had reservations about them or not was immaterial. He had to accept their offer. No matter what restrictions were in place.

"That much? Can the weekly amount be adjusted when I've reduced the balance somewhat?" Doing some mental calculations, he was filled with dread as he contemplated how strapped for cash he'd be when he accepted their offer. He didn't need an electronic calculator to work it out. What he needed was a miracle to help him convince Vicky it was the right thing to do. But in his heart he knew he wouldn't risk telling her the truth. He couldn't rely on her approval to let it go ahead. And regardless of how much pressure he'd be under to meet the repayments or the fact he'd be deceiving his wife, he wasn't going to back out now. Borrowing that money was something he knew he had to do, something he hoped would make a difference.

"I don't have a choice, I'm afraid. I'm up the walls. It's either work late or risk missing the deadline on those accounts."

Ben held the phone away from his ear, Jenny's high-pitched annoyance liable to deafen him. He waited till her tone had dropped a few decibels before putting the phone back to his ear again.

"You go ahead and eat, love. I'll pick up a takeaway on the way home."

I shouldn't have bothered calling, he thought, wishing

he'd had the good sense to send her a text instead. Running his fingers through his greying locks and listening to Jenny's warning about carbohydrates and increasing cholesterol, he let her words go over his head, having heard it all before.

"You'll miss me when it's too late. You won't realise what a catch I am until I'm gone," he teased, regretting his choice of words as soon as they were out there between them, her silence on the other end of the line indicating her change in mood. "Jen, I'll be home as soon as I can," he reassured her. "I know how much you hate me working late."

His wife's exaggerated sigh came down the phone line. He knew he should hang up now, end the conversation promptly, but he hesitated and then inevitably heard the same pleading words he'd heard a million times before.

He listened patiently and didn't dismiss the ancient obsession she was clinging to. "I will, Jen. You know I'm doing everything I can to help."

He fell silent again, listening to her regrets and what-ifs, twirling the telephone wire around his finger as he waited for an opportune moment to interrupt.

"We both know you had no choice at the time, Jen. You have to accept it now. We've come to the end of the road with this. We have to respect her decision."

Fintan yelled into his mobile phone, his cheeks flushed, his jaw set in a grim line. "This is the one and only time. Do you understand? Don't think for a moment it's going to give you a hold over me!"

He fell silent then, infuriated by the sneering sarcasm coming down the line in short, snappy bursts.

"I'll let you know when I can organise it. When it suits me. Then I never want to hear from you or your snivelling wife again," he finished, disconnecting the call and flinging his phone to the furthest end of the room.

How on earth did I let myself get mixed up in this, he thought, grabbing his keys and making to leave the house, dashing back to retrieve his phone at the last second.

Better not risk Vicky finding it and taking a call. She was giving him a hard enough time as it was over absolutely nothing. He didn't dare imagine how furious she'd be if she actually did have something to hold over him. His body rigid, his head feeling as though it were about to burst, he clutched the steering wheel with both hands and made a split-second decision on where to go to relieve some of his built-up frustration.

A place where he could be himself. A place where he didn't have to pretend. A place he'd discovered by accident when he'd needed somewhere to work things out in his head. A place where he could release some energy in the most normal fashion ever.

Chapter 4

When Ariel left the consultants' meeting, she had dark circles under her eyes and bright pink spots on her cheeks. She hurried back to her office, moving swiftly to ensure she kept ahead of the four male consultants who were trailing behind her, deep in conversation about the weekend's sporting fixtures. They had already put the meeting's in-depth detail to the back of their minds, in direct contrast to Ariel who was unable to think of anything else.

"I don't suppose you'd fancy joining me for a quick drink in The Bailey?"

Vicky looked up at the sound of Ariel's voice, stifling a yawn and fighting against the strain of a pretty hectic afternoon. "I was going to head straight home to be honest. I'm pretty knackered." She wasn't lying.

"Please, Vicky," the other girl begged. "I promise I won't keep you out all night. After the day I've had, I don't relish the thought of an empty flat with only the television for company."

Every bone in Vicky's body ached and psychologically she had already switched off her professional side. She wasn't sure she'd be capable of holding a conversation with her husband when she went home, never mind going for a drink and socialising! She'd been looking forward to leaving the stress and strain of the office behind and standing under a hot shower as soon as she got inside her front door. She had no interest in sitting in a noisy bar, more in the mood to spend her evening relaxing on the couch in front of a roaring fire.

But the pleading in Ariel's words was difficult to ignore and she found it impossible to refuse her invitation, particularly as she was curious about the outcome of the meeting. Watching the consultants troop past her desk, she couldn't help but notice that Ariel was the only one with her head bowed, the only one with the weight of the world on her shoulders.

"Why not?" she relented after a moment's thought. "But I'm only staying for a short while."

Ariel's face brightened. "Thanks a mill, Vicky. I do appreciate it."

Being the only two females employed in Ellis Enterprise had brought the women closer by default. Yet they didn't make a habit of socialising outside office hours, at least not alone. On the odd occasion when they did, they were accompanied by some or all of the other staff, sharing a meal or a drink to toast a healthy end-of-quarter or an achievement worth celebrating.

Vicky found socialising with them overpowering. She felt a lot more comfortable chatting to them from behind the safety net of her desk and computer. She categorised herself as the odd one out, the only worker in the company without a degree to her name, its absence a constant reminder of why she didn't match up.

Shrinking in company wasn't anything new for her. She'd had a lifetime of being excluded: initially from her parents and later from her peers in the private boarding school she'd attended for five arduous years. Falling in love with Fintan had been the turning point in her battle for self-confidence, calming her craving to fit in and saving her from herself.

"Can you give me a sec, Ariel? I need to give Fin a call and let him know I'll be a bit late," she said, picking up the receiver and dialling his number.

"Of course. There's no rush. I have to freshen up my make-up anyway. I can't go anywhere looking like this!"

Vicky raised an eyebrow and shook her head as she dialled Fintan's mobile number. Ariel's natural beauty could shine through any amount of jaded shadows but it seemed she couldn't see that, so Vicky knew it would be a waste of time pointing it out.

"Fin?"

"Hi, there . . ."

Vicky's fingers tightened on the receiver as Fintan's voice drifted in and out, a weak network signal making it very difficult for her to hear his response, convincing her that he was not at home where he was supposed to be.

"Where are you, Fin?" She strained to listen. "I can't hear you – but look, I only wanted to tell you I'd be a bit late. I'm going to The Bailey for one." She gave up the battle to hear him and hung up, her heart echoing loudly in her chest. Where on earth was he?

Within seconds, her mobile vibrated.

"Fin?"

His signal had improved, the connection perfect. His words floated down the line.

"Just going to The Bailey," she explained again. "I shouldn't be too long. Where are you now?"

She listened to his response, her eyes straying to Ariel once more, watching as she expertly applied pale pink lipstick, touching it up with frosted gloss, emphasising her soulful eyes with dark kohl eyeliner, those few simple touch-ups transforming her daytime office look to a sultry evening one, managing it so deftly that even the dark circles beneath her eyes appeared to be part of her look.

"No, I haven't eaten. Dinner would be lovely," she said, unable to ignore how quickly he'd muttered something about running some errands before changing the subject to what he was cooking for dinner. Why is he being so vague, she wondered. Her thoughts began to wander, any number of explanations coming to mind, explanations she fervently wished weren't true. She dragged her attention back to what Fintan was saying, her mouth watering at the promise of his tasty chicken chasseur. There wasn't any point in quizzing him about his movements over the phone. She'd need to be able to see his eyes to distinguish truth from lies.

Saying goodbye, she cut the connection, leaving the issue of her suspicion to be dealt with later.

She tidied her desk to leave, then put a dab of perfume behind each ear and smeared on nude lipstick. Buttoning her coat, she watched Ariel make a few quick changes – removing the cravat she'd worn inside the collar of her white blouse, undoing two more buttons and liberally spraying Chanel on her wrists and cleavage before exchanging black court shoes for a pair of strappy stiletto sandals that she pulled from her enormous handbag. She made the transformation look so simple, made Vicky wish she had the foresight to be quite as prepared.

By comparison, she felt decidedly underdressed in her knee-length navy skirt, pink-and-white pinstriped shirt and flat comfortable shoes. The term 'desperate housewife' came to mind – and not the glamorous TV programme either but an actual housewife who was desperate – and for one horrible moment, she almost felt responsible for Fintan's cheating ways. Almost.

A buzz of conversation reverberated through the busy bar as they made their way to a corner in The Bailey.

"Chilled white?" Ariel offered, taking off her fitted black suede coat and tossing it carelessly onto the seat.

"Coors Light with ice for me," Vicky replied. She unwrapped a lavender scarf from her neck, placing it neatly beside her winter-white wool jacket.

"One Coors Light and one white wine it is then."

"Thanks." Vicky massaged her temples, trying to

ease the dull ache that had been settling there since she'd hung up the phone from Fintan.

She smiled graciously when Ariel arrived back with their drinks.

"Cheers!" she said, raising her glass.

"*Sláinte!*" Ariel responded, taking a sip of her chilled white chardonnay. "God, that sure tastes good." She sighed heavily, leaning her head against the soft velour of the seat. Closing her eyes, she rolled her head gently. "What a day! It's been one thing after the other from first thing this morning."

"Are you bringing work home with you?" Vicky pointed to her bulging briefcase.

Ariel's eyes shot open. "I've no choice. My head will be on the block if I put down another week like this one. I'd be happier to go through everything with a fine toothcomb. On hard copy as well as disk. At least I can use as much paper as I like at home." She patted her briefcase. "Looks like this piece of leather is going to be my very best friend for the foreseeable future."

Vicky neither agreed nor disagreed, deftly moving the subject away from work. "Is Roger home or away this weekend?"

Ariel's pause made her wonder if she even knew where he was but after another sip of chardonnay she responded.

"Last I heard from him, he was about to fly over Dubai, and then he has a twenty-four-hour stopover after that. It looks like I've a lonely weekend ahead, I'm afraid."

Her relationship fascinated Vicky. Thanks to Ariel's independence and self-confidence and Roger's career as an airline pilot taking him out of the country for several days each week, the majority of their time was spent apart. And yet, it seemed to work like a dream.

Having worked with Ariel for eighteen months, Vicky truly believed their arrangement suited her and that, if she were honest, she wouldn't have room in her life for a full-time partner. Her energy levels and drive were amazing, something Vicky admired yet never wanted to replicate. Striving to be a successful financial consultant – and perhaps the best – in Ellis Enterprise was only one part of Ariel's ambition and drive to succeed. She also spent several hours every week competing on the golf course as well as playing in her local tennis club. She had hinted to Vicky that it would be a dream come true to become the golf club's next Lady President. Vicky had no doubt, knowing Ariel's commitment to anything she set her heart on, that she'd do everything in her power to secure the position and she'd be the best Lady President the club had ever had.

"Aren't you ever tempted to accompany Roger any more? Dubai sure sounds more than tempting. He can still get a travel concession for you, can't he?"

When the girls had met first, Ariel had been forever jetting off to exotic locations, taking full advantage of the perks of Roger's job, enjoying many long weekends in faraway locations.

Ariel placed her glass on the table, staring at the gold liquid for a moment. "One hotel room becomes like any other after a while and it isn't much fun sightseeing alone. I seldom tag along now – I leave him to get on with it."

"But don't you miss the breaks? They'd become such a big part of your life."

Ariel shrugged. "We prefer to take proper breaks now. Breaks where he doesn't have to work. At least then we get to spend some real time together."

"But surely it gets lonely at times?" Vicky persisted, absent-mindedly shaking her glass, the ice cubes clinking noisily.

"Huh?"

"For Roger, I mean. Night after night in a lonely hotel room has to get monotonous after a while. Aren't you ever worried or concerned that . . . ?" She allowed her voice to trail off, already regretting the impulsive question she'd thrown into their conversation.

"Worried that Roger might stray, you mean?"

Vicky nodded. "I guess. Men need more attention than we do – think with their trousers as it were."

Ariel sighed. "No way! You haven't met Roger, have you? He's the straightest guy I know. Crikey, he's the only person I know who informs the Revenue if he has underpaid his tax!" She paused for a moment and then continued. "Whatever else might come between us, infidelity isn't a threat."

Vicky swallowed hard, a sharp stab of jealousy lodging itself in her throat. Why can't I feel that secure about my relationship, she thought. Why can't it be me who's that confident for a change? And what else, she couldn't help wondering, could Ariel possibly have to worry about if not infidelity?

"Is that your secret to long-lasting happiness?" she said. "Long distance?"

Ariel mulled over the question for a moment before answering. "I'm not sure being apart would work for everyone but up to now it hasn't caused us any major problems."

"But do you miss him?"

"Of course, I miss him." She stared into the distance before continuing. "Weekends can be endless without him around to keep me company. But it's not as if he has a choice. I knew he was a pilot when I met him. I knew it could never be any different."

Vicky couldn't pinpoint anything in particular but definitely suspected an air of wistfulness in Ariel's response. "How long have you two been together now?"

"Five years, give or take a little."

"Long time . . ." It was on the tip of her tongue to enquire if they'd ever discussed getting married but then she thought better of it.

"I guess. But the years have rolled by, one slipping into the next."

"I suppose he'll never have a job with regular hours?"

Ariel shook her head. "Unlikely." She looked at Vicky directly. "To be honest, Vicky – and I've never said this to Roger – I'd give anything to have him around more. I'd swap everything I have right now to happily snuggle up on the couch with him every weekend. But don't ever tell him that!"

"Don't worry. I've never even met him so I'm hardly going to spill the beans." Vicky stared into the pale gold liquid in her glass, a hollow feeling settling at the pit of her stomach, a familiar nauseating sense of desire coming over her. Other people's lives weren't perfect either and yet they seemed straightforward in comparison to hers. Why do I always end up wanting the relationships other people have, she thought.

"So fill me in," said Ariel. "What's it like having a man around all the time? What am I missing out on?"

"That's a tricky one to answer!"

"But what do you two get up to? What have you got that I don't? Come on. Share!"

Vicky pulled a face. "Fin works most nights at the club so our social life is pretty limited. But he is home a lot of afternoons. One big advantage is that it's great going home to a tidy house and a cooked meal."

"See, Vicky," Ariel laughed, catching the barman's eye to order another drink, "that doesn't make you much different from Roger and me! I don't have a big house to clean so that cancels that. And you spend a lot of your nights alone too."

"When you put it like that, I suppose." Vicky forced herself to laugh, a strained laugh. Ariel's comment had left her with increasing doubt. She'd have to have words with Fintan. Something had to change. Where was the point in being married if she was alone most of the time? "Enough about men," she announced with a sigh. "I meant to ask you how did your meeting go? You were in there quite a while."

30

"Hmm?"

"The consultants' meeting with Ben and the others?"

"Oh, that! What a disaster!" She shook her head in disgust, tapping her nails on the table. "At least it was a disaster for me. Some of the others fared very well though. Can you believe Ben took two of my biggest clients and gave them to Marcus?"

Vicky, surprised Ben had made such a decision, opened her mouth to offer some words of consolation but then thought better of it and shut it again. What could she possibly say that would help?

"I was mortified. Marcus. Of all people. Not that I begrudge it to him or anything and I'd probably feel the same no matter who Ben passed my work on to. But you know how it is between Marcus and me."

Vicky knew only too well why Marcus getting her accounts was a difficult pill for Ariel to swallow. She had knocked him off top position only months before and he'd beaten her a short while before that. There was a definite unspoken competition between them and now he was getting a chance to rise to the surface again while Ariel's performance was taking a sharp nosedive.

"Taking two from you is a bit extreme, Ariel. Surely Ben will even things up a little and give you something else in exchange? Maybe he has something new coming in with your name on it?"

"Nope. He thinks I need to get back on top of my game before he'll even consider giving me back my normal workload. Very little commission for me this month!"

Though she made an attempt to smile, Vicky noticed it didn't come anywhere near her eyes.

"I presume he delivered his announcement to you in private?"

Ariel shook her head, her lips pursed in visible annoyance. "I wish he had! But he didn't put a tooth in it, just laid into me in front of the others. I couldn't believe how shocking my results looked as part of an overall picture. On the bloody overhead projector at that! In bold red font if you don't mind!"

"Ouch!" Vicky winced, imagining the other girl's embarrassment. And the men's gloating moment.

"I did my utmost to defend my case but, if you ask me, he had his mind made up before the meeting had even begun. He pointed out that too much ground was being lost, too much time being wasted going over material instead of signing off on it."

"Life is such a bitch at times." Vicky took another sip of her drink, its cold tartness clinging to her palate. "Especially when you feel you don't deserve it."

"Downright unfair if you ask me! And to make matters worse, all those smarmy men sat around the table acting concerned and offering their opinion on what I needed to do. Aagh!"

Oh, Vicky thought, it's no wonder she arrived back in the office with a big red face. "I'm presuming you'll fight back? As bad as this feels now, you're not going to let it best you?"

Ariel raised an eyebrow. "Of course, I'll put up a fight. But sometimes it's tough being the only woman on the team. I feel I've no guaranteed back-up, that I'm fighting a silent war."

"You're upset, Ariel. I don't blame you. But don't let your imagination run away. I'm sure they're not ganging up on you."

Ariel turned around in her seat to face Vicky. "If you'd seen the smug looks on their faces, I'd say you'd agree with me. Except Marcus, of course. He was looking at me with pity in his eyes. So infuriating! I don't want people feeling sorry for me. I want to feel I've earned their respect. No matter how liberated we might think we've become, there's always a divide, always an element of one-upmanship from the men. At least in my experience of working in a male-dominated business."

"Come on, you can't be serious?"

"I wish you could sit in for a meeting and watch. They'll never accept that women can rank as high as they can."

"But they're all so nice to talk to. And Ben – he's never struck me as being unfair in the past."

"Why didn't he spare me the embarrassment at least? Jeez, why didn't he tell me when he had me in his office? Or at least give me a hint that he was about to take my companies from me. He didn't have to do it so publicly. I deserve that much surely?"

"Could he have acted in the heat of the moment?" Though, remembering his remark about 'shuffling things up a bit', she knew of course that he hadn't.

"Ben isn't one who normally acts in haste." Ariel

pushed her hair back from her face, the light overhead catching the diamonds in her ears.

"Hopefully they'll have forgotten it by Monday morning. You know what men are like. They deal with things head on, no sparing of feelings or breaking the news gently. They launch straight into the heart of the matter, without dwelling on it or bitching about it like we do."

"Don't I know it! God, I'm such a misery guts today. You must be sick of me!"

Vicky reached out to rub the other girl's arm but then thought better of it, feeling as though that would be crossing a line in their work-relationship. "But look, it's not the end of the world. And knowing you, you'll have put this behind you and risen to the top in no time!"

Ariel shrugged, examining her nails as she answered, her lowered eyelids shielding her expression. "I'm not sure I'd trust myself to tender for a new contract at the moment. Between you and me, Vicky, my confidence has taken a battering. And even if I did have an account to chase – which I don't, by the way – it's highly unlikely Ben would let me go for it. At least not without insisting that one of the other consultants was holding my hand and walking through every step of it with me."

"Maybe you should concentrate on your other work and see how things go for a short while? Let the dust settle."

Ariel sat back in the seat, crossing one leg over the

other. "They might think they've won this battle, Vicky, but believe me they're a long way from winning the war! Ben included. Feckers! I'll show them I'm every bit as good as they are!"

Vicky looked at her watch and drained her drink in one go. She needed to get home. Fintan would be leaving for work and she didn't want to miss him. "I have to be off, Ariel. I want to catch Fin before he leaves. Will you be okay on your own?"

Ariel nodded, blushing when two handsome guys – dressed as if they'd stepped straight off surfboards even though it was dark and cold outside – walked by their table and stared straight at her.

Vicky watched as they nudged each other, appraising Ariel swiftly with admiring glances and completely ignoring her. She might as well be invisible for all the notice they took of her! Probably think I'm Ariel's mother, she decided, definitely feeling it was time to leave. She was weary and wanted to go home. *Home.* The word alone sank her further into despair. She missed what it used to represent. Before.

"Thanks for today," Ariel said to Vicky when she stood to leave.

"Aren't you playing tennis this weekend? You'll be able to take your frustrations out on court and forget what's going on in the office until Monday morning."

Ariel slapped her forehead with the heel of her hand. "Yes. God, thanks for reminding me! I'd actually forgotten all about it. I can't believe I let the most important match I've had in years slip my mind."

"Something different to distract you at least. Is it a club comp?"

Ariel took another sip of wine, wiping the lipstick trace from the rim of her glass as she put it back on the table. "Yeah. It's the final of the mixed doubles in the Leinster Senior League. I'm teamed with a guy called Gavin."

"Is he good?"

Ariel nodded. "One of the best. But we're up against it, I can tell you. We're hopeful though. And with a bit of luck on our side, we might manage to pull it off and win the cup."

Vicky fastened the buttons on her coat. "Now that sounds more like the Ariel I know!"

The other girl smiled, a smile that reached her eyes this time.

"Where do you get your energy to keep going seven days a week?" asked Vicky. "Do you ever stop and put your feet up?"

"Rarely. I get a great buzz out of bashing balls back and forward. Our opponents' club has won the league the last two years running. We were knocked out at semi-final stage both times. So hopefully this is the year for Sutton Lawn. One more match and the trophy could be sitting in pride of place in the club trophy cabinet."

"By the sounds of it, you're already planning a celebration?"

Ariel smiled and nodded enthusiastically, crossing her fingers and holding them up for Vicky to see. "Drawing Gavin as partner was a real stroke of luck. He's out to win as much as I am."

"Life's all about luck, Ariel, isn't it? Everybody wanting the same thing and only one person lucky enough to end up getting it." Vicky fixed her gaze on the flickering candles lined up along the narrow mantel over the open fire, her mind drifting to the only thing she'd ever truly craved in life: contentment and peace of mind.

Ariel wasn't fully in agreement. "I believe we make our own luck, hard work being the essence of most success stories."

Vicky sighed. So much of her life had been an endless battle, a battle to love and be loved and no matter how hard she worked at it, she'd never even come close to success. She'd thought she had with Fintan but these last few weeks she'd felt it slipping away, felt him slipping away from her to a place where she didn't belong.

What jury was used to decide these situations, she wondered? Was it merely a jury of conscience? Where the little person living inside our heads makes subconscious decisions, leading us to places in our lives we never planned on visiting.

Chapter 5

Ben Ellis tidied his desk and looked at the clock. Handing a few of the files over to Marcus had saved him time and he hadn't had to work as late as he'd thought he would. Jenny wouldn't be expecting him. He had at least an hour to call his own. His swimming gear was in the boot of the car. An hour in the pool easing the tension from his muscles would be the ideal way to end a long, stressful week.

Checking he'd switched everything off, he left the office, stopping to talk to Pete Scavo, the night security man, on his way through the entrance hall. A large burly gentleman in his early sixties, Pete was the epitome of reliability, his tanned skin and unusual surname the only traits he'd inherited from his Italian grandfather.

Ben liked Pete, liked him a lot. And not only because he felt he was leaving the Ellis Enterprise premises in good hands. Pete held a special place in his heart, as did anyone who put their talents to good use on his behalf. And Pete had taken one such task far above and beyond the call of duty, bringing fulfilment to Ben's life – and Jenny's – in a way that nobody else ever had.

"I'm last to leave, Pete. You'll be able to set the alarm and get on with the crossword in peace now!"

"Did you see the Chelsea versus United game last night? Chelsea very nearly threw them!"

Ben nodded, grinning. "I'm glad that TV we had installed is keeping you up to date with the soccer. 'Twould never do if you were missing out."

"Best security gig in Dublin, Ben," Pete laughed, grateful to his boss for making his job a lot more comfortable than was necessary. "Still hate taking money for it!"

"Goodnight, Pete." Ben left the building with a smile on his face.

"Hi, Fin!" Vicky called as soon as she got inside her front door, slipping her feet out of her black leather shoes and into a cosy pair of slippers. She hung her jacket and scarf on the antique coatstand, relieved to be finally home.

"With you in a sec!" Fintan called from the kitchen.

Sitting at her desk all day, getting through the workload as best she could as well as keeping in tune with office politics had been distracting, had kept her mind off her problems. For most of the day at least. Once inside her own front door, however, the stone fortress she'd built around her heart crumbled away, clearing a pathway and allowing her real emotions to rush in and torment her once more. She leaned against the oatmeal-coloured wall, suddenly exhausted as the familiar emotions of hurt, despair and insecurity floated through her veins and rose to the surface.

She heard Fintan rattling about and guessed he was putting the finishing touches to their meal. For a fraction of a millisecond, she allowed herself to believe that everything was normal, at least as normal as it should have been between any husband and wife. Life wasn't perfect for anybody. She knew that now. Although there had been a time when she'd clung to the fantasy and hope that when she grew up she'd have the life she'd read about in fairytales.

"I'm going to take a quick shower before dinner!" she yelled over the din of crashing saucepan lids.

"Sure, but don't be too long – it's almost ready," he replied, sauntering into the hallway, a waft of herbs and spices following in his wake. "Enjoy your drink?"

She shrugged. "It was okay. Nothing exciting. Ariel has a few issues at work. She needed to let off a little steam, someone to listen, and I was there." She moved automatically into his outstretched arms, savouring the exotic blend of cooking aromas from his well-worn Dublin GAA jersey as she leaned her head against his broad chest and wished she could remain wrapped in his warmth forever. "And you? How was your day?"

How she wished she could forget about everything else that was going on around them. Wished what had happened hadn't. Wished her heart hadn't hardened against him. Wished she could forgive and forget. Wished she hadn't gone to visit him in the club the night she did.

Fintan's voice interrupted her musing, his words vibrating in her ears.

"Oh, same old, same old. The usual lunch-time rush."

"What time did you get out?"

"I made my escape at the first opportunity, needing a few hours' break before heading back in. Tonight could be a late one, I'm afraid. There's a 21st and an engagement party booked in."

And there it was: yet another reason to cause an alarm bell to ring loudly in her head as he slipped in the fact he'd be working late, even later than normal. Again. She pulled out of his arms, her personal defence mechanisms rising like automatic bars on a prison cage. She clenched her teeth, resentment building inside her, her heart hardening into an impenetrable lump of steel.

"Surely you can get somebody else to lock up for a change, Fintan?" she asked, using his full title to demonstrate her annoyance. "You're only *one* of three managers in that place! Yet you're the one who's called upon for all the shitty jobs. When is the last time you had a weekend off?" Her eyes flared accusingly.

Fintan exhaled loudly, running his hands through his short brown hair. He didn't need this, not on top of the day he'd had.

There was a time Vicky would have made a joke about his hair standing in spikes. But today the hair didn't even raise a smile.

Fintan felt smothered by her insecurity, a quality that had endeared her to him in the beginning. Why did she make such a big deal out of the smallest thing and read into non-existent detail, letting her imagination conjure up all sorts of ridiculousness? Why was she always searching for more? What on earth did Vicky expect him to do? Leave his job? Tell the owner he wanted to work nine to five? Tell him that his wife was throwing a little hissy fit at home and to placate her he'd have to do what he was told?

"Sweetheart," he responded, struggling to remain calm, "you're being totally unreasonable! Regular weekends off are a luxury I gave up when I accepted the management role. It's not that long since you and I were jumping around in delight and toasting the prospect of a healthy pay rise on the strength of extra responsibility. Can you imagine the boss's reaction if I told him I couldn't work Friday and Saturday nights?"

He paused a moment, watching Vicky's guarded expression before pointing out the obvious. "He'd be perfectly entitled to demote me or maybe sack me altogether!"

"Now who's being dramatic?" Vicky shot back at him. "You're hardly going to lose your job because you ask for a few weekends off every now and again!"

And losing my job to go and stand in a lengthy dole queue is something I'm going to avoid at all costs, he thought silently. Particularly with the extra debt I'm about to take on.

"Believe me," he said, "I'd like nothing better than

spend every evening here with you. But unfortunately I can't."

"You *won't*, you mean!"

Dead right I won't give up a good job, he retorted silently, knowing at first-hand how unemployment could affect a family. He'd been too young to make a difference when his father had injured his arm in an unfortunate accident, leaving him unable to continue in the electrical trade, the profession he'd worked in since leaving school. Over time, his father had succumbed to a life of handouts from the state, falling into the trap of believing that's all life had to offer, allowing bitterness to replace ambition, standing by and encouraging his sons to do likewise, no longer seeing the point in even trying to make something of his life.

But I'm not that young boy any more, Fintan thought vehemently, and it isn't my parents I have to convince that I want to reach out and grab opportunity as it comes my way. It's my wife, the woman I love, the same woman who stood beaming at the altar rails and promised to love me through sickness and health, for richer and poorer. Staring into those same eyes now, he missed the spark of gaiety that used to shine back at him, missed her trust, missed her unfailing support.

He took a deep breath. "I'm not going to risk my job, Vicky."

"But I hate being here alone, evening after evening. It's just like . . ." Her voice drifted off.

He put a hand on her shoulder, his tone softening, knowing only too well what her reminder represented:

the loneliness she'd experienced growing up as an only child in a six-bedroomed period house on the Hill of Howth, being cared for by a string of au pairs, while her parents divided their time between their legal professions and an outrageous amount of late-night socialising.

"As long as you've known me, it's never been any different, sweetheart. And you never took issue with me working late before. When we lived in the apartment?"

"I was so busy organising the wedding I didn't notice."

"So why now? What's brought this about? I thought you loved living out here. Far less travelling for you getting to work?"

"I know, I know! But I feel we're being pulled apart. You're here during the day. I'm here at night. I'm in bed asleep when you come in. You're asleep when I'm tiptoeing around the room early in the morning trying to get dressed without turning the lights on."

He kept one hand on her shoulder, the other moving to stroke her flushed cheek. "What's going on in that head of yours, Vicky? We call each other a few times every day. You know where I am. So what's wrong? What has changed?"

But I *don't* know where you are or who you're with half the time, she screamed silently. That's the problem!

She reached deep inside her soul to find an answer to his question, a plausible one, an explanation he'd accept without telling him the truth. She couldn't tell him what was going around and around inside her head. Not until she had proof. And maybe not even then. She wouldn't be able to bear hearing him laugh out loud and dismissing her suspicions as figments of her imagination. Fixing a smile on her face, she brought her hand up to clutch his. "We're married now, Fin. All my life, I've dreamed of having a normal family life. But look at us. We barely have the time to go for a walk together, never mind anything else!"

She let go his hand. Her pause hung in the air between them.

Unable to bear the serious direction their conversation was taking, he took the opportunity to lighten the atmosphere. He slowly released his hold on her, daring to tease her gently. "Maybe I should get you a dog for company? Then you'd never be stuck for a walking companion!"

"Don't mock me, Fintan! Meeting at the front door and sharing the odd meal for the rest of my life is a far cry from the marriage I'd envisaged."

Marriage, he despaired. Only six months into it and it's already becoming a rope around our necks. Why did a simple piece of paper have to change things, demand more expectation? He had never loved anyone the way he loved Vicky. If only she'd relax and let him prove it to her. If only she'd believe what they had was real. More than anything, he wanted to be the knight in shining armour she desired: flawless and faultless, someone who would never give her a moment's concern. But unfortunately life had already dealt him some challenging cards, cards he was careful to keep close to his chest, cards he knew had left him guarded and occasionally secretive.

"But it won't always be like this and our hard work will pay off, Vicky," he said. "It will help us guarantee as good a future as possible."

"To be honest, Fin, I'm a lot more concerned about *now* than the future."

The unsureness in her eyes as she stared up at him reminded him of how she'd been when they'd first met.

He was working in the club that night he'd first noticed her, keeping an eye on the dance floor, watching out for broken glass or any hint of trouble. Spotting her standing alone, blonde highlights glistening, he'd instantly felt an inexplicable protectiveness and kept an eye out for her until her friends returned. He'd felt compelled to follow her every move, noticing the way she allowed her friends to take the lead, happy to follow in their footsteps and go with the flow.

Sighing, he let the memory go and brought his attention back to the present.

"There's no reason to be concerned, Vicky. Honestly. But that doesn't change the fact that I have to work late tonight, love. Unfortunately." He leaned against the staircase, wrapping his fingers around one of the walnut spindles.

She let out a long sigh of disappointment. "Aren't you flattered that your wife wants to spend more time with you?"

"Immensely so!" he laughed.

She wasn't sure if he was laughing at her or with her. But then she wasn't sure of anything any more.

"Although I have to point out that you left me here

alone this evening while you went off boozing with your friend." He raised an eyebrow, waiting for a reaction. She didn't disappoint.

"But I told you on the phone. I had no choice. Ariel put me in an impossible position. I couldn't say no!"

"I rest my case," he said, planting a kiss on her forehead.

He didn't dwell on things like she did, didn't place the same importance on spending quality time together. He loved her. She said she loved him. That was more than enough. They were in the lucky position of having two well-paid jobs, a comfortable home and a decent car. In his opinion, they were a lot more fortunate than many twenty-eight-year-old couples. And he wasn't about to jeopardise that.

She wriggled under his touch, pushing his hand away from her face. "The other two guys working with you are single, right? Surely they could do the weekend graveyard shifts?"

Fintan sniffed the air, a distinct smell of burning drifting into the hallway. And though he wanted to run in and remove the casserole from the oven, he knew better than to move away now. Vicky would take it personally and they'd be right back to where they began.

"You don't honestly think that single guys want to spend their weekends working anti-social hours any more than I do?"

"Have you even asked?"

He squeezed her hand. "I'd better turn off the oven or we'll be tucking into burnt offerings!"

"Any excuse to get away from our conversation."

Fintan sighed deeply and folded his arms, the physical action building an invisible barrier between them. He looked at his wife, recognising her defiance in the firm line of her chin, her hands on her hips as she refused to give up on her argument. She reminded him of his grandmother, a tiny slip of a woman who had stood up to a grumbling grandfather and anyone else who'd dared threaten her happiness.

He preferred the angry Vicky to the unsure and defeatist one. He wanted to pull her in his arms, kiss her hard on the lips, mould her slight body to his and whisper in her ear that everything was okay and she had nothing to worry about. But she was too angry and upset to listen. He knew she wouldn't believe him. He knew she'd want more.

"Vicky, we can't keep going over the same ground. Long nights, days off mid-week, late starts – that's what you signed up for when you married me."

"But you've got seniority, Fin! Can't you use it to pull rank and rearrange the rotas? Cut down at least?"

Her blue-grey eyes bored into his, reaching right into his soul to try and connect with him, to try and make him feel guilty. Or responsible. Or both.

He shook his head. "Not a hope."

"Well," she said with conviction, "I can't see the attraction in working through the night when I'm lying here in bed. Alone. Or maybe that's the way you prefer it?"

She could hear the whining tone in her voice, the

cold hand of jealousy pushing its way through her body, closing its fist around her heart and lungs, suffocating her, making it impossible to breathe without difficulty. She wanted him to blurt out the truth, to own up to what he'd done. She wanted him to know that she knew. But she wouldn't be the one to disclose.

She watched the softness in his eyes disappear at the sound of her words, sensed his exasperation as he clenched his fists and punched the knuckles of one hand into the palm of the other. But despite knowing she was driving him mad, irritating him beyond belief, she couldn't help herself descending on yet another freefall of self-destruction.

Fintan turned away from her and stormed into the kitchen.

She followed him, matching his hasty pace.

He turned down the oven temperature and took the steaming dish from the wire shelf, stirring the mixture and releasing the pieces of chicken that were sticking to the earthenware, all the time keeping his back firmly to his wife.

She guessed he was trying to formulate a response that wouldn't cause her to erupt even more. But she couldn't wait. No. Instead, more insults and accusations flowed from her lips.

"All those glamorous babes draping themselves over you! Pushing their fake boobs in your face! Why would you stay here with boring old me when you can have a different girl throwing herself at you every hour? Really ego-massaging, I'm sure. It's no wonder you never hear me getting out of bed in the morning. Probably exhausted keeping them all satisfied!"

She felt as though she was standing at the edge of a movie set watching a scene unfold in front of her eyes. She barely recognised the stranger that was cast in the role of Vicky Jones. And the sad truth was that she didn't care. She knew exactly how much damage she was causing and couldn't get herself to stop. She'd been holding her emotions in check all day, all week . . . all three weeks.

He turned to face her.

"It's not as if you own the nightclub or anything!" She stood glaring at him, digging her nails into the palms of her hands, her eyes boring into his, the stone fortress of self-protection rebuilding itself around her heart.

"And if I did own it, Vicky? Would that make it any different? What would you want then? That I only open in the afternoons? Breakfast, lunch and early evening meals? Get real. The place would be shut down in no time."

He turned away from her and covered the casserole, returning it to the oven once more. Storming into the utility room, he muttered under his breath with every step he took, escaping through the back door to breathe some clean air into his lungs. When he came back inside, she had left the room.

Vicky could hear him banging utensils and opening and closing drawers as she ran up the stairs and into their bedroom, shutting the door tightly to block out the sound of him taking his anger out on their walnut kitchen presses. Why had she started yet another argument? Why hadn't she kept her big mouth shut and pretended for even one evening that she was the normal woman he believed he'd married? Hell, there were times when she actually wondered about her sanity! Surely it couldn't be normal to obsess about a single isolated incident? An incident she had only witnessed for barely a minute, an incident that had been haunting her ever since, making her scrutinise his every move and analyse every word that came out of his mouth.

She couldn't get it out of her mind, found it impossible to erase those moments three weeks before when she'd entered the club where Fintan worked, her eyes scanning the scantily lit room for her husband. Instead of the enthusiastic welcome she'd expected, her spontaneous visit had instead opened the door to an appalling revelation. And she couldn't stop reliving it over and over and over until it had become the only thing inhabiting her mind. It wasn't as if it was the first time she'd ever seen Fintan chatting to a pretty woman. Of course not! But the animated concern on his face as he'd looked at *her*, the way his hands rested on *her* shoulders, the way his fingers had stroked *her* hair, how he'd put a protective arm around *her* and, heads close together, led *her* through the door marked '*Private*' with a covert glance back over his shoulder, had brought Vicky out in a cold sweat. Her imagination had already got to work, creating vivid, distorted scenes of what was going on between Fintan and *her* behind that door.

The more she relived those moments, the more suspicious she became, jealousy eating her up inside, making her question every aspect of her marriage, wondering if there were other evident signs she had innocently overlooked.

Catching sight of her reflection in the bedroom mirror, she took in her wild eyes and lank hair. Another Friday night. End of a third miserable week. She turned away from the mirror and flopped onto the bed in despair. Yawning widely, she stretched out and allowed the events of the day to wash over her. She would have loved to slip into a dreamless sleep but instead of winding down, her steady heartbeat picked up speed and galloped at an alarming rate in her chest. She lay completely still, keeping her eyes closed and her ears open. She listened. *Thump-thump, thump-thump, thump-thump* . . .

Her head reeled. Her anger slowly abated. She hated what she'd become. Her insecurity was now her enemy and she despised the neediness that had developed inside, the self-confidence she'd spent years developing peeling away layer by layer, leaving her as exposed as the shy, retreating teenager she'd once been. In her wildest dreams she had never believed that she'd find – and keep – a kind, generous man like Fintan. He was everything she'd wanted in a husband, everything her parents had never been. His easy-going, friendly disposition, his popularity – the traits she'd fallen deeply in love with. But now her intense love for him was being coloured by suspicions, primarily about his place of work and what went on there. That had become a huge problem for her. Temptation leaning across the counter, staring at him, catching his eye, flirting with him, making him offers any man would find difficult to refuse. Wasn't that how she'd met him herself? Yielding to his gentle charm, laughing at his jokes?

Stop! Don't even go there!

She held her head in her hands and shook it from side to side before jumping from the bed and rushing into the en suite bathroom to run a hot shower and attempt to drown out the voices that had risen to a screaming pitch. How she wished they would disappear down the plughole!

As she lathered her body with warm suds, the soothing rhythmic movements helped her to regain control and slow the pace of her breathing. Then the memories of that Friday night wormed their way into her subconscious again as she squirted shampoo onto her wet hair and massaged her scalp vigorously. Closing her eyes to prevent them from stinging as the mixture of shampoo and water poured down her face, she recalled how she had steeled herself to follow Fintan and *her*, to approach *that* door and raise her trembling hand to the handle. And how she had recoiled and fled, too terrified to open the door, too terrified to reveal the truth. Too terrified to try the handle and find it was locked.

She had tortured herself with 'if only' for days afterwards, wishing she'd remained padded in ignorance, regretting more than anything that she hadn't stayed curled up in front of the TV with her large bar of Galaxy and new novel.

"Dinner's on the table!" Fintan stuck his head around the bathroom door, his voice startling her, his words shattering her reverie, bringing her back to her senses, back to the present. "How long more will you be?"

"Coming!" she shouted over the din of the electric shower, giving her conditioned hair one last rinse before pressing the power button and silencing the noise. If only she had a power button in her head, she thought. How lovely it would be to silence the voices.

Chapter 6

> Hi Rog, missing you like crazy, Had d most awful day at work 2day. Restless now. Can't settle. Let me come home please! Forgive me!

Ariel stared at the screen on her mobile phone, reading back over the text and laughing out loud at the absurdity of what she'd keyed in. As if I'd ever send a pleading text like that to Roger, she thought, pressing and holding the cancel button until every letter had disappeared and the screen went blank. She tossed her phone onto the footstool, its silence a reminder of the lack of contact she'd had from him. She hadn't heard from him in over two weeks. Not since . . . not since she'd had to come clean and tell him why she couldn't travel to Dubai.

He'd organised flights, reserved a hotel room and booked time off work. A spontaneous surprise. Excuses had poured out of her. But none that he'd believed. Eventually, when she knew he was interpreting things incorrectly and her excuses were convincing him that she wanted to cool things between them, it was easier to come clean and tell the truth.

Roger had grabbed his jacket and made for the door of the apartment, instructing her to leave her keys on the table and be gone by the end of the week. She hadn't blamed him, had understood why he felt she'd deceived him, was convinced he'd return when he'd cooled down. She'd waited and waited but the silence between them lengthened and she finally accepted he wasn't coming back. She'd made attempts to contact him, giving up on her efforts after he'd cancelled her calls numerous times. Pulling out her suitcases and holdalls, she'd packed every stitch of clothes, took everything that was hers from the apartment and left.

Shaking her head to dispel these negative thoughts, she placed the files she'd been working on back in her briefcase, pushing it off her knees and onto the old-fashioned threadbare couch, cringing when she spotted woodworm on the ancient teak arms. Hugging her arms around her body, she rubbed her hands up and down, up and down, trying to instil some warmth into her freezing bones. The heating had packed up again. The old-fashioned two-bar electric fire was a luxury she could ill afford, shoddy though it was, the fuse-board buzzing loudly as the electricity units spiralled each time she plugged it in. She'd spent her last €20 cash in The Bailey – a small price to pay for a little companionship in her opinion – but she'd have to organise getting some coal and firelighters as soon as her next monthly pay cheque was lodged in her account. At least then she'd be able to light a proper fire in the old-fashioned tiled fireplace. Maybe then it would feel more like home. Maybe then she would unpack her suitcases and accept the fact that this was where she lived now.

Sliding across the ancient floorboards in her chunky hiking socks, she went into the tiny bedroom and searched in her suitcase for a Shetland wool cardigan, buttoning it right up to the neck to try and keep warm. The silent television stared mockingly at her, the disconnected cable hanging loosely from the wall behind, as she re-entered the living room that doubled as a kitchen. Cable TV, she remembered with irony, from the Internet description advertising the flat. They forgot to mention it wasn't connected. And the television itself looked so ancient with its enormous knobs and brass-coloured dials that it could very well have qualified for antique status. The only sign of life in any of the rooms was the geranium she'd placed on the window-sill, her one attempt to put her stamp on the place. Finding a flat to lease at such short notice had been difficult. Finding a flat within her current budget had been next to impossible, leaving her with little option but to settle for a place that in all honesty could only be described as a hovel.

"Pasta or gratin potatoes?" Fintan asked when Vicky padded into the kitchen, wrapping a velour dressing-gown around her scented body, her hair damp and tangled.

"Pasta is good," she said, taking a seat at the table and watching him serve.

The atmosphere between them had resolved itself once more. She presumed he was expecting an explanation for her earlier outburst. Trouble was, coming up with one was far from straightforward. She couldn't tell him what she'd seen in the club that night and the effect it had on every moment of every day since.

"Looks great, Fin. Thank you," she told him, placing her hand over his as he put the plate in front of her. "I'm sorry I was a bitch earlier."

"Lunatic!" Fintan laughed, taking a seat opposite and tucking into his meal with gusto. "Feeling better now?"

"Think so," she shrugged, savouring the taste of chicken in her mouth and chewing thoughtfully, being reminded for the umpteenth time what a good husband he could be and what an utter fool she'd be to let anything or *anyone* come between them.

"Fin?" she began, wondering how she should broach her request. It was a tall order but she was confident it would work. And if he could prove that he was fully committed to their relationship, perhaps then she could let go of her suspicions and look to the future. "Hmm?" he said between mouthfuls.

"I know you love working there . . ."

Fintan swallowed the food in his mouth and looked across at his wife, giving her his full attention. "I presume there's a 'but' coming next?"

She nodded. "But I don't want to be home alone any

more. I want you to look for a job with normal hours, hours that allow time for us to have a relationship."

He sighed in exasperation, then laid his knife and fork on his plate, his expression grim. "I've slogged for years to get a respectable position in the bar trade, Vicky. A decent position with a very decent salary. A salary, I might add, that we depend on to keep this roof over our heads. And a salary that would decrease drastically if I decided I wasn't prepared to work unsociable hours. I am not walking out of a good job to end up in the dole queue!"

"I earn too!" she shot back quickly.

His brown eyes softened. "I know that, love, and I respect it. But we couldn't survive on what you're earning. We need everything we're bringing in now and a bit more too."

She pierced a chunk of chicken with her fork, the metal of the fork scraping against the plate.

"I'm not walking away from a management position," he went on. "It's all I know. I'm lucky to be in a club that's busy seven nights a week. How many businesses have gone to the wall?"

"You have experience with the public. You'd pick up something else."

"I wouldn't, Vicky." He reached across the table and caught her hand in his, rubbing his thumb across her fingers. "I didn't stay in school like you. I don't even have a Leaving Cert to fall back on. I'm not qualified to do anything else."

She chewed thoughtfully. "Okay, well, what about

opting for mostly day shifts? Even for a while. Working five nights out of seven is crazy! Until four in the morning, sometimes later. Apart from anything else, it's not good for your health. And what if . . .?" A piece of chicken stuck in her throat, choking back the question she needed to ask. She took a sip of water from her glass, averting her eyes from his.

"What if what, Vick? What if the house was broken into? What if the car broke down? You know you only have to call me and I'll be straight home." His voice was reassuring, his fingers applying gentle pressure on hers.

"No, Fin," she said quietly. "What if we had a baby? What then? The baby would hardly know who you are."

He inhaled sharply. "That's a long way off. We're not even thirty yet! Barely off our honeymoon. We'll cross that bridge when we get to it but, believe me, I'm nowhere near ready to take on that responsibility!"

She slipped her hand from beneath his and put a large forkful of pasta and chasseur into her mouth to prevent herself from announcing that it was all she wanted, that she couldn't wait to be a mum and share parenting with him. It also helped her hold back another retort, a retort about that painful subject she tried not to think about, the subject that had cost her several nights' sleep long before this recent nightmare had robbed her of her rest.

Fintan shook his head, mistaking her silence for agreement and continuing with his justification. "You're hilarious, Vick. You had me going there! A baby? As if." He took a slice of bread and mopped the left-over sauce from his plate. "We're still paying for the lavish wedding – your bright idea to refuse your parents' offer of financial help I might add – and the garden needs landscaping. And then the car will need changing. If we can afford it. The list is endless. We're a long way from being able to afford another mouth to feed."

She sat in silence, listening to him list off one reason after the other, without even asking her for an opinion.

"And what about the cost of childcare? I see the pressure my brothers are under buying nappies and baby food, never having a week without a visit to the doctor. No. It's not for me, not for a long time yet, thank you." He picked up his glass of water and drained it in one go, trying his best to ignore how fast his heart was beating, trying his best not to think about the five-year loan he'd agreed to. Until that was repaid, his cash flow would be well and truly curtailed. And when the time came for him and Vicky to become parents, it would be when they were both ready, not when they stumbled into it.

That was the longest speech she'd ever heard him make, even longer than his wedding speech which was cut short by one of his brother's children unplugging the microphone and taking off around the hotel with it.

"Would it be that bad, Fin?" Beads of perspiration dampened her skin. What was he saying? That when the recession was over, they could bring it up as a topic for discussion! The disaster that was her life was getting worse by the minute. And what did he mean by saying paying for the wedding was my idea, she wondered. He'd been as adamant as she about showing her parents they were capable of doing things alone. He'd had his own agenda that day.

"Vick! We've lots of time for all the serious stuff in life. We should still be living life to the full! And when the time is right we will be the best parents ever, sharing as much of the childcare as possible between us so that our baby will actually know who we are!"

That's low, she thought, suspecting he was referring to her childhood experiences. That's lower than low. She was speechless. He could talk the talk better than she'd realised. But could she believe him? Or was he simply placating her to get everything his own way? She opened her eyes wide, feeling as though she were seeing clearly for the very first time.

He began to clear his side of the table, stacking his plate, cutlery and glass into the dishwasher, restless and uneasy, boiling the kettle and making a fresh pot of coffee.

She remained motionless, still unable to find any words to respond. Gingerly placing her knife and fork on the plate, she pushed her chair back from the table.

"You're right, Fintan," she said eventually. "Life is for living! I probably only need a night out on the town to remind me of that. Or maybe a pampering weekend with the girls is in order. Let my hair down."

She waited with bated breath, waited for him to invite her to join him in the club for an after-hours drink. In the same way she had so many times before they'd got married and moved from their apartment in Ballsbridge to their new home in Malahide.

"My next night off I'm all yours – promise," he said, pouring two cups of coffee from the coffee pot and bringing them to the table. "We'll do something special. A meal and a movie? Go clubbing? The choice is yours."

"Or maybe I could put my glad rags on later tonight and keep you company while you're waiting for all the partygoers to go home?" she suggested, gutted he hadn't come up with the idea himself, storing it as another grain of evidence. He wasn't doing anything to hide the fact he didn't want her near the club. Didn't he understand that it was him she wanted to spend time with? She had zero interest in clubs or movies. It wasn't a sparkling social life she was missing. It was *him*!

Turning away from her to get milk from the fridge, he dismissed her idea. "I'll be too busy tonight with all those parties going on. You'd be sitting there on your own at the bar watching me buzzing around. Best leave it. Anyway, the owner doesn't approve of staff partners hanging around after hours any more. Especially with all the new health and safety regulations . . ." He added milk to their coffee and began to clear the table again, never once meeting her gaze.

"No need to elaborate," she responded testily. She'd heard enough. "I know where I'm not wanted!"

"Ah jeez, Vicky, don't be like that!" he said, coming behind her and wrapping his arms around her, nuzzling his head in her hair, inhaling the smell of conditioner. "I'm going to work for God's sake. It's not as if I'm a guest at the party! Maybe you do need a break with the girls?"

Why tonight, he thought. Why does she want to pay a visit tonight of all nights? He was expecting a visitor at the club, a visitor Vicky would highly disapprove of.

She sat rigid, not daring to turn around. She assumed he was wearing an expectant expression at the thought of her going away for a few nights, giving him the freedom to do as he pleased, to be with whom he pleased. She refused to respond to his attempts at affection, furious that he thought he could humour her as you would a pet dog!

'Live life to the full,' he'd said. The words left a bad taste in her head, never mind her mouth! Whatever went on at work was obviously part of *him* living *his* life to the full and nothing whatsoever to do with her or their marriage. At least that's what the voice of suspicion kept whispering. And that's what Vicky thought too.

Pulling out of his grasp, she rose to her feet. She was damned if she was going to give him a licence to destroy them. She'd had enough of other people controlling her happiness. It was time she took control of it herself.

Conversation was minimal for the hour or so between dinner and when Fintan left for work. She'd scrolled quickly through his mobile phone while he'd taken a shower, disgusted to see he'd deleted every message and cleared his call log. She'd heard the mobile ringing as he'd walked up the stairs, had heard his muffled voice in the bedroom. So why was his call log empty? Vicky only needed one guess to figure that out.

She barely lifted her head to say goodbye when he popped into the lounge to tell her he was leaving, planting a chaste peck on her cheek. Although she did take the time to notice how pristine he looked. And she couldn't but inhale the strong scent of Burberry cologne that lingered in the room long after he'd shut the door. Recognising the efforts he had gone to with his appearance did nothing to ease her concerns. Her intuition was on full alert. Had he always used cologne for work? She couldn't say for sure but didn't think so. Whose benefit had he sprayed it for, she wondered. Certainly not hers, judging by the speed at which he'd left. He'd hurried from the room without even adding coal to the fire or bringing her a fresh coffee, something he generally did before heading off for a night at work, his interest in leaving the house more evident than any he had in staying. Was he rushing because he had somebody interesting waiting or was he rushing to escape any further nagging from her? She had a strong feeling it was a combination of both.

Feeling restless and uneasy, she gave up on the book she was reading and banged it shut. She'd been staring at the same page over and over without digesting a single word. She couldn't get the thoughts of what Fintan might be up to from her mind, couldn't stop thinking that he was out there laughing and giggling with another woman. With *her*. The ticking of the mantel clock – a quartz timepiece encased in magnificent red mahogany that Fintan's grandmother had given them as a wedding present – acknowledged every second that passed since he'd walked out the door. And the house was empty without him. She was empty without him. And it wasn't only because he wasn't there in body. She couldn't feel him in her heart.

Time crawled by. She shifted in the chair, turned the television on, flicked through about four hundred channels – twice – and turned it off again. Another endless night alone with an overactive mind, a mind that wouldn't stop thinking.

She wanted to be ordinary, with nothing to worry about except what to buy for the following day's dinner. She wanted to be able to relax like other people. She wanted to be able to get on with her life and look forward to things. But instead she sat transfixed, powerlessly allowing her suspicions to take over her life. She'd been like that for exactly three weeks: wondering and questioning, watching and imagining, hurt, furious and scared.

The numbness she'd become accustomed to was beginning to wear off. She was starting to feel again, confusion being the most prevalent feeling of all. Confusion and love. She couldn't stop loving Fintan, not even now. What was wrong with her? Was it because she'd been deprived of love as a child? Was that why she couldn't give up on the one person who had shown her true love? Was it because reacting to situations had been frowned upon? Was it because she'd been brought up to believe it was more appropriate to suppress true feelings? Was that why she had turned on her heel and run away? Was that why she hadn't gone charging through the door marked '*Private*' and pulled them apart, made them face up to their actions? Or tried that handle to see if it was locked . . .

Vicky let the book slide off her lap and drop to the floor. The sharp thud woke her from her reverie, bringing her to life. She jumped to her feet and fixed the spark guard in front of the open fire, reluctant to leave its warmth, yet anxious to get upstairs and do something constructive to help shake the crazy doubts that had deep-rooted themselves into every corner and crevice of her mind. She wished there was a code of ethics to follow when a person suspected they were being cheated on. Confronting him would be a pure waste of time. If he had the audacity to cheat in the first place, denial would be a walk in the park. She'd read enough problem pages and watched enough soap operas and soppy movies to know that much! No, she wanted – actually she needed – proof. And there had to be a way of finding it. Tucked away in the tiniest crevice of her mind was a lingering hope that she'd misread the situation, a lingering – probably misguided – hope that things could go back to the way they were. Before.

The door to his wardrobe swung open as she entered their bedroom, prompting her to begin by searching through his clothes. She started in fright when his clock radio buzzed on the hour, startled by the unexpected noise and surprised by how jumpy she was. What was she looking for? She wasn't sure but knew she'd recognise it if she found it. A phone number perhaps, a slip of paper with a date and time, a cloakroom ticket, another woman's tube of lipstick? Any or all of those things. But preferably none. That was the real truth she was hoping to find.

With renewed energy, she took a deep breath and pushed the clothes hangers to the left-hand side of the rail, starting in the pocket of his one and only winter coat, sliding it across to the other side when her search was done. Rifling through his jackets, jeans and trouser pockets proved fruitless. Not a thing. Unless she counted a total of fifteen tissues, three paperclips, a cocktail stick and some coins. She rooted in the pockets of his favourite denim jacket and couldn't help smiling when she found a photo of him and her, laughing hilariously on one of the rollercoasters in Disneyland, Florida.

Moving to the window ledge, she leaned against it, gazing at the photo, reliving the memory of how they'd screamed with fear and whooped for joy as the rollercoaster dipped and twirled from dizzying heights to dangerous swirls. Running her finger over the glossy print, she traced the outline of his face, his smiling lips and his hand holding hers, their fingers entwined tightly.

Her eyes locked on his hand, staring in disbelief as the image became distorted and his fingers unwrapped themselves from hers. Her eyes darted to his face to see his lips shaping into a sardonic sneer. She knew it wasn't real. She hadn't totally lost her mind. But she was losing control over her thoughts.

Her mouth went dry and a familiar emptiness settled in the pit of her stomach, a sense of entrapment taking hold inside. Her breathing quickened, a ticking pulse beating rapidly at the base of her throat. Confusion replaced her nostalgia. She flung the photo on the floor, watching as it landed on the varnished boards.

Slowly the image receded.

She scanned the room frantically, her eyes darting all around, searching for a sign, unable to tear herself away from the support of the window ledge, convinced her legs wouldn't hold her up.

Where else could she look? There had to be evidence. Surely if he was up to something she shouldn't be the last to know. Fintan, by his very nature, had a tendency to be careless, often misplacing things, easily distracted (more than she'd ever have imagined as it turned out) and hopeless to tidy up. If he is carrying on behind my back, she thought, he'll have left a clue.

She clutched her chest, a physical ache groaning across her breastbone. She wondered how she could live her life without him, lying awake night after night when he didn't come home. Ever again. She didn't want to lose him. She loved him. She'd invested her trust in him, had listened to his account of his rather colourful past, had shown understanding and acceptance. She wanted – no, she needed – to keep him. He was her husband after all. For better or worse, her life was nothing without him in it. But she needed to know what she was dealing with. And living with. More than anything, she just needed to know. But how?

She forced herself away from the window ledge and began to pace the room, thinking and thinking, trying to make sense of the craziness going on in her head. The buttermilk walls began to close in around her. She dropped her gaze to the floor instead, tightening the belt of her dressing-gown and shoving her hands into the deep patch pockets as she circled and circled the room.

She stopped pacing and leaned her elbows on the cream chest of drawers, staring at her dishevelled appearance in the mirror. *Maybe my weakness is another reason why he's seeking attention elsewhere?* "Now I'm being utterly ridiculous," she said aloud, her voice echoing in the otherwise still house. She stooped to take the photo from the floor, gazing at it for a moment before replacing it carefully in Fintan's pocket. "Fintan loves me. He loves me. He's not a cheat. He's hardworking and confident and only has our future in mind." The words had a semi-soothing effect.

She moved towards the window once more and stared into the darkness outside, forcing herself to believe the words she'd uttered aloud. She chanted them over and over in her head until eventually the positive statements drowned out the weaker voice, the husky whisper frantic to be heard which begged her to face facts and not to be so damn blind and stupid.

She hummed a tune to escape the mental debate, swaying in time to the rhythm of an old Stevie Wonder number, *Superstition*, until finally she shut out the voices that were fighting for her attention. The music had the desired effect, helping her to relax and get her breathing back to normal. She looked up, relieved to see the bedroom walls were back in their rightful position.

She waited a moment, listened attentively but all was quiet. Her head was her own again.

She took her hands from her pockets and ran her fingers through her hair, regretting that she hadn't dried it properly as she pulled against the fine knots, imagining them as an extension of the tangles inside her brain. She closed the door of Fintan's wardrobe, her attention shifting to the matching lockers at either side of their bed.

Each locker had three drawers. She didn't know what was inside his; hers were filled to capacity with jewellery and an assortment of accessories. But his were an enigma, an enigma she'd never felt the need to investigate. Until now. She pulled out each drawer in turn, unsurprised by the jumbled mess lurking within. She upended them on to the bed, emptying their contents into three separate bundles so she could put them back in the same order she'd found them, dumping the solid wooden drawers on the floor, beyond caring about scratching either the floors or the furniture.

After yet another futile search, she calmly returned the refilled top drawer into its original slot, calmer still as she replaced the middle one. First impressions told her she'd find nothing in the third drawer either. Silent relief flooded through her as she slowly picked her way through the array of cards and ticket stubs, old match programmes and silly mementos. Nothing. She thanked God for that and replaced everything in a messy way similar to how it was to begin with.

Kneeling down on the floor, she pushed the drawer

into its slot, only to find it wouldn't slide in completely. "Damn," she said through gritted teeth, unable to get it home. Something was blocking it. She pulled it out once more to investigate. And there, jammed against the back of the unit was a bright orange box, a box about twice the size of a pack of cards. She reached in to get it.

Blinking, she read the bold black writing on the label: *'Billy Boy, The Experience Pack. The ultimate Billy Boy experience, the excitingly different condom. We not only sell condoms, we sell Billy Boys!'* Squinting, she could just about make out the tiny writing at the bottom of the box: *'Coloured, flavoured and natural. Made in Germany.'* Flipping it over on to its side, she read: *'A multi-pack of condoms, containing one twelve-pack and two six-packs'*.

A cold shiver ran the entire length of her body.

Her hope was lost, her fears a reality.

She felt the blood drain from her face but apart from that she couldn't have been more surprised by her reaction. She'd lain in bed night after night waiting for Fintan to come in, trying to imagine what it would be like to actually discover real proof that he was cheating. She had truly believed she'd lose control. But the reality proved to be nothing like what she'd envisaged.

Instead of the rising anger and gut-wrenching hurt she'd anticipated, she was overcome by an uncharacteristic sense of calm and acceptance. And relief. Yes, relief was probably the strongest emotion that flooded through her as she stared at the orange box. Relief that she wasn't actually going mad after all. Relief that she hadn't been imagining the signs, and relief that six months of marriage hadn't turned her into a clingy, possessive partner. It wasn't her. It was him. Fintan's actions were to blame.

They didn't use condoms. They didn't need to. She'd always taken responsibility for the contraception in their relationship.

So what was Fintan doing with a multi-packet of condoms shoved at the back of his drawer? A good hiding place at that, a place where he knew she would never come across them.

She flopped on to the floor, leaning her back against the bed, turning the box over and over in her hands, finally giving in and opening it to see how many condoms remained. He'd used both six-packs, the twelve-pack was still untouched. With whom? And when? And, most importantly, why? Why did he need to have sex with another woman when he had a wife waiting at home, a wife who loved him?

She stared at the third drawer on the floor beside her and had another sinking thought. If he had brought *her* home and made love to *her* in their bed, his condoms conveniently hidden at the back of the bedside locker, where was she herself at the time? Out at work earning a salary to help keep the roof over their heads, as he'd so defiantly pointed out earlier. If he was conducting an affair in their home while she spent eight hours every day working her butt off in Ellis Enterprise, it was unforgivable. She could no longer defend him. Not even in her head where a storm bubbled dangerously beneath the surface and her desire for revenge became internal terror, the powerful force behind that storm.

Chapter 7

Ariel stared at the closing balance of the account she was working on, pulling the quilt up around her neck, nipping at a loose thread on the fingerless gloves she wore to keep her hands warm and still allow her the flexibility to turn pages and use a pen. The zeros before the decimal point swam in front of her eyes. She scanned the list of credit and debit entries, the blank spaces at the end of the ledger flashing at her like a neon light. The amount she'd need would be a mere bubble in a bottle of champagne when compared to her client's vast wealth. Who would notice if she added another expense or charge, found a way to embezzle enough cash to solve all her problems?

"*You* would, you idiot!" she said aloud, dismissing the notion as quickly as it had entered her head. She'd never embezzled as much as a cent in her life and no matter how bad things were, she was not about to sink to that level.

She signed her name at the end of the page in bold black ink, a signature she could stand over, a signature she could always be proud of. Whatever else she might have lost, she was not about to throw away her integrity. She tiptoed across the cold floor to turn out the light, stubbing her toe on her tennis racket as she fumbled her way back to bed through the jumbled floor mess. And though her toe stung like crazy, she couldn't help smiling at the thought of her game the following day. Win, lose or draw, she thought, at least running around the court will keep me warm for a few hours. That in itself would make the effort worthwhile.

Marcus leaned against the smoking shelter, inhaling the nicotine from his Rothmans cigarette. He stared into the starry sky, the absence of street lighting making a pleasant change from the hustle and bustle of Dublin's nightlife. The woman in the red dress – complete with plunging neckline – sitting on the silver patio chair directly in his line of vision was doing nothing to hide her interest in him. But she was wasting her energy. Another time perhaps she might have stirred his interest. But not that evening. Even if she'd peeled the red satin straps from her shoulders and revealed every tanned inch of her shapely figure, she'd have had her work cut out. There was only one female Marcus had on his mind. At least where romance was concerned.

Taking another drag on his cigarette, he flicked the ashes away from him, blowing smoke rings into the night air. Coming to Enniskerry for the weekend had been a mistake. He'd realised that as soon as he'd stepped inside Edel's cottage. Taking one look around and seeing the trail of discarded clothes leading to the bedroom in the otherwise pristine lounge, he'd walked back out again, got into his brand new Audi A5 – the extravagant luxury he'd treated himself to for his thirty-ninth birthday – and broke every speed limit he'd driven through on his way to the village pub.

Swallowing a double shot of Southern Comfort in one quick gulp, he paid the bartender, ordered a second one and brought it outside with him. The whisky burned his throat, the alcohol succeeding in easing the knot of tension that had been lodged in his chest since the consultants' meeting that afternoon. Ben's announcement, though favourable for him in a business sense, had come as a huge shock. He hadn't expected it, hadn't been prepared to be singled out so noticeably. And despite his colleagues slapping him on the back as they'd returned to their respective offices, Marcus hadn't missed their exchanged glances. Business was tightening and it was every man (and woman) for themselves. Marcus didn't want to be different, didn't want to be the one taking the largest accounts from a colleague, earning the highest commissions while others were negotiating fees and costs in order to encourage return of business. Yes, he'd enjoyed his successes, but they'd been as a result of hard work and not the misfortune of others. He was happy to be one of the lads.

Taking a second cigarette from the box, he placed it between his lips, sucking on it longingly as he lit it from the butt in his hand. He finally allowed himself to dwell on the one person whose face had been haunting him all evening: Ariel.

Her ghastly pallor hadn't escaped him. Nor the way she'd chewed on the inside of her cheek and failed to find words to retort to Ben's announcement. Her reaction unnerved him, made him wonder why she hadn't lashed out, why she hadn't defended her figures, why she hadn't fought back. And what, he wondered, was behind the haunted look that had recently invaded her eyes, lurking forebodingly, dimming her natural sparkle.

His spontaneous dash to Enniskerry finally made sense. It hadn't been about surprising Edel or attempting to rekindle what remained of their relationship, no matter how much he tried to convince himself it was. He knew that now. Rushing away from the office had been about putting distance between him and Ariel. He hadn't trusted himself to be anywhere in her vicinity. He hadn't trusted himself not to follow her to The Bailey and quiz her, find out what was upsetting her, show his concern, cross the line between personal and professional, let his true feelings be known.

He banged his empty glass on the wooden picnic table, jingling the car keys in his pocket, annoyed with himself for drinking so much. Annoyed with himself for falling under the spell of someone whose feminine attractiveness and stark vulnerability could weaken the resolve he'd made a short few months before.

The woman in the red dress stood up from her chair and brushed past him.

Yet again, he ignored her.

I have no option but to stay the night now, he thought, under no illusion about how far in excess of the legal alcohol limit he was for driving. Slipping out through the rear entrance and around to the front of the building, he checked he'd locked his car properly and began the long walk back to Edel's to eat some humble pie and ask for a bed for the night! Walking at a steady pace while his eyes adjusted to the darkness of night, he lit up another cigarette, stayed close to the grass margin along the country road and hoped he'd be saved the embarrassment of confronting Edel's visitor.

Pete Scavo flicked between the screens on the security camera, checking all zones and zooming in on all access areas. Pushing the computer mouse away from him, he adjusted his soft tweed cap on his head to shield his eyes from the glare of the flickering screens. The cap wasn't part of his security uniform but that didn't bother Pete. It served its purpose, prevented him from having to make eye contact with all and sundry. He slid down in his chair, wriggling until he felt comfortable. In the space of a few seconds his eyes were heavy with sleep and began to close, his chin flopping on to his chest, the dull hum of the blow heater at his feet lulling him into a dreamless sleep. As it did most nights he was on duty.

A fourteen-hour night shift. Many would hate it, find it exhausting, boring and monotonous. But Pete opted for as many shifts as he could possibly get, furious that the new health and safety regulations prevented him from working around the clock. Every hour he spent working as security guard was an hour less he had to be at home. An hour less he had to listen to the groans and squeaks in the old house he'd been living in since he'd married Barbara, squeaks and groans he'd never even heard when she'd been in the house. An hour less he had to look at the empty chair where his wife no longer sat.

At home, he found it impossible to sleep in the king-size bed Barbara had persuaded him to buy. She'd joked with him in the furniture shop, convincing him they'd appreciate the space between them in their old age when their joints were inflamed with arthritis and their poor circulation forced them to toss and turn at night. Except she hadn't survived to old age. And now he was left to carry on without her.

By the time he arrived for work every evening he was shattered.

Which explained why he wasn't as alert as he should have been that Friday night when Ellis Enterprise had a surprise intruder, an intruder who unlocked the main door, unset the alarm and tiptoed past a snoring Pete, knowing the exact route to take to avoid being detected by the eye of the security camera.

Chapter 8

Saturday morning

Vicky didn't wake till eleven. She couldn't believe how well she'd slept, the first restful night she'd had in three weeks. She snuggled deeper under the covers, content in the knowledge that she didn't have to get up and go to work. Nestling into the comfort and warmth of the duvet, she felt the gentle vibration of Fintan snoring lightly beside her. Still in that not-fully-awake state, she reached out to touch him. But a millisecond before her fingertips reached his skin, she remembered. Instantly, she felt clammy. Dirty.

She flipped over onto her side, away from him, moving towards the edge of their bed. Her eyes smarted with tears as she recalled the box of condoms she'd pushed back behind his drawer. And though they were out of sight, they were very prominent in her head. Suddenly she was wide awake.

She remembered everything that had followed

finding the condoms: every breath threatening to choke her, paralysis freezing her limbs and weighing her down, and then the flood of energy, the rage, the fierce desire for revenge . . .

"Hey there, your eyes open yet?" Fintan's sleepy voice cut in on her thoughts.

She gripped the edge of the mattress. "Not quite," she responded, her voice light, her body tensing when she felt his hand snaking around her waist and onto her abdomen. Her thoughts immediately turned to a distorted image of him with *her*, his hand on *her*. She shuddered within, her skin crawling at his touch, betrayal breaking her in two.

Fintan's hand was beginning to travel southward. It didn't take a genius to guess what he had in mind and she was having none of it. For all she knew, he could very well have been with *her* before leaving work the previous night, his hands massaging *her*, stroking *her*, loving *her*!

She pulled out of his loose grasp, threw back the covers and jumped out of bed.

"I'm taking a shower and then I'm going shopping," she announced, shivering as her feet touched the cold wooden floor. She needed to put some space between him and her, as well as giving him enough rope to hang himself. Maybe he'd seize the opportunity of a free house to have his lady friend over, she thought, disgust threading its way through every drop of blood in her body. After all, he still had twelve condoms to use. Now that she knew where they were, it'd be easy to check later whether they had been touched or not.

"Why don't I come with you?" Fintan sat up in bed, fixing the pillows behind his head. "We could have breakfast in town, you could shop, then we could take in a movie, talk –"

"You want to come shopping?" She stared at him in disbelief. Was he having her on? Fintan offering to come shopping was a first. What on earth is he up to, she wondered, convinced he was showing definite signs of a guilty conscience.

She slipped her feet into her slippers, pulled her dressing-gown around her and padded into the bathroom, closing the door firmly behind her. The sight of him sitting up in bed playing the role of perfect husband was enough to make her gag. Which she did. Over and over until her stomach hurt and her throat burned.

He was still sitting in the same position when she returned to the bedroom, his brown hair tousled, his eyes bleary and bloodshot from yet another late night. He reached his arms out for her, intent on making another effort to get closer to her. But she was too quick for him, pulling away so that all he got hold of was the giant-sized bath towel.

"Come back to bed, Vick? I love it when your skin's damp . . ."

I bet he does, she thought, her eyes narrowing in distrust, her breath quickening as a surge of resentment overcame her. The unbridled lust in his voice disgusted her.

She sashayed around the bedroom naked, her skin glistening with body oil.

His eyes followed her every move.

She watched him through the mirror.

He was too interested in the curve of her butt to notice that his reflection was in her line of vision.

Her heart hardened. She refused to think about how well his hands knew her body or how much their intimacy had deepened since their very first meeting. She was torn apart instead by the fact that those same hands had explored another woman's curves, his strong fingers stroking *her* face, running through *her* hair. Vicky fought for control, struggling to rein in her thoughts and make the graphic illusionist who was drawing vivid images in her head stop and erase.

She wanted to hit Fintan, draw back her hand and lash out, leave the mark of her fingers on his cheek.

He wanted to cup her breasts, massage her damp skin, pull her into his arms and hold her so tightly that he could forget the rest of the world even existed.

She wanted to repeatedly punch that smug grin off his face and hurt him.

He wanted to move inside her and take her to dizzying heights, bring them to a place where only he and she existed.

She wanted to crawl into a hole and die.

Bile rose in her throat, bitterness building and building, suffocating all other emotion. She struggled to think of something to accuse him of, something that would hurt him like he was hurting her. She tried to keep her mind off the obvious, the secret he had confided in her about his past, as the battle between remaining calm and lashing out raged loudly in her head. Once more she couldn't help herself. She was in self-destruct mode, a loose cannon that was seconds away from exploding. And what was more, she knew it. She continued to watch him through the mirror.

"What's with the sudden interest in coming shopping with me? And a movie? Don't you think it would be more in your line to do something dutiful and call over and see your parents? Or maybe pay a visit to your nieces and nephews? When was the last time you bothered?"

He shook his head, licked his lips expectantly, completely misreading her signals. He thought she was playing with him. He couldn't have been further from the truth.

"Everything I want, Vicky, is standing right here in front of me."

She turned around to face him, ignoring the lust in his eyes as he scanned her body from head to toe, feeling cheap instead of flattered. "Isn't family important to you, Fin? How long has it honestly been since you've visited Rathcoole?"

He shrugged his shoulders, his lack of interest evident.

Her nagging persisted. "Unless I'm mistaken you haven't seen them since our wedding day. That can't be right."

He sighed in exasperation, gently picking at a loose thread on the mulberry-coloured cotton sheet. Women! They were impossible to please, he thought. The previous evening had been shit! The visit he'd been expecting occurred, bringing with it threats and innuendo.

Consumed by a mixture of guilt and fury, he'd thought a relaxing day with his wife would take his mind off things. But what had she done with his offer? Only thrown it back in his face. She was unbelievable!

"You were moaning last night about us spending more time together. I'm trying to make an effort here." He threw his hands in the air.

"So an afternoon at the movies is supposed to do it?" Men, she thought, they would never have a clue what women wanted.

"Oh I can't win with you, Vicky! There's no pleasing you lately. And what obsession have you taken with my family all of a sudden? You've never shown any interest before."

She shrugged but didn't reply.

This time he persisted. "What's with you pushing me to call over there? And why now?"

She lowered her voice, fighting against the intense urge to scream at him and tell him what a lying cheat he was. "I think you need to acknowledge some of your responsibilities. That's all."

Fintan let out a long, slow breath, his hands by his sides now. "My relationship with my family – or lack of it as the case may be – is working perfectly as it is and technically is none of your business. In fact, I always thought it rather suited you that we kept ourselves to ourselves. Isn't it better to live our lives our way instead of allowing others to interfere? Aren't you happy with things the way they are?"

Happy? The word floated around inside her head.

What planet was he living on? How could she possibly be happy when he was screwing another woman right under her nose? He's become conceited, she thought, shocked that she hadn't noticed before. Or was his newfound self-confidence a direct result of the attention he was getting from *her*? She wondered about the other changes she'd missed. Exasperation? Impatience? Intolerance? Were they all signs of his increased confidence? Increased libido too no doubt! Were they traits associated with infidelity?

"Well, Vick?" His voice was softer this time.

Her assuredness began to waver. She recapped the situation quickly, still not responding. His passionate refusal in response to her suggestion about visiting his family certainly spoke multitudes. He was adamant about not revisiting his roots. Or his mistakes. Not even in a conversation.

And there she found her route to revenge. She'd found the key to unlock the door to the path she should take, a direction she'd never expected to travel. But his recent actions had been his own undoing. She'd stop at nothing – not even this – to make him suffer similar pain and experience similar betrayal to the one ripping her heart in two. She watched his face muscles contract, noticing a moody darkness replace the flippancy that had been there only moments before. She realised without doubt that she had indeed touched a nerve and exposed his vulnerability. His dark eyes held the tiniest frisson of fear, giving her something to cling to.

She turned to the mirror again.

Running a brush through her hair, she twisted her thick blonde mane into a tight knot and secured it with a silver grip. Fintan loved it when she wore her hair up and in that instant – standing in front of him in their bedroom – more than anything she wanted to turn him on. She wanted him to want her. More than that, she wanted him to experience the disappointment of not having her. And even more, she wanted his unsatisfied desire to disturb him, to make him wonder why she didn't reach out for him and respond to his efforts. To make him question if her rejection was because of something he'd done. To make him doubt himself. To make him unsure.

She snapped out of her daydream, conscious that he was still waiting for her response. Smearing some clear gloss on her lips, she wished she could toss the question he'd left hanging in the air right back at him. Was she happy indeed? How would he have reacted if she'd turned the tables on him and asked him why he'd gone looking for more, why he'd changed the way things were? Had he been unhappy? Would that be his justification?

Smacking her lips together, she turned around to face him, finally ready to answer him.

"Happy? I'm not sure I can give you a yes or no answer, Fin. Things don't always stay the same and we can't sign off on our happiness without giving consideration to others. Whether we like it or not, making time for family is the right thing to do. We can't live in a cocoon, ignoring everything going on around us, ignoring those we turned our backs on. Surely even you agree with that?"

He muttered something inaudible.

She spoke over his muttering, defiance in her tone. "I'm a member of that family now which means I've got a part to play too."

"Pot. Kettle. Black. You're a fine one to talk." He raised an eyebrow, scorn written all over his face.

His insinuation was valid but she didn't react. She was well aware of her hypocrisy. But that wasn't the issue at stake and she pushed it aside. "We ought to make more of an effort. Starting now. Hasn't it ever crossed your mind that two wrongs don't make a right? Do you believe in karma? What goes around comes around. How would you like it if we had children and they grew up to despise us and cut us out of their lives? In exactly the same way they'd watched their father do to his family?"

Her political-speak was nauseating, even to herself. She wanted to throw up again as she listed her arguments out to him.

He threw back the covers and sat at the edge of the bed, staring at the varnished floor. "Is that what's worrying you? That my family history will come back to haunt us in years to come?"

She shrugged non-committally.

He continued. "Even if I wanted to, it would be impossible to call there today. I'm working later on. By the time I'd driven all the way out to the Naas Road in Saturday traffic, it would be time to turn around and come back home again. I'd be lucky to spend ten minutes in the house!"

Her negotiating skills had fallen on deaf ears but she wasn't quite finished yet. "Are you saying your parents and family aren't worth the trouble? Don't you think it's about time you grew up, Fin? What if anything happened to any one of them? Could you live with the *guilt* of being too involved in your own life to pay them a little attention?"

She was still naked, still glistening.

He was still staring at the floor, meekness replacing the lust he'd been parading around a short time before.

"I don't do guilt, Vicky. I've made my decisions where my family are concerned and have no intention of changing my mind. It's perfectly fine as it is. So leave it be." He looked up at her for a brief moment, a lifeless stare clouding his brown eyes before he shifted his gaze back to the floor. He'd thought she'd understood him as regards his family. She'd certainly given him that impression. He'd explained honestly how things were, hadn't expected her to turn the tables on him.

As Vicky stared at her husband, a brief glimmer of pity passed over her. She wondered what his lover would feel for him now? Would *she* feel the same magnetic attraction to him if *she* saw him with his head dropped between his knees and his confidence bruised?

This thought spurred her to push him further, her hands on her hips, her stomach held in. "Is that how you see relationships, Fin? A bit like a used car? When it's no longer interesting or exciting simply discard it or trade it in for a newer, more improved model?"

He turned his gaze on her once more.

She wished she had clothes on.

He continued to stare at her as though she were a stranger now. If only you knew, he thought. If only you knew.

She was conscious of how irrational she was being but she didn't care, her only focus being to hit back at him. Had she reminded him of a different time, a different life? Had she transported him back there? Had she reminded him of issues he'd told her in confidence, issues he'd trusted her with?

"If that's what you want to believe, Vicky, go right ahead. But be very clear about one thing. If you take on my family and open up old wounds, you're on your own because the consequences could jump up and bite you in the ass."

The coldness in his tone was unnerving, unsettling and ever so slightly threatening.

She lowered her voice and asked one final question, gauging his expression carefully to see if by any stretch of the imagination he was starting to piece the jigsaw together and understand that something lay beneath her accusations.

"Is that what I have to look forward to in middle age? Being ignored. Shoved aside for bigger and better things if I don't match up to your expectations?"

She waited and watched.

He got up from the bed, moving slightly towards her but then stopping abruptly. His face was grey, his forehead slightly damp, his hands visibly trembling. "I'm not listening to this bullshit. Whatever your problem is, Vicky, you are not going to use me as a scapegoat! My family business is history! And as for your mention of bigger and better things," his voice dripped with sarcasm, "why don't you call and see your own parents? Attend to your duty? Or do you need to make an appointment in case they're too busy ignoring the fact you even exist?"

Ouch! That stung. But she didn't flinch, never moved a muscle. She was glad he couldn't read her mind. And equally glad that he couldn't hear another bit of her heart crumbling away.

He marched the few short steps into the bathroom, banging the door behind him.

At the sound of him turning the key, she collapsed on to the bed, hugging her arms around her body and curling up into a tight ball. She wasn't proud of her accusations but had found it impossible to control the necessity to lash out. No matter how much hurt she'd inflict on him, she knew nothing would ever match the pain she was experiencing inside, the pain that was becoming impossible to bear, the pain that was sawing through her flesh with rusted jagged teeth.

Chapter 9

Marcus yawned widely, stretching his arms high over his head, his body cramped, his clothes wrinkled. Sleeping in the car had been out of necessity, not choice.

Edel hadn't only refused to let him stay. She'd also taken the key he had for her house, shouted abuse at him and warned him against calling unannounced in future. And she wasn't about to change her mind, particularly after the way Marcus had interrogated her 'guest'!

Standing outside her closed door, he'd felt very sorry for himself. It was dark. He was freezing. He'd smoked his last cigarette and the battery in his mobile phone was dead!

He'd looked left and right. Not a sign of a car on the quiet country road. He knew there wasn't a hope of a taxi coming along. He didn't dare try to get back inside to use Edel's phone. The walk back to his car took him twice as long as it had from the village to the cottage first time round, the effects of his whisky long since worn off, sobriety easing its way back inside his head, bringing with it the problem he'd run away from to begin with: Ariel and the haunting effect she was having on him.

Fixing the driver's seat into an upright position once more, he rubbed the palm of his hand over his tightly cut fair hair, checked his reflection in the rear-view mirror and groaned. I look a wreck, he thought. It's no wonder Edel called me a bum!

Reaching into the glove compartment, he took out his battery razor and ran it over his face and chin, feeling somewhat human the next time he checked his reflection.

Turning on the ignition, he pulled the Audi on to the road and looked left and right again: left to Edel and right to Ariel. He revved the engine gently, deliberating his options, the magnificent expanse of rolling hills and picturesque landscape in his line of vision doing absolutely nothing to distract or cheer him.

Ariel held her mobile phone to her ear. "Sure, Gav, I'll meet you at the club. Yes, don't worry. Of course, I'll be on time!"

She laughed at the intensity of Gavin's instructions. He really does take his game seriously, she thought, draining the last of the grapefruit juice into a glass and sipping it slowly as she listened to her tennis partner relaying some strategy moves and going over a few last-minute techniques.

"That's all very well, Gav, but we're both playing long enough to know that a lot of it is down to luck on the day. And anything can happen in a final. Competition finals are the most difficult to predict." She moved towards the bedroom and picked up her tennis racket, gripping it loosely and practising some wrist movements.

"And, Gav," she added, when they came to the end of their conversation, "make sure you have your acceptance speech ready!"

Gavin gave her what-for on the other end, warning her against being too presumptuous.

"Okay, okay, we can improvise then if the moment arises. I'll meet you there thirty minutes before we're due on court."

She ended the call and swung her tennis racket backward and forward, her stretch severely limited by the amount of space in her room.

Her phone rang immediately again.

"What now, Gav? Have you dreamed up another winning formula?"

But it wasn't Gavin on the other end. Ariel let her tennis racket drop slowly, tears welling in her eyes when the person on the other end gave their identity, their purpose and their instructions.

That Saturday morning was the very first time Vicky had ever questioned her husband's relationship with his family. As Fintan had graphically pointed out, they had never been part of their daily lives. She'd come to understand very early in their relationship – after a couple of crazy hours in his mother's house one afternoon – why he'd chosen to leave home to move into a city-centre hostel before he'd even turned sixteen.

Fintan had never made a secret of what had gone on in the Jones household. A long time before he'd proposed on top of Howth Head on a clear summer's day, getting down on bended knee and surprising her with the most exquisite diamond ring, he'd filled her in on his background. In great detail.

Fintan's three older brothers were a force to be reckoned with, each broader and taller than the next. All three of them were married to local girls and living a stone's throw from their parents' home. They were unemployed and unemployable and happy to spend their days hanging around betting shops with buggies and children in tow while their wives went out to work to try and earn enough to make ends meet.

But Fintan had different values. He'd always been different, had always been impatient to escape the downbeat atmosphere at his parents' home.

Growing up in the shadow of a man who had allowed a knock in life – albeit a severe one – to shatter his self-esteem and bring an end to his working days had been more than enough to make him want and expect a whole lot more from life. He found it difficult to accept his father's defeatist attitude and hated to see him sitting in the armchair day after day, the sports pages of the newspaper laid out on the table in front of him and the television remote control in his good hand.

Fintan obsessed about escaping the entrapment associated with clinical depression. He fantasised about leaving the darkness behind in favour of the light mocking him from a distance. More than anything, he wanted to live. He wanted to breathe clean air. He wanted to be happy without feeling guilty for laughing or attempting something different. He wanted the opportunity to look forward to each day when he got up in the morning instead of tiptoeing around his parents and gauging their moods. He wanted to become somebody, a person other people respected and admired. He wanted a place he could call home.

Vicky stared at the bathroom door, imagining Fintan on the other side brushing his teeth or shaving or perhaps standing leaning against the cold tiles until he heard her leaving the room. Had he become the person he'd wanted to over the last decade or so? She would have thought he had. She had certainly admired and respected him, appreciated the strength of character he possessed that gave him the courage to walk away and make it alone.

But since he'd crossed their line of trust and cheated, she didn't know any more. Lying next to him that morning, he'd felt like a stranger beside her. She moved off the bed now, away from the coldness it represented, away from his bedside locker.

Slipping into matching navy silk underwear, she reached into her wardrobe and selected a faded but very comfortable pair of jeans from the rail, struggling to pull them up as they clung to the oil on her legs and thighs. Gritting her teeth, she remembered his comment about loving her damp skin. A shudder ran through her. There was a time, such a short time before, when ...but it was best not to think about that. Best not to look back.

She zipped up her jeans slowly. She couldn't believe Fintan had stared at her naked body yet remained blind to the evidence staring him in the face. He hadn't even noticed how upset she was, how betrayed she felt. Was he only interested in one – or two – things? Sex? Success? He'd already walked away from one family. Was he about to walk away from another? Was he a 'love 'em and leave 'em' kind of guy?

She pulled a pale pink fleece on with her jeans, inhaling the distinct smell of fabric conditioner as she pulled it over her head.

She moved to the window and pulled open the gold-leafed curtains. Staring mindlessly at the row of houses across the street, she shuddered at the prospect of taking her revenge to the next stage. She switched her attention to a playful puppy in the open green space at the top of the cul-de-sac, unable to prevent a grin spreading across her face as she watched him pull frantically at a discarded paper bag, gnashing and biting until he finally ripped the bag open to see what lay inside. His gnawing persistence helped her to see things a little more clearly.

Fintan would be nothing without the wrapping he'd carefully layered around himself: his confidence, his profession and his home. But how would he be after a revelation, a revelation that showed him in a brand-new light? What better way to find out than invite his parents to Malahide for a meal and drop the revelation in their laps right after serving coffee? Their inaugural visit to their youngest son's home. What better way to celebrate it than with a shocking announcement? Hell, she thought, I'll invite his little nephews too, turn it into a real family gathering, have the consequence of his indiscretion right there in front of them.

Saturday at noon

Pete Scavo stared at the clock on the mantelpiece. A long sleepless off-duty weekend loomed ahead. He couldn't wait for Monday at six when he'd be back in the fold of Ellis Enterprise. Until then he'd have to content himself as best he could: tackling crosswords, betting against himself as he watched horse-racing on TV and making his Saturday night and Sunday morning visits to church stretch as far as possible.

Every Saturday evening he took his place in a pew towards the back of the church long before anybody else arrived for six o'clock Mass, nodding his acknowledgement and shaking hands with neighbours and acquaintances as they trickled into the seats around him. Pete was an avid contributor to the whispered conversations held at the back of the church but as soon as the choir began and the priest and his altar servers appeared in their robes, Pete dropped his head in prayer and took solace in the message of God.

Not only was Pete first to arrive at these services, he was also last to leave, remaining in the pew watching families and singletons make their way back down the aisle, a buzz of muffled conversation following them, a sense of camaraderie present in the ancient church.

Using his ailing knee – an old hurling injury – as an excuse, he took his time leaving the seat, joining his hands and saying one final prayer before finally strolling into the porch at a leisurely pace, fixing his cap on his head as soon as he was outside the church gate and leaving society behind once more as he made the short journey to his home.

He repeated this routine on Sundays, this time attending ten o'clock Mass. On the colder mornings, he enjoyed a hot bowl of porridge and cup of sweet tea before wrapping a navy scarf around his neck, slipping on his grey woollen overcoat and making the ten-minute walk to the church where once again he felt closeted in the warmth of people around him.

Serving as Garda Sergeant in the area for several years had gained Pete respect and encouraged everyone to trust and have confidence in him. But unfortunately, over the years, his position had also afforded him a certain distance from people in his locality, a distance that he'd never managed to bridge, a distance he hadn't noticed until loneliness had enveloped him, increasing and deepening with every passing day since losing Barbara, his best friend, his favourite person in the world.

Chapter 10

Telling Fintan what she'd done, Vicky leaned casually against the walnut kitchen units, sliding an emery board across her nails in sharp even strokes. She counted the seconds in her head as she waited for him to explode.

She only got to count as far as four.

"You've done *what*? You've given them this address!" His eyes opened wide in disbelief. He fiddled nervously with the zipper on his tracksuit top, pulling it up and down, up and down, his pulse quickening, heat coursing through his body.

She repeated what she'd said in calm dulcet tones. "I've invited your parents – and your nephews – for a meal. It'll be lovely to have an excuse to use the dining-room for a change." As it turned out the two little boys were at Fintan's parents' house when she phoned – apparently their grandparents took care of them every Saturday. Vicky took it as a sign that the fates were on her side.

"*We* could have used the dining-room! God damn it, you didn't have to turn the occasion into a circus – giving my parents ringside seats!"

She ignored his sarcasm. "Your mother sounded pleased at the prospect actually. I'm expecting them at around four, so that will give us a couple of hours with them before you'll have to head into work." She held her breath.

Finding their number on Fintan's phone had been easy. It also gave her the opportunity to take a sly glance at his messages and call log. But yet again there was nothing. Why was he being so careful about deleting them? What was he afraid she'd find?

After what felt like an eternity, he spoke again. "I resent this, Vicky. You've no right to push a visit on me at such short notice. Not like this." His anger had abated. His tone lacked any trace of emotion. It was as if the light inside him had been quenched.

Vicky frowned in concentration, paying particular attention to her thumbnail, watching his changing expression from beneath her lashes. His confidence and swagger had disappeared. His sense of place had begun to wobble, a definite result in her opinion.

"They're my parents-in-law, Fin, and I made the call you hadn't the guts to make. The right call, the first attempt to bridge the gap between you."

"The right call? Right for who? And how dare you accuse me of being gutless!" he barked. He banged the palm of his hand against the doorframe, his anger returning with a vengeance. What on earth is she trying to do to us, he wondered. Why can't she leave things alone? And what is she playing at, inviting the boys over too?

Vicky ignored his question and his rising aggression, bouncing question after question back at him instead. "Don't you have a conscience? Your parents are ageing. One day it will be too late to build bridges with them, to let them know you care. Or is that what you're waiting for?"

"Don't be so damn dramatic," he grumbled between gritted teeth, shaking his head and glaring at her as though she'd totally lost her mind.

To catch him off guard and diffuse the sulk she could see him getting into, she switched to the softly-softly approach. "Why are you making such an issue of this, Fin? I'm doing you a favour. Life has moved on for all of you. It's not going to be how it was all those years ago. You're a totally different person now, not the small boy who did as he was told and stayed out of your father's way. And they have had their problems, Fin. They've been stuck in a rut for years, following the same routine week after week. A change of scenery will do them good."

She pulled a recipe book from the stack of barely used editions sitting on the deep window ledge, flicking through it to find something simple and manageable that she could put together without too much stress.

"You should have left things. I was going to call over at Christmas."

"Well, they're coming *now*!"

His face hardened. "Why did you invite the children, Vicky?"

"It's my house too," she retorted. "I'll invite whoever I want."

"Enjoy your afternoon then because I won't be here."

She stared at him, her mouth gaping open. He couldn't do that. He had to be there. Her plans were hinging on it now. It wouldn't have the same impact without him in the room. "But y-you can't!" she stammered, struggling to think of a valid response.

He turned and left the kitchen.

She heard the front door bang in his wake and the sound of him revving the car engine a few moments later. God damn him! How dare he leave things hanging in the air like that!

She stood there, looking around their immaculate home, a home they had pieced together bit by bit. A home they'd chosen carefully after months of searching, one they'd hoped would serve them quite happily for the rest of their days. And though the four-bedroomed detached in a well-sought-after cul-de-sac in Malahide had been way out of their price range, Fintan had worked long hours to ensure they could meet the bridging balance between the asking price and the mortgage. They had wanted to make the right choice first time around and not end up trading up and coping with the upheaval of moving house the way so many of their friends and colleagues had. They'd wanted their first home to be forever. They'd wanted their marriage to be forever. What they hadn't bargained for, however, was that forever (for them at least) would be so short-lived.

Her plans thrown into temporary disarray, she

tapped her fingers nervously on the spice carousel on the counter, then swivelled it on its axis, remembering the day Fintan had brought it home as a surprise. Oh yes, surprises were his speciality.

Would it matter if he didn't return for the meal? Should she go ahead and follow through with her plan anyway? Yes, she felt, yes, she would still go ahead.

Fintan's expression as he'd left the kitchen was ingrained in her mind. She knew she'd crossed the line and taken things a step too far in his view. Now they were both pushing boundaries. Would they ever be able to come back? Would Fintan even want to try?

She pushed the spice carousel away from her, burying her face in her hands. An ache filled the spot where she once held his love in her heart. She swallowed the lump in her throat. Where had he gone when he'd left the house? She wished she knew. Had her irrational invitation driven him even further into *her* arms?

Her mind raced. Pushing him closer to *her* certainly hadn't been her intention when she'd brought his family into the equation. Though now it seemed obvious, inevitable, that it would have that effect. Why hadn't she realised that?

She began to pace the kitchen, stepping onto cream porcelain tile after cream porcelain tile, walking in circles around the island unit, her pace speeding up until she was marching in an up-tempo beat to the rapid succession of thoughts invading her head. She couldn't visualise anything apart from Fintan's stony glare as he'd stormed away. What if I've pushed him too far, she fretted, biting her lip, clasping and unclasping her fists. What if he leaves me for good and goes to *her*?

She screamed at the top of her voice, not bothered about the open windows, neighbours or passing pedestrians. She pleaded with the silent kitchen for a miracle, shouted at the ceiling about the unfairness of life, dropped to her knees in tears as she begged an absent Fintan to return home and admit all. To return home to her. To reassure her, to put her mind at ease, to tell her he loved her. To return to the life they'd enjoyed. Before. But her pleading and wailing was all in vain. Nothing happened. The ceiling didn't fall in. The earth didn't move. The kitchen was exactly as it had been, everything in its rightful place. And her mind was still filled with turmoil though its pace was calming somewhat.

Shutting the recipe book with a bang and replacing it in its rightful place, her sweaty palms leaving imprints on the glossy hardback, she contemplated what lay ahead of her that afternoon. Her body trembled, her mouth went dry. She stared through the window, the pathway to her future breaking into a spaghetti junction of routes, the secret she was guarding the focal point of that intersection.

Chapter 11

Ariel pulled the door of her flat closed, tugging the large doorknob a few times to ensure it was shut properly. She'd been horrified one evening to come home and find the door swinging open – she remembered her heart pounding in her chest as she ran down the stairs and got the doorman to check if she had an intruder. Thankfully, however, all was intact and she'd realised to her embarrassment that she hadn't pulled the door shut properly on her way out. Since then she'd realised that there was a problem with the lock and it needed a really hard bang to shut it

In the neighbourhood where she was living, she couldn't be too careful. And after the phone call she'd received that morning, she was still feeling decidedly shaky, her concentration in disarray, her confidence undermined. How long more would she be able to keep him at arm's length? How long more before his threats transferred to a cold harsh reality?

Poor Gavin, she thought, as she began her walk to the tennis club, he'll have his work cut out for him on court today.

Standing at the traffic lights waiting for the pedestrian light to flash in her favour, she felt the vibration of her mobile phone in the pocket of her track pants. Her breathing quickened. She knew without checking who was calling. She'd disconnected their call the previous time. She increased her pace, not wanting to dwell on it. Not until after she'd played her game at least. She hiked her tennis bag onto her shoulder and continued walking, winning the match the only thought she allowed herself to focus on, the only thing keeping her sane in that moment in time.

Marcus arrived back to Dublin in record time. Pulling into a petrol station forecourt, he filled the tank with petrol and paid for it along with a newspaper.

If he hadn't been scanning the headlines as he walked back to the car, he would have noticed Ariel power-walking by the garage, her psychedelic pink tracksuit impossible to miss on such a dull and damp day, and it would probably have altered the course of his day as well as preventing him from making a hugely significant chance discovery. By the time he'd lifted his head, however, she'd disappeared around the corner.

Starting the engine, Marcus slowly manoeuvred the car onto the road and drove in the direction of Ellis Enterprise. It was not somewhere he generally visited on a Saturday but suddenly it was the only place where he felt he'd be able to relax and ease his mind, hoping after his crazy dash to Enniskerry and a fitful night's sleep, he might finally be able to get the vision of Ariel out of his head.

How could a sane, intelligent human being lust after and detest the same person at any one time? He didn't understand it himself, didn't understand the intensity of the feelings she evoked in him. He hadn't expected any woman to awaken excitement inside him again, to make him feel alive, make him flush like a schoolboy. One minute he wanted to wrap his arms around her and sink himself into her body like she was the only woman on earth and the next he wanted to close his hands around her throat until she wilted like a dying flower in his grasp, killing the temptation he was fighting to resist. The way she made him feel – the way her presence in the office had given him reason to start wearing aftershave again, to have something to look forward to when he opened his eyes in the morning – was also the reason he detested her, the reason he didn't trust himself around her, the reason he hated her for exposing his vulnerability to the female sex. He didn't want to give his heart to a woman, didn't want to bear the brunt or be badly burnt by the blindness of love. Not again.

Vicky's index finger hovered unsurely over the redial button, her head pounding, her vision slipping slightly out of focus. What excuse could she give her mother-in-law for cancelling their invitation so soon after issuing it? She contemplated inventing an emergency. But what? And wouldn't that bring them running to Malahide even faster?

Nausea rose inside her as she glanced around her house, picturing the Joneses arriving. Imagining being trapped in the house trying to entertain what could only be described as strangers, while Fintan deliberately stayed away, was enough to make her run to the bathroom once more and retch and retch until there was nothing left inside apart from the lining of her stomach.

After rinsing her face in cold water, she resumed her deliberation with the phone in the hallway, holding the receiver in her hand and wondering what on earth to do. She racked her brain, her heart rate beginning a high-speed gallop in conjunction with the ticking pulse in her neck. Her mind was blank. She swayed slightly on her feet. She couldn't think of a single rational reason to give Fintan's parents for changing her mind. At least not fifteen minutes after calling them in the first place! Whatever Fintan's opinion of them, Vicky was very confident of one fact: they weren't idiots. Far from it.

What kind of a fool am I though, she thought. Then again she'd spent a lifetime wondering about that, wondering what it was about her that clearly didn't measure up. Being with Fintan had helped her get past it. Gradually over the last few weeks, however, the self-deprecating doubts had reappeared and were back in full swing. After years of self-analysis, poring over self-help books (all without any positive results), she didn't expect to find an answer to that particular question any time soon.

She dropped the receiver back into its cradle without dialling, swallowing hard, cringing at the acidic taste that lingered in her mouth. It was one o'clock. She had three hours before they'd be standing on the doorstep ringing the doorbell. What would she do if Fintan kept his promise and didn't come back on time? How was she going to get through the visit? How would she keep an eye on his two nephews as well as cook and serve a meal? Would they cry if she asked them to sit down quietly? Should she buy some toys for them to play with? What ages were they? What would they eat for dinner? Should she make the children a separate meal? She didn't know the first thing about entertaining children.

They had kept his family at a distance and she'd been so wrapped up in the contentment of their relationship that the arrangement had suited her absolutely fine. But now that she was within two hours and fifty-nine minutes of having some of them arrive in on top of her, she regretted ignoring them. She could have done with an in-laws helpline or at least a friend to call to help her get through the situation without falling to pieces. No such luck unfortunately. What she was about to do was something she couldn't divulge to anybody – friend or foe! What she was about to do was something she could only do alone and live with the consequences thereafter.

Fintan drove around in circles, frustrated and confused, emotions resurfacing that he'd been convinced he'd left behind forever. But no such luck. I've overcome a lot worse situations in the past, he thought, so there's nothing stopping me from getting things under control again. Nothing apart from the promise I've made, the promise I chose to forget to share with my wife, the promise that could very well explode in my face and ruin everything I've spent the last decade building.

He pulled over the car and took out his phone, his eyes drawn to a picture of Vicky on his screen. She grinned mischievously at him from the still shot, her lips turned up at the corners, her eyes like slits as she squinted against the sun.

Fintan missed her suddenly. Missed the person she'd been when he'd met her first. He wasn't too sure about the person she'd become lately but hopefully soon, very soon, he'd be able to give her his full attention and the old Vicky would come back. He'd have run to the end of the world to keep her happy but she wasn't making it easy right now, she wasn't making it easy at all.

Tapping his fingers on the steering wheel, he thought for a second before dialling the number he'd memorised, the number he hadn't dared save onto his phone, the number he was careful to delete from the call log after every use. With a bit of luck, he thought, it won't be too long until I can delete it from my memory completely and everything will go back to the way it should be: normal.

Chapter 12

Ariel made straight for the water fountain when she arrived at the tennis club. Filling a paper cup to the brim, she brought it to her lips and took a long cold drink, gulping in fright when she felt a strong grip on her arm.

"What the – ?" Turning around, she was surprised to see Gavin. She was even more surprised to notice that his face was like thunder.

"What's wrong, Gavin?" she asked, pulling out of his strong hold, spilling the remains of her water onto the ground in the process.

"*What's wrong?*" he said incredulously. "We've been withdrawn from the competition, *that's* what's wrong!"

Ariel frowned in confusion. Her blood ran cold. Had the committee found out something about her? Did they deem her an unsuitable candidate to represent the club?

"You should have been honest with me, Ariel."

Gavin's voice was low but distinct. "I would have understood pre-match nerves. I've suffered them myself often enough."

"What? I'm not suffering a bout of nerves, Gavin! Honestly. What are you talking about?"

"So why did you telephone the club office to cancel, saying you were ill!" He stood directly in front of her, clutching his racket and waiting for an explanation.

"But I didn't . . ." she said, bewildered.

The secretary of the club chose that moment to approach.

"Ariel. Gavin. You're both here? But, Ariel, I thought you said –" She broke off without finishing, frowning in confusion. "I don't know what's going on with the pair of you but will you follow me to the office, please? We need one of you to sign our records, proof that you've forfeited the final of your own free will."

Ariel inhaled sharply. "Forfeited? Our own free will?"

Gavin looked at Ariel and shrugged as if to say 'I told you so'.

Ariel shook her head firmly. "But I didn't make any call!" She continued to shake her head, unable to believe what was happening. There had to be a mistake.

The secretary threw her a sceptical look. "Well, someone called Ariel Satlow did."

"What!" said Ariel. "That's impossible! Did you take the call yourself?"

"Yes!"

Ariel was slowly coming to the fearful realisation

that somebody somewhere was playing games with her. And it wasn't tennis! She brought her hand to her pocket, her fingers curling around her mobile phone. *Is it because I didn't answer my phone to him? Is this my punishment? Jeopardising one of the few pleasures I have left.*

Vicky was role-playing in preparation for her visitors. Standing by the front door, she visualised how she'd welcome them when they arrived, playing out various scenarios, each one more disastrous than the one preceding it. As a gesture of generosity, she'd offered to pay for their taxi when it arrived. Should she be outside to pay or should she wait until they rang the doorbell? She ran upstairs and got her purse. There were a few €20 notes tucked in the back.

She shoved what notes she had into the tiny drawer in the hall table, grabbing a blue pen and placing a large X on her hand as a reminder to withdraw more cash when she went to the village later to shop. To be on the safe side.

Her dash upstairs had brought blood rushing to her head. Suddenly the hallway began to spin. In slow motion she moved to the lounge and flopped on to the cream leather couch. Dropping her head between her knees, she closed her eyes and waited for the dizziness to subside.

She wished fervently that she'd chosen a more natural course of revenge. *Why didn't I go on an outlandish shopping spree,* she thought. *Inflict hurt on him through* his pocket? Why didn't I scratch his precious collection of rock CD's? Or cut up his favourite shirts or football jerseys like most half-crazed women setting out to get their own back on a cheating spouse or partner?

Her breathing slowed a little. She raised her head. And though she was definitely more in control, the argument still raged on loudly inside. She kept her eyes closed and let it continue, wishing she had any other option apart from reaching into Fintan's soul and squeezing and squeezing until it shattered into tiny shreds. It's nothing more than he's doing to me, she thought.

She pushed further back into the chair, her mind still reeling. She stretched her fingers, opened and closed her fists, rotated her shoulders clockwise and anti-clockwise and leaned her head from one side to the other, trying to relieve the tension that invaded every joint and muscle in her body. Still the debate in her head raged on. Am I out of my mind to contemplate unveiling Fintan's well-kept secret to his family, she wondered? Forcing all of them back to five years before and the consequences of a brief passionate encounter that he had been able to conceal? If only there was a code of ethics to follow on teaching a cheating husband a valuable lesson. All Vicky had to rely on was gut instinct. And judging by the look on Fintan's face and the droop in his shoulders when he'd left the kitchen earlier, she was convinced the guests she'd invited were the correct ones to force a reaction from him. It was too late for damage control. The damage had already been done.

Finally the voices inside her head calmed somewhat, the hum of traffic through the open window being the only sound she could hear. She got up from the couch, relieved that her feet were firm underneath her once more, her body no longer swaying and her mind in a more focused state. Her fear had subsided. Her confidence had reappeared. She was ready to take things to the next step.

The tennis club secretary remained tight-lipped, a clipboard held tightly to her chest. "Now, can one of you please follow me? We've wasted enough time on this already. Ariel? Gavin?"

As the secretary stalked off, Ariel swung around to face Gavin, the absurdity of the situation sinking in, her face reddening a little when she noticed passers-by giving them odd looks. We're obviously the talk of the club, she realised, this latest disappointment a fist pummelling against her heart. The tennis match had been an essential distraction for her, the only thing keeping her sane with everything else that was going wrong in her life.

"There's been a mistake," she said. "I'll get them to check their caller ID –"

"What difference would the number make?" Gavin interrupted. "They got the call and that's that."

"But we have to prove it wasn't us!"

"It wasn't '*us*'," said Gavin sharply. "I had nothing to do with this debacle!"

"And *I* had?" Ariel challenged him, tears springing to her eyes.

Gavin banged his racket – the racket he'd paid an absolute fortune for – onto the rough concrete. "We were this close, Ariel." He indicated the tiniest distance with his thumb and index finger. "We could have won. We both know we were ready for it."

Ariel stepped back from him. His racket was his most treasured possession. It was obvious he blamed her. And she had no way of proving otherwise. She only had her word and that, it seemed, wasn't good enough.

"I'm going home, Ariel. No point in hanging around here."

"But, Gavin, maybe we can still play! If only we can convince them I didn't cancel –"

"Too late," said Gavin. "The match has been called off."

"You have to believe me! I didn't make any call to the club!" Ariel protested.

But her words were wasted. There was nobody there to listen. Gavin was already disappearing into the changing rooms.

Her heart sank. This can't be happening, she thought. Not on top of everything else. First I tell Roger the truth and he walks out on me. Then I get into all sorts of trouble at work. And now this. It has to be more than a coincidence. Her mobile phone vibrated in her pocket. Once again, she ignored it, hurrying to catch up with the secretary to try and discover the truth behind her game being sabotaged, not to mention trying to redeem her long-standing reputation in the club.

As for Gavin, she doubted he'd ever partner her

again. And who could blame him? If the situation had been reversed, she'd probably have felt the exact same way.

Entering the competition office, she was met with icy stares from behind the desk. Taking a deep breath, she flicked her dark hair over her shoulder and painted a smile on her face. She'd been a member of Sutton Lawn Tennis Club for too long to be dismissed without at least a hearing.

Despite Ariel using every ounce of her strength, trying every conceivable angle she could think of to try and get them to do a turn-around on their decision, nothing she said convinced the tennis club committee that she hadn't been responsible for cancelling the final. Gavin was right – the fact the call had been made from a private number rather than her mobile meant nothing to them.

"But surely my years of loyalty to the club stand for something? All the silverware I've helped the club to win?"

"It's too late now, Ariel, anyway. The damage is done. The game is off. We've given our word to the other finalists."

"But it's so unfair!"

"Isn't it just?" the club secretary agreed tightly, thinking of the bar-takings they'd miss out on because the tournament celebration party had also been cancelled. "Why don't you get off home, Ariel? Enough has been said already."

Ariel raised an eyebrow. She's dismissing me, she

thought, blinking to hold back the tears threatening to spill. "I'm not signing that form because I didn't make the call. You could at least have rung me to confirm it wasn't a hoax." Her voice quivered.

The secretary's eyes narrowed.

Ariel could see she didn't like to be challenged. Stuck-up cow, she thought uncharitably.

"A hoax? Why would I think that? The game is off, Ariel." The secretary lowered her head and attended to some paperwork, her conversation with Ariel clearly over.

Mortified, Ariel sloped away from the club, through the gate and out on to the road once more to make the return walk home.

Her phone vibrated in her pocket. And this time, instead of ignoring it, she answered the call, having a good idea it would be more bad news, more threats.

"God damn you! What do you want?" she growled into the phone, releasing her pent-up frustration with every syllable that left her lips. "I've told you. I have no more to give you. I'm cleaned out! Happy now?"

"You know what I want," the voice on the other end responded. "Then you and your elderly parents will be rid of me forever."

I might have lost a lot already, Ariel fumed, and I'm probably out of my mind for even responding to these threats but I'd rather eat dry bread for the rest of my life than have my name dragged through the courts for something I haven't done. After this latest debacle, I'm already holding onto my integrity with my fingernails but if I can just hold out for a little more time . . .

There was a low menacing laugh came down the line. "Cat got your tongue?"

"I'm not going down for you. Over my dead body!" she spat, her fingers clutching the slim phone tightly.

"Don't think it can't be arranged. I see your parents' cat had kittens. Wouldn't it be a shame now if the mother cat went missing . . ." These were the last words Ariel heard before the line went dead.

She shivered slightly, the phone clutched tightly in her fist, a picture of her vulnerable parents foremost in her mind. She came to a stop, unsure where to turn, unsure whom she could trust, terrified her parents would get hurt – or even worse.

Her phone vibrated in her hand. Her breath caught in her throat. She was afraid to answer, afraid of what she'd be told next. But then a flashing name on the screen caught her eye. It wasn't *'private number'* as she'd been expecting. It was Roger. Finally.

"Roger," she breathed heavily into the phone, her eyes brimming with tears of utter relief. "Thank God you've called at last – oh thank God it's you!"

Chapter 13

Leaning over the piano in the alcove, Vicky took her wedding album from the shelf overhead. Blowing the dust from the leather cover, she sat at the edge of the piano stool, rested the book on her lap and flicked through page after page until she came to the glossy shot of the groom's family portrait.

To anyone who hadn't been there that day at the Deerpark Hotel in Howth, it could easily have been mistaken as the group shot. Fintan's parents, three brothers, their wives, twelve children (all girls but for Callum and Olly), and the aunts, uncles and cousins who'd refused to accept that immediate family didn't include them were gathered around the bride and groom, grinning for the camera as though they were all the best of pals and regularly sat around a family dinner table.

Staring at the print a little more closely, however,

and analysing the expressions behind the fake smiles and cheap wedding outfits, Vicky could see beyond the illusion it presented. The obvious divide between Fintan and his father: the sleeves of their jackets weren't even touching. His three brothers stood tall and proud, their ties slightly askew and a telltale sign of alcohol in their bloodshot eyes. Their wives, who gave the impression of being firm friends when out in public, had been captured unsmiling, their attention very firmly focused on Vicky's exquisite satin wedding dress, the scorn in their eyes a sure giveaway that their interest was far from admiring.

She tried to remember having a conversation with any one of the three women on that day. Not a single line came to mind. In another family, being married to brothers would have been enough to bring four women closer, sharing the competitive edge against in-laws as a common ground. But in this case, marrying into the same family had driven them further apart. Vicky continued to stare at the colour shot, with a vague recollection of the trio passing occasional comments about the weather or how classy the hotel was, but she couldn't honestly say she'd got any further than "Are you enjoying the day?" with any one of the other Jones wives.

Focusing on each heavily made-up face in turn, she wondered – and not for the first time – how much information the three women shared. She wondered if Suzi (spelt with a 'z' and an 'i' as she so regularly pointed out), the wife of Fintan's eldest brother George, had filled them in on her drunken shenanigans on the day of her first baby's christening. Somehow Vicky doubted it. After all, owning up to having unprotected sex with her youngest brother-in-law in a darkened alcove of a hotel corridor was hardly something to boast about, especially when it was closely followed by a pregnancy announcement.

Sighing, Vicky's gaze returned to Fintan, scrutinising his image closely. Fiercely handsome and sophisticated in his black tuxedo and white fly-collared shirt, his ruby cummerbund and bow tie matching the bridesmaids' dresses, she thought he looked uneasy. And why wouldn't he with the mother of his child inches away from him?

Deep in the throes of love and adoration a mere few months into their relationship, Vicky had listened agog to the story Fintan had told her, flattered he'd confided in her, recognising his confession as proof that their relationship was serious.

"Stupidest thing I've ever done," he'd concluded, holding her hand tightly in his. "How could I have been so thick?"

They'd been sitting in his car outside the flat she was sharing with three friends, friends she'd met at secretarial college, when he'd chosen to divulge his darkest regret.

"But, if you were out of your head on shots and she's ten years older than you, surely it was her taking advantage of you?" Vicky was quick to jump to his defence, happier to put the entire blame on Suzi. And even though she'd never even met her at that point, she'd already made up her mind to dislike her, disgusted that a married woman with a tiny infant could do something so despicable. And with her husband's brother!

"I don't think my big brother would have seen it like that. Do you? He'd be quick enough to remind me that at twenty-two he'd been well able to control himself, no matter how drunk he was!"

"I guess you're right."

Fintan heaved a sigh. "And then . . ." he ran a hand through his hair – it was longer then, curling around his ears, the back reaching below the collar of his shirt, "around two years later, she tried to come on to me again. This time, it was at my other brother's wedding."

"No way? Has she always had a thing for you?"

"Anything in trousers, I'd say," Fintan scoffed, his apathy for his sister-in-law evident.

"You didn't have sex with her again? Did you?"

"Absolutely not! I've barely stood in the same room as Suzi since that one time, apart from the occasional family gathering – and I've made sure to give her a wide berth then too! I didn't go to the second christening and by the time Darren's wedding came around, I was two years older and wiser and had cut well back on my drink binges." His expression darkened.

"Go on," Vicky put a hand to his face, applying gentle pressure to make him look at her.

He inhaled deeply before continuing, the memory as bitter as the day it had occurred. "Suzi didn't like being rejected. She turned nasty when I pushed her off me. I told her to go and play with her kids instead of her relations!"

Vicky listened attentively.

"And that's when she hissed that one of those kids was mine."

Vicky was thunderstruck. "But – but – how could she know that? How could she know for sure the baby was yours? She was obviously having sex with her husband too?" And who knows how many others, she couldn't help thinking.

"Yes, she must have been. I don't know why she thought it was me. Something to do with the dates? The fact we had unprotected sex? Of course, I'd had my suspicions – or fears – when she got pregnant and when Olly was born. But, to be honest, I didn't want to know."

"Did she want to take it further?"

"No, she didn't. I knew by the look of horror on her face that she hadn't meant to blurt it out. She wasn't stupid. She wasn't going to be left alone holding two babies. As tough as George might appear, she wears the trousers in that house. He has a dog's life. Stuck at home with the kids all the time while she swans around the place dressed like a tart! He must be blind if he doesn't realise she's playing away from home. But that's none of my business and I had no intention of making it so."

"Did she take back the admission?"

Fintan shrugged. "If you can call storming off taking it back!"

"So . . . do you think you're the father?"

He stared through the windscreen, his attention

drawn to two young boys pedalling their bikes furiously as they raced along the path nearby. "I could be."

"Only because the dates coincide though? And no protection?"

He'd looked right into her eyes then. "I couldn't get her words out of my head. Every time I saw a boy of his age, I found myself wondering. So I did a paternity test. I ordered it online."

"But Suzi?" Vicky paled slightly. It was a lot to take in.

"Suzi will never know. Ma minded the kids every Friday morning so I made a point of calling over and taking a swab from his mouth when nobody was looking."

Vicky shuddered at his subterfuge. "The result was positive?"

He nodded. "Yes. I could be his father. But unless I got George to do a test too, I'll never know for sure."

"And can you live the rest of your life without knowing for definite?"

"It's better for the little fellow this way. He's growing up with his brother and Suzi's just had twin girls now. I wouldn't want to jeopardise his happiness. Or my brother's – regardless of the fact we don't get on that well, his life is messed up enough. I've no intention of adding to that."

His selflessness had impressed her. She'd leaned across and kissed him, hugging him tightly to her.

"I didn't want to keep it from you," he'd whispered huskily into her ear. "I don't want anything to ever come between us."

Her heart had melted at his words and any doubt or concern that had flitted through her as she'd listened to his tale instantly disappeared.

She remembered the conversation as if it was only yesterday, his sincerity, her awestruck acceptance of every word.

And now? Well, now she could see it with older, more experienced eyes. Fintan had messed around, got caught and walked away. Nothing too different to what he was doing now with *her* except he was being more careful about using contraception.

Hell, she thought, didn't I find his multi-pack of condoms to prove it? What was it written on the box again? Oh yes! 'The Experience Pack'. How appropriate. Fintan definitely had tried and tested experience in that department.

The wedding album weighed heavily on her knees, almost as heavy as the weight of realisation in her heart. If Fintan could cheat on his brother, of course he could cheat on her too. All the proof she needed was staring her right in the face: Suzi. After that indiscretion, it seemed to her he was capable of giving into temptation with any woman: relation, friend or otherwise.

Looking at the photograph again, she stared at her own image in the same shot, noticing the fixed smile on her lips and the sense of unease in her eyes. It was only now she realised how tense she'd been. From beginning to end, the day had been stressful. And in a way she knew it served her right. Fintan had been in favour of disappearing to a tiny church on a foreign island. He'd begged her to forget about wedding planners and trimmings and had tried his utmost to convince her to tie the knot without any of the fancy accessories she was planning. But Vicky had dug her heels in and gone the whole hog, setting out to prove to her parents that she too could throw a lavish affair.

But on the day itself, she paid a high price. Smiling at people she barely knew and pretending to be the apple of her father's eye as he introduced her to the numerous guests he'd insisted on inviting had been painful. Shuddering slightly at the memory, she quickly flicked over a few pages of the photo album until she came to the picture of her family. The bride's entourage.

Vicky took in her mother's perfect pose. "What a joke!" she said aloud. Looking at her brilliant white smile (a smile that had no doubt cost a fortune at a private clinic) and the way her eyes rested on Vicky and Fintan as though they were the most precious people in her life. Vicky was convinced she'd practised it in the mirror for weeks before, her expression making a mockery of all that was true. But credit where it's due, she thought sardonically, she managed to pull off her best stage performance yet. She actually made us look like the perfect family. At least for one day. An image to match the illusion she'd portrayed for as long as Vicky could remember, an image in total contradiction to the coldness she exuded in real life.

"It's all about giving the right impression, dear," was one of her mother's favourite sayings. It was her attitude to almost everything in life, when in reality she seldom bothered to even pick up the phone and check if Vicky and Fintan were alive. Fin had been right in what he'd insinuated earlier. Vicky knew that without question. Both of her parents did go out of their way to ignore her existence. And if it were possible, their aloofness had become more prominent since their daughter's wedding day, the circles each couple moved in becoming further and further apart.

Leaving the introductions between both families until the evening of the wedding rehearsal had been deliberate on Vicky's part. She was aware of how unfair and immature it was – to all concerned – but she didn't regret it. She had watched her mother's face falling (at least it would have fallen if it weren't for the numerous sessions of Botox injections she'd had) when she led her parents into the church where the Jones clan were already instated. It had given her the tiniest sense of payback for a lifetime of embarrassing and humiliating moments. Vicky's mother had assumed that while the Jones family wouldn't quite match up to her standard, they'd at least be of similar status to Fintan himself. She hadn't been prepared for the boisterous gathering waiting to meet her and, as Vicky sensed her stiffen beside her, she'd safely have bet that she wasn't the only one experiencing a tiny voice of apprehension in her head as they waited for the priest to get procedures underway.

Banging the wedding album closed, she returned it to its rightful place where it would gather several more layers of dust before she'd bother looking at it again. Staring at photographs hadn't given her much solace, the farcical day a memory she'd gladly forget. Apart from reminding her of another reason why it was imperative for her marriage to survive. She didn't want to give her parents – her domineering mother in particular – the satisfaction of telling her that Fintan hadn't been good enough for her to begin with and that if she'd listened to her advice and co-operated with her various attempts at matchmaking, she'd at least have a healthy bank balance to fall back on when the whole charade came crashing around her ears.

Pushing all thoughts of her mother's taunting to one side, she made a beeline for the kitchen once more. Basking momentarily in the unexpected heat from the warm sunlight flooding through the large French doors, she came to a very quick decision about what dish to cook for her guests. Lasagne! A simple recipe, a dish her mother would have frowned upon, a dish she felt she'd actually be able to manage without messing up. As if on cue, her stomach growled loudly. Not wanting to keel over in the local supermarket, she made a cup of tea and some wholemeal toast – the first bite she'd eaten since Fintan's casserole the previous evening, a meal that felt like an eternity ago now.

If only I'd been more cautious from the outset and looked beyond his soulful eyes and cheeky grin, she thought with regret, I'd probably have recognised his capability for deception long before now.

Why are you so surprised?

Heat coursed through her body, the little voice of conscience disturbing.

It's not as if you haven't witnessed something like this before! Did you think you'd left it all behind?

Her toast fell from her hand, oil from the butter oozing onto the square white plate, spreading like a vicious rumour on nasty whispering tongues. The voice in her head refused to be silenced, jeering and nagging until she was forced to rewind to another time.

Growing up in the shadow of rich successful parents, Vicky had despised the two-fold existence: years of lonely evenings without as much as an English-speaking nanny for company coupled with the flip-side of loud, extravagant parties where she was paraded around the drawing-room like a prize calf, kissed and cajoled until the after-dinner drinks were introduced and she was suitably dismissed. Hating the invasion the all-night parties brought to their home even more than the loneliness of the other nights, she'd lain awake for hours listening to the distinct bass of eighties music, coming to her own teenage conclusions about the occasional squeaking floorboards and smothered giggles on the landing outside her room. And while she was sorely tempted to leave the warmth of her single bed and tiptoe to the door and peek outside, the fear of what she might discover kept her very firmly buried under the cocoon of blankets she'd pulled over her head.

But I'm an adult now, she thought, no longer the young girl who used to stick her fingers in her ears and run and hide behind closed doors.

What, she wondered, draining her tepid tea in one final go, would Fintan's parents' reaction be to the revelation that their youngest son could well have fathered the child his brother was bringing up as his own? She would soon see.

And Fintan – could it be that deception had always been part of his agenda? Is that what she was about to find out? Underneath all his supposed independence, did there lie a devious bar manager with his eye on a substantial inheritance from her parents?

His little-boy-lost story about his family not understanding his ambition had given him the key to Vicky's heart, making her love him even more if that was possible, making her feel they were kindred spirits – each with their own reason for escaping their childhood homes.

Maybe over layers of mince, cheese and pasta, I'll unravel the underlying plot in the chapters of the fable he's invented, she thought, and maybe then I'll discover the motivation behind his cheating ways.

Chapter 14

Marcus scratched his head and unzipped his cardigan. He'd been poring over the correspondence on Ben's desk since he'd arrived, having gone into his office on the innocent mission of finding any notes Ben might have had on the new files he'd passed over to him. But the documentation lying open on Ben's desk proved a lot more interesting and informative than client files.

What on earth is he playing at? he wondered. Why didn't he share this information with us at the consultants' meeting instead of keeping these problems to himself? Or at the very least send me a memo to keep me abreast of the situation? We need to get new business in. We need to get it in fast.

As a prominent shareholder in Ellis Enterprise, Marcus felt he had a right to be kept in the loop. He'd insisted on keeping his shareholder status anonymous, not wanting to isolate himself from the rest of the team.

Ben had agreed to his anonymity without question. Marcus hadn't demanded special attention, would have been in prime position to insist on promotion but had been content to remain as he was: just another consultant, nothing more, nothing less, his shares in the company serving him as nothing more than a security blanket for his family's future.

A few short years before, he'd been at the helm of his own financial consultancy organisation, hiring and firing, making decisions and carrying hefty responsibility. Marcus allowed his thoughts to drift back to that time, recoiling from the memories it evoked. By the time the receivers came in, took over his company and liquidated his assets, he'd been at his lowest ebb, convinced he'd never secure work in the financial trade again.

Once in any lifetime was more than enough to suffer such a loss, both personally and professionally. But he'd licked his wounds and picked himself up, succeeding in building his professional life from scratch again, even if it was as an employee and not employer.

But past experience had taught him to keep a close eye on business and never take his eye off the ball. It only took one mistake to change a company's course of action forever and Ariel's recent mistakes could have been enough to run Ellis Enterprise into the ground if the errors hadn't come to Ben's attention so swiftly. The thought niggled and niggled, Ariel's recent inexplicable vulnerability making her a loose cannon in his opinion. He pushed his attraction for her to the back of his mind, separating it entirely from business, as only a male mind can do.

Scanning through the handful of letters from disgruntled clients on Ben's desk, Marcus quickly assessed that something needed to be done – and done quickly – or it would only be a matter of time before the company felt the pinch of business downturn and they'd have a case of weakening reputation on their hands as well as a fall in profits. And if that happened, both his job and his investment would be worth nothing yet again.

I'm not about to stand by and watch everything I've struggled for go up in smoke, he thought. It's not as if I'll have the same opportunity to rebuild my life a third time in the current economic climate.

His probing was done for that day. He began to stand up from the leather chair, freezing as his eyes fell on the photograph on Ben's desk, a photo he had never seen before as it was always faced away from him, his face paling as he stared at the face of his boss's wife. But sitting in Ben's chair for the first time, he was seeing things from a different perspective, a perspective with very shocking implications.

Frowning, he picked up the 6x8 print, holding the black plastic frame in both hands, wondering how he hadn't noticed the similarity when he'd met Jenny in person. But thinking about it now, he realised he'd never caught more than a fleeting glance of the woman. In his brief lifetime with the company, she hadn't attended any social occasions and had seldom fraternised with the staff. But Ben mentioned her on a daily basis which explained why Marcus imagined he knew her better than he actually did.

Staring at the outline of her smiling face, Marcus was reminded of Edel's high cheekbones, her wide blue eyes and full lips, the likeness uncanny, the startling coincidence more than a little scary. There has to be a connection between them, he thought. And if that was the case, he wondered if it was the explanation he was most afraid of, the moment he'd been dreading for many, many years. Continuing to stare until his eyes watered, he replaced the photo exactly as he'd found it and left the building as quietly and discreetly as he'd arrived, his mouth drying, his palate resembling rough cardboard as he tried to make sense of his discovery and deny the explanations screaming to be heard in his head.

Thinking back to the beginning, he tried to fit jigsaw pieces together, recalling how he'd first been introduced to the vacancy with Ellis Enterprise. Even then, he'd been taken aback by the ease of his acquiring it. The position had practically fallen at his feet and he'd been unable to believe his good fortune to be offered the job after a short informal interview without too much investigation or scrutiny.

"Anyone can fall on bad luck," Ben had commented when Marcus explained in great detail why he'd decided to draw a line under his company and let it go to receivers.

"It was either that or invest more and more money into an already sinking ship," Marcus had continued, more confident now about giving a true picture following Ben's understanding comments, "and following a lengthy and frank consultation with my legal team, we felt letting it go was the right decision."

And that had been as much as Ben had questioned him on the subject, leaving the past behind them and displaying a lot more enthusiasm about the expertise Marcus could bring to his company.

Starting the engine for the umpteenth time that day, Marcus pulled out of the office carpark, stalling the car at the entrance, his feet unsteady on the pedals. On his journey home, he took two wrong turnings and went around the same roundabout three times, unable to concentrate, trying to rationalise, wishing there was somebody with whom he could share his burden, wishing he didn't feel as though he were a pawn in a chess game. The road blurred in front of him, Edel's face floating in the film of rain on the windscreen as he hurried home to find an envelope of documents he hadn't looked at in years, an envelope whose contents had once made him the happiest man on this earth.

Chapter 15

Fintan had little choice but to wait. After a lot of deliberation, he'd made his call, offered his suggestion on how the money situation should be handled and now he had nothing to do but hold tight until he got a response. He couldn't go home, couldn't risk the return phone call coming through while Vicky was in the vicinity. And after the bombshell she'd dropped before he left the house, telling him she'd invited his parents and the boys over, he wasn't sure he wanted to return. At least not yet.

Driving aimlessly to pass the time, he eventually came to a stop at Malahide Castle and parked the car near the football pitches. Getting out of the car for a breath of air, he joined the spectators at an under-age soccer game.

"Which side are you supporting?" one of the enthusiastic fathers beside him enquired.

"Neutral, to be honest," Fintan responded, watching the game with interest. "They're handy with a ball for their age all the same."

"You should see the premier side . . . oh look, here's a goal! Go on, Declan, strike!"

Fintan nodded and relaxed, temporarily forgetting his woes and becoming engrossed in the progress on the pitch instead.

What he was unaware of was that a spectator on the opposite side had spotted him as soon as he'd stepped out of the car. The same spectator had been unable to believe his good fortune when Fintan had appeared unexpectedly. He'd been prepared to make an effort to find him, never expecting Fintan to be handed to him on a plate.

Talk about falling at my feet, he thought, rubbing his hands in glee before striking a match and lighting a cigarette. Ostensibly watching the game, he kept a close eye on his prey, casually strolling around the perimeter of the playing field as Fintan sat into his car once more. Memorising the registration number on the Audi, he quickly saved it to the memory of his phone, knowing it would come in very useful when the time came to locate the exact house Fintan was living in.

Fintan, on the other hand, was making his way back to the village, sinking deeper and deeper into depression, his day getting progressively worse. The only reprieve from doom and gloom he had that afternoon was the few minutes he'd spent watching the under-age game and the light-hearted call he received from a friend who had asked for his help to arrange a risqué stag night.

Vicky kept her eyes peeled for Fintan as she walked the short distance to Malahide village, glancing at every passing car, willing it to be him. She scrutinised every tall, brown-haired guy walking or jogging along the main road. But nothing. And then as she turned the corner to make her way down Main Street and into SuperValu, she spotted him in the distance. He sat alone on a wooden bench in the people's park at the top of the village, his black and red Manchester United tracksuit a dead giveaway.

As she stood watching him, her heart softened the slightest fraction, the intense love she felt for him rising to the surface, momentarily submerging her jealousy and suspicion. She leaned against a tall building, scrutinising him. Should she approach him? Try and talk him into coming home? She couldn't be sure whether it was worth the effort. But eventually, unable to deny the feelings of love gushing to the surface of her heart, she decided to make one last attempt.

Taking a couple of tentative steps towards the park, she slowed when she noticed him sit up a little straighter on the bench. She saw him reach into his pocket for his mobile phone, halting dead in her tracks, holding her breath and watching closely. She was too far away to hear anything he was saying, his body language the only thing she had to base her assumptions on. From where she stood at the corner of the street, it looked as though he was answering a call and not making one. And then to her utter disgust, he threw his head back and laughed out loud, his eyes crinkling at the sides the way they always did (she couldn't see the little fan-like lines, of course, from that distance but she knew they were there). His laughter mocked her, tossing her last attempt at reconciliation back in her face. She was dying inside, furious that she'd allowed him to make a fool of her all over again, enraged that he was laughing out loud while she was rotting away inside.

Her feet froze on the concrete. He's not upset at all, she thought. That was wishful thinking on my part. Feelings of jealousy and suspicion returned with a vengeance, swimming through her body as though their life depended on them touching off every ounce of flesh before finally shooting right through her heart. Her love for him retreated into hidden crevices, drowning in the wake of jealousy's victory.

Vicky's mind – already overflowing with distrust – went into complete overdrive. She hadn't imagined how miserable he'd been when he'd left the house. Of that, she was certain. So who had the power to make him laugh like that? A deep, throaty laugh that up until recently had regularly echoed through their home. Had he called his mistress to meet him once he'd stepped outside the front door? Maybe I played right into his hands, she thought, giving him an excuse to barge out. He hadn't wasted much time, had he? Was he arranging a rendezvous with *her* to take his mind off his boring, irritating wife and what she was planning at home? In his head, had he already moved on? Vicky felt her blood run cold, his deception unbearable. With every nod of his head, every movement of his hands, she suffocated a little further. She couldn't stand there watching a moment longer.

Breaking into a sprint, she ran down the street, running and running, charging straight past the supermarket and down the hill towards the pier. Breathing so hard that her throat felt as though it were on fire, she came to an abrupt stop when she reached the water's edge. She hadn't any intention of running into the pier and drowning herself. She wasn't suicidal. Oh no. She was furious. But she wasn't about to give him the satisfaction of killing herself. Or allowing him off the hook for his brazen, deceitful actions. Or out of their marriage without at least putting up a fight. She was adamant that people should see what a two-faced lout her husband was, not shroud him in sympathy at a lonely graveside because his wife had slipped into the pier in an unfortunate 'accident'.

She leaned against the old cannon, using it as support as she struggled to regain control of her breathing. The stitch in her side was agonising. She doubled over, placing her arm across her midriff and clutching it tightly, pushing against the pain until it finally began to ease. The stench of seaweed and discarded waste wafted from the water. The tide was out, the bare seabed exposed as layers of hidden filth, a mocking reminder of what lay beneath her misguided impression of the man she'd married.

"What a bastard he is!" she whispered into the water, pausing between every word as she gulped for air to spit out what she wanted to say. "Sniggering into his phone like a bloody school kid! Making a show of us in public!"

"You okay, Vicky?"

She jumped at the sound of a male voice – a familiar one at that.

Oh no, she groaned inwardly, glancing over her shoulder and recognising Simon Guilfoyle – one of her neighbours – standing right behind her. Mortification washed over her. She found his close proximity unnerving. He has to have heard me talking to myself, she thought. He probably thinks I'm losing the plot completely. Who could honestly blame him? If I came up behind someone and heard him or her having a full-blown conversation with themselves, I'd suspect a touch of lunacy too.

Had she been speaking loudly enough for Simon to decipher every word or had her proclamation only been audible to her? Honestly, she couldn't be sure. Her mind didn't seem her own any more.

Painting a smile on her face and putting on some semblance of normality, she straightened up as best she could – darts of pain shooting around her waistline as she rose to her full height – and turned around to face him.

"I'm fine, Simon. But I'm not as fit as I thought." She gave a silly laugh and pushed on with her excuses. "I made the mistake of power-walking all the way from the house and now I've got a stitch in my side as my thanks. I'll be right as rain in a few minutes. A bit too ambitious in the fitness department I'm afraid. I was never very good at easing into things gently."

"You're fairly white in the face, Vicky. Can I offer you a lift home?"

His tone was serious, his concern evident.

She raised a hand in polite refusal. "Not at all. I need the exercise. You know yourself, when you're stuck in an office all week . . ." Long sentences were proving a bit difficult. She was still gasping for breath.

"Look at you!" he laughed. "It'll take you all day to get home in that state. I'll be driving up your way in a short while. Why don't you hop in and take the weight off your feet?"

Oh why not, she relented eventually. If only to get him off my back. She hadn't the energy to argue. Besides, taking him up on his offer would give her a bit more time to prepare a nice meal and make an effort with the table.

"Well, I've a bit of shopping to do and I don't want to delay you."

Simon nodded. "I can meet you outside Gibney's pub in twenty minutes. Would that give you enough time?"

"Perfect," she said, spotting the X on her hand and remembering her reason for putting it there. She'd make a withdrawal as she'd intended but it would be from Fintan's account. Not hers. Wasn't she already paying a high enough price for his mistakes? She certainly thought so. Now it was his turn to pay. And reducing his bank balance was only the beginning. "I'll be as fast as I can."

"Twenty minutes then."

Chapter 16

Marcus stared out the window of his two-bed town house, the precious envelope and documents he'd been so anxious to find strewn on the coffee table. He ignored the overgrown shrubbery and rough grass, focusing on the windmill twirling gently in the breeze instead – one of the few remaining reminders that Edel had ever lived there with him.

Wallowing in self-pity was alien to him. He generally found ways to stave off unexpected pangs of loneliness: a fast ride in his car, an energetic game of squash, a few sociable drinks or simply throwing himself at the mercy of work. But today, for the first time in weeks, he didn't fight the emptiness that wormed its way around his soul or the dullness that threaded through his heart. He didn't try to find a bright side or force himself to keep busy, keep moving.

Instead he allowed himself just to be, feeling justified

in that luxury, particularly if his suspicions were founded and his 'trusted' boss had been carrying a lot more on his mind than his business acumen when he'd approached Marcus at a trade-fair stand he was freelancing on, brought the conversation around to the vacancy within his company, handed him his business card and encouraged him to contact his secretary for an interview.

How could I have been so stupid, Marcus thought, opening the window a fraction to let in a bit of air and let out the smell of smoke. And what does he really want from me? And all this business with Ariel – giving me her companies, improving my status within the organisation. Is it a set-up? Is she part of Ben's plan to lull me into a false sense of security before he . . . before he . . . before he what?

But Marcus couldn't think straight, couldn't figure out what Ben wanted with him or from him, couldn't piece any of it together. The only thing he had to cling to was that Edel was with him. Even if their relationship was going through a bad patch. She was still in his life. He would never allow anyone or anything to change that. He'd move heaven and earth, go on a rampage, seek out anyone who'd even try to get in the way of what they shared.

And then his thoughts turned to Ariel and, instead of his heart rate increasing lustily, his mood darkened and he began to wonder if perhaps her 'mistakes' were contrived as part of Ben's overall manipulation. He'd been made a fool of by one woman already. He wasn't about to let another turn his brains to mush so she could chew him up and spit him out when she was done.

He threw the cigarette butt out the window, fastened the metal clasp in place and returned to the folder of documents he'd discarded only moments before. Focusing his attention on Edel was his sole intention and if that meant being cruel to Ariel in the process, then so be it. Only time would tell whether she was truly involved but for that time at least, he had every intention of treading cautiously.

"Thanks again, Simon," Vicky said, sitting into his car, her shopping bags at her feet. "You're an absolute lifesaver."

"Hardly," he laughed, pressing the ignition button on the dashboard to start his white BMW.

Today you are, she thought silently, meaning every word.

They fell into a relaxed conversation. She was happy to let him lead the way and do most of the talking, listening attentively as he regaled her with details of a charity project he was involved in, its main purpose being to provide increased assistance for under-privileged children.

As she listened to his tale – shocked by the horrific domestic conditions he described – her worries slipped unnoticed to the back of her mind. Quizzing him on the part he played in the fund-raising for this needy cause, she became engrossed, totally surprised to feel an unexpected fizz of adrenalin as a few ideas began to germinate in her head. Feeling alive was an alien emotion of late and though she didn't harbour much hope that it would last for too long, she basked in its warmth like a baby in its mother's arms.

"You know I'm working for Ellis Enterprise?" she told him.

"The financial consultancy group in Howth?"

"The very one," she agreed. "Our clients are always getting involved in sponsorship deals and very few of them are as worthy as this I can tell you."

He raised an eyebrow, his interest evident. He let her continue.

"I think, with a little bit of persuasion, I might be able to drum up a little funding for you."

"Yeah?" Simon asked, half turning his head to look at her, yet careful to keep his attention on the road at the same time. "That'd be fantastic. But please don't feel you have to. And don't put yourself – or your boss – under any pressure."

"Don't worry. I'm not going to twist any arms. It'll be a simple yes or no."

"All the same," he added, preferring – from experience – to err on the side of caution, "I prefer to work with willing volunteers. Otherwise things get messy and eventually the charity seems to fall by the wayside."

"Leave it with me and I'll mention it to Ben first thing Monday. If he shows even the slightest interest in getting on board, I'll set up a meeting."

"My business card is there," he said quickly, pointing to the compartment behind the handbrake. He wasn't about to pass up on the opportunity. "Take a few and pass them around to any interested parties."

Vicky took five from the small pile that were held together by an elastic band, impressed by the quality gold script etched on the high-gloss business card. "Of course, Ellis Enterprise will stand to benefit too," she added, slipping the cards into her black patent handbag, "particularly if the company ends up being favourably associated with helping under-privileged children."

"Well, I hardly thought they were going to be involved for the good of their health," Simon laughed.

She smiled at his directness and welcomed the sense of light relief that came with that smile. "I can't promise anything definite because to be honest it'll be entirely up to Ben Ellis. And he's not an easy man to cajole. But it won't hurt to ask. And all going well, it could prove to be a win-win situation."

He nodded in agreement. "Okay, why not give it a go then. Some of the situations we help out are heart-wrenching so if he has any compassion at all, he'll find it very difficult to refuse. I take it he's a family man himself?"

Vicky made a face. "He's devoted to his wife, Jenny. But it's just the two of them. No children."

"That's how it goes sometimes, isn't it? Certain things in life are outside our control."

She responded without thinking. "Yeah, it's a bit of a gamble for us all, Simon."

He brought the car to a stop outside her house.

"I meant to ask," he added as she opened the door, "how's Fintan's swing coming on? Do you know if he's ready for that game yet?"

Vicky went cold inside, letting go of the shopping bags and gripping the door handle tightly for support. What on earth was Simon on about?

"Fintan's swing? What game? I'm not sure I understand?" She averted her eyes from his until she'd recovered her composure. It was the first she'd heard of Fintan practising any swing!

The wheels in her head were rolling faster than ever, round and round as her imagination began to pick up pace, pushing her to jump to all sorts of conclusions. She turned slowly around to face Simon, praying he'd offer some innocent explanation, an explanation that would neutralise her doubts.

"His golf swing, Vicky. He's been practising. Didn't he tell you?" Simon took off the Red Sox baseball cap he was wearing, his shock of dark hair flattened underneath. After giving his head a quick scratch, he fixed the cap back on again, messing with the peak until it was curved in the way he liked it. "You're not one of those wives who disapprove of her man having a bit of fun, are you?"

She opened the top two buttons in her coat and stepped out of the car, feeling extremely clammy as a vision of Fintan indulging in some fun came to mind. With *her*! Was he trying to impress *her* with displays of grandeur on the golf course?

"Oh, I'm your regular modern woman," she lied, surprised when she managed to laugh. "And I do remember him mentioning something about practising his golf swing now that you remind me. I've got so much going on in my mind at the moment that I completely forgot about him taking it up. Sometimes we're a bit like ships that pass in the night to be honest: me coming in from work, him going out. You know yourself? Are you two getting together for a golf outing or something?"

"Nothing definite yet. I'm finding it hard to pin him down if you want to know the truth."

Probably too busy with *her* every spare moment he has. The thought ran into her head, leaving a vile aftertaste in its wake. "I'm sure he'd love the competition."

"We bumped into each other at the driving range a few times," Simon explained, "and I challenged him to a game at the club. He fobbed me off by saying he had to improve his swing before he'd be ready for competition! I didn't have him earmarked as someone who liked to win."

"Oh, that describes Fin to a T! Always striving to come out on top. And not only in golf."

Simon snorted and swallowed a snigger, unable to hide his amusement at the idea of Fintan always being on top!

Vicky ignored his male humour, not at all in the mood to entertain sexual innuendo. Her thoughts were very firmly rooted on the 18th hole and what was attracting Fintan to it. And how come I haven't noticed a set of clubs in the garage, she wondered idly, unable to prevent her thoughts from straying. Where was he hiding them? Around at *her* place? She wouldn't put it past him.

"As a matter of interest, Simon," she asked, "what club are you a member of?"

He put his hand on the gear-stick, getting ready to put the car into first gear and inch the short distance to his own house. "Marina, the local one here in Malahide."

"A golf club voucher might be a nice surprise for Fin seeing as he's taking his game seriously," she said then, imagining the shock on his face if she presented him with one. "Not a word to him though." She put a finger to her lips.

Simon laughed. "Great idea! I wish my wife would be as intuitive when it comes to choosing presents. I always end up with DIY tools for birthdays and Christmases. As well as a list of jobs to make sure I put them to good use! Don't worry, your secret's safe with me. Fintan's a lucky guy. I hope he appreciates it!"

A sinking feeling settled in the pit of her stomach as she grabbed her shopping bags and banged the door closed.

Fintan is too busy with his other life to bother appreciating me, she thought in disgust, wondering whether he'd only taken up golf to impress *her*, his athletic bit on the side. Was life one huge round ball of whispered secrets, like a million elastic bands bound together, everybody adapting their own version of events to help them get what they wanted from those around them, all the little secrets amalgamating into one large mound?

"Thanks again for the lift," she said through Simon's open window, the cheeriness in her voice hiding the heartache she felt inside.

Her hands shook as she searched in her handbag for her house keys. Ben Ellis's words came back to her in that instant: him asking her if she'd acquired a maths degree to help him out of a sticky situation. Well, she didn't need a qualification to figure out Fintan's formula! She knew exactly why he was practising his swing and the person he was planning to share a caddy with as they cruised from one green to the next, their fingers entwined lovingly or his hand on *her* leg as she steered. And it's certainly not me he's trying to impress, she thought, venom causing her stomach to churn.

But while he might have thought he'd covered all angles in the charade he was playing, he should be more careful if he didn't want a detrimental golf handicap to match that ever-improving secret swing of his.

Chapter 17

Pete Scavo folded his newspaper and laid it on the arm of the chair. Another crossword completed. Or almost completed. In Pete's book, having only one unsolved clue at the end of a task was complete enough for him. In all the investigative cases he'd worked on over the years, it wasn't uncommon to have a few unsolved clues and still manage to close a case satisfactorily. Loose ends, he thought, moving from the sitting-room to the kitchen to make himself a cup of tea, mulling the words over in his head.

"Did I ever think I'd end up being a loose end myself?" he muttered, dunking a tea bag in a mug and pouring boiling water over it.

He no longer bought or used tea leaves, unable to bear seeing them at the bottom of the cup and being reminded of Barbara and the readings she did for her bingo and bridge friends, readings that had brought fun and laughter to their home at all hours of the day and night.

Letting out a long sigh, he stared into the partially empty fridge. He missed his wife's touch about the place, missed the presence of life that accompanied her wherever she went and missed her culinary talents more than he'd ever appreciated them when she'd been alive.

"Cheese and ham? Or ham and cheese?" he said aloud, exhaling a long slow breath as he took the block of Cheddar from the shelf, snipping the mouldy bits from the edges with a small sharp knife. He closed the fridge door, not bothering with the ham when he noticed the edges were beginning to crust and curl. Nothing tasted the same any more. Eating had become something to pass the time rather than fulfil a hunger.

"You'd have plenty to say about that, Barbara, if you were here," he mumbled, putting the milk jug and sugar bowl on the table and setting his place, one of the few household rituals he'd continued since her death.

"As for you," he said, pointing a finger at the ginger-haired cat lying preening herself on the mat inside the back door, "what would she say if she saw you shedding hair all over her house?"

Biting into his cheese sandwich, he chewed mindlessly and allowed his thoughts to stray to happier times when his wife sat across from him at the table, her cheeks red from fussing around him, her chatter constant as she filled him in on the latest village news, snippets she'd heard while running her daily errands. They'd drained pots of tea between them, sinking their teeth into fresh home-made soda bread and thick layers of real butter, neither of them worried about raising their cholesterol. And by the time Barbara's failing heart had made its presence known, it was too late to cut back so she enjoyed her real Irish butter right up to the very end.

He was happy to let go his daydream when the phone rang, the instructions he received giving him reason to break the routine of a late Saturday afternoon, his mood instantly lifting at the prospect of being busy for the next couple of hours.

"I should still make it back in time for evening Mass," he said to the cat, taking his missal from the shelf and slipping it into the pocket of his overcoat, planning on going directly to the church on his route home.

Leaving the house, he didn't bother to take the time to tidy the kitchen table, a smile on his face as he imagined how Barbara would have disapproved of his carelessness, a tug in his heart when yet again it hit him that she was no longer there to do it for him. But his Garda training was ingrained in his psychology and he knew only too well that untidiness gave the illusion of an occupied house, an illusion he clung to every time he returned home. If only for that initial split second when he fooled himself into thinking there was somebody there to greet him, somebody there to welcome him home.

As Pete Scavo was going about his business, Vicky was welcoming her guests. Everything was ready. The table was laid. It was time to get the party underway. Literally.

Newbridge cutlery and condiments gleamed brightly on the brand-new tablecloth. White Wedgewood and Galway crystal adorned the place settings, a yellow (symbol of friendship) scented candle flickering gently yet safely out of little children's reach as a striking centrepiece.

Vicky had done rather a good job of the presentation under the circumstances. And she was pleased with her efforts. But it did nothing to lift her spirits. Instead, she was filled with a sense of desolation that they were about to sit down to the Last Supper.

Crying the whole way through organising the lasagne and salads, she'd been on the verge of flinging the lot in the bin and crawling back under the covers at several points, planning to stay buried and not to answer the door when the Joneses arrived. But she'd pushed against her reservations, fighting the panic and ignoring the salty tears that dripped into the minced beef as she'd stirred it in the pan.

Using the cuff of her fleece in place of a tissue, she'd then folded some red serviettes into cone shapes and popped them in the wine goblets Fintan's parents had given them as a wedding gift. Displaying at least one of the presents they'd received from the Jones side of the family had been a deliberate ploy on her part. The part of her that could still feel emotion wanted to please them, wanted to make them feel welcome.

But now that the hour of reckoning had arrived and

they were actually under her roof, a set of glasses was the least of her worries.

Fintan had failed to come home. She was alone with people who were like strangers to her. And suddenly the purpose of her invitation began to waver in her mind, her strength of conviction weakening.

Fintan's parents and their two grandsons arrived exactly on time. They hadn't taken the slightest notice of her red-rimmed eyes or how edgy she was. In fact they'd been more than complimentary when she'd greeted them.

"Lovely house, Vicky," Joan, Fintan's mother, said, taking her time as she made her way through the hallway, having a good look around her.

"Is it a nice area?" Ed enquired gruffly. "Looks fairly posh outside. Boys," he added then, "be careful with those ornaments. I'm sure they're not for playing with."

Vicky appreciated her father-in-law's interference but wished he'd follow his words of caution by actually getting the children away from her ornaments.

"We like it here anyway," she answered, covering both questions with one response. "It's generally very quiet and the people we've met so far seem friendly."

The two little boys were busily checking out Vicky's arrangement of owls that were sitting on the walnut radiator cover in the hallway. She cringed inwardly, her owl collection looking very vulnerable as two little sets of hands fiddled with them, turning them upside down to check them out and lining them up army style in two neat rows, making them look as if they were ready for battle.

Like myself, she sighed. Here I am lining these people up and preparing them for an emotional struggle between their sons when I drop my bombshell later.

"Give it a few years," Ed commented, removing his cap from his head and shoving it into the pocket of his wool jacket, "and there'll be youngsters playing and fighting on the street. Then it won't be as peaceful. It's always the same in these new developments."

"A bit of life will be nice around the place," Joan added in attempt to soften her husband's harsh words. "Boys, don't you have a gift for Vicky?"

The taller of the two grabbed the bag Joan held in her hand, pulling out a small wrapped package and shoving it at Vicky.

The younger boy forgot about the owls and looked on with interest, waiting for her to open it. "It's from the two of us," he announced, obviously in the habit of sticking up for himself. "Not just him!"

She guessed by its shape it was chocolate. "Why don't you open it for me when we're sitting at the table," she offered, anxious to get things underway, get through the meal and then find the right moment to make her announcement.

Ariel had cursed and cursed. Her phone battery had died as soon as Roger's voice came on the line. Half running, half walking, she'd hurried back to the flat as quickly as she could, clutching to the lifeline that Roger had finally made contact. She'd hoped it was to offer his help. But, first and foremost, she'd hoped it was because he'd forgiven her and could see it in his heart to take her back.

Ignoring the gang of teenagers blocking the entrance hall – the same gang she generally sneaked past to avoid their intimidation – she'd run through them and up the stairs to Number 105. Searching through the untidiness in her bedroom, she'd eventually found her phone charger hidden under a pile of dirty laundry. Plugging it in, she'd waited impatiently while it renewed the life in her battery.

Now, taking a deep breath, she punched in Roger's number.

"I'm so sorry, Roger," she breathed into the phone as soon as his soft Cork lilt came on the line. Luckily Ellis Enterprise paid her phone bill. Otherwise she wouldn't have been able to call him back.

"Why didn't you tell me what was going on, Ariel? While it was happening?" Roger was nothing if not direct, never minced his words and considered dishonesty in any form an atrocity.

His icy tone worried Ariel. How she wished he were beside her, holding her in his warm embrace, reassuring her that everything would work out fine. But he wasn't and she knew she wasn't out of the woods yet. Not by a long shot.

"Would it have made a difference if I'd told you every step of the way?" She couldn't help jumping to her own defence. "I can't honestly imagine you'd have stood by me if I came home from work one day and told you I was being taken to court for embezzlement!"

"So you decided it would be better to lie to me?"

"It's not as straightforward as that, Roger. I was thinking of you too. How could I put that worry on you when you were in charge of flying an aeroplane to the other side of the Atlantic? And I'm innocent, Roger. I swear to you I'm innocent!"

"So you keep saying,"

Ariel flopped onto the unmade bed, hugging her knees to her chest. She'd beg if she had to. But first she'd tell him everything. She'd tell him the truth. "Roger, if you have time to listen, I have time to talk."

"Is that beeping an incoming call for you?"

"Yes, but before I can take it, I need to know if you'll fly somewhere for me?"

Pete Scavo was out of breath by the time he reached the old army barracks, his woollen overcoat weighing him down, his cheese sandwich sticking in his throat for the entire bus journey and short walk it had taken to get there. Closed since the mid-1900's, the forbidding barracks had been converted into a block of flats, the exterior walls restored to their original grey brick, the windows replaced in keeping with the original style, flag poles extending from the ledge over the first floor. Developing the outside of the building in line with planning had eaten into the property developer's budget, leaving very little funding to cover the rest of the project. The interior had been completed to the cheapest standard possible, seriously under regulation, which probably explained the low rent tariff as well as accounting for the type of clientele renting there.

"There you are, Pete. We were about to give up on you. They're screaming upstairs to get the water switched back on."

Pete halted at the door, nodding at the two burly men standing in his path, employed no doubt to keep control of the houseful of less-than-ideal tenants living in the one- and two-bedroom flats there.

"What's it this time?" Pete enquired. "Leaking tap? Someone pull a cistern off the wall?" He shuffled from foot to foot, waiting for guidance on what DIY job needed doing.

"Bit of an altercation in Number 101 last night, old man. We had to get the heavies in this morning to evict them! Whoosh!" He kicked the air with his foot.

"Much damage?" Pete hadn't brought his overalls with him, forgetting them in his hurry to get out of the house and on with the maintenance jobs Ben had put his way.

Military House wasn't one of the six developments Ben had invested in but the owner was part of a network of property developers he knew very well. Ben had limited his investments to up-market buildings, ideal for business people looking for a home – and address – to be proud of. He regularly put work Pete's way, sensing he had more time on his hands than was good for his sanity.

"You'll see for yourself when you get to the door. I hope you've nothing planned for your Saturday night, Pete? No water damage but everything else you can possibly think of! They must have had a right to-do up there."

Pete fixed his cap on his head. "I'll make a start then." He'd been in Military House before and knew his way round, which was why he chose to take the stairs and not the lift, not trusting it to make the journey to the first floor. Once – and once only – had he risked stepping into the rickety metal cube, the experience leaving him shaken for quite a while afterward. And it wasn't easy to unnerve Pete. He clutched the missal in his pocket and offered up a silent prayer as he came to a stop three steps up. He stood aside and let two tenants past, the smell of stale alcohol forcing him to hold his breath. But he continued up the staircase. Keeping busy, no matter how undesirable the circumstances, was a whole lot better than sitting at home doing nothing. Alone.

Chapter 18

"No salad for the boys," Joan, Fintan's mother, said quickly as Vicky placed a bowl of green salad on the table. "I'm afraid they're not the best at eating vegetables."

"I'm sure most children are like that," Vicky commented, glancing at the two little innocent faces staring up at her. "You still haven't told me your names," she said, looking from one to the other, as they stood side by side near the table.

They spoke at the same time, their enthusiasm making her smile.

"Why don't you go first?" she suggested to the youngest.

She went down on her hunkers so she could look at them properly, her eyes automatically straying to the littlest one.

"I'm Olly and I'm five," he said. His face broke into a smile, his eyes crinkling at the sides.

Oh God, she thought, her breath catching in her throat as she stared at him. His eyes were the exact shade of brown as Fintan's, the way they crinkled up at the sides also reminding her of her husband's infectious smile.

"And I'm Callum. I'm six and a bit. I'm the eldest."

Vicky snapped back to attention. "You're tall for six!"

"And I'm the tallest in my class at school," Olly cut in, vying for attention.

If it weren't for the glint of devilment shining in their eyes, she'd have believed that butter wouldn't melt in their mouths.

"Where's Fin? I thought he'd be here to greet us?" said Joan.

"Eh, he's . . ."

But Vicky didn't get to finish before Joan had cut in again.

"I was only saying to Ed we haven't seen him since the day of your wedding! And he's only rung a couple of times. We're only on the other side of the city after all. Surely he'd be able to squeeze one hour into his schedule. He is going to be here, isn't he? He's not working or anything?"

Vicky fumbled with the bread-basket, taking it from the table and stalling a moment before answering. It was the one question she'd been dreading. Of course Joan had expected him to be there to greet her, no matter how strained the relationship between him and his father.

"I sent him to the shops for dessert." The lie slid from Vicky's lips like cool melted ice cream slipping along her palate and down her throat. She bit into her lip, hating the untruths she was resorting to, her cheeks burning in shame.

Inside her head, a stage performance was already getting underway, the curtains coming up as a screenplay came to life.

The word 'dessert' had instantly conjured unwelcome thoughts for Vicky, her mental lens zooming in on an action shot of *her* topped with cream – the sumptuous dessert her husband had become obsessed with recently. The scene rolled on. She couldn't block out the image of Fintan licking his lips in anticipation of relishing multiple courses of *her* fruitiness. The film kept rolling, the next shot a graphic image of her husband and *her* doing it right there on the dining-table, laughing hilariously as he wrapped himself around *her* on the walnut tabletop that was designed to sit eight people around it – not have two lying on top.

Vicky tightly clutched the rim of the basket in her hand, splinters of wicker piercing her skin. She fought against the compulsion to scream, the scene in her head refusing to disappear. Picturing them clambering all over each other and rocking rhythmically on the table made her want to pull the tablecloth from the surface and send everything crashing to the floor.

But she didn't. She couldn't. She had to hold it together.

"I can't imagine what's keeping him," she said quietly and slowly, the words sounding trite to her ears.

She dropped the basket on to the table, watching as it wobbled dangerously, slices of brown and white bread jumping up and down like a chorus of dancers. Putting a finger out, she stopped it, glancing at Joan and recognising the stark love in her eyes, an emotion that was impossible to mask, an emotion she herself had fallen under the spell of too. Because, after all, Vicky knew that both she and Joan truly did love the same man.

Will I be able to go through with my plan, she wondered, momentary remorse filling her as she imagined for the first time the pain she'd be inflicting on the other people involved. How could she justify such selfishness?

She glanced briefly at Ed who was making his way around the dining-room looking at the wall hangings and other artefacts, the permanent frown on his face an indication of the bitterness he'd been carrying on his shoulders for years. Sensing the gloom veiled around him, Vicky could understand why Fintan had felt the need to escape that atmosphere, lest it drag him down too.

She shuddered, partially in dread and partially in anticipation, as she imagined Ed's reaction to the news that Fintan had sex with his brother's wife. Would he receive it with his usual disinterest or would it force a reaction? Would it be the catalyst to break the bubble of depression he'd been living in?

As if he'd read her thoughts, Ed's voice cut in on her thoughts and brought her attention back to the people around her once more.

"Gone out for dessert is a likely story! Typical Fintan, always avoiding things he doesn't want to face."

"Sit over to the table and we can get started, Ed," Vicky told him, ignoring his loaded comment, attempting to distract him instead.

Regaining the teeniest bit of confidence by reminding herself that they were after all in her house, under her roof, she forced herself to feel in control.

Joan was direct and agreeable, excited at the prospect of spending time with her son and seemingly without animosity about the length of time he'd left without contacting them. Ed, on the other hand, didn't hide his resentment of his son's success or his impression that Fintan had left his family behind.

Taking the silver server from the centre of the table, Vicky carefully cut the lasagne into even squares. Nodding and smiling at regular intervals when Joan included her in unimportant chatter, she filled the plates with generous helpings of food and placed them around the table. But all the time she was smiling, her mind was elsewhere, plotting and scheming until she had things neatly in place in her head: a twin set of revenge, his and *hers*!

But while it all sounded great in her mind, transferring her idea from her head to reality wouldn't be easy. The Jones family weren't an easy group to steer. She was already discovering that. As it was, she couldn't get Ed or the boys to come and sit at the table even though their food was ready and waiting.

Ed was still making his way around the room at a

snail's pace, picking up every ornament, turning it upside down and checking it underneath – for what reason she wasn't sure. She didn't think he'd be interested in the manufacturer – more than likely looking for the price tag instead to decide if they were worth anything! Once he was done with the ornaments, he proceeded to investigate the photographs on the pale cream walls.

"Don't see any of us in these snaps," he commented to anyone prepared to listen, pawing the glass with his grubby prints. "Not good enough to show off on his walls, I s'pose."

"We're only getting around to hanging some wedding photos," Vicky said by way of explanation, her cheeks burning guiltily. Though Ed had only cast blame on Fintan, she was in little doubt but his comment was designed to embarrass her too. And privately, she could only agree with him. She hadn't exactly encouraged any family photos to be out on display for all to see, quite happy for the family pictures on her wall to be all about the two of them, quite happy to ignore the extended members as if they didn't even exist.

Until now, she thought. Until it suits me to get them involved. What does that make me, she wondered? A manipulative bitch?

"Next time you call, Ed," she promised in a bizarre moment of remorse, "I'll make sure the Jones family portrait is up for all to see. I'll show you the album later and point out the shots I have in mind for framing."

"Well, if we're as long waiting for the second invite as we were waiting for this one, I won't even resemble the man in the wedding photo! It's about time you and that son of mine started remembering you have relations."

His sarcastic tone brought an end to their light-hearted discussion, his large bulk making the room look untidy, his stern glare causing a shiver to course down her spine. She didn't think he was joking, convinced he meant every word. She didn't respond immediately, preferring to let his words melt into the room. Continuing to watch him from the corner of her eye, she struggled to suppress her rising irritation as he pulled opened the door of glass unit where she kept their most precious trinkets: a selection of crystal and delicate wedding presents as well as *Lladro* figurines she'd been collecting for a number of years.

Was he going to spend the whole time scrutinising their personal belongings? She wanted to tell him keep his fingers off but wouldn't dare be so rude or unwelcoming. Not to his face. What went on in her head was one thing but what she allowed out of her mouth was another. She knew that as soon as they were gone out the door, she'd be running around every frame and glass, every ornament and shelf space with the polish and cloth, rubbing every fingerprint and smudge until all evidence of his handling had well and truly disappeared.

"Lasagne is nicest straight out of the oven, Ed," she said as sweetly as she could, hoping he'd take the hint and make his way to the table before he dropped the heart-shaped crystal clock he had in his hand. "Yours will be cold if you don't come and sit down."

A sharp screech from Joan completely distracted Vicky's attention from her father-in-law and the glass cabinet.

"Callum, get back here!" Joan's tone was a high-pitched warning.

Unfortunately, however, it fell on deaf ears.

The elder of the two children had bolted through the double doors into the lounge. He jumped straight onto the piano stool and banged the piano keys with all his might. As if that wasn't bad enough, he then climbed on to his knees, turned around and put his bum on the keys to see how many notes he could play at once.

She groaned inside, the harsh notes from the piano cutting right through her. Why hadn't she thought to lock it and keep it safe? Or indeed lock the lounge door altogether! But it was too late for that now and if she had turned the key to keep them out, she'd probably have got more sarcastic barbs from Ed about not trusting them, which could have resulted in all sorts of accusations and insinuations.

Damn! Her heart sank as Callum jumped off the piano stool, narrowly missing his eye off the corner of the mantelpiece. All she could do was try and keep as close a watch as possible on the little boys for the few hours they were in the house. In their opinion, she presumed, the piano was the only plaything they'd seen since they'd arrived. Watching Callum climb back onto the piano stool and kneel again, this time waving his backside and hitting every key with it, she realised it wasn't going to be an easy task to lure him away from it until he'd at least had a chance to make plenty of noise. Or she offered him some sort of alternative temptation.

His behaviour remained unchecked. Ed was oblivious to his antics and Joan, regardless of her initial screech, had already forgotten about him.

Though it was on the tip of Vicky's tongue to tell Callum to stop, she kept her mouth firmly shut. Her protectiveness would probably have appeared over the top to people with such little regard for household items and the atmosphere between her and Ed was already icy. But there had to be some way of getting Callum away from her piano.

To Vicky, her piano symbolised so much more than an ornament or piece of furniture. It held a lifetime of memories – good ones mostly – and was one of the few possessions she'd insisted on bringing to Malahide from her parents' home, having built a close attachment to it over the years.

As a young girl, she'd lost herself in the oblivion of music, whiling away many lonely afternoons perfecting some of her favourite melodies and practising for piano exams. Her musical talent was one of the few things she'd excelled at, one of the few things her parents couldn't find fault with and one of the few things in which they'd ever displayed even a semblance of pride.

As she listened to Callum banging out tuneless notes, she hoped against hope that the ebony and ivory keys were designed to last. But they at least could be retuned. She wasn't sure she could. She was fragile, easily broken.

"Why don't I teach Callum and Olly how to play a little tune after dinner?" she suggested, smiling and tossing Olly's hair, choking back the urge to run into the lounge and yank Callum away from her precious piano.

They weren't bad boys, she suspected. But they were wild and, if her intuition was right, the piano was only the beginning of their exploration. The noise coming from the lounge was reducing, Callum's interest in banging the keys waning. She decided to wait it out.

But she found it impossible to concentrate and couldn't resist glancing toward the lounge again. The bronze vase standing on the hearth caught her eye. She hoped that both it and the plant growing inside would escape Callum's heavy hand. Giving a cursory glance at the mantelpiece, she couldn't prevent a sharp intake of breath as the ornamental statues she'd brought home from a New York shopping trip seemed to grow sets of eyes and stare pleadingly at her, begging her to save them from being shattered into thousands of pieces.

Ah, to hell with the serving and waiting, she thought, dropping her silver-service act and moving as quickly as she could towards the piano just as Callum had started to use his fist on the keys. Catching the small blond boy by the hand, she gave him little option but to return with her to the dining-room, whispering the promise of a surprise in his ear if he was a really good boy.

His eyes lit up and he was the epitome of good behaviour as he took his place at the table.

"It's dinner time now, Callum. You must be hungry?"

He shrugged his shoulders. "Kind of."

"And don't forget," she reminded him, "if you clear your plate, you'll get something really nice from the goodie jar."

He tucked into his food with gusto, happy to eat up as fast as he could in order to get a treat.

"You too, Olly," Vicky encouraged, unable to resist ruffling his hair again, grinning when it stood in tufts. Just like Fintan's. "And maybe you'd like to learn how to play chopsticks on the piano as well?"

"Like a real piano player?" His jaw dropped open.

She grabbed her small window of opportunity and closed the doors to the lounge, resisting the urge to turn the key and pocket it. Only then, when everyone had finally begun to eat, did she sit down and join them.

"How many bedrooms in this house?" Ed enquired between mouthfuls of lasagne.

"Four, but they're not huge. Pretty average to be honest," Vicky said modestly.

"That son of ours is doing better than he's letting on, Joan."

"Isn't that a good thing?" His wife came to her youngest son's defence. "At least one of them has something to show for himself instead of sitting around waiting for the work to come to him."

Vicky watched and listened to their exchange, understanding the hidden accusation against Ed in Joan's words.

"It wouldn't kill him to give his ma and da a helping hand with a few bills and stuff. He hasn't as much as brought us a litre of milk since he walked out."

"And the other three have?" Joan's question was loaded.

"They have children to feed and clothe," Ed retorted. "Fintan only has himself to look after. Young Vicky here has a fine income of her own."

Vicky was furious, feeling she might as well have been invisible. She played with the salad on her plate, her face flaming.

Inside her head, she screamed at Ed. The cheek of him sitting at our table, she thought, eating our food and slandering us! No matter what my grievances are with Fintan, his father has a cheek coming here and carrying on as if he owes them in some way. Fintan had been right about his father. He was only happy when he was complaining. He wasn't one bit proud of the person his son had become.

"That's enough, Eddie," Joan hissed, reaching an arm around Callum and turning up his sleeve to prevent it from falling into the ketchup he'd squirted liberally over his food and plate. He'd even managed to get some onto the tablecloth. "Fin's a good one," she went on. "Always was. It's a pity you can't see that. You never let up on him. Not ever! You never had a good word to say about him, not even when –"

Ed dropped his cutlery, glaring across the table at this wife. "Well, why did he –"

Joan withered her husband with a look, silencing him in that instant. "He's the only one who ever gave me a bit of time, Ed. Kept me company when you wouldn't get out of bed for days on end and his brothers were gadding about the place bringing trouble to the door! It doesn't matter what you say now. You can't ever change that. We can't turn back the clock."

Vicky found their outspoken behaviour shocking, a direct contrast to her parents' suppression of any subject liable to give rise to an argument. Sitting in Ed and Joan's line of fire, feeling increasingly uncomfortable in her own home, she was reminded of the numerous mealtimes she'd rushed through to escape the lingering silence between her parents. Living with a lifetime of unresolved issues being shoved under the proverbial mat had been every bit as difficult to deal with as the Jones' method of holding nothing back and embarrassing all those around them.

Ed huffed and puffed and fidgeted in his chair, bunching his serviette into a tight ball. But surprisingly, he didn't offer any retort to his wife's admonishment.

"Who can blame him for getting out while he could?" said Joan. "There was no future on offer if he'd stayed with us. He'd have been dragged into the same hole the other three are stuck in, the same hole we fell into ourselves all those years ago. Can't you be happy for him for once in your life, Ed, instead of always being ready to put the boot in? He's doing well. Leave him be."

Joan's strength of character was unexpected, a quality Vicky found admirable, particularly when faced with years of Ed's grumpiness day in and day out.

"'Scuse me," Olly piped up from beside Joan, his voice distracting Vicky from the sombre mood that had fallen on the table, "how come your dog isn't here?"

Vicky's heart softened instantly as she looked at the innocent little boy sitting across from her, his brown eyes wide in anticipation, his light brown hair standing up in tufts on his crown. Looking into those deep eyes reminded her of Fintan and she suddenly wished more than anything that she did have a dog lying in the back garden. Then she wouldn't have to disappoint Olly. But the only things living in her back garden were the few trees and shrubs that had survived her pathetic attempts at gardening. It wasn't as if she could pull a cocker spaniel or terrier out of thin air, so she shook her head and gave him an honest reply.

"No, sweetheart, I'm afraid we don't have a dog. I –" But before she could get another word in, Callum interrupted rudely.

"Told you, Olly," he shouted cheekily, sticking his tongue out at his brother. "Told you it wasn't a real dog! Ma got it wrong as usual."

Vicky frowned in confusion. What had Suzi said? "What are they talking about? Where on earth did they get the notion that we had a dog?" She looked from Joan to Ed and back to Joan again, but instead of answering her question or explaining to the boys that it wasn't Fintan and Vicky who had a dog, they both took a sudden interest in the food on their plates.

"Eat your garlic bread, boys, and don't be annoying Vicky," Joan said hurriedly.

"Yeah," Ed added. "She's gone to all this trouble. Didn't she tell you she has something nice for afters? Now be good or you won't get any."

He's changed his tune, Vicky thought. He's actually praising me! He has to be up to something!

And she wasn't the only one who believed that. The boys weren't having any of their grandparents' subterfuge either. They were not going to be silenced, both of them already insisting again, one fighting to be heard over the other. They had something to say and nobody was going to stop them.

"My ma said Fintan had a bitch," Callum piped up, his words clear and distinct. "A lapdog, Ma said. What kind of dog's that? Has she a long tail? Is it like a hunting dog?" He folded his arms, pouted his lips and waited.

"A bitch is a girl dog, isn't it, Vicky?" Olly looked directly at her, his tone gentler, his expression transparent.

Though he was the younger of the two, he was by far the sweetest. Vicky's heart melted as she listened to his questions, her resolve to make him the subject of her revenge faltering. But the more she looked into his eyes, the more she felt there was a possibility that she would actually be doing him a favour. Fintan would make a great father, if only part-time in Olly's case.

"Yes," she told him. "It's a girl dog."

"Where is she then? The girl dog, where is she? Ma told us there was a bitch living here. Can we bring her in the house after tea? Can we play with her? Please!" He opened his eyes as wide as saucers, his questions coming in quick succession.

"Stop annoying Vicky, you two!" Ed growled, reaching across the table and giving Callum a clip on the ear. Then he glanced at Vicky, his expression difficult to read. "Take no notice of their whining. They're always making stuff up and goofing around. You couldn't be up to them." After that he turned his attention to Olly, glaring across the table at him. "Didn't I warn the two of you about behaving today? You know what will happen if you don't!"

Vicky's heart sank as she contemplated what could happen to little Olly, scrutinising him closely and watching his reaction to his grandfather's scolding. His face had fallen. The look of anticipation he'd worn moments before had totally disappeared. The poor little boy, she thought. He hasn't done anything wrong. He was told we had a dog bounding around somewhere. She was positive he hadn't made up the story of the girl dog.

Watching the changing expressions on the faces around the table – Joan rolling her serviette up into a tight knot, fraying the edges as she pulled at it and looking as though she wished she were anywhere but where she was, Ed's upper lip twitching as he glared at his grandsons, Callum's eyes narrowing as he listened to his grandfather's threats and poor little Olly's crestfallen face, his lip wobbling and tears brimming at the edge of those big brown eyes – it dawned on Vicky what was going on. She knew exactly what the boys meant. She knew exactly who the *girl dog* was meant to be. It's me, she thought! I'm the bitch Suzi was talking about. How dare she? Just how dare she? Vicky felt her cast for revenge stretching slightly further to include her latest enemy in the net. I might as well kill two birds with one stone, she decided firmly. That'll teach *that* bitch to keep her hands off my man!

It had been Ed's threats and his panic about silencing the children that had alerted her suspicion. Children were nothing if not blatantly honest. The boys hadn't made up the dog story. Of course not. They'd simply repeated what they'd heard, the true meaning behind their mother's mocking escaping their innocent minds. She forgot about the people around her, ignored the bustle of conversation and hushed tones between them, even the crash when Callum knocked against his glass and spilt his glass of orange over the lace tablecloth and the sticky liquid seeped from the table onto the polished floor.

She painted a smile on her face and rose slowly from her chair, burying her hurt and humiliation behind the smile.

"I'll run and get a cloth to clean the spill. No harm done I'm sure." Her tone was even. Emotionless. The confidence she'd felt earlier melted like chocolate on a hot summer's day, the light at the end of her tunnel quenching like a candle in the wind.

"Oh, Callum, look at the mess! What do you say to Vicky?" Joan prompted her grandson, rubbing her temple in slow circular movements.

Vicky guessed the strain of the afternoon was making her head ache. And if that were true, she wasn't alone.

"It's a beautiful piece of lace," Joan commented. "I hope it doesn't leave a mark."

"I hope not either but," Vicky added with a sigh,

"some things just can't be erased." Her words had little to do with her brand-new tablecloth.

"But what about the dog?" Olly found his voice again, dropping his fork on the floor when Ed barked abuse at him.

With a growler like that around, who needs a dog, Vicky thought.

Olly clambered down off his chair to pick up the fork, disappearing under the table. He's probably trying to stay out of Ed's way, Vicky thought, watching for his little brown head to reappear. But he seemed reluctant to leave the comfort of his hideaway.

"Come with me, Olly, and I'll tell you." Her intervention surprised herself more than the child. Where on earth had that come from, she wondered? What am I doing sticking my neck out and coming between my father-in-law and a child I barely know?

She hadn't any idea what she was going to tell Olly. That his mother very obviously despised his Aunt Vicky and had called her a bad name? That she was the only bitch living in this house? Unlikely.

"Okay," Olly agreed, crawling out from beneath the table, his little legs moving at lightning pace as he scurried to her side. He kept as near to her as possible, skipping instead of walking, while they covered the short distance to the kitchen.

"So tell me about you and your family, Olly?" Vicky asked as soon as they were out of earshot, lifting him up and sitting him on the island unit so she could look him in the eye. "I've never been to your house so you have to tell me all about it. Then I can paint a picture in my mind." As if I haven't enough going on in there, she thought sadly, now I'm going to add a picture of a family who despise my very existence!

"We don't live in a big house like this," he started, waving his arms around, his eyes darting around the lavish kitchen. "And our place is always messy 'cos we've six people altogether."

"Six?"

He nodded and began to list, using his fingers so he wouldn't forget anyone. "There's me, Callum, the baby twins and Ma and Da."

"And do you have a dog?" She refrained from adding a sarcastic comment about Suzi. He was only a child. It wouldn't have been fair. She wasn't going to sink to Suzi's level.

Olly shook his head, his hair flopping gently with every movement. "Nah, we're not allowed. When we ask Da, he says he can barely feed us, never mind a mangy old dog."

His candid honesty was refreshing and Vicky found herself warming more and more to him, his overt innocence being his greatest appeal. She wondered in the warmth of that moment whether any babies she might have would resemble the cousin – or very likely their half-brother – sitting in front of her. She gave a quick glance at the flatness of her stomach, imagining a baby lying on its back inside watching all that was going on outside of the sky of its world. One day, she promised herself. One day.

And then, finally, she'd have her ally, a little person who would love her unconditionally, a little person who'd take her side no matter what. At least she was hoping so.

"I think your mummy must have made a mistake," she told Olly, wishing she could make him smile again. "We've never had a dog in this house. But what do you say you and I make a little deal?"

He frowned suspiciously. "What's a deal? What's that mean?"

She stroked his cheek, his skin like satin to touch. "A deal's a promise, pet."

"I never break a promise," he told her proudly. "Not even when my big brother tries to make me."

She was convinced she'd seen him stick his chest out the tiniest bit. His manly instincts brought a lump to her throat. "I bet you're the best boy at keeping promises. And I always keep my promises too."

Looking somewhere to the left of Olly's face, her eyes glazed over slightly as the promise she'd made to herself the night she searched Fintan's pockets vividly came to mind. She still had a long way to go to fulfil that promise. Blinking repeatedly, she regained focus and smiled at the patient little boy waiting to hear the deal she had to offer him, his intensity endearing, his innocence arresting.

"So, Olly," she continued, holding out her right hand and indicating for him to shake hers in true 'deal' style, "I'm promising you that if I ever get a dog, I'll make sure that you can come over and see him as soon as he arrives."

His cheeks reddened, his little body jigging with excitement. "Really? Can I walk him? And teach him how to give the paw?"

"Of course." Vicky made to lift him down but just as she'd slipped her hands under his arms, she couldn't resist a moment of childish curiosity.

"What do your ma and da say about your Uncle Fintan?"

Now I'm scraping the barrel and stooping to the lowest level, she thought. She wasn't proud to be gleaning information from a five-year-old boy – just desperate.

Olly shrugged. He didn't look very interested in answering that one.

He rolled his eyes around a little and thought for a moment. "I dunno. When Nana said she was bringing me to your house, they said he has big boots or something, I think. Has he got big boots, Vicky? Are they even too big to fit under the bed?"

Once again, his gaze held hers as he waited for her response. His short attention span had already strayed from the non-existent dog. His tiny face was animated by an inquisitive mind. She was tempted to wrap him in her arms to protect his innocence, a mad compulsion to protect the temporary adoration he was showing her, feeling it was about the only show of true affection she could depend on that evening.

"Do the boots fit or not?" He began to wriggle on the counter top, his impatience evident, his adoration fading with every moment she delayed.

"They fit under some beds," Vicky confirmed sadly,

a lead weight where her heart should be as she forced herself to accept that Fintan's boots (or whatever footwear he happened to be wearing that day) could quite possibly be under *her* bed at exactly that moment.

"Can me and Callum play football with Uncle Fin when he gets back?" Olly changed the subject, his interest shifting swiftly to the long back garden as he glanced longingly through the window.

"I don't see why not," she agreed instantly, wishing things could have been less complicated and she could have enjoyed his company so much more.

"Your garden's nearly as big as the green at the end of our road!" Olly craned his neck to see how far back it stretched. "I play really well. Da says I get it from him. He used to trash Uncle Fin at football when they were boys like me. He said Uncle Fin's useless at . . ."

His unfinished sentence hung in the air, his jaw dropping open as he fixed his eyes on something behind Vicky.

She knew instantly that they weren't alone. Distracted by Olly's ramblings, she hadn't heard anything, but the look of embarrassment on his face was a dead giveaway: his cheeks reddening, his fingers scratching at the edge of the counter and his mouth contorting into a variety of unusual shapes to hide his self-consciousness.

"What did your da say about my soccer skills?"

Vicky froze at the sound of Fintan's voice, the floor tile she was standing on becoming the perimeter of her life in that moment, shielding her from everything else around her. She wished the ground would open and the two-foot-square porcelain tile would drop unexpectedly like a lift in a theme park or a cage in a special effects movie. But it didn't. And she had no choice but to remain standing, rooted to the spot. She found it impossible to move, couldn't bear to turn and look into her husband's eyes, the fear of what she might see much more imposing than her desire to get back at him. At least in that split second it was. Manipulation, scheming and second-guessing was exhausting. More than anything, she wanted the madness in her head to stop.

Chapter 19

Vicky remained standing with her back to Fintan. Exhaling slowly, she let out the breath she'd been psychologically holding since he'd left the house earlier that morning. But she wasn't ready to face him. Not yet. Instead, she continued to focus on Olly's face, watching his expression carefully as he stared at Fintan, attempting to gauge what was happening through the child's eyes. Remaining aloof was extremely difficult but not impossible. Her stomach turned somersaults. Her pulse rate increased. But she didn't flinch. An outward calm slipped around her in a cloak of protection. She guessed by Olly's glance sideways that Fintan was moving a little nearer, his footsteps silent in his training shoes, the slight crinkling of his nylon tracksuit the only audible giveaway.

His close proximity filled her with a mixture of relief and trepidation: relief that he had come home and trepidation as she tried to second-guess what mood he was in and how he was going to receive their guests. Or her for that matter. Would the presence of his parents make any difference? She wouldn't have long to wait to find out. Still she kept her eyes on Olly, afraid to meet Fintan's eye.

And then, just as she was about to move away, he came and stood right beside her. Her short intake of breath was audible as he reached out his arms. Not for her. For Olly. He didn't even turn his head in her direction. His eyes were firmly focused on his five-year-old nephew. Exactly as Vicky's were. And both adult parties were wondering the same thing. Was Olly Fintan's son?

The small boy delighted in jumping into Fintan's arms and was oblivious to the drama unfolding before him.

Fintan rested Olly on his hip, a casual arm around his waist to support him. She couldn't resist taking a peep at them, the resemblance between them stark. He swung the little boy around in the air before finally – when Olly's high-pitched laughter was getting slightly out of control – placing him gently on the floor and bending down to talk to him. Fintan's natural ease with Olly filled her with emotion, his warmth and affection good reason to hope he'd welcome a baby of his own with open arms some day. When the time was right.

Vicky stepped away from them, remembering her reason for coming to the kitchen in the first place. The stain would have taken hold by now. She was surprised that Callum hadn't come scurrying in to find out what was delaying them. Rinsing a dishcloth under the hot tap and wringing it out, she allowed more time to pass and listened to the exchange between uncle and nephew. Their familiarity surprised her, particularly as Fintan had only met the child a handful of times in his short lifetime. At least that's what he'd let her believe. And if that were true, then there could only be one explanation for the natural way they had bonded: blood-lines – the invisible silk thread holding families together, a thread that ravels and knots and sometimes even looks as if it has disappeared altogether, a thread that might weaken in parts but – apart from the most exceptional circumstances – rarely snaps.

She stalled at the sink, deliberating her next move, her heart pounding. Should she encourage Fintan and Olly to go and join Ed and Joan or should she wait for him to make his choice without prompting? Yet again, she found herself in a rabbit-and-headlights situation, she being the rabbit and Fintan's presence being the imposing blinding glare.

Fintan's voice cut in on her thoughts.

"Who else is here, Olly? Your brother?" His question, though delivered slowly and casually, reverberated around the room.

Polite small talk it's not, Vicky thought, understanding him well enough to read between the lines. He was sneakily casing an itinerary of what was facing him, seeking out a chance to assess the situation before going to meet it head on.

His stalling mechanisms were testament to his

discomfort. Excellent. She gave a silent whoop for joy, part of her shocked that her deviousness was actually paying dividends.

She slowly turned around.

Olly moved from foot to foot, pulling at the sleeves of his khaki-coloured jumper and scrutinising Fintan as he spouted his answer.

"Just me and Callum. He wasn't supposed to come 'cos he was grounded for the whole week but then Ma said he could come so she could have quietness." He shoved his hands into the pockets of his jeans, unable to stand still for a single second.

"He must have been very bold to be grounded for that long. Going to tell me what he did?" said Fintan.

As if he cares about Callum, Vicky thought, wishing he'd just get his act together, quit stalling and go and meet his parents.

Olly nodded enthusiastically, delighted to share a tale about somebody else being in trouble, his fine hair bouncing with every move. "He went to the shop. He wasn't s'posed to. He went to the one that's at the other end of our village. He walked all the way with his friend and it was really dark. Ma was looking everywhere for him. And she shouted at him when she got home and –"

"So it's just you and Callum and Nana and Grand-dad?" Fintan interrupted, keeping Olly to the point and finally acknowledging his parents' presence in the house.

Olly nodded his head. "Me and Callum stay with Nana and Granddad every Saturday now while Ma and

Da are out. Do you want to know what Callum did in your house?"

Fintan's head jerked slightly in his wife's direction. For a split second, she thought he was going to look directly at her for a reaction.

But he changed his mind. "What did he do? I hope it wasn't something bold?"

"He sat on your piano!" Olly tripped over the words that spilled from his mouth, unable to get them out fast enough, his eyes never once leaving his uncle's face.

Fintan brought a hand to his mouth in mock horror. "No! Did he break it?"

Olly shrugged solemnly. "I don't think so 'cos Vicky's going to show us how to play sticks or something. Aren't you, Vicky?" He turned to look at her.

She nodded, unable to find her voice to speak.

"Can you play that?" He turned to Fintan once more.

"Nah," he said, rising to his full height and easing his legs out. "I'd rather kick a ball than mess with a silly old piano."

Olly beamed and nodded his agreement. "Me too. Want to go outside now 'cos it's nearly dark?"

"I'd best go and say hello to your brother first," he said.

Olly looked disappointed. At a guess, Vicky felt sure he'd enjoyed being centre of attention, not something that was likely to remain in place when he rejoined Callum. "All right so. He's in there. And Nana and Granddad are inside there too." He turned and pointed through the door towards the dining-room.

But Fintan still didn't make a move to go inside, simply rested a hand on the island unit, his other hand in his pocket as he looked down at Olly. Waiting.

Once he steps inside the dining-room, Vicky thought, I'll be a step closer to payback time and he won't be able to reach a hand out to the locker drawer and ease a condom around himself for protection. This time he'd be on his own. This time he'd be the one left standing alone while a door shut firmly in his face. This time he'd be the one suffering.

Chapter 20

Marcus went over and over the documentation, each time taking a different interpretation and changing his mind about what to do next. Quite honestly, there were no answers in the envelope. But there were questions, plenty of them, all of them unanswered. For so many years, he'd been holding his breath, expecting an intrusion between him and Edel. But not like this, not a situation that could mess up the rest of his life, every tiny aspect of it. After staring at the paperwork until the faded ink blurred in his jaded vision, he tidied every slip of paper away, deciding to leave it until Monday morning when he could challenge the parties involved.

Marcus didn't believe in coincidence and in this instance was convinced that everything was happening for a reason: getting the job with Ellis Enterprise, the best accounts falling on his lap like pennies from heaven and the growing divide between him and Edel.

Ariel jumped into the shower, screaming at the top of her voice when the freezing cold water cascaded over her hair and shoulders. She'd completely forgotten about the water problem. Shivering with the cold, she gingerly stepped out of the flow of water but continued to lather herself with lavender gel.

Roger was on his way from Dublin Airport. She didn't want to appear a snivelling mess when he arrived. She gritted her teeth and stepped back into the flow of icy water, her scalp numbing from the cold as the shampoo ran down her face and skin. But at least I'll be clean, she grimaced, turning the water off at the earliest possible moment and wrapping herself in a huge yellow bath towel before slipping her arms into the chunkiest dressing-gown she possessed.

Catching her reflection in the cracked mirror over the bathroom sink, she noticed black rings underneath her eyes. "Bloody hell," she said aloud, "I'd better get my make-up on fast or Roger won't recognise me when he gets here."

She couldn't deny how flustered she felt: blotching her foundation as she rubbed it a little too roughly onto her cheeks, parting her hair on the wrong side as she ran a comb through it before attacking it with the hair dryer on full power. When she'd finished repairing the damage, she slipped into a pair of dark denims and hand-painted slinky top. I might be at the lowest point in my life, she thought, smacking her lips together to even out the gloss, but I still have my pride.

Filling the kettle with water, she plugged it in to boil, wishing she had espresso to offer Roger instead of the jar of instant sitting on top of the fridge. But a few minutes later the kettle still hadn't boiled and when she put her hand to the side of it, she realised it was stone cold.

"God damn it! I've paid my rent. The least I'm entitled to is running hot water and electricity!"

She ran to the door of the flat. There has to be a caretaker around, she thought. It's probably only a fuse. She dashed mindlessly onto the first-floor landing and crashed right into a burly gentleman, a burly gentleman who swung around to face her once he'd steadied himself, his mouth dropping open when he recognised who she was.

"What are you doing here?" Ariel asked, frowning in confusion and forgetting about the kettle that wouldn't boil in that split second. She'd given Roger her new address in desperation. But she hadn't wanted anyone else to know the levels she'd been reduced to. Too late for that now, she thought, her stomach sinking. It'll be all over the office by Monday evening.

Chapter 21

Vicky stared at the stranger inhabiting her husband's body, expecting a rush of emotion to charge through her as though it were a bull racing after a red rag. But nothing happened. No love, no bitterness. Nothing except an icy numbness running alongside the blood in her veins. A sensation of being outside her body.

Time had stopped for her. Or at the very least slowed down to a crawl with everything in the house on live pause, everything other than the kitchen scene. In her head, she pressed the imaginary play button, deciding it was time to get things moving.

"My goodness, Olly, we'd best get back inside. The others will think we've forgotten about them! And they must be ready for dessert by now. You coming?"

Two could play mind games, she thought, holding out a hand for the little boy, ignoring Fintan as he had her.

But, to her utter disgust, Olly shook his head and instead of accepting her offer slipped his small hand into his uncle's, gazing up at him before making a plea for some fun.

"Can we play ball now, Uncle Fin? Please. Look outside!" He pointed through the window to the darkening sky. "It's nearly night-time. I promise I'll eat my food after. I promise, Uncle Fin!"

"Don't worry about the time – we've got brilliant lights outside!"

"Like a real football pitch? Like Croke Park?"

Fintan laughed.

Vicky had to prevent a loud gasp escaping her lips as she watched them communicate, Fintan's eyes crinkling at the sides, his laughter genuine, the resemblance between him and Olly uncanny. Was it just a family resemblance? No. There was no doubt in her mind about Olly's biological father, no doubt whatsoever. Maybe one day, they'll thank me for forcing them together, she thought, trying to find a positive in her devious scheme.

"Not quite like Croke Park but strong enough all the same. Now, food first, and then we'll see how good you are with a ball! Come on, let's get the hard part over with and then we can have some real fun instead of sitting around having boring conversations."

She walked ahead of them into the dining-room. Clenching her teeth together in the fakest smile she'd ever worn, she held her head high and did her utmost to appear upbeat and chirpy. And her performance would go down as one of her best yet, the spring in her step ringing a resemblance to Dorothy as she stepped along the yellow brick road in *The Wizard of Oz*.

"Sorry for the delay – Olly kept me chatting," she said brightly, reaching for the tablecloth and immediately attacking the orange stain with the damp cloth, her unease increasing with every passing second as she waited for somebody to speak: Fintan or his parents.

Time ticked by slowly. Very slowly for Vicky. Her knuckles burned as she continued kneading the material, the ornate lace design rough against her skin, words hopping around inside her head as she tried in vain to think of something to say. Why, when she needed it most, wouldn't a funny or smart comment come to mind?

The silence around her got louder. At least that's the way it felt. She pleaded inwardly for somebody to speak. In that instant, she was actually tempted to send Callum back into the lounge to bang on the piano. Even the out-of-key sounds he'd created earlier would have made a welcome change from the pressure of silence in the room, the growing concern that she had created a situation she might not be able to handle.

She lifted her eyes for a second and gave a quick glance around the table to try and make a quick mental assessment. Fintan's stance was casual. He rested his elbow on the back of a chair and chewed on the inside of his lip. Contemplating. Game-playing. Stalling. As though she were watching a tennis match, her eyes flickered across the table to Ed. His surprise at his son's return was evident, the grim look on his face a reminder of the fact there was no love lost between father and son. Deuce. Next score: match point. Both were building up to it, an unspoken defiance between them about whose serve it was.

Callum was too busy using crusts of bread to build a road around the remainder of his lasagne to notice somebody new had entered the room. And Olly wasn't moving anywhere away from his new playmate.

Beside Vicky, Joan picked at a slice of wholemeal bread, blissfully unaware of the tension polluting the air around her, lingering like the smell of incense in a church long after the coffin had been shouldered down the aisle.

The lump in Vicky's throat became unbearable.

Then Fintan finally opened his mouth and began to speak: to Callum.

The sound of his voice instilled life into the others in the room, spiking the inflating atmosphere and bursting it into tiny pieces.

"You've grown quite a bit since I saw you last, young man, and I hear you've been having a go on the piano? Did you manage to get a tune out of it?"

Callum blushed. At first glance, Vicky thought he was embarrassed to be centre of attention. Although, considering his earlier outburst, that notion didn't quite ring true. In her short estimation of him, he'd inherited more of his grandfather's crassness than any other recognisable quality. And on closer scrutiny, she abandoned any notion that he was suffering from embarrassment and recognised a deeper intensity in his eyes, a defiant look of appreciation for his uncle.

What was that about, she wondered? Olly's reaction had been very similar. Instantly impressed. Awestruck. Open admiration for a man they barely knew. Why, she wondered, if nobody ever had a good word to say about Fintan, did both little boys view him as something of an icon or a long-lost hero? And while their appreciation was noble, she'd have welcomed some assurance about the version of hero he was in their eyes. A runaway teen who'd considered living with this family the equivalent of a stay of execution? Or the prodigal son whose absence had heralded him as the golden-haired boy?

Joan swivelled around in her chair at the sound of her son's voice, her face breaking into a broad grin as her eyes met his. She opened her mouth to say something but Callum managed to get in there first, leaving Joan to swallow her welcome and save it for later.

All eyes and ears were on the exchange between Fintan and Callum. Joan's. Vicky's. Ed's. Even Olly's.

"I was only messing at the piano." Callum shrank down a little in his chair. "I didn't do no harm to it."

"I don't think you'd be sitting here enjoying your meal if you did! That piano is treated with more respect than me in this house!"

"Huh?" The six-year-old screwed up his face in confusion.

Poor Callum, Vicky thought. Fintan's barb went right over his head. The pathetic sneer made Fintan sound like a spoilt and demanding child, a little boy jealous of the time his mother gave to a new baby – or a musical instrument in this case. What was the real reason behind his remark? Was it fuelled by jealousy, she wondered? Could he be resentful of the time she spent idling on the keyboard? Unlikely. Was it reason enough for him to seek attention elsewhere? No. But he was more than likely using it as an opportunity to hurt her.

"Maybe instead of trying to be a musician, you could join me and Olly for a kick-around in the garden? I'll go in goal and you two can play out field against each other. What do you think?"

The little boy's blue eyes lit up. "Cool! Can we go now?"

"Shortly. There's still food on your plate."

And that's when I'll break the news, Vicky decided. While the boys are in the garden playing football.

"Is this your place here next to me?" Callum pointed at the empty chair beside him, looking expectantly at his uncle.

Damn, she thought, a slow blush creeping from her neck to her cheeks. She stopped rubbing at the stain, dropping the cloth on top of the ugly brown mark. She hadn't set a place for him. Double damn. It hadn't been a conscious decision to leave him out. At least she didn't think it had. Her subconscious, on the other hand, had obviously been working on a table plan of its own. Not one Fintan was part of. Not a very sensible one on her part. Easily remedied if she'd wanted it to be. All she had to do was grab more cutlery and a place mat from the nearby drawer. But making a fuss now would be admission that she hadn't expected him home. In her heart, she couldn't deny that was true. But he didn't have to know that. He didn't have to be sure of what was going on in her head.

She stole a look at her watch. Five o'clock. She stole a look at Fintan. His expression was unreadable as he toyed with the idea of taking a seat. Was he still in the same mood he'd been in when he'd left the house? Upset? Annoyed? Or had he indulged in something or someone to cheer himself up? To feel wanted. In control.

He'd been away from the house for five hours. Where exactly had he spent that time? And how exactly had he spent it? With *her*?

"Come and sit down, Fin. Let me get a proper look at you," Joan said then, turning around to her son once more. "Or are you going to stand behind me breathing fire down the back of my neck? You've barely said hello to us yet!"

Vicky moved away from the table ever so slowly, monitoring their interaction as discreetly as she could. The gentle pleading in Joan's eyes, the tinge of confusion and annoyance in his, how quickly she'd sensed his discomfort, how he'd overcome his awkwardness by communicating through the two young boys. What was the true relationship between mother and son, she wondered? And where did Fintan's father fit in? Did he resent their closeness?

Ed's fury at his wife's pleading was visible, the sides of his nostrils whitening, his eyes flashing dangerously. "You shouldn't have to beg him to have a bloody conversation with you, Joan," he snapped at her from across the table, wiping drops of spit from his mouth with the back of his hand, ignoring the numerous serviettes sitting on the table. "If he can't take the time to greet his own family, he hasn't the manners he was brought up with." He pushed his chair back, chipping the paint as he banged it off the wall behind. He didn't notice. And in spite of Ed's rising temper and the look of disgust on Fintan's face, she found herself wondering if they had any paint left over so the damage could be repaired. How could she possibly be worried about the paintwork at such a time? Perhaps because she had control over a paintbrush and tin of paint while she had no control whatsoever of the family feud erupting around her dinner table.

Ed continued to glare at Joan. Fintan continued to glare at his father. If it's this bad now, she thought, what will they be like later? After I've made my disclosure?

"Bloody upstart who thinks he's too good for his own family!" Ed's slandering continued but not once did he look at or speak directly to Fintan.

Vicky gasped at his rudeness, shocked that he'd launched into such an aggressive tirade moments after Fintan had stepped into the room. The animosity between them was palpable, Ed's worsening mood impossible to miss. Did he think Fintan was invisible? Or deaf? I've obviously underestimated him too, she thought. By a long shot. I'd been prepared for him to treat his son – or both of us for that matter – with reserved hostility, but not outright audacity. He'd arrived with clear intent. To cause upset. Then again, am I any better, she asked inwardly? Haven't I set everybody up in the hopes of fireworks?

The confusion in Fintan's eyes had disappeared. He let go of the chair he'd been holding and opened his mouth to speak. "Don't speak about me as if I'm not here, Da. Can't we make an effort to get on for a change?" His tone was low, his words loaded, his naturally sallow complexion a red-and-white patchwork canvas.

As soon as the words had left his lips, Vicky noticed him glancing at Olly, his arm moving instinctively around his slight shoulders, pulling him towards him, the small boy's arm looping tightly around Fintan's thigh.

Was Fintan trying to protect the young boy from the wrath he himself had suffered at the same age? Or was he the one in need of someone to hold?

Chapter 22

It was one of the few Saturdays Pete had missed evening Mass since Barbara's death. It wasn't that he'd been delayed repairing the damage in Number 101. He'd been on his way along the corridor, after returning the toolbox to the storage cabinet, when the occupant in Number 105 came bounding out of her flat and bumped right into him.

Under normal circumstances, he'd have spared her a few moments' conversation and moved along. But he'd always been a sucker for a woman in distress, that often being his downfall when it came to gathering evidence during his time on duty or indeed spending hours of personal time taking a case right through to the end. Which was why he'd promised Ariel he'd stop by once he'd finished filling out a report for the owner of the building, to see if there was anything he could do to help. And that was how he ended up being in her flat when her boyfriend arrived and jumped to the wrong conclusion.

Vicky's heart thumped loudly. Things were spiralling. Moving along. Not necessarily in a good way. But there was a definite change in temperature. And a definite change in Fintan. She picked up the cloth once more and walked as quickly as she could back into the kitchen, escaping the madness of the dining-room, yet unable to shake the crazy thoughts in her head. Standing with her back to the island unit, clutching the counter top for support, she stared into space and struggled to get her emotions in check and come to grips with the mixture of feelings knotted up inside.

More than anything, she'd wanted to meet Fintan's gaze and figure out whether they were on speaking terms or not. While Ed had shouted obscenities at Joan and antagonised Fintan by talking about him instead of to him, she'd wanted to reach out and grab her husband's arm. And if he had given the slightest indication that they were on some form of communication terms, she'd have offered silent support with a sympathetic look or understanding smile.

I'm going crazy, she thought, clutching clumps of her hair in her hands as she tried to make sense of the twists and turns and miles of unending roadway in the roadmap of her mind. One minute she was cruising in one direction, going out of her way to make Fintan suffer, to punish him for deceiving her and trying to gain the retribution she felt she deserved. And the next she was reversing dangerously on a roundabout, doing a complete turnabout and wanting to gaze lovingly into his eyes and let him know she supported him! God help me, she thought, but I can't make sense of it all.

Only somebody deluded could be so irrational, she decided with a sigh, taking her hands from her hair and smoothing it back into some semblance of shape with her palms.

She approached the table with a plate of mini desserts in her hand. "Ed, you look ready for dessert?" Transferring the little pastries and creams onto the tiered crystal cake-stand, she went back again and got two bowls of jelly and vanilla ice cream ready for the boys.

As she placed one dessert bowl in front of Callum and the other at Olly's place, she remembered the extra treats she'd offered them and ducked back into the kitchen to get the goodie jar.

"After your jelly and ice cream, guys, you can take whatever treats you want," she said.

"Cool!" Callum picked up his spoon and began to mix the ice cream with the jelly, stirring and stirring until he'd blended it all together.

Olly took his place back at the table, reluctantly letting Fintan's hand go.

Vicky fussed over the table, topping up the boys' glasses with more minerals and moving things around to make room for a plate of after-dinner mints.

"You've gone to a lot of effort today, Vicky. Thank you."

"Oh, eh right, you're welcome." Vicky caught Joan's eye briefly. And in that shared glimpse, they made a connection. At least Vicky thought they had.

But Vicky knew that when the moment came and she told Ed and Joan about Fintan's secret, she would bolt out the front door and leave the Jones family alone for quite some time.

"I'll get a plate and come and sit beside you for a while, Ma." Fintan put a hand on his mother's shoulder and squeezed it gently. "You can fill me in on what's been happening. Come on, Olly, you haven't touched your ice cream!"

"I'm eating my jelly first and then I'll have my ice cream." He licked the back of the spoon before putting it back into the jelly once more.

Joan gave a little shrug, feigning indifference yet blushing a little at the attention he was paying her, picking up their conversation as soon as he'd returned with his plate of food. "My life is very dull. In fact it's not much different than when you were at home, son. I've replaced children with grandchildren but our routine is pretty much the same."

Vicky looked at Ed. His expression was stony.

"I'd rather hear all about that busy lifestyle of yours," Joan went on, " the things you do every day that don't allow you any spare moment to pay us a visit!"

Ouch, Vicky thought. And I'd been feeling sorry for her! Joan wasn't beyond tossing a remark or two around either. She knew exactly how to pull her son's strings.

"Ma, I work in a pub. It's no big deal! The most

exciting thing about it is tossing a few drunks out on their ear on a Saturday night." He threw his eyes to the ceiling and shook his head at the two little boys. "She's been asking the same questions and giving me the same interrogation since I was your age. I bet she does the same to you? Wanting to know every little detail?"

Callum and Olly snorted first, then giggled and finally nodded enthusiastically. Neither of the boys was very concerned about their nana's questions, however, concentrating instead on being on their best behaviour. Getting out into the back garden was all they wanted to do and if nodding their heads and agreeing with Uncle Fin got them out there faster, then so be it. They continued nodding.

"Don't talk about your mother like that," Ed warned Fintan. "And you needn't mind filling the young lads' minds with nonsense either!"

Fintan sat beside his mother, ignoring his father completely. He knew there was no point trying to humour Ed, not when he was in the mood he was in today, picking fault with everything, making out the world owed him.

Vicky started to pray.

Ed's expression was venomous. She tried to distract him by gabbling on mindlessly about the recent budget speech. Not that she knew too much about it herself. While the Minister for Finance had been delivering his speech and listing the drastic measures being taken to prevent the economic downturn from completely taking hold, she'd been coping with the recession going on in her own little world, coping with a downturn in the bedroom department and trying to prevent the institution that was her marriage from collapsing completely in the absence of cabinet confidence (Fintan and her being the only two cabinet members deemed eligible for opinion).

But Ed wasn't having any of it.

"What difference does a budget make to those of us not working? Budgets are for the likes of you and yer man here." He wagged a finger at Fintan. "The people the sun shines on."

"Those days are long gone, Ed." Vicky couldn't resist putting him straight. "Even though we're working, we're still finding things as difficult as most since the recession hit. But look, enough doom and gloom. I didn't invite you over here to be miserable. What about a drink? Can I get you something?"

Vicky realised that she had forgotten to open a bottle of wine when they'd sat down to eat and it was probably the wrong time to even suggest it with Fintan tucking into his main course and Ed already on dessert.

"What have you got?" The promise of a drink perked Ed up considerably, the deeply etched frown lines fading ever so slightly as he raised his eyebrows a notch.

Joan shook her head, catching her husband's eye and frowning in warning. "You'd better not, Ed."

Fintan frowned too but kept his attention on his plate and scooped up a forkful of lasagne.

Vicky didn't understand. Had Ed a drink problem to add to that aggressiveness of his? The combination of the two could be lethal. She looked at Joan but couldn't catch her eye as her gaze was fixed firmly on Ed.

Damn. She'd offered him one now. There was no going back. Joan must have had good reason to advise him against it. Would she suffer later as a result? Or was she concerned about the effect alcohol would have on his behaviour while he was in the company of his youngest son?

But Ed was waiting for Vicky to bring him a drink.

"Eh, we have some wine. I'll check what's on the rack. Or there might be a few bottles of beer in the fridge. I've been meaning to get some in." She didn't want to give him the impression they had a stock of bottles that he could work his way through while he sat there trading insults with Fintan.

She was about to go to the kitchen to see if there was a beer for Ed when he directed an interesting question at Fintan. Instead of moving out of earshot, she slowly made her way to the drinks cabinet at the other end of the room, listening carefully to every word, wishing she could record their conversation and read between the lines, their expressions containing the punctuation and intonation of every sentence.

"You were in an awful hurry last week, Fintan," Ed began, his tone civil towards him for the first time that evening.

But it was the civil tone that alerted Vicky's suspicion.

"Darren said you drove right by him and didn't even stop and offer him a lift! What were you doing over that side of town anyway?"

"If you've something on your mind, Da, why don't

211

you spit it out? But remember Callum and Olly there beside you. It wouldn't do to let them see what you can be like, now would it? I've heard you're trying to prove yourself a better grandfather than you ever were a father."

Vicky dropped to her knees in front of the drinks cabinet, turning around to catch a glimpse of the two men in the room. Looking from one to the other, she was surprised at the similarity between them: tall, strongly built, brown-haired (although Ed's was tinged with grey) and both scowling as though they'd been handed a cent after losing thousands.

Fintan hadn't held back. In one sentence, he'd covered two major issues: his father's parenting skills as well as the example he was showing his grandchildren. Was he deliberately provoking Ed? Was that for Vicky's benefit or his own? She couldn't be sure. Or was he simply pushing his father out of his comfort zone, letting him see he hadn't changed his opinion on him?

She pulled the first bottle of wine that came to hand from the wooden rack, disappearing from the room to get a corkscrew. Her hasty exit went unnoticed. Ed was too busy glaring at his son. Callum and Olly were on their best behaviour as they waited for the promised game of soccer and Joan, surprisingly, was the calmest of all as she pushed her plate away and settled down to converse further with Fintan. They looked as though they'd last met only yesterday.

For a moment Vicky wondered if they had. Could he have been lying about his visits to his parents too? As the thought festered in her head and all sorts of connotations began to form, she expelled it. His mother's comment earlier negated that ridiculous theory. But as soon as one concern extinguished, another arrived. What about his father's comment about Darren? What was that about? Was there more to it than Fintan passing him by? Ed's smugness was worrying, gave her reason to believe he was leaving something out. Deliberately holding it over Fintan. The more she thought about it, the more she wondered about its significance. She twirled the top of the corkscrew around with her finger, tipping the drawer lightly with her hip and watching it slide closed.

Where was Fintan when he'd driven right by his brother? The question popped into her head, appearing from nowhere, magnifying out of proportion as she searched for an answer. She attempted to block it out, clutching the wine bottle in her hand, her fingers tightening and tightening around its neck.

Had he somebody with him when his brother caught sight of him? A gorgeous, sexy dark-haired someone?

She released her tight hold on the bottle and shook her head, fighting against this latest assumption, refusing to dwell on it. Her mind was already in a muddle with all that was going on. But pushing the vision from sight and imagining it in a zip-lock airtight plastic bag wasn't enough to obliterate her worries completely. A still image of Fintan and *her* sneaking off to places to be together flashed vividly in her mind's eye, the echo of *her* laughter ringing loudly in their wake.

"White wine, Ed?"

"If it's all that's on offer, I'll take it," he grumbled, watching the golden liquid plop into the glass as Vicky poured.

"Wine, Joan?"

She shook her head.

Vicky deliberated about offering Fintan a drink but decided against it. "The bottle's there if anyone wants a top-up."

"You know you shouldn't be mixing alcohol with your medication, Ed," Joan pointed out quietly. "You know the effect it can have."

"Oh stop nagging, Joan! What's seldom is wonderful. Cheers!" He held up his glass to the others around the table.

Vicky inhaled slowly. Cheers, she returned silently, trying to think of the right words to use to formulate the toast she had in mind.

Chapter 23

Pete had changed the fuse, fitting one that was strong enough to allow Ariel boil the kettle and charge her phone simultaneously. He couldn't believe the antiquated system installed in the building, corners cut on spending at every opportunity. Neither could he guarantee it was as safe as it should be.

"I don't plan on wasting too much of my youth here, Pete. I'll be moving on as soon as I get a few things straightened out."

"Glad to hear it," Pete said. "A professional lady like you has no business in a place like this."

Ariel's face burned with shame, Pete's kindness more than she could handle on top of everything else. "A place like this is plenty good enough for me, Pete. In fact, I know a few who would probably say it's too good for me."

Pete rubbed his arthritic knees in circular movements,

his gaze directed firmly away from Ariel. "Never waste your energy on what others say or think, my girl. Once you have a clear conscience, that's the most important thing in life."

"And I do, Pete. I do," she found herself returning. She hovered around the table, making a pretence of tidying the newspapers and magazines into a neat bundle, stalling for time, craving the opportunity to offload her troubles to someone she could trust, someone who wouldn't judge her and hopefully someone who might be able to offer advice. And who better than an ex-sergeant? A knock on the door interrupted her musings.

"That's probably Roger now," she told Pete, taking a mouthful of coffee and going to answer the door.

Her stomach churned. How would Roger be? Friendly? Aloof? Angry? But she wasn't to find out just yet as it was only a pizza delivery boy who'd stopped at the wrong flat.

Closing the door once more, she caught a glimpse of Pete in the reflection of the television, his head lowered, his shoulders stooped. She knew from the minimal amount of information going around the office about him that he was a very private man, a lonely widower, a kind, reliable employee.

"Can I trust you with something, Pete," she spluttered, making a spontaneous decision to share her troubles. "I'm in trouble, big trouble, and I don't know where to turn. I'm in way over my head."

Pete stared at the old-fashioned floral couch, the orange, red and brown swirls blurring into a blob of abstract colour. Should he encourage her to confide in him, he wondered. Was he the right person to be sharing her troubles with? Once the information was out in the open, there would be no going back. He'd have a decision to make about what he should do with it, whether he could mind his own business and let the story stop there.

He raised his head, the anxiety in her brown eyes arresting, his decision already made for him.

"Maybe I can be of some help," he offered. "I've heard a good many stories in my lifetime, stories I'll take with me to the grave. You can trust me with anything."

Ariel nodded. She believed she could.

"So, Fintan," Ed said to his son, the wine loosening his tongue, "you're doing well for yourself? Driving a big Audi and holding down a management position at work. Not too bad at all now for a young lad from Rathcoole!"

"Don't sound so happy for me, Da. It doesn't suit you." The accusation spilled from Fintan's lips, his tone harsh, a difficult-to-read blend of hurt and anger in his eyes.

The look on Olly's face brought a lump to Vicky's throat. He was staring disbelievingly – with his mouth hanging open – at Fintan, visibly shocked to hear him snap at his father. It wasn't difficult to guess why. The little boys had considered Fintan to be different from the rest of the family, had him raised on a pedestal. The way they'd treated him had been proof of that. But now that he was snapping at his father and the fall-out from

217

his anger echoed silently around the table, he was no longer playing the part of coolest uncle.

The men resembled two boxers in a fighting ring, circling each other, each one watching and waiting for their turn to pounce. It'd be far better to leave them fight it out for themselves.

Vicky's body began to shake, not visibly but internally. She needed an excuse to get out of the room. She couldn't bear to see the distress on Olly's face for one more second. She gave one last cursory glance at Fintan, the man she'd married, the love of her life, the man she was about to destroy.

"Joan," she squeaked in a voice that barely resembled hers, "if you've finished eating, why don't I show you around the house?" She placed the wine bottle on the table between Fintan and Ed. She had completely forgotten it was still in her hands, her fingers numb around the cold green glass.

Green: the colour of jealousy, the emotion that had smothered all that was good inside her.

Now that the moment of truth had arrived, she was panicking. She knew that. But at least the sense of panic was something to cling to. She was scared, scared of losing him, scared of waking up alone every morning. She loved Fintan with all her heart but he had hurt her badly. And for that he had to pay.

Chapter 24

Ariel stared at the floor as she began telling her story, leaving nothing out, sparing no detail.

"You're up on trial for embezzling a total of two million euro? And you say you're being framed on top of that?"

Ariel nodded, sniffing loudly, struggling to bite back her tears. "And blackmailed."

"What proof have they got against you?"

"I had control of mortgage funding. The transactions in question."

"Remind me what they were again," Pete asked, his hands wrapped around the fresh mug of coffee she'd given him – black, as she'd run out of milk.

"God, Pete, it's embarrassing enough saying it once!" She got up from her chair and began to pace the room, her unease evident.

"Maybe so," Pete said, knowing that she was

already regretting sharing, "but the devil is generally in the detail."

"Don't make me feel I'm on trial!" She pulled at the sleeves of her top, chewing her bottom lip nervously.

"I've Garda blood, Ariel. I can't help it. You shouldn't have told me if you didn't want an interrogation." He smiled at her, pulling his coat around him.

Ariel stared at the elderly gentleman. Poor devil is sitting here listening selflessly to me for the last half hour. He's freezing. He's missed his visit to Mass (everybody who knew Pete knew his weekly ritual). And I'm treating him as though he's the enemy. What's wrong with me?

She dragged a chair over so she was sitting directly in front of Pete. "I'm sorry. You must think I'm very ungrateful."

He smiled, a warm smile that reached his eyes, the skin on his face crinkling like a silk shirt washed at a hot temperature.

She took a deep breath and tried to explain again. "I was in charge of mortgages in the last financial company I worked in. We offered independent mortgage advice, a type of one-stop shop for customers buying property. They told us what they wanted and our job was to get it for them at the cheapest possible rate. Obviously our company made a profit from the transaction too." She didn't want to leave anything out, anxious to give him a true account.

"I'm with you so far," Pete said, wincing as the black coffee hit the back of his throat. He only liked it with milk but for politeness' sake he continued drinking. "And you were meticulous when it came to transferring funds to clients' accounts as well as calculating their expenses?"

"Meticulous," Ariel repeated, remembering all the nights she'd stayed in the office till midnight to keep accounts up to date, particularly during the boom when mortgages were being released without question. But she'd taken pride in her work and reaped the rewards in commission – which allowed her the luxury of filling her wardrobe to overflowing with designer clothes and shoes – so she had never minded.

"And then there was a mix-up in accounts?"

"Yes." Ariel inhaled sharply, the pain and embarrassment associated with the event as severe as the first day she'd been hauled in by the General Manager. "We had just released mortgages for two O'Brien families. Two brothers who'd bought houses next door to each other with a view to renting the properties."

"Made sense, I suppose," Pete muttered, remembering how much Barbara had wanted him to invest in property to inflate their retirement fund. He was glad he'd been cautious now. And not only because property prices had deflated. What good would money be when Barbara wasn't there to enjoy it with him? From now on, all he needed was enough to live on. He wouldn't be going on expensive holidays, had sold his car, considering it an unnecessary luxury and happier to use public transport as a means of getting wherever he needed to be.

He let go of his ramblings and brought his attention back to Ariel.

"I was on holidays when the deals were going through with the building society. Roger and I were travelling southern Australia at the time."

"Amazing experience, isn't it?" Pete interrupted. He'd spent a month down under with Barbara, thanks to the travel vouchers the Garda Siochána had presented him as part of his retirement package.

Ariel checked the time, anxious to get on with her story. What was delaying Roger? Had he changed his mind?

"Oz was the ideal holiday. Although in a way," she added with regret, "my being away from the office for four weeks left the door wide open for what followed."

"Expenses?"

Ariel nodded. "Both brothers received their house keys on the same day: one in the morning and one in the afternoon. The cheques were released to the property developer and amounts were also deducted for expenses . . ."

"Were they listed?"

"Of course. The properties were brand-new so there was nothing unusual: registration of transfer deed, mortgage registration, wayleave . . ." She'd been studying her fingernails as she rattled off the list, financial-speak coming second nature to her. But she realised when she looked up at Pete that she was losing him in jargon. "Sorry, Pete, I'm getting carried away. Anyway, the main expense item was stamp duty, a compulsory payment because they were purchasing investment properties. And then, of course, there were our professional fees. These were usually set at a given percentage at the time of negotiation with the client."

"Fair enough. You couldn't be expected to do it free gratis."

She squirmed in her chair. Free gratis would have been a lot easier to live with than the robbing one of the O'Brien brothers suffered. "So putting it simply, the total cheque came through to our organisation from the bank – or building society in this case – and we divided it out, giving our client a statement of account at the end along with a cheque for any remaining funds."

Pete picked up the mug, drained the last of the putrid-tasting coffee and plonked the empty mug back on the table. He took a cotton handkerchief from his pocket and wiped his mouth. He was finding the sequence of events easier to follow now that she'd elaborated and given him more detail. And it was getting interesting. His inquisitive mind was already figuring out what might have happened, trying to piece the jigsaw together, getting things into chronological order, fitting characters into prototypes.

"Were you in the office on the day the cheques were released, Ariel?"

She let out a long sigh. If only she could go back in time, she thought for the billionth time, running a hand through her dark hair, wishing, wishing and wishing.

"Yes. It was my first day back. I was still jet-lagged, up to my eyes in paperwork, and quite honestly I never checked the calculations on the O'Brien accounts. I assumed my colleagues had been as thorough as I – big mistake now as it turns out – and I just scrawled my name at the end of the document and moved it along to have the cheques released."

Pete took his cap from his pocket, twirling it around in his hands, his eyes on stalks as he waited for the next instalment. "How did it all come to light? What happened next?"

It had been so long since he'd had anything as riveting as this to exert his brain, the *Irish Times* cryptic crossword being the most taxing item he'd challenged in the last few years.

Of course, there was that other investigative matter, he remembered now, a matter he'd pushed to the furthest crevice of his mind so he wouldn't make the mistake of mentioning it to a living soul. He'd been well compensated to keep his mouth shut. And he had no regrets. What harm had it caused? No harm in the world that he knew of.

Ariel watched Pete with interest, the eagerness in his face confusing. Is he taking satisfaction in my story, she wondered with a pang of concern? Is he enjoying my pain? But on closer inspection, she realised it wasn't delight spread across his face as she'd first suspected. It was animated interest.

She picked up the story where she'd left off. "I forgot all about the case, filed it away and got to work on the huge backlog waiting for me after my trip."

"Isn't that the worst about being away?"

Pete could remember many summers where he'd come back from his three weeks in the sun – or travelling the furthest corners of Ireland in a camper van – to a mountain of paperwork and court case hearings.

"It certainly is, Pete. But I can tell you, I will never be so careless again!"

As her determined promise left her lips, her thoughts turned to the errors Ben had found only the day before. She knew, though she had yet to prove it, those errors were not of her making. But that was another day's work. Perhaps it was something as simple as a computer glitch. With a bit of luck, she thought, refusing to believe that the only stroke of luck she was having was bad luck. But now there were more pressing things to be dealt with, things she hoped had absolutely no connection with the events in Ellis Enterprise.

Pete sat forward in the chair, waiting expectantly for the climax of the story. "Well, Ariel, don't stop there."

"A few days later, I had a visit."

"The O'Brien brothers?"

"Exactly. They had done a comparison of expenses and one had been charged significantly more than the other for identical transactions."

Before she had time to continue and finish the story for Pete, they were interrupted by a loud knocking on the door.

"That must be Roger!" she exclaimed, her tone rising in pitch.

Pete recognised her panic and put a hand on the table to support his weight before rising to his feet. "Maybe I should go, Ariel," he offered kindly.

"Em, oh right so. Roger and I have a lot to talk about so I suppose it might be best if we were alone."

Pete eased his body into a standing position at the same pace as usual, slowly and carefully, while Ariel ran to the bedroom and checked her reflection in the mirror, her heart racing as she smeared gloss on her lips, shaking hands causing her to go outside the line of lipliner she'd applied earlier.

"Roger, this is Pete," she said hurriedly as soon as she'd opened the door.

Roger's eyes narrowed when he noticed the elderly man standing by the table, a man he'd never met before, a man who was sizing him up from beneath the peak of his tweed cap.

"And what's he doing in your flat?"

"Pete changed the fuse for me," Ariel prattled. "The kettle wouldn't boil with the phone charger plugged in."

Roger folded his arms in front of his body, standing with his feet shoulder-width apart.

Pete was disappointed to leave without at least hearing the end of Ariel's story but knew it would have to wait for another time. Judging by the glowering expression on Roger's face and Ariel's incessant fidgeting as she waited for him to go, he had no choice but to leave the estranged pair to sort out their differences and bide his time to work out what happened next. Already the wheels in his head were in motion, the snapshots of information she'd given him placed haphazardly on an imaginary case board.

"I'll be seeing you, Ariel," he told her. "Good luck with everything. Hope it all pans out in the end." He

226

ambled from the flat at a steady pace – a pace he'd perfected over the years, designed to irritate – irritate Roger in this case – pulling the door shut behind him.

Roger immediately launched an attack on Ariel.

"What did he mean 'good luck with everything'? What have you been telling him? Am I the only fool that hasn't been in on the truth?"

"No, Roger! I haven't been telling him anything!" A warm flush spread from her chest to her neck, creeping into her cheeks.

Roger dug his hands deep into the pockets of his pristine beige chinos. "Then why are you blushing?"

"He's just a kind old man who changed a fuse for me. He was in the right place at the right time to help me out. What's more, I know him. He's the security man at work and he sometimes does odd jobs in places like this!"

"So you called him up and invited him over to change a fuse?"

He looked down his Roman nose at her, making the height difference between them seem a lot more than the two inches it actually was.

"No! That's not how it was. He was in the building anyway."

She put her head in her hands, tempted to weep, her obstinacy the only thing holding her tears in check. Everything was going wrong. Everything. Why did I have to invite Pete to stay for coffee, she thought. Why didn't I just let him change the fuse and leave? Or why didn't I put up with the dodgy electrics and wait patiently for Roger to arrive?

Roger was in a mood now and unless she could coax him out of it (which she knew from past history would take a lot of cajoling and sucking-up), there wasn't much chance he was going to oblige her.

There wasn't much chance he'd take a flight (free in his case) to London to find her brother, Ryan, and bring him to Dublin.

Ryan was her only brother. He'd bought a one-way ticket five years before and had never set foot on Irish soil since, his only contact being the phone call he made to their mother every year on her birthday.

Chapter 25

Vicky watched Joan's lips move but couldn't grasp the meaning behind her words, the fuzziness in her head playing havoc with her hearing. Not until the other woman had repeated them twice.

"I said I've always wanted to see the inside of a house like this, Vicky." Joan paused a moment, probably to make sure she'd heard her that time.

"It's nothing special, Joan."

"Boys," Joan pointed a finger at Olly and Callum as she rose to her feet, "if these two start fighting and arguing, move away from the table and come and find me or Vicky."

Vicky gave a nervous giggle. She had to be joking. Surely she didn't expect things to get out of hand and take a nasty turn? Or did she?

But the boys nodded their heads, looking at each other in confusion.

Olly was crestfallen. Callum appeared unperturbed but it was difficult to be sure. Both of them seemed unsure whether their grandmother was serious or not. Vicky had no doubt but that sitting at a boring dinner table listening to two grown men arguing wasn't their idea of fun. She watched them exchanging glances, nudging each other until at last Callum spoke.

"Uncle Fin? You said you'd play football with us if we finished everything on our plates. Well, we are finished! Look!" He tilted his dessert bowl enough to let Fintan see that he'd eaten every bite, even going as far as licking the inside of the bowl to get the last bit of jelly out. "Can we go outside now? Please?"

"Yeah, please, Uncle Fin!" Olly supported Callum.

"A few more minutes and we will. Here, let me open the treat jar for you." Fintan leaned across the table and unscrewed the top of the jar to disclose a variety of chocolate snacks and sweets. "Take a couple and we'll go outside then. Promise. I just need to keep an eye on your grandda and make sure he doesn't end up talking to the bottom of that wine bottle too soon."

"If you have something to say, son, why don't you just spit it out instead of fif-faffing around like some sort of pansy! Don't think you're ever too old for a clip around the ear."

Ed reached for the wine bottle again, topping up his glass right to the brim. He glared at his son and banged the bottle roughly on the table. Then he turned the same threatening look on his wife, sending her a silent warning message when her cheeks flushed at the sight of him helping himself to more alcohol.

"I'll just nip to the loo if that's all right," Joan said quickly.

A little stunned by everything that was going on around her, Vicky waved her mother-in-law in the general direction of the downstairs bathroom and left her to find it herself. There was something about Joan that confused her. Watching Ed drinking had brought out her vulnerable side. Strange in light of her earlier ability to stand up to him. Or, Vicky thought, is Joan another woman who has so much going on in her head that she finds it impossible to be all things to all people and easier to switch off when faced with situations that didn't suit.

Fintan was still fuming at his father's rebuke. I'm not taking this treatment, he thought. I'm not taking it in my own home. Red mist floated in front of his eyes, all traces of maintaining control slowly slipping from his grasp.

He ruined my teenage years, he thought, his heart hardening as he remembered the humiliation he'd experienced at his father's hands, the amount of times he'd had to answer the door to moneylenders, lie and pretend, shiver in fear when his father took his frustration out on him and his mother and keep a tight lip all the other days when Ed had sat weeping in the chair or had refused to get out of bed.

I've made something of myself now, he thought, his eyes straying to Olly for a moment, remembering himself at that age and wanting so much more for the innocent child sitting nearby, wishing – as he'd done as a young adult – that things could have been different.

And fuck Darren, he thought. Why did he have to tell Da he saw me last week? Fintan had spotted him the day he was on his way to meet George. He'd been standing at the bus stop smoking. Fintan hadn't looked his direction, had kept his eyes firmly focused on the road ahead, praying that Darren hadn't noticed him. But no such luck.

Vicky would give him a hard time over that later. He'd noticed how she'd stalled at the drinks cabinet listening to Ed's snide remarks. He hadn't missed the filthy look she'd thrown in his direction when she'd returned to the table with the bottle of wine.

Though he despised himself for being lured and manipulated and dreaded the day Vicky found out about the Credit Union loan, looking at Olly now he knew it was worth it. That little boy and his brother and twin sisters deserved a chance. But once the money was handed over and he'd bought his brother out of trouble this one time, Fintan was determined to get social services involved at whatever cost. He'd do his best to ensure a safe and supervised upbringing for his nieces and nephews – all four of them, not just Olly. It wasn't right they should suffer as he had. Not when there was help at hand. Not when they had an uncle who cared.

Before Vicky left the room, she watched Fintan struggling with his emotions, tensing a little when he forked up the last of his lasagne, scraping the plate with metal. She couldn't watch much more, couldn't watch her husband metamorphose into a person she didn't recognise, into his father.

She felt sorry for the children and didn't agree with them being left in the room to referee two older men, men that should have been mature enough to act responsibly, men that couldn't look at each other without sniping and might actually be a danger to the little boys beside them.

"Come on, boys, you've waited long enough," she said, taking the decision out of Fintan's hands. "Your uncle still has dessert to get through. He can follow out when he's ready. I'm sure you two are well able to kick a ball without a referee."

Guiding them to the garden and telling them where they'd find a football, she stayed in the conservatory to watch them, leaving Ed and Fintan alone for the first time that evening.

Hearing the children's laughter a few minutes later as they banged a football off the concrete garden wall, she longed for the day when she'd be sitting there watching a child of her own playing out there. In her daydream, Fintan ran alongside their toddler, turning back every now and then to smile at her.

But in reality, all she could hope was that he'd stick around long enough to see that day materialise.

"So, Vicky," Joan said, coming to stand beside her in the conservatory, her overpowering sweet perfume causing Vicky's stomach to churn, "what is it exactly you want from me?"

Vicky's blood ran cold. What on earth? Were her intentions transparent? She hadn't expected that. Not from Joan. Stupidly she'd thought she could pull her strings and manipulate every conversation and happening to her own advantage. But Joan was no puppet on a string, hadn't been for a very long time. And neither was she blind to what went on in other people's relationships. Far from it as Vicky was about to find out.

Chapter 26

"Edel, don't hang up. If you do, I'll stop paying for that cottage you're living in!"

It was the fifth time in quick succession that Marcus had dialled her number – the first four times she'd disconnected. Issuing threats wasn't his usual way of getting her to talk to him but the line was still live so his words had obviously succeeded in keeping her listening. He wasn't too convinced it would make her talk to him, however.

Despite his good intentions of leaving things until Monday morning, impatience had got the better of him, Edel's mobile number whirring around and around in his head, and he'd been unable to keep his fingers away from the phone.

"Why won't you listen to me?" Edel pleaded now. "Don't you get it? I need time alone. I need time to find out who I really am. I don't want you around me, fawning over me, assuring me."

Marcus sighed, a weariness washing over him. At least she's talking to me, he thought with relief. At least that much. He had that to cling to.

"What have you to think about, Edel? Why you walked out on me after eighteen years? Without rhyme or reason? The first I heard of it was when an Enniskerry landlord called me for a reference and a cheque for your deposit, promising me a set of keys as soon as the bank had cleared my payment! Surely I deserved more honesty than that?"

Silence from the other end. And then a gush of jumbled accusations.

"I'm too much of an inconvenience for you. You're better off without me burdening you."

"Don't speak on my behalf, Edel. Don't assume you know what I'm feeling."

"But it's the truth!"

"You've already replaced me, haven't you?" He undid two of his shirt buttons, his chest tightening, the finality in her tone making it difficult for him to breathe.

"No."

"Don't lie to me. I can help you through this." His words were barely a whisper.

"No! It's not like that. You don't understand, *Marcus*."

He heard a click on the other end of the line. She'd hung up on him. Again. And she'd called him Marcus. She'd never referred to him by his first name before. Another nail in their relationship.

He dropped the phone and lit a cigarette, his nicotine dependency increasing daily. Monday, he thought, on

Monday I'll get to the bottom of this. I'll find out why she's turned against me.

Vicky couldn't look at Joan. And neither could she find any words to respond to her question.

What is it exactly you want from me?

The words echoed in her ears. Her mouth went dry, her lips cracked from sinking her teeth into them. She brought her gaze to meet the older woman's eyes.

"It's okay, Vicky, I'm not about to jump down your throat," Joan reassured her, aware that her frank announcement had startled her daughter-in-law. Shifting her eyes away, she turned her attention to the garden outside, the strong lighting illuminating the little boys as they dashed around, fighting over the football and sliding on the damp grass.

"Em, Joan," Vicky stuttered, clearing her throat before continuing, rubbing the palms of her hands together, "I don't want anything. I thought you'd be interested in seeing around the house, that's all. And there was something . . ." Her voice trailed off. She couldn't get the words out. She couldn't say it. Not yet.

"Oh, yes, I'd love to see the rest of the house!"

"And we really should have invited you here long before now. I'm truly embarrassed."

Joan pulled her eyes away from the garden outside, focusing on Vicky instead of her grandchildren. "I don't know what Fintan has told you about me but one thing I'm not is blind! There's something going on in this house today, something you've decided to drag us into.

236

I don't know you very well but it's plain to see how jumpy and uncomfortable you are."

"I'm not . . ."

Joan raised an eyebrow and shook her head, disappointed Vicky had denied the truth in her observation.

Vicky's legs were like jelly. She flopped into the chair nearest her, indicating to Joan to sit in the rocking chair beside her. And she did sit. In her own good time. Not instantly as though she were doing what she was told. The tables had turned. Now she was the one in control. And Vicky was the one waiting for what came next.

"Inviting us here is your doing by my estimation. My son doesn't want us here," Joan stated in a very matter-of-fact fashion. "That's blatantly obvious."

Vicky paled, guilt flooding through her.

Joan continued. "Maybe not to his father – then again, those two haven't got on for years. Not since Ed refused to try and get back into the workforce. Fintan never understood how difficult it was for Ed after the accident – I presume he told you about that?"

Vicky nodded but remained tight-lipped.

"And then Ed became more and more depressed and it took years to regulate his medication, and for an ambitious teenage boy with the world at his feet, all those things were impossible to live with."

"I can imagine."

Joan doubted very much that she did but she let it go. "But never mind the past. What's done is done. It's what's going on between the two of you that's concerning me."

"There isn't –" Vicky blurted in defence.

Joan put a hand up, her eyes narrowing slightly. "Let me finish like a good girl. I only want to help you. I do know my son, no matter what you might think."

Vicky gulped, her heart filling with dread, tears very near her eyes. She didn't want Joan to be nice to her, not after her awful game-playing, not after bringing her to the house under false and very selfish pretensions.

And certainly not before she told her about Fintan betraying his brother.

Joan reached out and patted Vicky's knee in a soothing fashion. "He hasn't even looked in your direction, never mind spoken to you. And you – well, you're like a waitress in your own home! Fussing and flustering, unable to sit down and relax."

Vicky slid back in the chair, clutching the arms for support, her determination to make Fintan pay waning.

"Now, I'm going to ask you again. What on earth is going on under this roof? You're only married a wet day! What were you thinking of inviting us here to be part of that atmosphere? Why are you putting yourself under that pressure?"

Vicky shook her head, unable to speak, a lump in her throat the size of a golf ball.

"You must have had some idea of what Ed's like? What on earth would you want him barking in your dining-room for? What you've done today isn't normal, Vicky, at least not where I come from. Inviting people to visit when you're not even on speaking terms with your husband. Unless of course . . ." She paused for a second and stared into Vicky's face, "you did it to antagonise him! That's the truth, isn't it?"

The tears Vicky had been holding in check started to flow freely down her cheeks. She wanted to run from the house and the mess she'd got herself into as far as she possibly could but her limbs were numb, her ability to move paralysed.

"I'm right, aren't I?" Joan persisted. "You don't even have to answer, Vicky. It's written all over your face."

Vicky sniffed, wiping the tears from her cheeks with the cuff of her fleece. "Not like that. It's something else . . ." She paused. The pause lengthened.

Joan took her silence as agreement and carried on with her assumptions. "But why change things now? In all the years you've been with Fintan, you haven't bothered about getting to know us. And I can't say I blame you. What would people like us have to offer somebody like you? I saw the type of people your parents are at the wedding. Rich and sophisticated. It's a wonder Fintan wanted to invite us there at all!"

"Joan, that's not true!" She found her voice at last, genuinely horrified by the woman's candid approach. "You're his family. Of course, we wanted you there!"

Joan shook her head gently, her expression open and honest, her voice gentle. "I'm not criticising you, Vicky. Nobody could have been happier for Fintan than I was when he introduced us to you and told us he was getting married. When he left home first, I did novenas on his behalf, prayed for a miracle to help him get a good wife, someone who would support those dreams of his."

"Thanks," Vicky muttered, a wave of relief washing over her, shame following closely in its wake, coming in a very near second. At least she doesn't hate me.

Vicky couldn't explain why but it was important to her that Joan didn't hate her. For the first time in her life, somebody had taken the trouble to analyse why she was doing something, why her brain worked the way it did, why she'd got so lost in the path of life. She bolted upright in her chair. I'm wrong, she thought. It's not the first time. Fintan took the same time and interest. But she'd thrown it back in his face.

Joan's voice cut in on her thoughts.

"Would you like to know a little more about that son of mine?"

Vicky nodded, her lips shaping into a smile, a genuine smile for the first time since Joan had set foot in the house.

Her mother-in-law returned her smile, her eyes the same hazel brown as Fintan's. It wasn't only his father he resembled. He'd inherited some of his mother's features too. Vicky felt consoled by that fact.

"Fintan is cut from different cloth than the rest of us. He's kind and considerate. He's caring and hardworking. That's why his father can't understand him. Because he's different. Because he has the confidence to get out there and try, regardless of the consequences. Ed has improved a lot since the boys grew up. He's not under the same pressure to be the breadwinner. But he'll always take Fintan's absconding as a personal insult."

She stared into the distance for a moment, closely inspecting the cane furniture and variety of soft furnishings surrounding her, her eyes straying to the ceiling and glancing admiringly at the pine boards shining in the light.

"You shouldn't have pushed Ed on Fintan. Fathers and sons. Ed gets on much better with our other sons because they're more like him, I suppose. And also because they don't judge him. Not like Fintan does." She sighed and paused. "You shouldn't have done it. Silly girl!" She shook her head and wagged her finger, her last two words sympathetic.

For me, Vicky thought. She feels sorry for me.

She struggled to ingest all Joan had said, unable to stop the tears that had started again, ignoring them as they fell silently on her cheeks, dripping soundlessly onto her chin before landing on her denim jeans.

Joan didn't react, didn't reach out to hold her, didn't hand her a tissue from the box on the coffee table beside her. She let her cry and cry, waiting patiently until her sobbing came to a natural end.

"Feeling better?"

Vicky shrugged. Foolish would have been a better description of how she was feeling.

"Okay, if you're not going to be honest with me, let me ask you a question. It might help you to be honest with yourself. Something a lot more important than your reason for bringing us over here."

Vicky watched Joan closely, holding her breath, waiting for what was about to come.

"Are you still in love with my son?"

241

Vicky opened her mouth but Joan put up a finger to halt her.

"I want you to think about this before you answer. If you are in love with him, why are you trying to hurt him?"

Vicky opened her mouth yet again but, hearing Joan's advice, she shut it again without uttering a single word. She stared at her mother-in-law, seeing her in a new light, oblivious to the black shadows under her eyes or the age lines ingrained on her sagging skin. The only thing Vicky was aware of was the intent look in her eye. It wasn't a look that held insecurity or accusation. It was an experienced look from a wise woman who had spent years analysing situations from behind those seeing eyes, while she probably learned that in her life there were times when it was best to keep your mouth shut.

Eventually Vicky answered. "I love him so much it hurts," she said honestly. "But what if that isn't enough any more? What if he doesn't love me back?"

"Love is never enough, is it? And there are so many types and levels of love. When we don't have someone to love, we spend our lives searching for it, and then once we've found it, we pick holes in it, test it, measure it . . ."

Joan broke off without finishing, her thoughts drifting to her experience of true love, an experience that ultimately qualified her to advise others now, an experience she would hold dear in her heart until the day she died.

"I think Fintan's cheating on me, Joan." Vicky's

honest admission slipped from her lips as little more than a whisper. Immediately she wanted to suck the words back in, wave a wand and make Joan forget she'd said them. But it was too late. The words hung in the air between the two women, between mother and wife.

Joan opened her eyes wide, shock and disappointment mingling into one. "The Fintan I know wouldn't cheat, Vicky. Are you sure you're not imagining this? Be very careful you're not wrecking a good relationship on suspicion alone."

"But I saw him with this woman in the club where he works. I saw him touching *her*, his arms around *her*. I saw them going into the private office together. I found condoms in his drawer. I'm on the pill so we don't even use condoms! And as if that isn't bad enough, the bitch works with me, Joan. She works with me. And now she's . . ."

Unable to finish, Vicky stood up and went to the window, shaking her head and wrapping her arms tightly around her body, her eyes blurring with tears.

She wiped her eyes. She practised the words in her head for what she was about to say next, to tell Joan about Olly and her biggest proof that Fintan was capable of cheating on all of them. Please let her understand why I have to tell, she pleaded heavenward. Please help me, God.

She looked out to where the boys were playing. To where the boys weren't playing any more . . .

Chapter 27

Ariel pleaded with Roger, prepared to drop to her knees and beg if she felt it would make any difference, willing to do anything to convince him to carry out her request.

"You expect me to do that without blinking an eyelid? Traipse around London – you'd swear it was only a small village – and find your brother? After you lied to me for months?"

Ariel nodded, clutching his hands in hers. "He's my only chance, Roger. He's the only one who can testify in my favour, disprove the allegations I'm being blackmailed with."

Roger grunted his disapproval, remaining tight-lipped, pulling his hands out of hers.

"You have contacts, Rog." Ariel's voice was filled with desperation. "You could get flight details checked. Crosscheck his date of birth and find his address. Please?"

"I'm an airline employee," Roger said stiffly. "I'm not at liberty to give out personal data. If I do what you're asking, I could lose my pilot's licence."

And you could lose me if you don't, Ariel thought silently. I could end up in jail for something I haven't done. But she didn't voice it, afraid that he'd dismiss the hope she was clinging to, afraid that he'd turn his back on her and refuse to help, afraid that he no longer loved her.

He's here, isn't he, she convinced herself. If he hated the ground I walk on and was ashamed of me like he said he was, surely he would have stayed away completely?

She flopped onto the couch, pulling her knees up under her, dropping the glamorous confidence she'd intended to uphold.

Roger remained standing, wrinkling his nose in disgust at the thought of sitting on any of the furniture.

She let out a long sigh as she watched him, the words 'silver spoon' coming to mind. She'd never noticed how much of a snob Roger could be. Then again, she thought, he's never fallen on hard times, has never experienced anything other than good fortune in his life. He'd been his parents' pride and joy, a straight A student in school and only ever hung around with other high achievers.

Perhaps, she thought, if I didn't end up living in this building, I'd be looking down my nose at the shabby furniture too. But despite its hovel-like status, Number 105 was home for now and unless she could beat the justice system and prove that she was not guilty, this flat might be a lot more comfortable than her next address:

a cell in the Dochas Centre women's prison on the North Circular Road.

"At least think about it, Roger," she tried one last time.

"I'll let you know my decision," he said, walking out the door without as much as a kiss or a hug or a half-hearted goodbye.

Uneasiness settled over Pete Scavo as he left Ariel's building. He'd listened outside the door for a minute before making his way carefully down the stairs, holding the handrail and bringing both his feet onto each step before descending onto the next.

Roger's entrance had brought an abrupt end to Ariel's storytelling. But that wasn't what was bothering Pete. Although, he had to admit, his curiosity was aroused and he was looking forward to hearing the end of the tale at the very next opportunity. What was running through his mind as he ambled along the footpath to the bus stop was the unnecessary quizzing Roger had given his girlfriend once Pete was safely outside the flat. Or was Ariel his ex-girlfriend? Pete wasn't sure what the current status of their relationship was. Snapping at her that way as soon as he'd stepped inside the door had been uncalled for.

He didn't rush to catch the bus that was pulling into the bus stop. Now that he'd missed his chance to converse with the locals in church that evening, he might as well stretch the journey home as long as possible because, once he was inside his front door, the only company he'd have for the evening would be the television.

Still, he thought, rising to his feet as the next bus trundled down the road, figuring out Ariel's predicament will be something to while away the hours too. Maybe, if Roger lets her down, I'll be able to come to her aid and give her the benefit of my expertise. Coach her from the side as it were. There weren't many situations he hadn't come across in his thirty-three years in uniform.

He settled into a seat beside a young mother and her baby. As the bus trundled along, stopping frequently to pick up Saturday shoppers returning home and socialites heading out for a night on the town, his mind strayed to the bunch of old newspapers stored in a metal filing cabinet in his garage. His face broke into a smile. The baby beside him looking strangely at the old man who appeared to be smiling at nothing.

But Pete had good reason to smile. The numerous occasions Barbara had threatened to toss the whole lot of his papers in a bundle and watch them go up in flames would always stay with him. But her threats had been idle. In the twenty-eight years they'd been married, she had never brought him a moment's upset, never going to sleep on an argument being their secret to lifelong harmony.

His reluctance to part with 'old news', as she called it, would go to the grave with him, as would the many cases and reportings he'd pored over for hours, trying to get to figure out the result long before it was in print.

It's a pity I didn't think to ask Ariel when exactly all

this happened, he mused, smiling again when the baby reached out to grab his tweed cap. Then again, he thought, shaking the baby's hand in his to try and distract him from the cap, it had to have happened before she came to work with Ellis Enterprise. That at least would narrow it down. And the majority of trials are mentioned for hearing within a few months of the crime.

He sat up a little straighter, watching ahead for his stop, staying on the bus until he got to the closest one. Mostly he got off one or two stops sooner, to get a bit of fresh air in his lungs and hopefully meet some of his neighbours as he walked the last bit of the way. He was impatient that evening, anxious to make a start on poring over his newspapers. With a bit of luck, he thought, his arthritis slipping his mind as he hurried off the bus at a much lighter pace than normal, I'll find a mention of the O'Brien hearing and recognise the name of the Guard associated with the case.

There's more than one way to skin a cat, he decided, chuckling to himself as Roger's scowling face popped into his mind's eye. In his opinion, Roger didn't deserve a beautiful girl like Ariel chasing after him. Instead of appreciating her and standing by her when she was in trouble, he was forcing her to beg.

Pete Scavo didn't believe people should beg for help. He believed in justice.

Chapter 28

Apart from the area of lawn lit up by the outside light, Vicky's back garden was in darkness, the football the boys had been playing with sitting in the corner of the goal, the garden gate swinging open.

While I was crying my eyes out and selfishly working out a way to get my own back on Fintan, she thought, staring in disbelief at the empty back garden, Callum and Olly were making their way out the gate and onto the busy road. Shit! They're only little. And they don't know the area. Not at all. She glanced at her watch. Six o'clock on a December evening. Why I didn't I watch them more carefully? Why didn't I pay them more attention instead of worrying about myself as usual? How did Joan and I miss how quiet things had gone outside?

The thoughts flashed through Vicky's mind in the split second following her discovery that the garden was empty and the little boys had disappeared.

Snapping into action, she swung around from the window and turned to break the news to their grandmother.

"Joan," she placed a hand on her shoulder, "Callum and Olly aren't in the garden. I can't see them anywhere. I'm sure they've just gone exploring but I'd best go and find them. Wait here. And call me if they appear from somewhere."

Doing her utmost to hide the panic building inside, she spoke as calmly as possible, not wanting to upset Joan. It didn't make any sense for the elderly woman to go chasing around looking for the children, not when she didn't know the area. There was only one person Vicky could ask for help: Fintan.

"Little monkeys!" Joan said, swivelling around to look out the window. "You couldn't trust them for five minutes."

And why didn't you tell me that, Vicky wanted to scream. I don't know the first thing about children and now I've gone and lost two! In the space of about ten minutes!

"Fintan!" she called, coming to her senses and hurrying back to the dining-room, beyond caring what was happening between him and Ed.

She stopped dead as she entered the room. "Oh my God, what's happened?"

Ed sneered. "Your precious husband! Didn't know he was capable of this now, did you?"

She watched blood seeping from a cut over his eyebrow, thick red droplets nestling in his grey-tinged eyebrows.

"The boys are missing," she whispered. "I need Fintan's help."

Vicky expected to wake up any moment. It had to be a dream. A nightmare. A living nightmare. Where was Fintan? And what had happened between him and his father?

He wasn't in the lounge either.

"He's gone. He got a phone call and left," Ed took delight in informing her, hiccuping loudly, the hiccup turning into a loud vulgar belch. "And good riddance!"

Her first thought – shameful in light of the urgency around finding the boys – was whether he'd returned to *her*! Was it *she* who'd phoned him?

She backed away from Ed, hurrying to get Joan to attend to him. No doubt it wouldn't be the first time and she'd know exactly what to do.

But the conservatory was empty too, the rocking chair swinging backward and forward, the ghost of Joan's sweet perfume lingering in the room. Where was she?

And Fin?

Then she noticed a reflection in the window, a shadow staggering behind her, a shadow with a bundle of bloodstained serviettes held to his head.

Chapter 29

Ariel's phone rang. Number withheld. She had a good idea who it was and, as she pressed the green button to take the call, she dried her tears, inhaled deeply and decided she was done with feeling sorry for herself.

Her life was on a downward spiral as it was. How much worse could it get? Her boyfriend hated her. Her boss was treating her like a child. Her bank account was in a pitiful state and her address was something she was ashamed of.

But at the back of her mind she knew she still had the most important thing of all on her side: her family. And they were worth fighting for. More than anything.

"Hello," she answered gruffly, waiting for the barrage of abuse to follow. She wasn't disappointed. She listened without hearing, interrupting as soon as the caller paused for breath.

"You don't scare me any more," she said with a lot

more conviction than she believed. "I've reported your threats against my parents. The Gardaí are taking it very seriously. They're keeping a very close eye on their house."

She held the phone slightly away from her ear, trying to block out his warnings.

"We'll let the courts decide who's right or wrong," she said. "I have my evidence now. I've nothing to fear. You can't blackmail me any more. My brother's coming home to testify."

She wiped one of her clammy hands on her jeans, her heart racing so fast she expected it to bounce right out of her chest.

"And Number 105? Are you settling in well?"

Click. The phone went dead again, the dial tone buzzing in her ear.

The danger she'd risked hit her with a bang. "Dear God, help me out here!" she pleaded, joining her hands in prayer, begging for her safety.

She dashed around, carelessly tossing the few items she'd unpacked into her bags and zipping them closed. Then she called a taxi and left Number 105. With a bit of luck, she thought – shuddering as she took one last look around the shabby excuse for a flat – I won't be returning any time soon. But she didn't hand in her keys. Not yet.

The radio continued to play long after she'd left, the tap she hadn't turned off properly dripping in poor time.

Chapter 30

"Not much of a hostess now then?" Ed sneered, letting some of the blood-covered serviettes fall on the tiled floor in the conservatory.

"Why don't you sit down? Your head must be sore." Vicky waved frantically toward the chairs, letting him take his pick of where he wanted to sit, no longer worried about him getting blood on the furnishings. Glancing behind him, she could already see a trail of red through the kitchen. Would she ever get it back to how it used to be? The thought ran through her mind, the bloodstains only a fraction of the mess she'd have to repair.

She brought her attention back to her father-in-law who was thrown on the couch, one arm along the back of it, the other hand still applying pressure to the cut on his forehead.

"The boys have disappeared from the garden. I have

to go and look for them." As well as their grandmother and their uncle, she added silently.

Ed threw his head back and laughed. "Fin probably took them. Seeing as he has no sprogs of his own!"

Vicky grimaced. How dare he, she thought. We're only married six months. How dare he cast aspersions at us? How bloody dare he? She could have shouted at Ed that Fintan already had a child but truth be told she was terrified of him in the state he was in.

She turned on her heel and left him sitting there, still laughing to himself. Creep, she muttered, glancing over her shoulder and watching in disgust as he wiped his bloodstained hand on the arm of her chair.

Aargh! she screamed inwardly, scurrying out the back door and into the garden.

What possessed me to invite that monster to my house? She didn't know where to start looking and did a quick search around the entire area in case the boys were skulking behind the wheelie bins or something. But nothing. Not a sign they'd ever been there apart from the discarded football and the mucky skid marks on the grass.

"Joan!" she called, hurrying out the side door and along the side of the house. "Olly, where are you? Callum?"

An eerie silence settled around her. She peered around the front of the house, holding her breath, afraid of what she might find there. One – or both – of the boys lying flat on the road after being knocked down. Their grandmother kneeling beside them, sobbing.

But the road was empty, a stray cat walking along a garden wall the only sign of life.

She ran to the gate, looked left and right, dashing to the green at the top of the road in the hope the little boys were playing there. Again, her search was futile.

It was only when she turned around and came back towards her own house that it dawned on her that their driveway was empty. Fintan had taken the car. God damn him! Where's he gone now?

She clenched her fists tightly and ran down the road, stopping halfway when she heard her name being called from behind her.

Joan! Where had she sprung from?

The damp evening air catching in her throat, she ran as fast as she could back to her mother-in-law.

"There's no trace of the boys, Joan! I don't know which way to go next!" She panted hard, her breath coming in short, fast rasps.

Joan put a hand out to steady her. "Relax, Vicky. It's okay now. Fintan's been on the phone. He has them."

Vicky saw red. The cheek of him! Had he any regard for anybody else's feelings? Didn't he know how worried they'd be when they noticed the boys were gone? And where the hell did he go with two children? What on earth was he playing at now? Vicky couldn't think straight, the pressure in her head mounting.

She marched into the house, a bewildered Joan following her, asking questions and answering them out loud when she received no response. Vicky buttoned her lip, terrified that if she opened her mouth she'd say something she'd live to regret for a very long time.

Going straight to the piano, she sat down on the

stool and played a scale, followed by two more, followed by a rendition of 'Amazing Grace'. After that she closed the lid of the piano, went into the dining-room and began to clear the mess from the table.

Her parents-in-law sat silently in the conservatory, Ed half asleep and Joan half amused. It had been the most unusual day they'd had in a very long time – it certainly made a change from the monotony of their life. They were reluctant to move from the warm and comfortable surroundings, both keenly aware that it might be quite a while before they'd be invited to visit again. They weren't in any hurry to leave.

Joan rested her head against the thickly padded cushion, holding her husband's bloodstained hand in hers, watching the gentle rise and fall of his chest, her heart filling with love for him as he slept. He was his own worst enemy. She knew that. But she couldn't help loving him. She'd loved him from the moment she'd first laid eyes on him at the tender age of seventeen, since he was a young boy with dreams and hopes of a successful life just like Fin's. And while Fin had cut loose and made his come true, Ed hadn't the education or courage to do something different after his accident. And so, with the passing of years and difficult times, Joan had watched her husband's dreams disintegrate, leaving only the bitter aftertaste of failure and disappointment behind. There was nobody more disappointed in Ed than Ed himself.

Joan sat very still beside her husband, thinking about the day, thinking about her son and his young wife. She hoped they'd weather the storm billowing around them. In all the years Fintan had lived at home, he'd shown her nothing but kindness: protecting her and loving her more than most sons should have to. It was her turn to try and help him now. She'd call him tomorrow and tell him how Vicky was feeling, what her suspicions were. It would be up to him to sort it out then.

Chapter 31

Fintan indicated and turned into McDonald's restaurant on the Naas Road, reluctant to say goodbye to Olly and Callum, remorseful for the way he'd snatched them from the garden. He'd enjoyed listening and joining in with their chatter in the back of the car, their innocence a joy to behold after the conversation – if you could call it that – he'd had with his father.

"Drive through or sit down, guys?"

"Sit inside! Sit inside! Can I have a happy meal?" Callum, as usual, was first to answer.

"Can I have a milk shake, please?" Olly piped up politely.

"Sit down it is," Fintan laughed, "and happy meals and milk shakes all round!"

He swung the car into a parking spot, opening the back doors for the boys to jump out. He'd been careful to snap the child locks on the rear doors, terrified to take a chance in case anything happened to either of them.

Grabbing them from the back garden and enticing them into a lift home had been an impulsive but not irrational decision. The mood his father was in, Fintan didn't trust him to care for the children. The wine had gone straight to his head, reacting with his medication and fuelling the age-old bitterness he held against Fintan.

But while that fact in itself was significant, it hadn't been the reason he'd taken his nephews to safety.

"Last one in's a rotten egg!" Callum screamed at the top of his voice, taking off across the carpark without looking left or right, narrowly escaping an accident as a car slammed on the brakes.

Fintan put a hand up in apology to the driver, swung Olly into his arms and rushed after his tearaway nephew. From nowhere, a vision of his brother George flashed into his mind. He'd been loud and boisterous as a young boy too, just as unpredictable as his son was now.

Beating Callum to the door of the restaurant, Fintan raised Olly's arms in the air, encouraging him to goad his brother.

"*You're a rotten e – egg! You're a rotten e – egg!*" the winners of the race shouted, much to Callum's disgust.

Watching the boys punch each other playfully, Callum jumping up and down trying to reach Olly in his uncle's arms, Fintan was overcome by nostalgia. Suddenly he was reminded of the fun he'd had with his brothers:

the incessant teasing, fighting and competing that went on between them, the excitement on Christmas mornings when they ran around the house playing Cowboys and Indians, complete with the holsters, guns and cowboy suits that Santa had left under the Christmas tree. He realised in that moment that he hadn't always been the odd-one-out. He hadn't always despised his brothers. Or his father. But that was a lifetime ago. Before his father's depression had taken hold. We're different people now, he thought with a pang. We're not those young boys any more. All that remains is the fact we are still family.

He put Olly on the ground beside his brother and gave their food order – unable to resist a Big Mac for himself. Keeping the boys close by (not trusting to let them out of his sight), he brought them to the children's area where he allowed them to run loose in the play zone until the waitress arrived with their food.

Callum came running back to Fintan's table and swung out of his uncle's arm, crossing his legs and shaking his bum. "I need to go to the toilet. I need to go! I need to go! Quick!"

Fintan couldn't but smile as he beckoned at Olly to come with them.

"What happened to your hand, Uncle Fin?" said Callum.

Fintan avoided answering by hustling Callum into the toilet. But Fintan didn't understand a lot about children. He didn't understand that they never forgot.

And so, as he was biting into his Big Mac, mayonnaise dripping down his chin, Callum repeated his question.

"You washed the blood off your hand. Did you see all the blood on his hand, Ol? What happened your hand, Uncle Fin?"

The younger boy closely inspected his uncle's hands, disappointed when he couldn't see any blood. "There's nothing there, Callum. You're making it up."

"I'm not!" he snapped crossly, pushing his brother out of the way and looking at Fin's hands himself. "You washed your hands! Didn't you? Ha!"

Fintan sighed, preferring to forget about where the blood had come from but unable to ignore the two pairs of eyes looking at him, the two pairs of eyes belonging to two little boys who weren't about to let him off the hook.

"Granda's wineglass smashed in his hand when he was taking a drink. He got a small cut on his forehead. I tried to clean it and must have got blood on my hand. Now if you don't stop all this chatter, your burgers will be cold!"

"Can I have a McFlurry? Pleeease!" Callum instantly moved onto the next item on his agenda. Fintan was spoiling him and he was going to make the most of it.

Where do they put the food, Fintan thought, looking at the two small little people sitting at the mushroom-shaped table beside him. They'd already cleared their plates for Vicky. He watched them eyeing the ice-cream menu, licking their lips in anticipation and couldn't but imagine the pressure their parents were under trying to keep their fridges filled with food.

Fintan cursed when his phone rang as he was

popping the last bite of Big Mac in his mouth. Probably Vicky panicking, he thought, wondering if the boys are okay. She probably has an SOS out for us, he sighed, taking his mobile from his pocket and answering it without looking at the caller ID.

"Fintan. That wasn't a very nice way to treat your guest, now was it? Your brother, George, won't be too impressed if I add another week's interest on for lack of respect. Tut, tut, tut!"

Fintan blanched, moving out of earshot, yet never taking his eyes off the boys. "How many times do I have to tell you? You'll have it Monday, every last cent."

"Make sure I do. That's a lovely little wife you have there. I'm sure she'd show me some respect if I paid a visit."

"I'll call you Monday as soon as I have it. Stay away from my family. Do you hear me?"

"Monday by noon."

The phone clicked.

Fintan sat back down and picked up the large Coke he'd ordered with his burger, sucking and sucking through the straw until the ice cubes were all that was left and his body had stopped shivering. He ran a hand through his hair and stared at the giant-sized plastic Ronald McDonald, envying him his easy life standing in the one position with the same smile on his face morning, noon and night.

"Look at Uncle Fin's hair, Olly!" Callum burst out laughing, pointing at Fintan's hair that was standing in tufts.

Olly laughed along with his brother, running his fingers through his soft brown mop to try and make it stand up too.

Fintan smiled at the boys' mirth, wishing he too had something to laugh about.

The few minutes before he'd left the house were ones he wouldn't forget in a hurry, ones he wished he didn't have to remember.

He'd struggled to remain in his chair and not retaliate while his father laid into him, delivering insult after insult, calling him a snob, reminding him of his lowly beginnings and warning him not to get above himself.

Gritting his teeth and concentrating on his food, Fintan tried his best to ignore his father's malicious jeering, tossing the odd jibe of his own into their heated exchange, surprised by the deteriorating change in the older man as the alcohol seeped into his bloodstream, weakening his attack and exposing him for what he'd become: a bitter old man who had wasted his chance in life.

Fintan snapped back to the present, relieved to see Olly and Callum playing with the dinosaur toys they'd got with their meals. Watching the boys wind up the toys and letting them toddle across the table, chuckling heartily when they plunged over the edge and picking them up to do it all over again, he tried to make sense of what had happened next.

When his phone had rung, he'd considered it a timely interruption.

"Still have no manners? Downright rude," his father

slurred into his glass when his son took his phone from his pocket.

"You're calling me rude?" Fintan couldn't help retorting.

The phone continued to ring.

"You wouldn't know manners if they hit you in the face!"

"Hello," he'd said into the phone, glaring at his father all the while.

"I'm at your front door," were the words that greeted him.

Fintan pushed his chair back awkwardly, his heart missing a beat when he recognised the voice on the line.

Ed drained the end of the wine into his glass.

"I said I'm at your front door. If I were you I'd open it right now."

Ed continued to slur obscenities at Fintan from across the table, the wine bottle still in his hand, a sneer plastered across his face.

The voice on the phone continued to goad him to come to the front door.

Fintan felt trapped. He took a step backwards, felt himself being sucked into a deep dark hole, felt himself being transported to a time when his life amounted to nothing else but a deep dark hole. And there had been moneylenders at the door then too.

He shouted into the phone. "Get away from here! How dare you come to my house!"

Ed laughed heartily in the chair across from him, wagging his finger as though he were scolding a young boy in trouble, the bottle very nearly slipping from his hand.

Fin reached across to grab the bottle.

But Ed was too quick for him and pulled it toward him, forgetting he had the glass to his lips at the time. The bottle hit against the wineglass, shattering it, wine spilling all over Ed's hands and sleeves, the broken edge of the glass catching him right above the eyebrow.

Fin stood and gawped, freezing on the spot as he had so many times as a young teenager trying to protect himself from the onslaught of his father's tongue.

Ed still had the stem of the glass in his hand. He glanced across at his son, holding his gaze for a moment, before releasing his fingers and dropping the broken glass on to the floor, letting go of the bottle – which was still in his other hand – onto the table.

Fintan watched as the bottle rolled toward the edge. In slow motion, without uttering a word, he reached across and saved the dark green bottle from falling, replacing it on the table, then turned on his heel and walked to the front door, his phone still in his hand, the caller still on the line.

He flicked the door-catch to open it, unprepared for the force pushing against him as soon as the latch was released.

It took him the briefest of seconds to take control of what was happening. Finding strength from somewhere deep inside him, he barged against the thickset man blocking his path. The man pushing the door against him had overstepped the mark. He was threatening his home and Fintan wasn't about to let him get away with it. Pushing and pushing with all his might until both he and the other man were out on the footpath, he exhaled in relief when he managed to pull the door shut behind him.

"Two nice little boys playing football in your back garden." The other man seemed unperturbed.

"You said you were going to call me on the phone, not turn up at my house. How did you know where I live?" Fintan's heart thumped loudly, his thoughts immediately turning to Olly and Callum, a fierce sense of protectiveness coming over him.

"I make it my business to know where all my clients live. Did you enjoy watching that kids' match today?"

Fintan flinched, finding the idea that somebody had been watching him nauseating. He curled his fingers into tight fists. "I am not your client."

"You've agreed to take over George's debt so as of now you are my client."

Fintan didn't waste his breath arguing with the man. "Monday. I'll have the money on Monday."

"Make sure you do." The man stood back from the doorstep, looking around him, his eyes wandering around the large four-bedroomed house, finally coming to rest on Fin and Vicky's two-year-old Audi. "Because if you don't bring me the cash, I'll be taking it in other ways. With interest."

Callum and Olly's squeals of laughter could be clearly heard through the side gate, the man's gaze straying towards them.

A few minutes stretched into eternity. Neither man moved or spoke. Finally, Fintan watched in relief as his guest left.

The moment he had disappeared from sight, Fintan ran to the back garden and asked the boys if they'd like to go for a drive with him, promising there'd be a decent treat in store, not just a chocolate bar out of the treat jar. Luckily the car keys were still in his tracksuit pocket and he'd been able to slip away unnoticed.

"Uncle Fin! Uncle Fin!"

He blinked profusely, letting go of the vivid memory and bringing his attention back to his nephews. "What is it, guys?"

"Can we have McFlurrys, please?" Callum and Olly shouted at him, unimpressed that he was daydreaming and ignoring them.

"You can have anything you want, boys," he told them, resisting the urge to pull them into his arms and squeeze them tight to his chest and hold them there for a long, long time, instead watching with interest as their faces lit up and they scurried to get a closer look at the menu, huddling together as they tried to decide what to have.

He knew in that instant he was doing the right thing.

Chapter 32

Ariel struggled with her bags, dumping them on the doorstep of her parents' house and indicating to the taxi driver to give her two minutes. Two minutes to borrow the taxi fare from her mother.

"Ariel? Whatever's the matter, love? Come in, come in. Paddy! It's Ariel."

She couldn't ever remember hugging her mother so tightly before. She couldn't ever remember needing such a tight hug before. "Can you lend me the taxi fare, Mum? I've no change but I'll pay you back. I promise."

"Of course. Let me get my purse. Pop one of your bags up on Paddy's lap there," she laughed, as Ariel's father wheeled himself into the hallway to greet his daughter.

Ariel leaned down to hug him, a dart of pain crossing her chest. After five years, it still broke her heart to see her father in a wheelchair, still broke her heart to watch him smiling through the whole ordeal.

Her mother took her purse from the drawer in the hall table. She'd kept it there for as long as Ariel could remember, always on the ready should anyone call selling anything, always on the ready to support a charity. Ariel smiled, relief washing over her for a moment, savouring the familiar warmth and security of home. But then she remembered why she'd had to come home.

She paid the taxi driver and walked back inside the house, closing the front door tightly, leaving the rest of the world outside.

"This is a pleasant surprise. How long are you staying, love?" Paddy asked his daughter, moving his chair this way and that until he had it in the right position to get near the sink and fill the kettle.

Ariel sighed. She had no answers prepared.

"A few days. Maybe longer. I'm not sure, Dad."

"Man trouble?" her father raised an eyebrow.

"Something like that," she said, glancing around the kitchen, the cat flap in the door reminding her of the menacing reference to her parents' ageing cat.

Nothing had changed. A starched white tablecloth covered the pine table, stainless-steel saucepans on the hob, no doubt filled with potatoes and vegetables prepared for the following day, the Sesame Street cookie jar that had been with them since their first family visit to London and the evening newspaper folded neatly on the countertop.

They of all people had a right to know everything that was going on.

But first, she decided, I'll enjoy a cup of tea and a

slice of Mam's delicious coffee cake. She couldn't remember the last time she'd eaten something so good.

"You'll sleep in your old room of course," Ariel's mother said in a matter-of-fact fashion after they'd had a pleasant catch-up about the comings and goings of her parents' neighbours as well as the latest updates on family and friends. "The electric blanket is on already. You'll be like toast when you get in between the covers tonight. You look as though you could do with a proper night's sleep! I'll only be a minute. I'm just going to put fresh towels in the bathroom for you. There's plenty of hot water if you'd like a nice long soak."

"Thanks, Mam." Ariel choked on her tears, her mother's kindness too much to bear.

"We're here if you need to talk," Paddy said when his wife had left the room. "And if you don't want to talk, don't feel you have to. You're home now. No pressure."

Ariel turned away from him, not wanting him to see the tears trickling down her cheeks, not wanting him to think she felt sorry for him. Because she didn't. It was herself she felt sorry for.

"I don't suppose," she began, clearing her throat, "I don't suppose you've heard from Ryan?" Her words came out in a rush.

Paddy answered immediately, his voice clear and distinct, devoid of any resentment. "It's your mother's birthday on Tuesday so we'll be expecting a call from him then."

Ariel nodded. "Will you talk to him, Dad?"

Paddy's gaze strayed to the red candle burning at the centre of the table. He couldn't imagine the table without a lit candle now. It had been five years since his wife had begun the ritual, blessing it with holy water every morning, convinced it would guide their son to return to them in his own good time. "Ah sure, it's your mother he wants to talk to. He hasn't been able to face me since." He wheeled his chair around, picking up the long-handled poker and stoking the coal fire.

"Have you forgiven him?" Ariel asked in a hushed whisper.

Her father nodded sadly. "I've learned to live with things the way they are now. He'll always be my son."

"Do you love him, Dad?"

Paddy closed his eyes and nodded.

But he doesn't know or believe that, Ariel wanted to scream. "Would you talk to him for me, Dad? If it was urgent, would you talk to him for me?"

Paddy opened his eyes, sighing heavily, his gaze firmly focused on the red and orange flames, the crackle of fresh timber overriding his daughter's voice. But not her words. He'd heard her distinctly. Urgent, she'd said. Leaning the poker against the white marble fireplace, he put his hands on the wheel rims and pushed himself back to the table. He couldn't stand back idly and lose her too.

"What makes you think he'll talk to me? What makes you think he'll stay on the line long enough?"

Ariel didn't speak, the expression on her face all the

words that were required, her trembling lower lip a factor her father couldn't ignore.

"I'll give it a shot."

Ariel reached out and clasped his hand in hers, convinced there was a glimmer of hope flickering in her father's eyes.

Chapter 33

Hours after she'd discovered the children were missing from the garden, Vicky called and paid for a taxi to take Ed and Joan home, heaving a sigh of relief when Ed managed to walk out the door without staggering, more than surprised when Joan pulled her into her arms and whispered to her that everything would be okay.

Thank God he didn't keel over from the combination of alcohol and the cut on his head, Vicky thought, as she stood at the door and waved them goodbye.

Any notion she had of making a dramatic gesture by telling Joan about the relationship between Fintan and Olly had well and truly faded following Fintan's hasty departure.

I will get my chance. Just not now, she thought, relieved to have peace and quiet back in her home once more.

Looking at the clock she was surprised to see it was after eleven. A dark cloud marred her short-lived relief at finally having the house to herself: Fintan. He was the dark cloud on her horizon. Had he gone to work that night, she wondered. He could have gone straight there after he'd delivered the children home, changing into the spare set of clothes he always kept in the back office in case of emergency. Or he could have gone somewhere else entirely, she thought with a sigh, intense physical exhaustion forcing her to surrender her jealousy – at least temporarily.

She moved toward the piano and sat down to play, losing herself in the movement of Bach's symphony, the voices in her head overruled by the ancient classical rhythm.

Chapter 34

The streets of Malahide were deserted on Sunday morning as Vicky made her way home, her feet burning from pounding the roads, her body exhausted from lack of sleep. She'd watched every hour go around on the clock the previous night, waiting and listening, straining at every sound to hear Fintan's key in the door, to hear him come home. She'd slept fitfully between midnight and three, waking up with a start every few minutes, convincing herself he was still at work and would be home at his usual time. At half past three she gave up on the attempt to get back to sleep, her ears peeled for an engine slowing to a stop underneath her bedroom window, willing it to be him.

At five o'clock, she began to pace the room, imagining all sorts: a car crash, a robbery at the club, a kidnapping.

By six, she couldn't stay in the house any longer, her

276

mind frayed to a nervous frazzle. She slipped into a grey fleece leisure suit, zipped up an oversized anorak belonging to Fintan, pulled a black beanie hat on her head, woollen mittens on her hands and left the house, melting into the darkness outside.

She didn't think about where she was going but kept moving, peeling off her mittens when she got too warm, increasing her pace as she circled the village, the world coming to life as dawn broke through. Every step she took kept time with her pulse, the same sentence going over and over in her head, one word per heartbeat. *Fintan – didn't – come – home – last – night. Fintan didn't come home last night.* Over and over, the same sentence repeated in her head. Over and over again. She didn't push the words away. Because they were true.

She walked for miles, her face falling in disappointment when she returned to find an empty driveway. Her prayers and hopes had been ignored.

She was on her hands and knees in the conservatory when he finally returned home late that evening. Pushing her hair out of her eyes with wet hands, she turned around to face him, her heart sinking when she saw he was still in his tracksuit, his hair dishevelled, day-old stubble on his face.

He didn't go to work last night. The realisation hit immediately, her reprieve from jealousy coming to an end.

"I know what you're up to behind my back, Fintan."

She shocked herself by saying the words aloud. But

she couldn't carry the burden any longer, couldn't fight for her marriage alone. She went back to her scrubbing brush, kneading and kneading as she tried to get the bloodstains out of the grouting between the floor tiles.

"It's not what you think," he answered quietly. "I got myself involved without realising. Tomorrow, Vicky. It'll be finished tomorrow. Then we can go back to how it used to be. No more lies."

Vicky kept her back to him, continued scrubbing, her tears mixing with the grey sudsy water, Ed Jones's blood on her fingers, Ariel Satlow's sexy grin floating mockingly in the bucket of water.

"Are you coming home tonight?"

"Can you honestly say you want me here?" he asked. "After yesterday and last night . . . the unbearable tension between us these last few weeks . . ."

His words hung in the air.

He's giving me a choice, she thought, her fingers stinging from rubbing the tiles with such venom, the skin on her knuckles grazed, her mind in a muddle. She needed him to reassure her regardless. Hell on earth, she thought. It's my living hell on earth. Why didn't he deny it? Like most men would have. She hadn't wanted it to come down to a choice. She didn't want to be the one to choose. Because she knew she'd choose him every time. But she'd never know if he'd choose her.

"How many times, Fintan? Was it only this once or have there been other times?" Sadistic as it was, she needed to know. She needed detail. And she needed him to know he hadn't got away with it, any of it.

Fintan brought both hands up to scratch his head. Damn, he thought. Damn. She obviously knows about the loan. But how? His heart began to pound. Had that guy come around and threatened her, he wondered. He swallowed hard, his mouth dry. He stared at Vicky kneeling on the floor, her vulnerability stark. But surely she wouldn't be calm if she had been threatened? It can't have been him, he decided, trying to figure out who else could have told her. Maybe it was George and Suzi? Oh God, he thought, despair flooding through him, I've let her down so badly. I've shattered our trust.

"How do you know, Vicky? Who told you?"

There was nothing for it but to own up. He knew that now. He actually felt relieved. He was sick of sneaking around, keeping things from her.

She still didn't turn around. "I know you think I'm stupid, thinking you can get away with this. But do you think I'm blind and deaf too? Nobody told me, Fintan. I saw you. I saw the two of you together. I heard you on the phone. I know you were deleting all those calls. So don't bother trying to lie your way out of this. Show me that much respect at least."

Oh shit, he thought. I tried so hard to be careful but things got out of hand. She saw me with that bastard yesterday. He inhaled deeply, struggling to find words to explain. "I've never lied to you about anything other than this. I swear to you, it won't happen again. Do you think you can forgive me? Please?"

She stopped kneading, watching as the scrubbing brush splashed water over the sides of the bucket when she let it slip from her hands, resting her bum back on her heels, afraid to turn and face him.

"And what about your sudden interest in playing golf? What's that all about?"

Golf! Fintan felt like exploding! Had she been spying on him? He'd released a bit of stress at the driving range. Big deal, he thought. One of the lads at work had suggested it. And he'd been right. He'd really enjoyed bashing the balls one after the other. He hadn't bothered mentioning it to Vicky, hadn't given it a second thought and certainly hadn't considered it to be of any great significance.

"I went to the driving range a few afternoons. Last I heard it wasn't a crime! I've played a few games of snooker too. Did your sources miss out on that?" He couldn't help his bitter tone. Her interrogation was ridiculous!

"But how can I believe you or forgive you when you don't tell me what you're up to. And I can't just turn a switch and forget what's happened! The memory will be staring me in the face! Week after week!"

Oh God, he groaned inwardly. She must be talking about the repayments now. Have the Credit Union called her because it's a joint account? How did I honestly think I was going to get away with this? "But it'll reduce with time," he tried. He'd do his best to clear the loan as quickly as possible. He'd sacrifice what he could. He'd work extra hours.

"And I have to –" Vicky began.

Then she stopped abruptly. She had been about to point out: 'I have to see *her* every day'. But as the words formed in her head, she realised she didn't. She didn't have to see her every day. She couldn't work with Ariel any more. She knew that now. Not after this, not if she was to give Fintan a second chance. Not if she was to have a hope of a life without anxiety.

Ariel would have to be removed from the picture.

"Do you want me to go?" Fintan asked.

"Is it finished . . .?" she found it impossible to continue and complete the sentence. She couldn't say the words, couldn't shout: 'Is it finished between you and Ariel?'

"Tomorrow," he said. "Things will be back to normal by tomorrow."

Hearing her husband close the front door a few seconds later, she dipped her hand in the bucket, groping around the lukewarm water for the scrubbing brush, a vivid image of Ariel's head lapping in the grey suds. Vicky pushed up on her knees, peering over the bucket, a shadow of a smile on her face as she stretched her fingers before squeezing them around Ariel's throat. The wire bristles from the scrubbing brush scratched the palms of her hands but Vicky felt nothing apart from relief as Ariel's image receded into nothingness.

Chapter 35

Monday arrived, a dark dismal day with lashing rain and howling wind sweeping the length and breadth of the country.

Pete Scavo's eyes stung from hours of scouring through newspapers.

Ariel didn't show up for work.

Marcus arrived at Ellis Enterprise long before anyone else, locking himself in his office to make a telephone call he hoped would give him answers.

Fintan listened to the rain bashing against the window of the hotel room he'd been staying in since Saturday night.

Vicky arrived at her desk at one minute past nine – the first time she'd ever been late (even if it was only one minute) for work in her life – with a face as long as a wet Sunday and a stare in her eye that would put many a psychiatric patient to shame. The sleeping pills she'd taken had been effective. Very effective. She'd slept for sixteen hours straight through. A dreamless sleep, a sleep of the dead.

"Morning, Ben," she said, when she noticed her boss approaching her desk.

"What a day outside! Any word from Ariel yet, Vicky? She's a no-show so far and I wanted an early meeting with her."

He stood with his hands in his pockets, his lips shaped in a grim line.

"I haven't heard a word," she answered, her stomach gurgling noisily. Waking up so late, she'd left the house without breakfast. And the last thing she needed on an empty stomach was a conversation about Ariel!

Searching in her bag for her favourite pen, her eyes were drawn to Simon's gold-embossed business card. It was the first she'd thought of either him or the charity. But she'd promised to make an effort and at the very least she hoped it might distract Ben from his precious Ariel.

"Actually, Ben, there's something I want to ask you," she began. "I promised a neighbour of mine I'd pass on his card."

"His card? What line of business is he in? Is he looking for financial advice?"

"In a manner of speaking," Vicky answered. "He's involved with a charity and he's looking for sponsorship."

Ben groaned. "Isn't everybody looking for sponsorship these days?"

"Oh come on, Ben. It's a great cause: under-privileged children. Ordinary children. Kids who don't get a chance in life. Kids whose parents are too young or too poor or too upset to take proper care of them." She detected from his silence that she had captured his attention and slipped the card across the desk to him before the moment passed. "Want me to set up a quick meeting with him?"

Ben shrugged. "I'll have a look at my schedule." He took a few steps away from her desk, turning back before he reached his office door. "If you can get him on the phone, I'll have a chat with him. I'll see what sort of thing he's involved in."

Vicky dialled Simon's number and hoped something positive would come out of the call.

And to her immense surprise, after a morning she had thought would never end, her efforts paid off.

"Can you get everyone in the office to fill these out, please?" Ben asked her, dropping a bundle of forms on her desk. "They're for Simon."

Vicky frowned in confusion.

"Because there's kids involved," he went on to explain, "everybody here needs to have Garda clearance before we can even become affiliated with the charity."

"Oh, right." She picked up the forms he'd downloaded from the internet, glancing along the page at some of the questions.

"When they're done, you might be good enough to drop them in to Simon and tell him to get the ball rolling?"

Ariel's was the only clearance cert left to fill. Vicky knew from her phone call earlier that she wouldn't be in that day. She hadn't bothered to enlighten Ben, preferring to get the other girl in trouble instead. Taking a closer glance at the questions, she realised all the information was available on Ariel's personal file. Rather than delaying things for Simon, she took the liberty of completing it on Ariel's behalf, surprised to notice on her file that she'd changed her address recently, even more surprised to notice where she'd moved to. It wasn't the posh area she'd have expected.

Popping the form into an envelope with the others, she put them in her bag to drop them off at Simon's house on her way home.

Home. She still hadn't heard from Fintan. And he'd promised it would be over today. How can I even contemplate taking him back, she thought, after he's admitted that there has been something going on?

The effect of Vicky's sleeping tablets had completely worn off, the voices in her head coming out in force, Fintan's absence magnifying in her head, Ariel's empty office staring her in the face, her new address flashing like a neon light. Has she split up with Roger in the hopes Fintan will leave me too? Is that it? Is that the next step?

Vicky clasped her fingers and squeezed them together tightly, her wedding ring pinching her skin. She took Ariel's form back out of the envelope, made a note of her address and slipped the form back in again.

The methods she'd been using were too slow and

drawn out. Her plan to hurt Fintan had been sabotaged, halted in the nick of time when the boys had disappeared from the garden. But that didn't mean it was over. Time for escalation, she decided, her eyes drawn to the empty office once more. I'll deal with Ariel first, get my own back on *her*. *Her* name will be mud by the time I've finished with *her*. See how she likes it!

"Marino Golf Club, please?" she asked directory enquiries. "Yes." She waited to be connected to the number.

"Marcus, have you a minute? Can you pop into my office? I'd like a quick word."

Marcus took a sharp intake of breath. He'd spent the morning trying to work up the courage to confront Ben. And now he'd been summoned to his office.

"Eh, I'm in the middle of something, Ben. I'll be there shortly."

He took the brown envelope from his drawer and spilled the contents onto his desk. He'd try phoning once more before risking a confrontation with Ben.

Dialling the number from the letterhead, he flicked through the other papers: a birth certificate, a baptism certificate and a St Martin's scapular. And that was it. The entire contents. And the only person able to fill in the missing pieces was at the unlisted number he'd just dialled.

"Can I have a word with Mother Paul, please?"

The nosy nun who answered grilled him with questions.

"It's a confidential matter," he insisted. "I need to speak to Mother Paul."

He seethed silently as he waited.

"My name is Marcus Cole and I'm looking for some information, please."

There was no surprise from Mother Paul.

"Mr Cole, this isn't your first time to call. You know I can't divulge any information."

"But I'm her father." He visualised the nun's rounded cheeks, her tiny frame and her sprightly manner, not taking the passing of years into account and assuming she was the same as she'd been all those years ago.

"And is that not enough for you?"

"I only want to know if there's been contact between my daughter and her birth parents?"

A long sigh, a rattling of keys. "Then I suggest you talk to your daughter."

"Can you tell me if somebody has been in contact with her recently? Or if she has initiated any attempt at contact? Can you please tell me that much?"

"I'm sorry, Marcus, but I'm not at liberty to say. But I can offer you a bit of friendly advice. Talk to your daughter. Try again. And don't worry. Even if there has been contact – from either side – it shouldn't threaten what you have together."

Easy to say, Marcus muttered, but maybe not so easy to live with. He tidied the documents into the brown envelope once more, planning to bring them with him to Ben's office. If the opportunity arose, he'd take it, but he'd go in with an open mind and see how things panned out.

Barging in there and asking his boss straight out if he was any relation to his adopted daughter, Edel, was not what one would call socially acceptable behaviour. But having lost two nights' sleep because the issue was floating around and around in his head had left him a little irrational and emotional so there was a possibility he might do just that. And anything could happen once he lifted the lid on Ben Ellis's Pandora's Box and exposed how he'd manipulated bringing their two families together.

Opening his briefcase, Marcus took a drink from a tiny bottle marked Rescue Remedy. He reckoned he would need all the help he could get to remain calm.

Chapter 36

Ariel sat back from the table, unable to eat another bite. "Tea or coffee, Mum? Dad?"

Her mother made to get up but Ariel put a hand on her shoulder.

"You've been running around after me since I got here. Now it's my turn."

Paddy laughed. "You're brave! Trying to order your mother around in her own kitchen!"

Ariel was enjoying the reprieve from real life, enjoying being at the centre of attention with her parents. "Come on, you two! In and sit down and let me tidy the kitchen."

"Okay," her mother relented. "But then we're going to talk. And this time, Ariel, no holding back."

Ariel pushed her dark hair behind her ears and stared at her parents in turn. Haven't they gone through enough already, she thought.

Her body visibly tensed as her phone rang.

"I'll get that," Paddy insisted, wheeling his chair to

the hall and picking up Ariel's phone. "It's Roger, love. Maybe you should take this one yourself?"

Ariel put the plates she was holding into the dishwasher, dropped a kiss onto her father's cheek and ran upstairs, her phone clutched tightly in her hand. There was a lot riding on the call.

"Roger?"

"Hi, Ariel."

A pause.

"Are you going to help me?"

"No." His voice was firm. "I gave the situation a lot of thought but I can't do it. I'm not using my position like that. You have to understand."

"Loud and clear, Roger. Redirect my post to my mother's house. You know the address." She put down the phone and stared out the window of the upstairs room, Dollymount Beach visible in the distance, angry waves foaming in the storm, pushing against the sand, washing up stones and sediment in its wake.

"Tea's made, Ariel!" her mother called.

She smiled wryly, glancing at the ring finger of her left hand. Stupidly, she'd always assumed she'd marry Roger some day but she was very glad now he'd deferred the conversation every time she'd broached it. She knew that when her broken heart mended she would see what a lucky escape she'd had from a life with a selfish, narrow-minded egotist.

Silence fell around the table at Ariel's announcement.

"Roger has finished with you because you're on trial

for fraud and you can't leave the country? Ariel! What on earth have you got yourself into? And why haven't you told us before now?"

Two red blotches appeared on her mother's cheeks, her father remaining silent at the top of the table.

"Five years ago, I set up a loan for Ryan," she explained, taking the story right back to the beginning.

At this point, Paddy's mouth dropped open, jumping to conclusions and assuming she was in touch with her brother without their knowledge. "You've been in touch with him all this time?"

Ariel shook her head. "I'm not, Dad. I mean immediately after the accident." She paused for a moment, her gaze firmly focused on her fingernails so she didn't have to meet the hurt in her father's eyes. "I helped him finance a loan. He wanted to pay for the damage he'd caused as well as having some money to tide him over when he got to London first."

"Ryan got you into the mess you're in now?" Her mother's voice was thick with emotion. She'd tried so hard to remain positive, clinging to the hope that one day all four of them would sit around her table once more. Suddenly she cupped her hand around the candle, about to blow it out.

"No, Mum!" Ariel shouted. "None of this is Ryan's fault. He's paid back every cent of the loan through his bank. It's all my own doing. I was upset at the time. I took a few short cuts. He had a few months to go to his eighteenth. I changed a few details because I knew he needed to get away in a hurry. He couldn't bear to stay here after what he'd done. I helped him out, believing at the time that space was the best thing for all of us."

"I wish he'd never left. It hasn't helped." Paddy stated. "If he'd stayed, we would have come to terms with things. Eventually."

"There was nothing here for him, Dad. His friends had been warned to stay away from him. He never came out of his room. Mum, you agree, don't you?"

"I did then. But I have a responsibility in all this too."

"No, love," Paddy said immediately. "Without you . . ." he cleared his throat.

But his wife shook her head. "I couldn't look him in the eye after he'd brought so much hurt to this family," she continued. "Drinking and driving and running his own father over right outside our front door. If he hadn't stopped when he did . . ."

"Mum, don't upset yourself," Ariel pleaded, seeing no point in reliving the incident again. "Ryan has suffered more than any of us – well, apart from Dad, of course." Her eyes strayed to her father's wheelchair, remembering how his legs were crushed between the front of the car and the house. His own car – Ryan had taken his father's car without permission that night. But at least he'd survived. Another few inches and he'd have been dead, the doctor had told them. "Ryan's lost his family. Ever since that night, he's been on his own."

All three looked at each other for a moment, their eyes straying to the empty chair.

Ariel was the first to speak. "Anyway, that's only

part of the story. As I said, Ryan repaid every cent to the bank."

"You're losing your old father here," Paddy remarked.

"Unfortunately, a guy in the office knew I'd put the loan through for Ryan. He kept the information to himself – apart from a few sly comments to me over the years to let me know he hadn't forgotten."

Her mother stood up from her chair. She didn't like where the story was going. "Blackmail?"

"Pretty much," Ariel conceded.

She chose not to tell them about the money he'd demanded from her, threatening her that he'd inform Ellis Enterprise about her past history if she didn't hand over cash. Which, after long deliberation, she'd paid him, feeling at the time it was better to lose a couple of week's wages than her job altogether! Between that and the deposit she'd had to pay on Number 105, her savings had been entirely cleaned out.

She had every intention of telling Ben herself once she'd settled in with the company but the longer she'd been there, the harder it had become. And considering her previous employer had been kind enough to give her a good reference – adopting the innocent until proven guilty mentality – she'd worried about getting him into trouble for not mentioning it either. But she knew it was only a matter of time before the whole sorry mess blew up in her face.

"You might as well tell us everything, pet."

Her mother topped up their tea.

"It turns out that this guy had been embezzling

funds from the company. God knows how long it was going on but he managed to drag me into it: overcharging customers – by several thousands I might add – and unfortunately he got me to sign my name to things a few times when he knew I hadn't time to check them properly."

"Is that why you left your job there?" her father enquired.

She nodded, turning around in her chair and reaching for the cookie jar, taking out a couple of Lincoln creams and dunking one in her tea.

"But surely your solicitor can prove what was going on?"

Ariel sighed. "You know how long these things take. Evidence is still being collected."

"Maybe you're worrying about nothing?" Her mother was hopeful.

"The guy in question is nasty. And clever. He keeps phoning me, threatening to drag my name through the courts, make it sound like Ryan and I were in on a scam for years if I testify against him. He has it all worked out."

Paddy shut his eyes, wishing his limbs were intact. Then he'd be able to sort that guy out himself.

"Mam, Ryan's licence was taken off him for five years. He should be getting it back now. I can't let this guy drag him down without reason."

"But what can you do, Ariel?" her mother asked. "What's your best way out of all this?"

"I won't lie in court and I can't deny signing the forms. But I'm hoping I can get people to vouch for my integrity." Although, she thought, after the weekend I've had, I'm not so sure any more. She pushed the thought to the back of her mind. "I really need Ryan to be there to testify. At least if he backs me up, the judge might show some leniency."

"Then you can tell that guy who's blackmailing you to take a running jump."

Ariel couldn't help smiling. Her mother never did put a tooth in it! She just said it how it was.

"I'm really happy with my solicitor. She's prepared to fight tooth and nail. But she says, without Ryan as back-up, I'm wasting my time pleading not guilty."

"Well, let's hope he keeps up tradition and calls tomorrow for my birthday."

"Maybe it's time I buried the hatchet," Paddy piped up, entwining his fingers with his wife's. "Put me on to him tomorrow when he calls. He's been away long enough."

"One other thing, Ariel. Is that guy dangerous?" Her mother's concern was evident.

Ariel remembered his tone, remembered his smug arrogance when she'd worked with him. But then she looked at the worried strain on her parents' faces. It galled her to tell them the truth, but for their safety she felt she had no other option.

"He has been tossing threats around, Mam, so please be very careful when you're answering the door." She looked at her father then, the stern line of his lips enough to demonstrate how infuriated he was. "Both of you," she warned. "Promise me you'll be extra careful."

"Don't worry about us," Paddy told her. "Just concentrate on what's important."

"But you guys are the most important thing to me," Ariel stated, her eyes filling with tears.

"And you to us, pet. Now let's change the subject. How are you getting on in the office?"

"You wouldn't believe the mistakes I've made there recently. And . . ." She stopped a moment, piecing together the horrible things that had been happening to her and wondering for the first time if it could have anything to do with that guy. But how could he have known about my tennis match, she wondered silently. And there's no way he could sabotage my files at work. He's capable of a lot but I can't see how he could organise that. She remembered her embarrassment on Friday when Ben announced the changes. She remembered Marcus's overt concern. She hadn't given it any serious thought until now but she couldn't help wondering if he had accessed her data and made a few adjustments to the files. She pushed the thought from her mind for now, having more pressing things to deal with. But she realised that it could well be a possibility. An image of a smiling Marcus came to mind. She'd always accepted his friendly nature, assuming it was genuine. But seeing as he was the one who had benefited more than any other in light of her mistakes, she couldn't help questioning how genuine he really was.

"Ariel?" Her mother put a hand on her arm. "You were going to tell us something else?"

"Somebody called the tennis club and cancelled my final."

"You're to stay here until this ordeal is sorted. Do you hear me?" her father insisted.

"Yes, Dad. Loud and clear."

"I take it that guy knows where your flat is?" Paddy asked.

She nodded. "Actually, Dad, I just realised I've left my briefcase there and I'd brought home lots of confidential files so I'll have to go back to the flat later. After that, I promise I'm not setting foot in the place and you're stuck with me until this mess is over. Or I meet a tall, dark handsome stranger who whisks me off into the sunset!"

"I'll start praying then," her mother teased, clearing their cups from the table. "But I don't want you going there on your own. I'll come with you. Let me know when you're ready to go."

"Not at all," Ariel returned immediately. No way on earth would she let her mother see where she'd been living. "I'm going to go for a lie-down now. I barely slept last night." Sharing everything with her family had been a huge weight off her shoulders. "You won't even miss me! Anyway, isn't Monday your night for bridge?"

Her mother conceded. "Well, don't make any delay over there. No point in playing into his hands. You have to show him who's boss!"

Paddy shared a smile with his daughter.

Chapter 37

Marcus was losing his nerve.

Ben had come clean with him about the problems the company was having, some of the Ellis Enterprise clients unhappy with the decisions they'd made on their behalf.

"We'll have to up our game, Marcus. Maybe supporting this charity Vicky was on about will improve our profile."

Marcus had other ideas. "Or has the time come when we need to go scouting for clients, Ben? It's been easy up to now. They've fallen at our feet. But nobody in their right mind will be throwing money away on advisors soon if they find they can do just as good a job themselves."

"Fair point," Ben agreed. "This group here," he added, pointing to a bundle of letters, "want to switch their pension funds. That's not going to be cheap, not with all the fuss in the market right now."

Marcus got up and walked around Ben's spacious office. "Are they threatening to pull away from us? You're talking about some of our bigger players I presume?"

Ben nodded, his face grave. "It's written between the lines. We need to instil a bit of confidence, let them know we believe in the product we're staking a hold in." He sat back in his chair and chewed on the end of his pen, watching Marcus pacing. And wondering why. "There's no need to worry about your investment. We have a lot of strong commissions coming in. The company is solvent."

"I've been at rock bottom before, Ben." Marcus gave a wry grin. "I'm in no hurry back there again." He ran a hand over his chin.

"Nor me, I can assure you," said Ben. "Set up a meeting with the accountant if you need more reassurance."

"Ah, there's no need," Marcus said, happy to take Ben at his word.

"But there's something else amiss, isn't there? Is it anything you want to discuss?"

Marcus felt his pale pink shirt stick to his back. "Ah. Things aren't going very well at home."

Ben frowned. "If you need time off, Marcus, you only have to ask."

The other man shook his head. "No. Work keeps my mind off things. Speaking of time off, where's Ariel today?"

"AWOL! And it's not like her. There's something up with that girl this last week. Her finger's not on the pulse, not like it used to be. She hasn't confided in you by any chance?"

"I'd be the last person she'd confide in." Marcus shook his head, his face flushing as he tried to shove Ariel's face from his mind and keep to the issue at hand. He looked directly at Ben.

"Ariel's work has always been impeccable." Ben clicked on his mouse repeatedly. "I'm hoping she'll get whatever is bothering her sorted and we'll see more of her usual form."

"So you're not tossing all the best accounts at me because I'm a shareholder? Or for any other reason?"

Marcus came back to the desk and took a seat in front of his boss once more, picking up the envelope he'd brought with him and turning it on its edge.

Ben was visibly taken aback by his enquiry. "You know your stuff, Marcus. That's why I passed them over to you. The other lads are under enough pressure bringing in new accounts at the moment. If you feel it's too much . . ." He broke off without finishing.

"No, no," Marcus backtracked, Ben's words putting some of his concerns to rest. "I'll get in touch with the clients and have a chat with them."

"Good man. I trust you'll do a good job. It's all hands on deck now to help us survive the slump."

Marcus inhaled deeply. This was his one and only chance. He knew if he bottled it now, he might never revisit the subject and he didn't think he could go through another night with it all going around in his head.

"So my daughter, Edel, has nothing to do with your decision either?" He shifted his gaze to the photo on the

300

desk for the briefest second, then back to the other man, watching his reaction closely.

Ben's jaw tightened as he clenched his teeth together, his forehead creasing into a deep etched frown, his complexion paling and losing its natural healthy flush. He was shocked by the question, totally unprepared, yet part of him felt relieved that finally he could broach the subject Jenny had been plaguing him about for the longest time. But how could he tell Marcus about that under such delicate circumstances? He had to consider Marcus's feelings in all of this too, had to put himself in the other man's shoes.

"What do you mean, Marcus?" Ben's voice trembled.

"Edel, Ben. My daughter, Edel. Don't lie to me. I know there's some connection between her and Jenny. There has to be." He swivelled the photograph around so they could both see it, pausing a moment and staring at it. Then he reached into his inside pocket and pulled out a photo of Edel, the most recent shot he had of her, taken by one of her friends at a rock concert. "A blind man could see the resemblance, Ben. Don't you agree?"

Ben paled, his eyes lingering on Edel's photo, his heart aching for Jenny who was blissfully unaware that he was looking at a picture of her most treasured desire, the daughter she had given up for adoption eighteen years before, the daughter whose loss had left a large gaping hole in her heart and her life, remorse and sorrow filling the void childlessness had left.

"I'm sorry for being so underhanded," said Ben. "Look, do you think we could discuss this somewhere else, Marcus? Somewhere outside of the office? I could meet you in The Bailey in half an hour?" He loosened his tie and opened the top button of his shirt, his unease and discomfort evident as he waited anxiously for Marcus's response, and his relief when he nodded his agreement.

Marcus picked up the envelope and his photo of Edel and left the room, his shirt wet through.

Ben had given him half an hour, enough time to slip home and have a shower before he had to face Ben's truth. And find out if his precious daughter had found herself a new father.

Chapter 38

Pete Scavo had forgotten to stop for lunch, becoming so engrossed in some of the newspaper stories he'd come across that he'd lost track of time, in particular enjoying the articles he'd been mentioned in himself.

If I don't move on to recent years, I'll be pushing up daisies before I ever find what I'm looking for, he thought, bundling some papers into a bag so he could take them to work with him later. He knew there were easier ways of tracking down the information he wanted – go to the library and put Ariel's name into a search engine or give the Garda Station a call, mention his name and the fact he'd served as sergeant for a decade or more and ask them to do a check for him – but none were as satisfying as reading it in context with everything else that was going on around the country at that time.

For once, he wouldn't be shutting an eye when he sat

in front of his monitors. He had more important things to get on with.

Vicky's steady hand surprised her as she applied ink-black mascara to her lashes, emphasising the depth of her eyes, making them stand out against the paleness of her skin (even after applying foundation). As she critically analysed her reflection in the full-length mirror, she couldn't help but stare. What an outer-inner contradiction!

To an anonymous onlooker, she would probably have exuded an air of confidence and self-assuredness, neither of which she possessed. To any male out on the pull late at night, she felt she might have tempted them to stop and offer conversation or a drink. She would have run a mile at the suggestion of either but she imagined that, dressed like she was now, she would certainly be in with the chance of an offer.

And to Pete Scavo? Well, God only knew what he was going to think when she turned up at the office in full make-up, dressed in black from head to toe (including a black beret she'd resurrected from her bottom drawer), and trying to convince him that she had an important task to attend to at ten o'clock on a Monday night. She'd checked the security schedule before she'd left the office, relieved to see it was Pete and not the other guy who was on duty that night. She had some chance that Pete might be sleeping but the other guy seldom even blinked while he was working, never mind taking an occasional doze. No, having Pete on duty will give me the best chance to get in and out without being noticed.

She had a plan if he was awake, the same excuse she'd had prepared on Friday night when she'd made her previous late-night visit.

She'd make it sound like life or death – or at least solvency or insolvency. If Pete displayed any doubt, she'd insist it was urgent. I'm never doing this again, she vowed, lightly dusting fluorescent powder over her foundation to finish her look. It's the last time I'm going to risk my job. After that night, she felt confident there wouldn't be any further need. What she was about to do would bang the final nail in the coffin of revenge.

She'd covered every eventuality, had a mixture of stories ready. International clients could prove useful, the time difference being an essential factor in her planned explanation. If she had to give one. She'd been lucky last time. Pete had snored through her visit, never even stirred when she'd slipped in and out through the main entrance, inching along by the wall, careful to remain in the narrow band of corridor the security camera didn't reach.

She prayed she'd be as lucky again. That had been the first time she'd ever returned to the office outside of working hours, the first time in ten years. Anything else she'd tampered with – adjusting Ariel's accounts files – she'd managed to do while Ariel was out of the office at meetings. And the quarterly results table she'd prepared for Ben, to make Ariel's performance look ten times worse than it actually was, had been prepared at her desk.

But she still had the thorny issue of keeping her visit a secret from her boss. Ben Ellis would probably suggest medical attention if he heard she'd returned to work after hours, particularly as she was the one usually lecturing him on getting his home work life balance in order. But that would be the least of her problems if a link was established between her inexplicable visit and the tampering with Ariel's computer.

A familiar pulse ticked loudly in her neck as she visualised getting past security, her reflection blurring slightly. Panic and self-doubt raced for attention, her body breaking out in a cold sweat. Pete was sharpness personified and for as long as Vicky had known him, she'd yet to see anybody pull the wool over his eyes. But she knew from talking to him that he did regular checks around the building. And he enjoyed a doze for a lot of his shift. With a bit of luck she'd manage to get in and out again without being noticed.

What am I thinking of, she wondered? Doing unto others as they have done to me. Will it be worth it? And most importantly, will I get away with it? What if it's my reputation I destroy and not *hers*? What then? Will Fintan and Ariel walk away into the sunset together while I join the dole queue or get locked up in a mental asylum?

Transparent blue-grey eyes shone back at her from the mirror, hurt and anguish flashing beneath layers of bronzed eye shadow and black mascara. Sunday and Monday had been the longest days of her life. Fintan's disappearance on Saturday night had pushed her to the edge. The quick appearance he had made, admitting to cheating, promising to end it, had left her numb. She'd shut down her feelings, sealing them into a stronghold compartment, a place symbolising limbo. Unable to deal with or confront the reality of what was going on in her life, her brain went into auto control, leaving her with the simplest of choices: sink or swim. She had to choose one or the other. For Vicky, there was no contest. She'd chosen to swim and survive.

She continued to stare in the mirror, nodding in acknowledgement, establishing a connection with her reflection. The other half of her: an identical twin. As a young child, she'd found solace in the belief that her reflection and shadow were indeed real-life human beings, human beings with only her interests at heart, human beings who – unlike so many others – would never hurt or turn their back on her. Regardless.

She understood the hurt hiding inside the person in the looking-glass. Understood that being made a fool of was the worst part. Feeling isolated, alone, scared, afraid of what the future held – all that all hurt too. But the harrowing pain associated with being humiliated stood apart from them all, the predatory lion swallowing all other emotions in one mouthful.

She switched off the light in the bedroom, her reflection fading into the darkness, a cloak of isolation descending over her. Pulling her long black coat from the hall closet and buttoning it through, she felt the soft wool fit snugly around her body. Checking that the television was unplugged and security alarm switched on, she left the house and closed the door firmly behind her, shivering slightly against the biting easterly wind, her heart sinking in dismay when she noticed the empty space where the Audi should be.

Damn! No car in the driveway! Formulating a step by step mental plan as well as fixing her hair, applying make-up and searching for the appropriate outfit to suit her frame of mind had taken all of her concentration, leaving little space for the practicalities involved. Such as getting to the office! It had completely slipped her mind that when Fintan had taken off on Saturday, he'd also taken the car.

Sharing a car seldom posed problems as she had the luxury of using the DART to get to work. She preferred the relaxation of travelling by train between her home in Malahide and the office in Howth, hating to battle the snail-like crawl of Dublin traffic. But at half nine on a Monday night, the skeleton train service in operation wouldn't be of any use. Without having to even look at a timetable, she knew she'd missed the last direct train travelling to Howth. Damn! Damn! Damn!

Her transport hiccup delayed her slightly. She hated the extra burden of travelling alone by taxi – not something she made a habit of – and was sorely tempted to abandon the whole idea. But returning inside to the emptiness of home was equally uninviting. Closing her eyes for a moment as she stood outside the front door, she recapped on what she had to do, her final outcome flashing in neon highlighter at the end of her mental list. Instantly she felt calmer.

There was work to be done and she wasn't going to get through it standing outside her house dithering about organising a taxi ride. Walking as quickly as she could, she made the short journey from her house to the village in record time, more focused than she'd been in days.

As luck had it, there was a taxi waiting on the rank and before she even had time to prepare a satisfactory explanation for her lack of a car for Pete, the taxi pulled up outside the doors of Ellis Enterprise.

"Do you want me to wait, Miss?" the taxi driver offered.

"No, thanks. I've no idea how long I'll be." As soon as the words were out of her mouth, she wanted to take them back. Why was she giving information to a complete stranger? Apart from anything else, she didn't want to draw any attention to her actions that night. Biting down hard on her lip to prevent any more unnecessary rambling, she gave the taxi driver a twenty-euro note and thanked him for the lift.

"Night so," he said, handing her change through the window before swinging the car around and heading back in the direction of Malahide once more.

Vicky inhaled deeply, pushed her shoulders back and walked toward the entrance doors to do her worst.

Chapter 39

Edel stood outside Marcus's house, her finger poised over the doorbell, stepping back in surprise when he opened the door before she'd built up her courage to press the button.

"You came!"

He wanted to pull her to him and hold her there forever. As he had when she was a tiny little scrap wrapped in a snow-white blanket and Mother Paul had placed her carefully in the crook of his arm.

"What kind of a weird message was that to leave me?"

She barged in past him, furious with the world, furious with her mother for walking out on her and Marcus to start a new life with a man half her age – a man Edel had introduced her to in the first place!

At eighteen, Edel had been busy with her own life, hanging out with her friends, studying for exams, too busy to notice that her mum was also getting on with life. And despite her anger and embarrassment, she couldn't deny that she missed her, missed her a whole lot more than she'd ever let on. They'd been like sisters. Or so Edel had thought.

Being rejected at eighteen had hurt her deeply. She blamed herself, convinced it was something she'd done, convinced she had been a disappointment from the moment she was born. Nothing could persuade her otherwise, no matter how often Marcus had insisted her mum was being selfish and thinking of nobody but herself.

As an adopted child, Edel had always carried an element of self-doubt and defensiveness, feeling she was somehow to blame for being given up as an infant too, making this second rejection by her adopted mother almost impossible to bear.

But the real irony for Edel was that her birth mother was trying her utmost to reunite with her now, continuously contacting her through the convent who'd organised the adoption. For Edel, it was eighteen years too late to bond with this stranger who'd given birth to her and handed her over to the woman she'd grown up calling Mum, the woman who had nursed her, played with her, taken care of her until eventually the novelty had worn off and she'd walked out on her too.

Marcus followed his daughter through the hallway and into the living room, unable to prevent the hope building inside him. At least she had taken the trouble to come. But now, the news he had to tell her – would it drive her away again? It was a chance he was prepared to take. For her sake more than his. To bring an end to a lifetime of waiting.

"Did Mum contact you about the course I'm enrolling for?" She picked up a newspaper, glanced at it, was unable to concentrate and tossed it back on the dust-covered coffee table once more.

"She sent a text," Marcus responded, disappearing from the room for a moment and returning with a tray to the living room, a tray filled with Edel's favourite snacks. "I paid the fee online. You'll get the details in the post."

"Thanks," she muttered ungraciously.

Marcus sat down, weary. He hadn't returned to work in the afternoon, his head spinning after the conversation he'd had with Ben.

"Why did you move all the way to Enniskerry? You're only eighteen. It's too far away for you on your own."

"I'm not on my own all the time," she retorted, wanting to hurt him, wanting to remind him that she was entitled to a life of her own.

Marcus bit back his retort, refrained from lecturing her about one-night-stands and guys who weren't suitable, masking his concern as best he could but not entirely. "All the same, it's a very quiet road you're living on."

But she had plenty to say to qualify her decision. "And nobody recognises me there. Or knows that my mother went off went a guy half her age!" She unwrapped a Twix and bit into it, pulling the caramel with her teeth. "Why did she do it to us, Dad?"

Marcus's heart broke, the love he felt for his daughter

spilling over him like a tidal wave. Being called Dad was music to his ears, gave him hope, encouraged him to think that she'd hear him out. But first he needed to offer reassurance, offer a needle-and-thread solution to the severed gash caused by her mother's betrayal.

"She left *me*, Edel! She still loves you."

"She left me too. She never even looked back."

Marcus could pinpoint the hour and minute their lives had changed.

Half past six on a Sunday evening, right after the News, three months before.

Dublin had been enjoying a much-needed, well-deserved, Indian summer. Marcus had barbequed every possible variation of meat, indulging his family in the outdoors during the better-late-than-never heat wave until they had come to take it for granted, the floods and high winds of July and August a distant memory.

That Sunday, like the preceding days, Marcus was sipping a beer and tossing steaks and sausages on the grill on a smoky patio, his skin tanned, his complexion flushed from the heat of the charcoal when his wife had come home from an afternoon with her sister.

At least that's where she'd told him she was going when she'd left home in a blur of perfume, waving away his offer of a cooked breakfast or a lift into town.

"Traffic's light on Sunday," she argued. "I'd rather be independent, free to come and go as I wish."

He hadn't even raised an eyebrow, familiar with her determined ways and knowing better than to try and insist.

He'd settled down to an afternoon's gardening instead, tidying beds and pruning, enjoying the feeling of heat on his skin, luxuriating in the simple pleasures in life. That stress-free afternoon was one he'd remember for a long time to come, the pruning scissors still rusting under the gorse bushes, the shrubs he'd been cutting back left unfinished, the barbeque standing out in all weathers since.

She had arrived home very late that glorious Sunday, a dreamy look spread across her face, her clothes dishevelled, her lipstick smeared.

"I'm leaving you, Marcus," she'd said, as though it were the most natural thing in the world, as though she were telling him to close the gate. "I'm giving up my job to travel."

The heat had gone from the sun by then, Marcus shivering in the wake of her words. "And Edel? Are you leaving her behind too?" had been his first question.

"Our daughter has her own life," she'd told him. "She's an adult now. I've been there for her all these years and I'll keep in contact. When I get an address she can come visit. But she doesn't need me around any more."

"There's somebody else? Isn't there?" He hadn't needed to ask but he had needed to hear her admission, words that clung to the membrane of his brain for a long time after she'd climbed on the back of a Honda 750, wrapped her arms around her young lover's narrow waist and tucked in behind him as they zoomed off in search of excitement.

Her face had lit up. She nodded. "He's young and vibrant. My life was dull before he came along. We were stalemating, Marcus. You'll meet somebody too. You'll see."

His heart had snapped in two, like a bright shiny lollipop dropping on a tiled floor. Her lack of empathy shocked him beyond belief. His wife was leaving him, the wife he'd spent a lifetime trying to please was walking away from him, without so much as a by-your-leave!

"It's because we've had to downsize, isn't it? I've let you down."

She'd stared at him and shrugged. "Ah, chill, Marcus. Life has so much more on offer than the number of bedrooms or reception rooms."

At that very moment, Edel had stepped out of the shadows.

"I hope you're very happy together, Mum!" she'd shouted before running to her room and locking the door. She'd heard every word.

Her mother had left without a proper goodbye, sending her a message by text instead, promising to keep in touch. And a few days later, when Edel had thought things couldn't possibly get any worse, she suffered the extreme humiliation of finding out exactly who her mum had replaced her and Marcus with – on Bebo!

Marcus pulled her into his arms now, not caring whether she pushed him away or not. "I know how much it hurts, pet. But she'll get this out of her system. She still loves you."

"But not as much as if I was her real daughter! She's

had her fun with me now. I'm past my sell-by date. She told me once she only loved babies, never had the tolerance for cheeky teenagers!" Edel pulled out of his arms, feeling suddenly claustrophobic.

"Sit down, Edel. There's something I want to talk to you about." He'd already broached the subject on the phone, gave her a vague outline of what he needed to discuss with her.

Taking a seat on the couch, he patted the cushion beside him for her to sit down.

She took a Bounty bar from the plate, nibbling the chocolate around the edges as she listened to him speak, spitting out the coconut filling when he dropped his bombshell.

"I know where your birth mother is. More than anything, she would love to meet up with you. Even once, to explain her side of the story."

Edel's face crumpled in hurt and disbelief. "I don't want to see her! I don't ever want to see her! She gave me up. She dumped me on a gaggle of nuns who wouldn't know one end of a baby from another." Her voice quivered as she shouted, refusing to entertain even a mention of her birth mother.

But Marcus knew that deep down, no matter what she believed or what words she was shouting at him, a time would come when she would meet the woman. And after that, *que sera, sera*. What would be, would be. And he was no longer scared, no longer felt threatened. Not after the conversation he'd had with Ben the day before. If anything, listening to what he had to say made Marcus realise how privileged he was to have had the pleasure of watching Edel grow from a tiny tot into the young woman sitting beside him now.

He reached an arm around her shoulders, pulling her close to him.

"I love you, Dad. Only for you . . ." She wrapped her arms around him and buried her head in his chest.

"I love you too," he whispered into her hair.

"How did she find me, Dad? When the convent wrote to me saying she wanted to make contact, I said no!"

"Her husband went to huge trouble to find you, pet. But they would never have taken it any further without you giving Mother Paul your permission to make contact. Only for the fact that I caught a glimpse of Ben's wife's photo on his desk and noticed the resemblance between you and her, I doubt Ben would ever have broached the subject with me."

Edel pulled her father tighter to her.

"You are the image of her, pet. If you do choose to meet her, it will be like looking in the mirror and fast-forwarding twenty years, give or take." He took her silence as increased interest. "From listening to Ben, she's a really kind-hearted person."

"Don't make me sick! How can she be kind-hearted if she gave her baby away?"

"That was a long time ago. Times were different then. But look, Edel, that's not my story to tell. You are under no obligation to meet her. None at all. Ben was adamant about how much both of them respect your privacy. And your wishes."

Marcus didn't go into any more detail. He'd given Ben his word that Pete's involvement in tracing Edel would never be disclosed. Using his investigative skills and contacts to extract the information from Mother Paul could lead to all sorts of trouble, for a lot of people. And while it wasn't ideal or above board, Marcus felt that in the long term there was a possibility that everything would work out for the best. Ben's intentions were all for the greater good, born out of love for his wife and a desire to bring fruition to her life's obsession: to meet up with the daughter she'd been forced to part with – the only child she'd been blessed to carry full term. He'd also come clean and admitted he'd headhunted Marcus and offered him a job in the hopes of providing Edel with financial security. And from a selfish point of view, he'd clung to the hope that through Marcus he'd glean snippets of Edel and her life, snippets he could report to his wife.

Edel sighed. "But it sounds like they're obsessed with me or something. What if she's weird? Have you met her?" She lowered her voice and licked the remains of chocolate from her fingers.

Marcus laughed. "I've only seen her in passing. She's not a bunny-boiler if that's what you're worrying about. But she is curious. And surely you must be too?"

Edel shrugged.

But despite her display of indifference, her body language told Marcus a different story and on that basis he decided to push her a little further.

"Don't you want to know why? Why she had to make the choice she did? How it's ruined every day of her life since? Why she didn't have an option except obey her parents at the time?"

318

She looked up at him, fear of the unknown evident in her eyes, the hurt Marcus's wife had caused by further abandonment adding to her confusion, regardless of the attempts she'd made to forget both her birth mother and adoptive mother had ever existed. She pondered on her father's words. "I don't know, Dad. I'm scared. I'm scared it will change everything. And what if she meets me and hates me? What if the memory she has of the baby she gave up eighteen years ago is nothing like me and what I'm really like?"

Marcus continued to stroke her hair, unable to speak, unable to entertain the idea that anybody would ever be disappointed in Edel. He rocked her in his arms, resting her head under his chin.

"There's no need to be scared."

"You won't leave me, Dad? You're not trying to push me onto some stranger?"

"Never. You were my baby, my little girl. My big girl now. I'll be beside you every step of the way. If you want me, that is."

She sniffed and nodded.

"Why don't you at least give it some thought?" he persisted.

"Maybe one day. But I'm not going alone."

They sat holding each other for quite a while, each lost in thought, Edel apprehensive, Marcus relieved.

She wanted him with her, wanted them to meet Jenny together. That was enough for him. He could let go a little bit. He could be generous. He could do that for his daughter.

319

Chapter 40

Vicky's hands shook as she took a large bunch of keys from the pocket of her coat. Standing in the beam of a streetlight, she went through each one, fumbling nervously, until finally she recognised the correct key to open the entrance door of Ellis Enterprise. From where she was standing, there was no trace of Pete in the front hallway. Perhaps I'll get in again without having to explain myself after all, she thought, slipping the key into the lock and turning it anti-clockwise. Her heart beat loudly in her chest, fear filling her airways, making it impossible for her to breathe.

Once inside the glass doors, she re-locked it immediately, punching the alarm code into the digital panel, unable to believe her luck second time around. She'd managed to get inside unnoticed again.

She shimmied along by the wall, avoiding the eye of

the camera as she had the previous time, her heart beating like a loud bass drum.

Pete Scavo sat in his office, poring over court-case details. Newspapers covered his desk. He'd brought a month's supply with him and had been totally engrossed in speed-reading every page, searching for a mention of the O'Brien case. Changing his focus from the newspaper to the camera screen for a brief moment, he frowned when a shadow caught his eye on screen one. Discarding the newspapers for a moment, he peered a little closer, but whatever it was seemed to have disappeared. He scanned the other cameras but couldn't see a trace of anything unusual. Slightly uneasy, he went back to his newspapers.

Pete prided himself in his ability to do his job, his years of experience in the police force arming him with the skills required. The newspaper articles had distracted him, had done so for the past couple of days. He hadn't even looked at his crosswords that weekend, too damn engrossed in searching for a mention of Ariel's case, too damn close to pull back now.

He scoured an entire broadsheet for any trace or mention of the O'Brien case, glancing up every couple of minutes to ensure he was still alone, his concentration disturbed, his evening upset, the shadow he'd noticed irritating him but Ariel's dilemma irritating him a hell of a lot more.

Vicky tiptoed along the office corridor, not quite sure herself why she was creeping around but it felt like the most natural thing to do at that hour of the night. Ariel's comment the previous week that the building might be haunted suddenly came to mind. An eerie sensation passed over her, causing her to shiver. The antiquated heating system kicked into life every few minutes, the only sound she could hear apart from the beating of her heart.

Taking on the persona of an intruder helped her to distance herself from the enormity of what she was about to do.

The corridor led into the dome-shaped open-plan area where her desk was positioned. It was more difficult to avoid the glare of the security camera there but she kept as close to the wall as possible, hoping to get away with it. At least there aren't cameras in the consultants' offices, she thought with relief.

While she enjoyed sitting on the fringes of the six single occupancy offices to keep abreast of what was going on and give Ben and the other consultants easy access to her desk, there were at least a few moments of every day where she would have enjoyed a little privacy. She would also have liked a break from every nuance and whim the five consultants and Managing Director felt she needed to hear. But then, it was all part of the job and without that insight into what went on behind closed doors, she wouldn't be armed with the know-how she needed now.

She stole past her desk towards Ariel's office, a knot of tension settling in her stomach, sheer hatred coursing through her veins. *Her* door, the same as all the other offices, had been left open – probably by the cleaning staff who did a thorough job of dusting and polishing every nook and cranny two evenings every week: Monday just happened to be one of them. Vicky pressed the light switch, blinking furiously when the spacious room filled with light and her reflection stared back at her from the wall-to ceiling windowpane looking out over Dublin Bay. She pushed over the door but didn't shut it, afraid it would make too much noise.

Ariel's perfume lingered faintly in the room, her presence prevailing despite the fact she hadn't been there since Friday. Vicky shuddered again, unable to ignore a disturbing image of Ariel watching over her, dark brown eyes piercing through her back as *she* followed Vicky's every move to sabotage *her* career and reputation.

The call she'd made to the Golf Club that afternoon was only the beginning of further decimation, the opening line in another trail of slights on her personality.

Destroying the other girl's rep in the tennis set had been easy and she was expecting the same success with the golf club. She'd actually had fun pretending she was Ariel on the phone, eloquently crying off playing the final, forfeiting the tennis match that was so important to her, the cancelled match hopefully leaving a stain on her reputation for a long time to come.

Panic lodged itself in her throat. She struggled for breath, a second image terrifying her, an enraged Ariel coming to life in her head. Vicky pictured her laughing hilariously – an ice-cold menacing laugh – as she caught her red-handed manipulating her files. She could imagine her delight in exposing her unprofessional efforts to humiliate her, and went cold at the thought of her finding out everything she'd done already.

Vicky's brain went into overdrive. She visualised being berated, having a very good idea of what Ariel would say under the circumstances, how she'd grab the opportunity to turn the tables around: "*Did you think that a jumped-up office assistant would be a match for me?*"

Vicky stood motionless in Ariel's office, wondering how on earth her life had sunk to the levels she was stooping to.

She wiped her brow. Her black satin shirt stuck to her clammy skin, the weight of her coat suddenly unbearable as her body temperature soared to dizzying heights. With trembling fingers, she unbuttoned the twelve brass buttons on her coat, struggling inexplicably with the last three, believing she was going to suffocate if she didn't get the heavy outer garment off as soon as possible.

Her breath quickened once more. Inhaling and exhaling slowly, she moved towards the office wall for support. Perspiration rolled down her back. She pulled the coat from her shoulders, flinging it on the ground, the room beginning to spin ever so slightly around her. Ariel's personal belongings flashed mockingly at her from every corner, surrounding her, closing in around her. She tried her best to ignore them but, regardless of which direction she turned her eyes, they were staring at her.

Her ornate paperweights danced to life on her desk, bronze figurines glaring at Vicky from the filing cabinet. A map of the world hung on the wall, big red X's flashing from several marked destinations.

On impulse, she darted to Ariel's desk and took a red felt-tip pen from the penholder before going to stand and stare at the map. Closing her eyes, she haphazardly marked a few more locations, smiling when she flicked her eyelids open and took a look at her handiwork. Some unknown desert in the Middle East and an obscure spot north of Greenland were amongst her efforts. She returned the offending pen as though it were hot in her hand. She hoped against hope that she had selected Ariel's next holiday destinations! As suddenly as it had begun, her dizzy spell eased once more, her breathing returning to normal and her panic and fear subsiding.

Unable to ignore the gnawing sense of unease that had taken hold in the pit of his stomach, Pete abandoned his hunt through the newspaper and scrutinised the camera screens thoroughly, watching for anything out of the ordinary. But again, there was nothing remarkable. At least nothing he could see on screen.

Vicky was seated at Ariel's desk with the computer switched on. She was ready. Getting to work quickly, she clicked on the mouse and watched as Ariel's computer screen came to life, the stillness of black opening into a vivid orange hue.

Orange! Its brightness was dazzling. She hadn't been

325

expecting anything quite like that. Typical of Ariel, of course, to be anything other than ordinary. Resentment filled her every pore as she stared at the personal profile Ariel had set up on her desktop. Attention-seeking. Nothing more. She remembered her natural femininity and how much interest she'd attracted in the short time they'd been in The Bailey. The acid taste of jealousy made her gag.

Why couldn't I have come up with the simple initiative of jazzing up my computer background a little, she wondered.

Because you're dull and boring, an uninvited and unwelcome voice responded instantly in her head, melting her earlier enthusiasm about taking further action, leaving her with a great big hollowness inside.

Flashy. Showy. Bitch. For every descriptive word that came to mind, she banged her finger on a different key, the keyboard shifting slightly on the desk under the unnecessary pressure. The cursor flashed annoyingly at her until she entered the service provider's four-digit code to bypass Ariel's personal password. The egg-timer icon appeared. Within seconds she was in. She took solace in her tiny trace of one-upmanship. Ariel might have the higher salary and posher title. She might be a man-magnet. But she didn't have access to all areas. Unlike Vicky.

She hovered the cursor around the desktop, her hatred and jealousy building with every passing moment. She was such a show-off, Vicky thought. A stuck-up cow who thinks it's her God-given right to have anyone she wants. Imagine having an orange screensaver on your office computer! Stupid. Childish. Dramatic. She frowned in concentration, opening and closing various client account files as she tried to decide how much damage she could cause in one sitting without raising huge suspicion and, most importantly, without jeopardising her own position. The possibilities are endless, she thought, recognising some of the bigger companies still remaining in Ariel's remit.

Taking a peek at her personal folder, she double-clicked on the mouse and opened Ariel's calendar file. Nothing either interesting or incriminating there that was worth bothering about. But as she was about to close it down, a germ of an idea began to form in her mind.

It was risky but that served to excite her all the more. She imagined the fall-out for Ariel. She'd need to compare her appointment schedule with some of Ben's appointments first. If only to be on the safe side. But that wouldn't pose any problem. She had the privilege of having direct access to his electronic calendar.

Dashing out of Ariel's office and running to her own desk, she quickly powered the computer and waited for the files to load. Flopping into her chair, every moment feeling like an hour as she watched the anti-virus programme flash on her dull grey screen – its lifelessness stark in comparison to the vivid orange hue on Ariel's. Why didn't I take notice before, she wondered.

Pathetic as it may have been, the whole orange-screen scenario had succeeded in making her feel even more dull and lifeless than she did already, exactly the same as her grey screensaver.

She focused her gaze on her fingers, diverting her attention away from the computer screen, watching them fly across the keyboard as though they had a mind of their own. She opened the file she required and selected Ben's scheduler. At a quick glance, she could see he had a busy week ahead. Further disturbance from Ariel would be the last thing he needed. But it was what he was going to get.

Vicky printed off the page detailing the events for the following few days. Grabbing the single page from the printer, she went to work once more at Ariel's desk.

Opening Ariel's appointments file thankfully eliminated the bright orange hue from the screen. Its disappearance made it easier for her to concentrate. Paying close attention to the mix of appointments Ariel had scheduled for both inside and outside the office, Vicky made a couple of adjustments to times and locations, making sure not to overdo it, making sure it would still pass for human error.

She cross-referenced the changes against Ben's calendar. It would be silly to mess with any he was attending too. Of course, the two she'd messed with happened to be appointments with some of their bigger clients, clients who had little time to spare for the inconvenience of somebody not turning up.

She was tempted to make a few more changes but bearing in mind that less was often more, she made a note of what she'd done and closed down the scheduler, taking her mobile from her bag and calling a taxi to come and pick her up.

Only one item left to attend to. She opened Ariel's email account, the grand finale in her evening's work.

Selecting Marcus's name from the address book, Vicky created a new mail, entering 'dinner' in the subject box. Swallowing hard, she paused for a moment before writing the text of the email. Would she let him believe that Ariel was coming on to him or would she try and keep it formal? She couldn't decide. Her fingers hovered as she imagined Marcus's reaction, confusion being top of the list as he tried to interpret the signs between the lines of the email.

'You know how it is between Marcus and me' was how Ariel had described their professional relationship. How would she feel if he knew how much losing her accounts had meant to her? Or if he thought she fancied him?

"Am I taking this too far?" she wondered aloud, her voice hollow in the empty office, letting her typing fingers decide what was going to be said in the email from Ariel to Marcus. The words came to life on the screen in front of her, a whole new string of assumptions being conceived in a few short simple sentences.

Marcus. Thought I'd write a couple of lines to say how embarrassed I am that Ben saw fit to pass on two of my best accounts. I can only imagine what a dork you think I am! However, I have to admit to you how delighted I am that he chose you to deal with them. I've admired your ability and performance for quite some time and know my body of work will be safe in your capable hands. Perhaps we could go for dinner to discuss or at the very least work on them together . . . that's if you're interested? (Your place or mine?!)

A

PS I had to build up my courage to send this email. Please don't embarrass me by mentioning it in person. I'll know by your reaction if you're interested in my offer or not. Actions speak louder than words.

Vicky read it over once, memorising the content and jotting a red X into her personal diary to keep note of the date she'd sent it on. Watch this space, she thought venomously. Watch this space!

Before the sensible side of her brain had an opportunity to point out the consequences involved, she pressed the *send* button and let the email off on its journey through cyberspace. Deleting all records of the message from the sent folder as well as the back-up storage file on the hard drive, she closed the account.

Her night's work was done.

Shutting down Ariel's computer, she was relieved to be getting out of the office once again, relieved to be getting out without being caught.

Pete found what he was looking for: a press cutting outlining the O'Brien case. *Yes!* Triumphant, he fixed his cap on his head and pushed his chair back from the desk, deciding it was high time to do a tour of the offices. Then he could sit down and savour his discovery.

Pete was all for modern convenience but watching the building through a computer screen would never match up to doing an actual tour on foot and checking every room with his own two eyes. I'm being paid and trusted to do a job, he reminded himself, easing out of his chair, his arthritic joints stiff from sitting down, and leaving the comfort of his office to put his mind at ease that the shadow he'd seen had been just that. Padding along the corridor, his limping step echoing in the darkened building, he increased his pace as best he could when he spotted a sliver of light coming from one of the offices: Ariel's office.

Instead of leaving instantly as she'd planned, Vicky moved across the office toward the window and stared into the distance, distracted momentarily by the lights shining in the darkness beyond and slightly unnerved when a single star became detached from a twinkling cluster and fell from the inky sky.

Is it an indication of my fate, she wondered. A sign telling me that I'm distancing myself from loved ones and I'll end up alone? She stood still and watched the star's descent, waiting for another sign, totally startled by the unexpected form in which it arrived.

"What do you think you're doing here at this hour of the night, Vicky Jones?"

The sharp accusing tone in Pete's voice made her physically jump. She'd failed to notice his reflection in the glass behind her as he approached.

"Pete, you startled me," she said, swinging around to face him. She quickly retrieved the excuse she had prepared for being in Ariel's office so late at night. "Eh, I needed to send an urgent email to one of our American clients. Completely forgot it earlier. Luckily the time difference saved my bacon."

"You should have let me know you were in the building, Vicky," said Pete sternly.

"You weren't at your desk when I arrived but I was going to say goodnight on my way out."

"But why are you using Ariel's office?"

"Oh, she wasn't in today and the attachment I needed was on her USB stick."

"USB's, UFO's, they're all the same to me. Turning on and off the alarm is as much as I need to know about technology." Pete shook his head in confusion, his concern for Ariel foremost in his mind. Why hadn't she made it to work today? What could have happened since he'd left her on Saturday?

Pete didn't trust that Roger guy to take care of her. He'd check up on her himself the following day if she didn't turn up for work, he decided. It might be nothing more than flu keeping her at home. He'd call around to Number 105 on his way home from his shift. He might even get to hear the end of her story and save himself from going blind squinting over newspaper print!

"Are you still playing a bit of golf, Pete?" Vicky asked him, pulling her coat on once more and fastening the buttons from the bottom up.

He shrugged his shoulders, a hint of sadness sweeping

across his face. "I haven't gone near the place since Barbara passed away. Found it too hard coming back to an empty house to be honest, missed having her there beside me. She enjoyed a couple of rounds every week as much as me. And it just didn't feel right going without her."

The poor man, Vicky thought, realising for the first time how lonely he was without his wife. She remembered when she'd died, passing away very suddenly from a massive heart attack. Unfortunately she'd passed away the same weekend as Vicky and Fintan's wedding, making it impossible for Vicky to attend the funeral. And by the time she'd returned to work after her honeymoon, Pete had seemed to be back to his normal self.

But I was wrong, she thought now, overcome by a pang of sympathy for the man standing in front of her, suspecting he was still grieving and wasn't coping quite as well with being widowed as he was letting on.

Poor Pete, she thought, feeling very small at the way she was deceiving him. Smaller than she'd ever felt in her life. She swallowed the traitor-like taste in her mouth, wishing she hadn't had to involve Pete – or anyone else for that matter – in her subterfuge. But it was Ariel's fault and she deserved to pay. She deserved to get her comeuppance.

Pete strolled slowly towards the door. "I'll do a bit of patrolling, check everything is in order. Earn my wages so to speak. Are you heading away now?"

Vicky nodded, picking up her bag and following him out of Ariel's office, turning off the light on her way, the events of the evening fading into the darkness. Thank God for that, she thought, letting out the breath she'd been holding. He seems to have accepted my excuse.

"I'll walk you to the door then," he said.

"Night, Pete," she said as he unlocked the door. "See you tomorrow, I'm sure."

"See you, Vicky," Pete answered, saluting the taxi driver waiting in the Ford Mondeo outside.

"By the way," Vicky added, pausing as she turned to go to deliver her masterstroke, "don't worry about me squealing to Ben. He doesn't need to know I got past your eagle eye without being noticed! It can be our little secret."

Chapter 41

Fintan hadn't gone into work that Monday night. Or the previous two nights. For the first time ever, he'd called into work sick. He spent Monday evening driving around in circles, thinking. Thinking about the happenings over the last few days. And weeks. And years. It was the first time since he'd left home all those years ago that he'd taken the time to stop and think, to stop and analyse what he'd been running from.

And then late that evening, his mother called him.

"Ma!" He was surprised to hear from her, his surprise immediately turning to concern. "Is everything okay, Ma?" And then irritation. Is she going to hound me now because they were invited around for one visit? "I'm a bit busy, Ma."

"I asked Vicky for your number on Saturday, love."

He indicated and pulled over onto the hard shoulder of the Malahide Road, needing to give this telephone conversation his full attention.

"Won't keep you a second, son. I'm on your father's phone. Don't want to be wasting his credit."

"What is it, Ma?"

"It's Vicky."

Fintan's grip tightened on his phone, his brow wrinkling in concentration. "What about her?"

"She thinks you're cheating on her, son, seeing another woman behind her back. She's in a really bad state over it."

"Seeing someone? No way, Ma! There has to be some mistake. I'd never cheat on Vicky. I'm crazy about her."

"But she's convinced you are, Fintan. And with someone she's working with. She's all distraught about it at the moment."

"Ma, I swear to you I wouldn't do that." The phone felt hot against his ear but then he realised the heat was coming from him and not the phone.

"She said she saw you, Fintan. In the club. Slipping into some private office with a girl she works with."

"Jeez, Ma, I wasn't with anyone. I swear I wouldn't do that." He racked his brain trying to make sense of it, running a hand through his hair, his hand clammy when he pulled it away.

"Well, son, that's what she told me. And she was in a right state, crying bitter tears. She was crying like a baby. You're only married six months, Fintan. That's not right."

"I'll have to talk to her about this. She's making a huge mistake." How could Vicky believe he'd cheat on her, he wondered, bewildered. He hadn't so much as looked at another woman since he met her. Unless she'd got the wrong end of the stick . . .

Joan's voice cut in on his thoughts.

"And there was something else. She said she found condoms in your drawer and that you and her never use them."

"What? I'll sort it out, Ma. You have to believe me – I'd never cheat on Vicky."

"I knew that, love. And I told Vicky you weren't like that. Listen, I'd better let you go. Your father'll be complaining if he catches me wasting his credit."

Fintan nodded, forgetting for a moment she couldn't see him, finding his voice when he realised. "Right, Ma. Go on. And Ma?"

"Yes, son?"

"Thanks."

"You're welcome, son. You're welcome."

He remained on the hard shoulder for a long time, mulling the details of the phone call over and over in his head, thinking about his wife's unfair and unfounded accusation. How could she think I'd cheat on her with someone else, he wondered, trailing his finger around the leather steering wheel. And condoms! They must have been in the drawer for years at this stage, probably well past their sell-by date. He couldn't believe she was that desperate for proof, couldn't believe she'd cling to something so ridiculous. She obviously hadn't checked the date on the box!

And then he remembered what else his mother had said. Vicky thought he was seeing a girl working with her. There was only one person that could be: Ariel. Vicky was always banging on that they were the only two females working with the company.

I don't even know the girl, Fin had thought. I wouldn't know her if she stood in front of me! He leaned his head against the headrest, wondering how to fix things, wondering how to make the madness stop.

Shaking his head in dismay and pulling the car out on the road again, he drove at a steady pace until he reached the entrance to the Travel Lodge Hotel near Dublin Airport. He'd driven straight there after dropping Olly and Callum home on Saturday night and had been staying there since.

He hadn't been able to return home and face Vicky. He'd been too angry, too confused and too uptight. He'd rented a room to give himself time to clear his head, to give himself time to decide whether he could pick up the pieces of his marriage again and to give him a neutral address where he could hand over the Credit Union money he'd borrowed to repay his brother's moneylender.

Hours later, he lay watching TV on the cheap single bed, his arms behind his head, relieved that the envelope of money he'd carried around in his pocket all day was now in the hands of somebody else.

At Fintan's insistence, the transaction had taken place in the presence of Olly's mother and a social worker. There was nothing illegal about the money changing hands, simply one man paying off his brother's accrued gambling debts. And while he resented handing over fifteen thousand euro to the lowlife who'd clasped his fist around the bundles of cash and grinned broadly at the high interest rate he'd been paid, Fintan sincerely hoped his nieces and nephews would benefit from the deal.

At least they wouldn't lose the roof over their heads. At least not this time. The social worker who'd witnessed the handover had promised to make regular visits to the family home. And Suzi, his sister-in-law, would be in direct receipt of a sizeable portion of their welfare payments. All thanks to Fintan's intervention, intervention he planned on following up by paying occasional visits to see Olly and his family when he could. He wanted to help them see that life could be different. Spending a couple of hours with his nephews had made him see he'd pushed away a lot more than his parents and brothers when he'd made the escape from home.

The moment he'd closed the hotel room door behind his visitors, Fintan felt a huge load fall from his shoulders. Inviting Suzi to witness it had been risky, particularly considering their past history. But Fintan wanted to push responsibility onto her too. Let her see for real the financial trouble her family were in.

"When George gets on his feet, we'll repay you," she'd said sullenly after the money had been handed over.

"I won't hold my breath," Fintan returned, clearly reading her unspoken message. *Don't think your money gives you a claim on Olly.* "Just take the way out for what it is and try and keep away from moneylenders from now on."

Suzi clutched her leopard-print handbag tightly, her eyes narrowing as she listened to his advice. "When you have family of your own you can preach," she told him, leaving with a parting message that was loud and clear.

Fintan looked after her as she left the hotel room, her shoulders back, her head held high. I must have been really drunk the evening we got it together, he sighed, or she must have been a lot more charming than she is now. Either way, it was a moment of madness. And no matter how much he romanticised about spending some real time with Olly, he knew the child was better off in the bosom of the only family he'd ever known. But he would play a small part in his life, the part of doting uncle. If only from a distance.

Once the social worker had left, Fintan turned his attention back to his own problems and the part he'd played in upsetting his wife and driving her imagination to the extreme. He was still trying to figure out how long she'd been driving herself wild with jealousy. The more he thought about it, the more things began to slot into place. Intense jealousy would explain her possessiveness, explain why she'd been questioning his every move and made sense of why she'd pleaded with him to give up working in the club at night. He tried to remember the last time Vicky had been in the club but he couldn't. Not since they'd married and moved to Malahide.

Then his mind flashed back to Sunday when he

stood in the kitchen and admitted he had been deceiving her and begged her forgiveness.

"Oh shit! She must have thought I was admitting to having an affair. Oh the poor girl, my poor darling!"

He spoke aloud in the empty hotel room, realising Vicky and himself had been on totally different wavelengths. Oh God! What had he said? He tried to remember, unable to recall his exact words, trying to think of a way to reassure her as quickly as possible.

"I am a cheat! Vicky's right. I am what she thinks I am. Is there a difference between cheating with another woman and lying about money?" He mumbled the question to himself, the words hanging in the air, the answer staring him in the face. "There's a huge difference! Lying about money is something we'd probably get over eventually. But cheating with another woman would have left permanent scars on our marriage!"

He pulled himself up in the bed, wanting to be with his wife more than anything in the world, wishing he'd had the guts to be honest, wondering whether it would have prevented her jumping to the wrong conclusion. He didn't dare imagine the hurt she'd been going through.

But if I'd told her the truth about helping my brother out, how would she have reacted? Would she have stopped me getting the loan? And then he remembered how she'd been around Olly. Wouldn't she have wanted to protect him and his siblings too? The same way Fintan had. The Vicky he knew certainly would. The old Vicky. The real Vicky.

I hope it's not too late for us, he groaned, wishing he

hadn't been so blind to what was going on. How can I make it up to her?

He gathered the few bits of clothes he'd bought in a nearby sports shop, stuffing them into a large paper bag, leaving the room without even turning off the television. Dropping his key into the letterbox at reception, he headed in the direction of home to prove his wife wrong. He hoped she was still awake. He hoped she was prepared to talk to him. He'd bring home CCTV evidence from the club if he she wanted further proof. He'd spend as long as it took making it up to her, proving his loyalty.

And hopefully after that, he thought, we'll put all this behind us, enjoy a ripe old age and live happily ever after!

Chapter 42

"She should have been back long before now, Paddy. I'm going to give her a quick ring to put my mind at ease."

"Ah, can't you leave the girl alone? She's been living away from home long enough to be able to take care of herself. Did you win anything at bingo?"

"Not a farthing! I'm calling her now. I didn't want her going over there alone in the first place." She glared at her husband.

Paddy closed his eyes. This wasn't an argument he was going to win.

But a few seconds after she'd dialled her daughter's mobile number, the melody from Ariel's phone could be heard in the upstairs bedroom. She had forgotten it at home. They had no way of contacting her. All they could do was sit and wait. And their wait wasn't made any easier by the repetitive ringing of their daughter's

343

phone. They weren't the only people anxious to speak to her that night.

It was Fintan's turn to watch the clock go around. He moved around the house, unable to relax. Where is she, he wondered. Has she left me already? Is that it? Where on earth would she go? His heart beat faster, his concern increasing. She's hardly out there getting her own back, he fretted, imagining her dancing in a nightclub, her blonde hair swinging loosely on her shoulders, the whites of her eyes flashing as the strobe lighting shone around her, her vulnerability a halo of light surrounding her.

Fin clenched his fists tightly, the thought of his wife with another man bringing bile to his throat. He refused to entertain the idea, his face contorting with anguish as he put himself in Vicky's shoes and got a sense of the pain eating her up inside, the harrowing hurt and humiliation obliterating her true self.

Explaining everything to her instantly became a matter of urgency.

He jumped to his feet and ran into the hall to answer the phone. "Hello, Vicky, is that you?"

He held the receiver tightly, his grip loosening instantly when he realised it wasn't her. "Oh right, thanks for calling. I'll collect it tomorrow," he said, when the receptionist from the Travel Lodge explained he'd left his mobile phone in the hotel room.

He wasn't going to leave the house, not until Vicky came home.

Vicky was still in the taxi when Simon's call came out of the blue, his reason for ringing very unexpected.

"Don't think I'm not appreciative of your help, Vicky," he began, "but there's a problem with one of the clearance forms you sent me."

Vicky assumed one of the boxes on the forms had been left blank. "I'm sorry, Simon. They were done in rather a rush. Are you missing some detail?"

"You could say that!"

"Damn, I should have taken a moment to glance over them instead of rushing them straight to you."

"Wouldn't have made any difference. Only the Garda computer could have thrown this error up."

Vicky clutched her phone in both hands and waited for him to divulge a little more.

"Can you get Ben to call me first thing?" he said.

Oh, I can't wait until morning to find out what's going on, she decided, not when I was the one who instigated the company's involvement with the charity in the first place. She felt she deserved to know what was going on.

"Tell me, Simon. Give me the worst."

"It appears you have a fraudster in your midst, someone with a serious court case hanging over their heads."

"No! Who is it?" She didn't attempt to contain her curiosity. "I swear I won't tell anyone. And I'll get Ben to call you first thing. You can take it through the appropriate channels then."

"I can't divulge information like that, Vicky. It's confidential. I've probably told you too much already."

"Spoilsport!"

"I'll talk to Ben first and then I'll check with the charity to see how they feel about the situation. I hate turning my back on a good offer. Damn her anyway."

Her! Simon had overlooked the fact that there was only one other *her* at Ellis Enterprise! "Damn *her* is right," Vicky responded. "The kids will lose out now because of *her*. So sorry about that, Simon. I had no idea."

"Don't blame yourself, Vicky. It was a very kind gesture on your part. You weren't to know. And all is not lost yet. We might still be able to work around it. I'll have a chat with Ben and see what we can salvage."

Sly, devious bitch, she thought, after she'd said her goodbyes to Simon. Vicky was livid, disgusted that Ariel's underhandedness was going to ruin this opportunity for a worthy charity. Why should *she* get away with ruining everything? And what crime had she committed? What was she up on trial for? Vicky wondered if she'd divulged that piece of juicy information to Ben when she'd applied for the job. She doubted it very much. More likely he was in for a shock when he heard from Simon. He'd have to take more action than simply passing the file onto somebody else. Trial and retribution! It tasted good.

Her phone still clutched in her hand, she made a spur of the moment decision and dialled Fintan's mobile number, her heart rate increasing, her mouth going dry as his phone began to ring.

The ringing stopped. A click on the line told her he'd picked up. She held her breath.

"Hello, I'm afraid . . ."

A female voice reverberated in Vicky's ear.

In an instant she was wild with fury, enforced hatred pushing her to forget where she was.

"You fucking bitch!" she screamed into the phone. "You fucking bitch!" Disconnecting the call with a sharp stab of her finger, she leaned forward in her seat and shouted at the taxi driver. "Turn around. You have to turn around."

"Take it easy, Miss. Are you okay back there?" he asked, trying to catch his passenger's eye in the rear-view mirror.

"I need to get to Fairview immediately!" Vicky scrabbled in her handbag to find Ariel's address, reading it from the light of her mobile phone. "Military House. You have to get me there now. Please hurry."

She closed her eyes and rocked from side to side, channelling every ounce of energy she possessed into remaining calm, storing it to use when she got to her destination. She knew what she had to do. There was only one way to bring an end to the madness.

Vicky rocked back and forward on the seat, her body thrown sideways as the taxi driver swung around quickly before taking off at speed in the opposite direction, a sense of urgency breathing through the car, a sense of dread making Vicky's temples pound. The voices in her head were still, her concentration fixed on one solitary thought.

Leaning back into the seat, she clasped her hands tightly in her lap, ignoring the pain penetrating her heart and soul. Soon, she thought, her gaze following the reflection of the moon on the sea, soon I will end this torture.

Pete was furious, Vicky's parting comments putting a

damper on the fact he'd found the article he'd spent days searching for. He punched in the four-digit alarm code, staring after Vicky's taxi as it disappeared around the corner.

He took a walk around the building, hoping it would ease his mind. And frustration. Passing Vicky's desk, he stopped short when he noticed the standby light on her monitor. That hadn't been on earlier. Aware of Ben's energy-conservation fetish, he watched out for any waste of resources and noticed these things. Placing a hand on the hard-drive box, he felt it was warm.

Happy that everything was as it should be, he went back to Reception and played back the last hour of security film. Pete leaned his elbows on the table, held the remote control in the air and flicked the recording onto slow motion.

"I have to be missing something."

He flicked from screen to screen, zooming in on the communal area when Vicky came into full view for the briefest moment before disappearing into Ariel's office. But there was no visible evidence that she'd been up to anything untoward, nothing at all except Pete's intuition that she'd been lying to his face.

On impulse he called the taxi firm she'd used – the same taxi firm Ellis Enterprise always used. And Pete was on first-name basis with them.

"How's it going? Pete Scavo here," he said into the phone, picking up the article he'd cut from the newspaper and double-checking the details before slipping it carefully into the inside pocket of his jacket. "You collected someone from the office a short while ago. She's left something behind. Was it home to Malahide you dropped her?"

He whistled softly into the phone while he waited for the telephonist to get in contact with the driver.

"Ah, I see," he said, gritting his teeth. "Nothing I can do so." He thanked him and hung up.

Now what's taking her there, he wondered, the silence in the building eerie around him, a sense of foreboding settling under his skin. His gut instinct told him there was something not right, yet his conscience reminded him that his job was to protect the premises. If he'd been more attentive to his job earlier, he wouldn't be in the dilemma he was in now. But he couldn't shake off the urge to check things out, couldn't ignore the hunch that Vicky had been playing him for a fool. It wouldn't take him long to follow her and check exactly what she was up to. He'd be back at his post in no time. In the years he'd been working there, he'd never had as much as a sniff of a robbery so hopefully he'd get away with this one absence.

After much deliberation, Pete called the taxi firm back and booked a lift to Fairview. Ariel could be in danger, her absence from work very out of the character. In his years in the force, Pete had learned a valuable lesson, several times over. Never ignore a hunch. "Call it an extended supper break," he justified to the empty reception hall, picking up the phone and dialling the number of Mountjoy Garda Station.

"Is Sergeant Brown on duty this evening? Tomorrow morning at six? Perfect. I'll call him back then. No message. Just an old friend trying to track him down."

Chapter 43

Ariel's shoes were soaked through, her socks wringing. There was half an inch of water on the living-room floor. She could see the problem immediately. She hadn't turned the tap off properly, the stopper had been in the sink and now most of the flat was a complete mess!

But I'm lucky, she thought. At least it's contained to this flat. It hasn't gone through the ceiling. And my briefcase was on the bed, so it survived any water damage. Maybe it's a sign my luck is changing, she thought, and continued mopping and squeezing, grateful to the doorman for loaning her a mop and bucket from the cleaning press downstairs. The physical exertion made a pleasant change from sitting at a desk staring at a computer screen punching in figures. Or worrying herself sick about whether Ryan would come home and testify in court. Yet she must hurry and get out of here – it wasn't safe any more.

She increased the volume on the radio and hummed along to one of U2's tunes, trying to quell her unease, unaware that two visitors were on their way to her flat, one to protect her and the other – well, the other to give her what she felt was due.

Vicky checked and rechecked the address. Military House indeed, she thought, glancing around the outside of the building, being reminded of an army barracks she'd visited once on a school tour.

The cheating cow must be down on her luck, she thought, letting the taxi driver go when she finally accepted that this was where her work colleague was living now.

Spotting the open lift in the entrance hall, she stepped inside and pressed the button to take her to the first floor. She leaned against the cold metal, her eyes gritty with tiredness, the events of the day and evening washing over her as she took a brief reprieve from her pent-up anger.

What will I hit *her* with first, she wondered, biting her lip as the lift climbed the shaft, creaking and shuddering as it moved slowly upward. Will I head straight for the jugular and tell *her* that I know *she's* been sneaking around behind my back with Fintan? Or will I ease *her* into it and tell her I know about *her* dodgy past? Corner *her*, scare *her*, threaten *her*?

Vicky clenched and unclenched her fists, overcome by a powerful sense that her vendetta with Ariel was on the verge of a climatic conclusion. She staggered when the lift ground to a halt moments after it had began to move. She straightened up, ready to jump out once the doors parted.

This is it, she thought, feeling slightly claustrophobic in the motionless lift. The moment of confrontation has arrived.

She inhaled deeply, a pulse ticking loudly in her ears as she waited for the doors to slide apart so she could make her way to Number 105. The quicker she got her ordeal over with the better. Her nerve and determination were already slipping. She exhaled a few times, looking around her for a button to press to open the doors. But there wasn't one. And she was still waiting five minutes later. Waiting, and waiting, her anxiety increasing, the small space closing in around her.

She picked up the lift telephone, pressing the call button, the receiver cold against her ear. But it was a waste of time. The line was dead, lifeless.

"Help! Help! Can anybody hear me?"

Chapter 44

Tuesday morning

Pete Scavo sat at the edge of his bed, his body sagging wearily, his brain like fluffy cotton wool. The second half of his shift had dragged in slow motion, the first time in quite a while he'd found it impossible to rest, the antiquated central-heating system – a sound he was generally comfortable with – scaring him half to death every time it kicked into life.

Somewhere at the back of his mind, he knew there was something he'd meant to do before going to bed but for the life of him he couldn't remember.

It seemed nobody had noticed he'd left the premises during his shift, deserted his post. For that he was grateful.

Pulling his shirt over his head, he slipped in between the sheets, sheets that hadn't been changed in quite a while, sheets that had been tossed and turned in for the months he'd been unable to sleep without Barbara.

But that morning, following the stressful events of the previous night, Pete Scavo fell into a comatose sleep in his own bed.

Fintan woke with a start when the doorbell sounded, rubbing his eyes in confusion as his eyes adjusted to the dim light he'd left on in the lounge overnight. He glanced at the mantel clock and jumped to his feet. It was seven in the morning. Was Vicky only getting home now? Where on earth was she all night?

He'd sat in the lounge, planning and preparing what to say to his wife, trying to string sentences together, trying to find words that would portray how empty his life would be without her, how much she meant to him and how much attention he'd pay her for the rest of his life to make up for the last few weeks. She couldn't but forgive him, he thought.

Inhaling deeply, he pulled open the front door, fully expecting to see her standing there after forgetting her key, totally unprepared for what was facing him.

"Mr Jones? Fintan Jones?"

Fintan nodded, rubbing the sleep from his eyes.

"Detective Superintendent Karl Wilson and my colleague Detective Sergeant Boyce."

Fintan was still half asleep, his eyes barely focusing on the identification badges being shown to him.

"It might be best if we come in for a moment, Mr Jones."

Fintan held the door open for them, rubbing his clammy hands on his Dublin jersey, as two plainclothes

Gardaí walked past him, standing in the hallway waiting for him to close the door so they could deliver their news.

Ben Ellis's cheeks were damp, the telephone receiver clutched tightly in his hand as he tried to digest the tragic news he'd just been given.

"No, there has to be some mistake. This can't be true."

He listened carefully.

"Yes, yes, of course. I'll make sure everybody is available to talk to you. How soon will you be here?"

An hour. Sixty minutes. The amount of time the Gardaí had allowed him to gather his staff and tell them their colleague had been found dead a couple of hours before.

Marcus opened his email inbox and scanned the list of senders, unable to resist double-clicking on one from Ariel before any other. He reached for his cup of coffee and brought it to his lips, the scalding liquid burning his tongue, the sting going unnoticed as he read and reread her mail. He ran a finger under the words on screen, the words she'd sent asking him to give her a sign.

He glanced at the time she'd sent it: after ten the previous night. Even more confusing, he thought, unless she had access to her email at home.

He didn't respond immediately, needing to give her suggestion some thought. Was she coming on to him or not? Or was he reading something into her words that wasn't actually there?

Paddy wheeled his chair into the porch and picked the morning paper from the floor with a long-handled claw, giving a quick glance at the headline as he returned to the kitchen.

"Turn up the radio, Paddy," said his wife. "They've just mentioned something about Ellis Enterprise."

By the time he'd wheeled himself to the radio, the news reporter had already moved on to a different topic.

"Take a look through the paper and see if there's anything mentioned there," his wife persisted, adding a drop of milk and some sugar to her porridge before beginning to spoon it into her mouth.

Paddy spread the tabloid open on the table, obeying her command, knowing better than to cross her when her stress levels were as high as they were now.

When Ariel had finally walked through the door the previous night, his wife's blood pressure had been elevated off the scale in Paddy's opinion. He'd had to take the phone from her hand on a few occasions to stop her reporting Ariel missing and though he daren't let on, Paddy was every bit as concerned about his wife's wellbeing as that of his daughter!

"Did you ask Ariel who was ringing her phone late last night?" his wife asked.

"No, I did not! She's not a baby any more! If she wanted to tell me, she would have!"

"I'm glad she's back at work today. She's safer there.

She left extremely early though. I hope there's nothing else wrong."

"Come on, you're overreacting," he said soothingly. "She's been out of work for two days. She probably has a lot of stuff to catch up on."

His wife remained tight-lipped.

Paddy reached a hand out for hers, noticing the wobble in her lower lip, recognising her fear and anxiety and wishing he could wave a wand and make their troubles disappear. But if that were possible, he'd be up on his feet by now. He wouldn't be sitting in a chair paralysed from the hips down.

"Ryan will come through for us, love. Try not to worry. You're making yourself ill."

"What if he doesn't ring, Paddy? What if he's forgotten us?"

Paddy shook his head in denial, refusing to even consider that possibility. "It's your birthday. He'll ring."

With his free hand, he reached out and lit the red candle standing at the centre of the table. Now all they could do was sit and wait.

"What are they doing in there?" Ariel whispered to Marcus.

"Checking for evidence, I'd imagine. Probably hoping to uncover something that will help them trace her movements last night."

They stood leaning against the reception desk, their offices out of bounds until the Gardaí had finished their search.

Ben strolled towards them, his face pinched and drawn. "They want to set up an interview room. To have a word with all of you about when you last saw Vicky. My office is probably the best. It's not like there's any work going on there anyway."

He walked away from them again. Though they'd all shown up for work it was far from business as usual and while Ben was tempted to lock the doors and send them all home until after the funeral, he felt his staff were getting some consolation from sticking to routine and being in each other's company.

Ariel and Marcus stared after him, lost in their thoughts.

"He's in shock like the rest of us," Marcus sighed, putting a hand on her arm. "He was her mentor. They worked alongside each other for over ten years."

She let out a long sigh. "More than a third of her life."

"Why did you keep this information to yourself, Ariel?"

Once the news had broken, she'd admitted openly that she'd already been questioned.

She stared into the distance and exhaled slowly. "I couldn't get the words out. I did try. But I couldn't."

"Would you not be better off at home? It's worse for you than any of us."

She shrugged her shoulders. "I can't sit around my parents' house being wrapped in cotton wool. When my mother hears this, she'll go berserk."

"Can't say I blame her!"

"The flat is still sealed off by the Gardaí – not, I might add, that I'm ever setting a foot in that building again. In my head, all I can see is the outline of her body drawn on the floor . . ." she whispered, her voice trailing off, her eyes misting over.

"I always thought these things only happened to other people."

"What if whoever did this was actually looking for me, Marcus? I keep thinking I must have been the target. To the day I die, I'll wonder what the hell she was doing there in the first place. I never even told her where I lived!"

She'd have to tell the Gardaí about the threats she'd been receiving. She'd known that from the outset, from the moment she'd received the call from Detective Superintendent Karl Wilson instructing her to come into the station for questioning.

Sneaking out of the house as quickly as possible, her heart pounding in her chest, her mind in a quandary, she'd fully expected it to be in connection with the embezzlement case, totally unprepared for what was facing her.

But her interview had turned into a preliminary questioning and at that had been cut short when Karl Wilson had been called away. The opportunity to inform him she was being blackmailed hadn't presented itself. Instead she was asked to make a statement about her movements the previous evening. She omitted her reasons for moving out of Number 105, avoiding disclosing it for as long as she could. In coming clean with the Gardaí, she knew she'd also have to risk telling Ben the full extent of her previous employment history and she was dreading the prospect of doing that.

Ben's visible upset convinced her that today was not the day to divulge her deceit. Today was a day to grieve. But she would tell him. When the time was right. She respected him too much for him to hear it from anybody else.

Marcus rubbed his head with the palm of his hand, her proximity making him uneasy. More than anything he wanted to pull her into his arms and display the emotion he'd been fighting against for weeks, the emotion he'd been trying to shun. How lovely it would be to seek comfort from each other, to help each other through this horrific ordeal.

Now that he'd laid the ghost and threat of his daughter's natural parentage to rest and was happy to wait until Edel was ready to take the next step, he could think clearly again. He realised he'd allowed his imagination too much free rein. The woman standing beside him had no agenda where he was concerned and whatever was causing her efficiency to waver had nothing whatsoever to do with him.

Ben had laughed – the one moment of mirth they'd shared in the course of their intense conversation – when Marcus had suggested she might have.

Marcus could see now that he'd allowed paranoia to colour his judgement. And more importantly, he'd allowed his wife's rejection to shut down his ability to trust.

Now he attempted to ease Ariel's concerns. "I suppose she could have got your address on your personal file. I'd imagine she had access to all those details."

"Hmm. But why? Why, Marcus? She was found face down on the floor in my flat. What was her reason for being there? " Her face paled, deep-etched circles under her eyes.

He put both hands on her shoulders, forcing her to look at him. "It was a vicious attack on a young woman. The kind you hear announced on the news several times every month in this city now!" He lowered his voice a little, aware that Gardaí were hovering around the building and probably had them all down as suspects until the perpetrator was caught. "You don't honestly think Vicky was a target, do you? Or you for that matter? I think it was a case of wrong place at the wrong time."

Ariel shook her head.

"How's her husband coping?" Marcus went on. "Weren't they only married six months?"

"Yes, I suppose it's far too early for any funeral arrangements?"

"I heard on the radio the body will be released after the postmortem. I presume she'll be waked at home. Under the circumstances, I wouldn't be surprised if it was a private funeral."

"Imagine she's dead. Vicky is actually dead!" Ariel shuddered, unable to believe it was true.

"Her poor husband must be in a state of shock. How's he going to pick his life up after this? My heart goes out to him."

Watching his own wife walk away from him had been beyond his worst nightmare. But the difference was choice. She'd *chosen* to leave their marriage. In the case of Vicky's departure, a cold-blooded murderer had taken control of any choice she might have had.

"She was crazy about Fintan." Ariel remembered the way her face lit up every time she mentioned his name, how she defended him no matter what. "She had so many plans for their future."

"Did she have many friends?" Marcus had walked by Vicky's desk several times every day and now that she was dead and he wouldn't have the chance to stop and chat ever again, he realised he knew very little about her or the life she led.

"I honestly don't know. Will we make the effort and call to the house to pay our respects? It might help her husband and family if we let them know how much she meant to us, the important role she played in the company."

Marcus stared into the distance, watching along the corridor for a sign of movement. "We take each other for granted, Ariel, don't we? Here in the office, I mean. We breeze past each other, bounce ideas and figures around until we're ready to move on to the next bigger or better account. And then what?"

She stared at the man standing beside her, recognising a softer side to him that she hadn't noticed before, recognising a man who displayed a genuine interest in other human beings.

"And then we do it all over again, Marcus! Because

unfortunately life's like that. We don't realise what's important until it's too late sometimes. Until it has disappeared. Honesty and integrity the most important of all."

"I read the email you sent me last night," he blurted out, seizing the moment and taking a giant leap into whatever life without his wife had to offer.

She frowned in confusion. "My email? What email? I wasn't even online last night."

Marcus blushed, fiddling with the silver cufflinks on his shirtsleeves. He'd misread the signs. "Ah, nothing. Nothing. It doesn't matter now. Honestly."

But Ariel knew by the look of embarrassment and mortification on his face that it did matter. It mattered a lot. What email was he talking about? Had she sent him something by mistake? And what did he mean last night? She'd been too busy mopping floors to email anyone!

Ben's return disturbed her thoughts, prevented her from getting to the bottom of the matter there and then.

"They want a word with you first, Marcus. And Ariel, they want you to stick around too. They're anxious to talk to you again."

Marcus made his way to Ben's office. He had nothing to hide, yet a feeling of guilt swept over him as he went.

"Actually, Ariel, will you cancel any appointments you'd set up with clients this week? I'll tell the others to do the same."

"Sure. As soon as I can get into my office. And Ben,

that media event we had arranged for Thursday needs to be cancelled. Vicky posted the invites on Friday."

Ben nodded. "I'll deal with that. I'll give the event management company a call to let them know we're deferring it. I have the guest list on my desk, so I'll get that sorted."

He gave a half smile before heading towards the canteen, at a loss to know what to do or say. Nothing could have prepared him for this. If only there was something he could do to help. But what help could you offer a family who'd lost the most precious thing of all: a life?

Ariel went and sat at Vicky's desk, her heart aching as she looked at the few items beside the monitor: her calculator and desk diary, her pens and a ruler. And that was it.

Why? She wondered. Why, why, why had Vicky been murdered? And what on earth was she doing in my flat late at night?

As she looked at the date planner on Vicky's desk, she noticed the date: Tuesday 5th December. Oh God, she thought, it's Mam's birthday and Ryan's supposed to call today.

Chapter 45

"Can I get you anything?" Ben felt sorry for Karl Wilson, the Detective Superintendent who'd been interviewing his staff in turn for the last couple of hours. His was the final interview.

"No, thanks, Ben. You've been extremely co-operative as it is."

"Do you have a definite line of enquiry?"

"We're investigating everything, leaving no stone unturned. At the moment we're still trying to piece together her movements in the few hours before her death. Can you think of anything, no matter how small or unusual, you feel might be helpful? Was she acting anyway different yesterday? Any lates or absences worth noticing? Out of character behaviour? Her work? Any changes there?"

Ben closed his eyes and thought about all the questions. He tried to remember the day before.

He'd been totally preoccupied with Marcus and Edel and could barely remember the events of the previous day, vaguely recalling having a few words with her before she'd left for the night. He mentally retraced his steps, thinking back to Monday morning and any interaction he'd had with her. And then something dawned on him, a fact that had completely slipped his mind until that very moment, something that might be well worth mentioning.

"There is something. Her neighbour – Simon something or other – she was to drop an envelope off to him on her way home. Have you spoken to her neighbours yet? I wonder if she made it to his house?"

"One of my colleagues is doing house-to-house calls but he's finding it difficult to get people in this early in the day. You don't have his number by any chance? Or can you tell me what it was in connection with?"

Ben opened his desk drawer and took out a gold-embossed card. "Here it is. Simon Guilfoyle. He's involved in a charity organisation fund-raising for under-privileged children. Vicky asked me to have a word with him about sponsorship."

"And did you?"

"I spoke to him on the phone yesterday morning. Vicky put the call through, to be honest. We chatted for a few minutes and he emailed me a Garda clearance form. I filled one out myself and gave copies to Vicky to distribute to the other staff. She said she'd get them completed and drop them into him yesterday evening."

"And you haven't heard from him since?"

Ben shook his head. "You know how long some of these red-tape things can take. I didn't expect to hear for a while. And Ariel was missing so Vicky probably wouldn't have had hers in the bundle."

"I'll give that Simon guy a quick call before I leave here and see if he saw her."

"At least it might pinpoint if she even went home yesterday."

"I think we've spoken to everyone by now. Our IT guys will be in later to take a look at Vicky's computer, monitor any activity over the last few days. That won't be a problem, will it?"

Ben shook his head, pain crossing his face. "Not at all. Do whatever you need, anything at all you feel will help find the monster who did this and get him behind bars. Vicky was my eyes and ears. She kept both this place and me going. I only wish I'd thought to tell her that more often, instead of taking it for granted she'd be sitting outside my door for a good many years yet."

Karl Wilson listened without sympathising, preferring to keep a professional distance. "That's almost it then. Are there any other staff I need to see?"

"Unless you want to speak to the other security guard – the one who was on duty last night?"

Karl Wilson thought for a moment. "Would his path have crossed with Vicky's yesterday?"

"A few minutes morning and evening, I suppose. Pete was on duty Sunday and last night so she probably would have bumped into him. Vicky had a word for everybody, took the time to stop and talk."

"I might come back when he's on duty so. Thanks again, Ben."

With that, Karl's phone rang and he was distracted once more. On with the job.

"Is it him?" Paddy asked his wife for the second time, his voice rising with impatience. She'd moved to the far side of the kitchen with the phone and he couldn't distinguish if it was Ryan or not.

She turned and faced her husband, tears in her eyes, a gigantic smile on her face. "Yes. It's him and he'd be delighted to talk to you."

Paddy held his hand out for the phone.

"How've you been keeping, son?" he began warmly, his eyes resting on Vicky Jones' photo on the *Evening Herald*'s front page. *A tragic loss for her heartbroken husband and parents,* he read, and decided enough time had been lost with his own son.

"Get a flight home, son. You've been away long enough."

"Still telling me what to do, Da?" was the response he got from the other end.

There'll be time enough to tell him about the court case when he comes home, Paddy decided, preferring to get him onto home ground before landing such a huge thing on him.

"I'll be seventy in a couple of weeks' time. I could do with a bit of help to blow out the candles."

Five years of sorrow and bitterness fell away, acceptance and forgiveness filling the breach left behind in its wake.

Ryan blew his nose on the other end of the line.

Paddy was grinning from ear to ear, delighted the childhood memory had evoked an emotional response.

"I'll be there, Dad. Order the biggest cake in Dublin!"

"Dad!" Edel shouted into her mobile, the signal in Enniskerry unreliable. "Dad, are you okay? I heard about the murder. It's the most awful news! Did you know her?"

"Don't worry about me, pet. I'll be fine. And, yes, I knew her. She was a truly lovely individual."

"Dad, I'll come home and stay with you if you want? Dad, did you hear what I said? Is the signal gone? Can you hear me? Dad!"

The signal was perfect. Her words were like music to his ears. His little girl was coming home.

"Do you want me to collect you?"

"Yeah, please. And Dad?"

"Yes, Edel?"

"Do you still have broadband?"

Despite the dreadful sadness surrounding him in the office building, Marcus couldn't but smile. Some things, thank God, would never change!

"I have you scheduled for two thirty on Friday." Ariel called the time and date from her scheduler back to her client.

That was the second call she was making to clear her diary for the week. Both of her clients had disagreed with the appointment schedule they were pencilled in for, contradicting the meeting times, dates and locations

Ariel had documented. But, thankfully, she'd reached them before their appointed time.

"I'll give you a call next week and we can set up another meeting."

Replacing the receiver carefully, she checked through her list to see what other clients she needed to call. And this time, she thought, I'm not going into time and date detail because as true as God, I'll bring in a ghostbuster if I find any more inexplicable cock-ups!

Chapter 46

Wednesday morning

Pete Scavo hovered in the hallway of his home, an inexplicable force preventing his arm from reaching up and opening the front door. He'd been standing there, unable to move, for over half an hour, the dreadful thing he'd done at Military House two days previously weighing heavily on his mind.

It hadn't been his turn to work on Tuesday night, his trip to the shop for the evening paper and milk being his only outing for the day or evening.

As usual, he gave a glance at the front page while he waited to pay, the stark headline shocking him, forcing him to grab the edge of a shelf. Using the counter as support, he shook the newspaper out and re-read the headline.

The body of a woman discovered last night when Gardaí were called to an apartment complex in a North Co Dublin suburb has been identified as that of a twenty-eight-year-old employee with Ellis Enterprise.

He'd left the shop without the carton of milk he'd paid for, craving the safety and privacy of home, his newspaper clutched tightly in his hand, the front page turned inward so he didn't have to look. He mumbled indecipherably under his breath, his words becoming jumbled with the short rasping breaths leaving his body. His front door came into view, the loneliness waiting for him on the other side inflating like a balloon, a balloon on the verge of bursting.

Pete unwrapped his scarf from his neck and tossed it onto the banister alongside his coat, the newspaper still clutched in his hand. Leaving it folded, he went straight to the metal filing cabinet in the garage and filed it away as old news. He didn't need to spread the paper open on the table and scan through every line. He already knew the details. He already knew what today's news was.

The fridge was practically empty, the milk carton discarded in the overflowing bin. He'd forgotten to put it out for collection. Again.

"No milk, puss," he sighed, shaking his head at the cat, having little choice but to drink black tea, the absence of milk reminding him of the putrid coffee Ariel had given him. He took ten scraps of newspaper from the top pocket of his jacket. Arranging them chronologically as three sides of a square on the kitchen table, the scanty detail of Ariel's case set out before him, he traced a trail with his finger around the space still waiting to be filled: the result.

But Ariel would be his last one, he decided, and only for his dear friend in Mountjoy Garda Station he doubted very much he'd be able to pursue her case either. He really was getting too old for this. It was time he took his retirement seriously.

On Wednesday afternoon, Fintan stared into his wife's coffin, the bruises on her forehead and face obliterated by expert make-up appliance, the results of the post-mortem prominent in his mind. Staring and staring until his vision blurred, he convinced himself she had opened her eyes and smiled up at him. All in his imagination, of course. She was stone cold. She was dead. What were those words he'd been told? *Head injuries consistent with a sharp blow to the head.*

Nodding his head to the many expressions of condolence he'd received over the course of the last two days, he barely acknowledged people as they passed through his home, some bringing casseroles and sand-wiches as their way of showing support. Already there was enough food on his kitchen table to feed an army. And no doubt there would be more to come, he realised, scratching the heavy growth on his chin, trying to concentrate on what the undertaker was saying to him.

"Is there anyone else you'd like us to contact? Any other instructions you want us to carry out?"

But Fintan was in a world of his own, the undertaker's words lost on him, remorse and regret welling up inside him.

Cream satin lining and a walnut coffin: the only two details floating around in Fintan's mind.

When they'd been choosing their kitchen units, she'd

been adamant that walnut was the best, singing its praises, selling it to Fintan on the basis of hard-wearing and long-lasting.

And when he'd stood in a room surrounded by coffins and caskets, samples made up in an array of shapes and sizes, he'd felt drawn to the walnut one standing on its edge in the corner of the room, knowing instinctively it was the one she'd have chosen for herself.

His heart weighed a ton, the buzz of hushed conversation wafting through the house an annoyance he could have done without, the intimacy and privacy he'd shared there with Vicky swallowed in the melée of people passing through. He knew they meant well, hovering around, helping themselves to tea and coffee, pretending they'd known Vicky a lot better than they had, showing an interest for the sake of finding out what was going on.

How he wished their words could bring Vicky back to him. How he wished he didn't feel so guilty. Or responsible. How he wished he could take a step back in time.

He reached into the coffin and caught her hand in his, remembering with regret the last time he'd spoken to her. Tears slipped down his cheeks. Why didn't I try harder to explain, he wondered? If only she'd told me how she was feeling, what she was thinking. If only, if only. So many questions he'd never find answers for, the main one being what she was doing in Fairview so late that night. And on her own.

He'd been questioned already, taken down to the Garda Station moments after they'd knocked on the door to deliver the devastating news that his wife had been found dead in suspicious circumstances. The details were sketchy in his mind, shock eliminating the actual facts, but he knew Detective Wilson would be back after the funeral. He knew they weren't finished with him yet.

Admitting he'd been staying in the Travel Lodge had been embarrassing. Proving he'd been home that evening had been difficult. Unless of course they'd looked at the hotel CCTV as he'd suggested and caught him on camera dropping off his key. But he'd watched enough detective TV shows to know that didn't offer him an alibi.

As they'd fired questions at him, he'd been too shocked and numb to think straight, not caring if he ended up behind bars for a crime he hadn't committed, the life he had before him, a life without Vicky, already stretching ahead like a lengthy prison sentence. To him, nothing mattered any more: not the debt he'd been so concerned about, not the job he'd considered his security, not his family . . .

"Fintan, we came as soon as we could."

He didn't need to turn around. He'd recognise their posh accents anywhere.

"A bit late now," he muttered, ensuring they were the only ones who heard his response. "She's not exactly up to visitors today. Not looking her best for you."

He heard the sharp intake of breath behind him. Instinct made him clutch his dead wife's hand tightly in his, attempting to protect her even now, his most important duty as her husband, the duty he'd neglected in recent weeks.

"We understand you're grieving, Fintan, but don't

you think we are too? We've just lost our daughter. How have you got it in your heart to be so cruel?"

Fintan half-turned to look at the wealthy pair standing beside him, taking in their stony expressions, dry eyes, pursed lips. Not a sign of emotion, their supposed despair impossible to recognise. He found it impossible to hold back, no longer having a reason to remain polite.

"You lost your daughter a long time ago. Correction: you cast her aside! You let what should have been the most important person in your lives slip through your fingers."

"Now look here, we gave you space. Victoria wanted it that way."

"All Vicky ever wanted was to be loved," Fintan informed them sadly, casting a net of responsibility over those who had let her down, including himself in that minority group.

Vicky's mother stood ramrod straight, never once reaching out to touch her daughter or kiss her waxen cheek, her husband's hand protectively in the small of her back.

"We rushed back from the Maldives as soon as we heard. My wife is distraught and jet-lagged. We need to pull together now, Fintan. Be there for her final journey. Let others see a united front."

Fintan swallowed the retort that jumped to his lips, his gaze lingering on his wife's corpse, his in-laws' concern about the outside world and what they might think bringing bile to his throat. Vicky had spent a lifetime struggling to be noticed by her parents, always wondering where she fell short, never in a month of Sundays guessing her death would bring them running.

At least your death hasn't been in vain, my love, he whispered silently. They have finally come through for you. I won't stand in their way.

Letting go of her hand, he stepped back slightly, encouraging her parents to move a little nearer and talk to her.

"We'll pay for her funeral, of course," said her father. "And we'd like her to be buried in the family plot." Vicky's father took the lead, followed in close succession by his wife, neither of them laying a finger on their daughter's body.

"Of course, there'll be room for you there too, Fintan, when the time comes," his wife added.

Fintan brought his hands to his face, closing his eyes, expecting to wake up from the nightmare any moment. They are some piece of work, he thought. Cold as ice. Nothing in the world like their daughter. He inhaled deeply before breaking his news.

"No, thanks, all the same. Vicky's wish was to be cremated and have her ashes spread from Howth Head, some of them flying into the sea and more of them landing on the rough grass. Her wish was to be free after death." As she wasn't in life, he added silently.

She'd joked about it the day he'd proposed. It had been the nearest they'd ever got to discussing burial wishes. But the fact she'd mentioned it at all was good enough for him. Her wishes would be followed in detail, the fact he'd be irritating her parents into the bargain simply an added bonus.

"Did Superintendent Wilson get to you yet?" Fintan

asked his mother-in-law, ignoring their outraged faces. "He's going to want a word."

"We're literally off the plane. But I've no doubt they'll get to us. If I don't get to them first. I want to know everything about her murder. Everything!"

Fintan didn't like the look his father-in-law was giving him.

"You don't honestly think I did it, do you?" Typical, he thought, blame the husband.

Vicky's father held his gaze, her mother's eyes avoiding it, straying to her daughter's coffin instead.

"Vicky was the love of my life," he told them, his hands shaking as he reached out to touch his wife's face. "She was the best thing that ever happened to me. We were happy together. Nobody can ever change that. And so help me God, if the Gardaí don't do their job and find whoever did this to her, I won't rest until justice is served!"

As they recognised raw emotion in his words, his pain and stark loss engrained in his face, Vicky's parents had the grace to look ashamed. And in that shame lay a well-hidden level of emotion for their daughter (a love they had never taken the time to display), a level of emotion that could have made a huge difference to the adult she'd grown into, to the insecurity she'd dragged around on her shoulders throughout her short life.

Chapter 47

"Can I go over the results of our technology check, Ben?"

Karl Wilson had returned to Ellis Enterprise again that afternoon, a lengthy report with him.

"Certainly." Ben been in the building from early that morning. He'd given everybody else the rest of the week off. He was exhausted but refused to go home, feeling his place was to be in the building and on hand for those who needed him..

"Were any of the staff on overtime this weekend or late at night?"

Ben shook his head. "I was last to leave on Friday, was probably here till half six."

"And Monday?"

"You'd have to ask Pete, the security guard. He was in early that evening. There were still a few here when I left."

"Our computer guys have located some late activity on two of your computers. And calls were made to a taxi company from the main desk shortly before ten o'clock."

Ben frowned. He'd like to have had the chance to investigate that himself. "Pete should be in shortly. He might be able to enlighten us, especially about the calls."

"The computer network is protected by password. Am I right?"

Ben nodded.

"So as it stands, staff can only access the data using their own computer?"

"That's about the size of it all right."

"And nobody has the administrator password?"

Ben thought for a minute. "Vicky had access. She had a bypassing code or something, not something we ever needed to use to be honest. But she wouldn't have had any reason to work late."

Karl closed his eyes a moment and thought about the findings his colleagues had come up with, deciding to analyse them further before releasing the information into the public domain.

"Do you have Pete's address by any chance? I want to tie as much of this up as I can before I go off duty. It would be handier to call to his house rather than traipsing all the way up here again tonight."

"I'll get it for you now. And Pete's one of your own. He'll be delighted to help."

Karl Wilson had been investigating murders for quite some time. He'd become adept, in so far as was possible, at reading expressions. And in his expert opinion, Fintan was neither a cheat nor a murderer. But his opinion wasn't enough. The murderer was still at large and Karl was too much of a professional to rely on instinct alone. And for that reason he wasn't finished questioning Fintan Jones yet, despite the fact his fingerprints had not been found at the scene.

"I know this is hard for you, Fintan," Karl sympathised, "but we're still trying to piece your wife's movements together. And I'd really like to speak to your mother again too."

Fintan sank into the chair, prepared for yet another gruelling. "She'll be at the house later for the funeral if you want to talk to her then." Who'd have thought his mother would be defending him? What a turnaround!

"We've been through your telephone records. The last calls made were to a cab company."

"My parents were visiting on Saturday. Vicky ordered a cab to take them home."

"But wasn't that the same night you didn't return home?" He flipped the pages of his notebook, checking his notes. "And didn't you tell me already that you drove your two nephews to Rathcoole?"

"Yes. That's correct."

"And would it not have made sense for you to take your parents too?"

"We had an argument. My father and I don't get on very well."

"Okay. And there was a call to Sutton Lawn Tennis Club?"

Fintan shrugged. Vicky didn't have any interest in tennis that he knew of.

He shook his head sadly. There were so many things he was finding out about Vicky. Things he'd never known about her. Her frame of mind was his main concern. Why would she have called a tennis club? Was she thinking of joining up? "I'm sorry. This is all news to me. And I wasn't at home for most of Saturday."

Karl read from Fintan's statement. "You drove around Malahide and then you called into the park to watch a game? After that you returned to the village and sat in the people's park to clear your head?"

Fintan nodded.

"Do you make a habit of loitering around on a Saturday?"

"No, Detective."

Karl's eyes were still on the statement. "Your employer. He says this weekend was the first time you ever called in sick? Pretty coincidental, don't you think?"

Fintan pushed his shoulders back. "I told you. I'd had an argument with my father. And there was –"

But again Karl Wilson moved the subject on without warning. "Your mobile phone, Fintan. Many of the calls are from the same number – short, snappy calls judging by the length of time you were connected. Can you explain these?"

He nodded again. He didn't care any more. He didn't care who knew what a wimp he was. "A moneylender. A loan shark."

Karl frowned, his brow wrinkling in concentration,

motive jumping into his head immediately. Life Assurance to clear Fintan's debts. "How much do you owe?"

"I don't owe anything. I wouldn't go near someone like him, no matter how badly off I was."

"So explain why you've been getting calls – what look like pestering calls at that – from someone like that?"

"Because of my brother."

"Speak up, Fintan," Karl said, two motives vying for space in his head at this stage. Life Assurance being the most obvious, followed closely by a loan protection policy.

"My brother George begged me for help. He has a young family. He'd got himself into debt, serious debt –"

"And your wife knew about this?" Karl cut in quickly.

"No. I didn't want to burden her. I thought I could handle it alone. And I was kind of ashamed of my brother too. Hell, I've spent most of my life ashamed of my whole family!"

"So you thought you'd kill your wife, lie low for a while and then collect your dividends?"

Fintan stood up. "No way on earth!"

"Sit down, Mr. Jones."

The distraught widower obeyed.

"Where did you get the money?"

"Credit Union."

"Was it a joint account?"

"Yes."

"Whose name is on top?"

383

"Excuse me?"

"Names! Whose name – yours or Vicky's – was the first name on the account?"

"I don't know." Fintan broke out in a cold sweat. The interview wasn't going well. He was being put in the frame for murder.

"What Credit Union are you with? The local one?"

He nodded, wiping his hands on his jeans. "I didn't do it. You have to believe me."

Karl stood up. "Pull yourself together and go home to attend to your wife's funeral."

He left.

Fintan felt the room begin to spin, the ceiling coming down on top of him, the net of insecurity he'd thought he'd escaped years before returning with a vengeance. He put his head in his hands and wept.

Pete ignored the doorbell. He didn't want to talk to anybody. Instead he sat at the table, staring into space, waiting for the time to come when he'd begin his journey to work for the evening. The pieces of newspaper were still on the table, one side of his square still waiting to be completed.

Chapter 48

Thursday

"Bloody rain!" Ariel muttered under her breath, holding the umbrella over her head and trying to see if she recognised anybody in the melée of people around her. Battling against the gusting winds that threatened to sweep the umbrella from her hands, she queued to get inside the church in Malahide.

As with the majority of tragic funerals, family, friends and neighbours had come out in droves to attend Vicky's last farewell. Garda presence – though the officers were doing their best to remain discreet – was palpable. An air of tension lingered among the congregation, most of them believing an arrest would take place immediately after the ceremony.

Rumour circulated through the community and beyond, each with its own suspect and motive in mind, all without proof.

Finally, moving inside the building, Ariel closed her

umbrella and squashed her way through the crowds to get past the main doors, relieved to be in the main body of the church. Every seat was packed to capacity, the crowd standing at the back spilling into the porch and outside.

Such a young woman, a woman with her whole life before her, a gentle, caring person who had never cast a bad word or deed were some of the sentiments floating around Ariel, the premature timing of Vicky's death a mystery to all. All except one person, one person who'd stood by and watched her drop to the floor, one person whose head was bent in prayer as the strains of 'Amazing Grace' filtered through the church.

Ariel was relieved to notice others slipping out of the church before the funeral procession came down the aisle. It made it easier for her to leave too. Feeling a hand on her shoulder as she made her way out the gate, she turned around expecting to see either Marcus or Ben, her jaw dropping open when a burly Garda in plain clothes discreetly flashed his badge and asked her to accompany him to the station.

"But why? I've already been interviewed. Twice."

"We're hoping you'll be able to help us further with our enquiries."

"How well do you know Mr Jones, Ariel?"

"Last night was my first time to ever meet Fintan." Ariel sat at the edge of the chair, her hands clutched together on her lap.

"And you weren't conducting a relationship with him?"

"Absolutely not! Why would you say that?"

Ariel gripped the edge of the table, fury emanating from every pore in her body, yet for no apparent reason there was a sense of foreboding lurking deep within.

When she'd introduced herself to Fintan the evening before, he'd taken one look at her and shouted at her to get out of the house.

"But what have I done?" Staring at the distraught man in front of her, she couldn't make any sense of his outrageous reaction.

Fintan's bloodshot eyes flashed angrily at her. "Just get out of my house. I don't ever want to see you again."

Luckily there wasn't anybody else in the room at the time so at least she'd been saved any further embarrassment. All she could do was put his outburst down to grief. But the more she looked at him, the more she felt she'd seen him somewhere before. And now she was being accused of having a relationship with him? What on earth could Vicky have told him about me, she wondered. Why did he flip like that?

"Having an affair isn't a crime, Ariel. For the purpose of the case, it's best if you tell the truth. We'll find out anyway."

"But I am telling you the truth!"

"Just like you told Ben Ellis the truth about the embezzlement case? That kind of truth."

Ariel opened her mouth and then shut it again.

"Ariel?"

"I needed a job. If I'd told him I was up on trial, he wouldn't have employed me. Nobody would."

"So you faked your reference?"

"No. I did not. My previous employer adopted an 'innocent until proven guilty' approach. Deep down, I think he believes I had nothing to do with fraud but his hands were tied and he had no choice but let me go."

"It's still dishonest," Karl insisted. "Lying by omission. You were hired under false pretences, young lady."

Ariel nodded. "Maybe so. But I was being blackmailed. I had no choice. And I've worked my arse off for Ellis Enterprise."

The Guard sat back in his chair and sucked on the end of his pen for a moment. "And why didn't you report this blackmail case? The Gardaí could have helped. Or is there other information on top of the affair and embezzlement that you're withholding from us?"

Tears welled in Ariel's eyes. I'm being set up, she thought. Somebody is setting me up.

He shook a tissue box in front of her.

Ariel cleaned her face with the heel of her hand. "No, thank you." She'd tell him the truth. Every single bit. And then let him judge if she was involved in Vicky's death or not. And if he still felt the Gardaí could help her, she'd be only too glad to accept his offer.

"Can you remind me where you were on Monday night last between the hours of six and twelve?"

She sighed but didn't flinch. "As I've told you already, I was in my mother's house first and then I called over to the flat to collect my briefcase. When I got there I noticed I'd left the tap on and the floor was covered in water."

"Did anybody see you there, Ariel?"

"Yes. I borrowed a mop and bucket from the doorman. And I gave it back on my way out of the building."

"And while you were in the flat?"

"No. I didn't see anybody."

"One of the other residents stated there was very loud music coming from your flat that night. Was that to cover up any arguing or screaming by any chance?"

"Will you please believe me? I was there on my own," she insisted, remembering mopping the floor to the strains of 'With or Without You'.

"And Fintan? How long have you two been an item? You might as well admit it, Ariel."

She held her resolve, kept her tone even, terrified her behaviour would get her into more trouble than she was in already. "We're not an item, Guard."

"A casual fling then?"

She shook her head in denial.

"And Marcus? Your work colleague? Is he your next protégé?"

"Excuse me? Where are you going with all this? That's defamation of character. I think I should have my solicitor present."

"That's your prerogative. Do you want to call him or her?"

Ariel thought for a moment but shook her head. How could she possibly pay for a solicitor? "Why are you accusing me wrongly?"

"There was a pretty suggestive email sent from your office computer to Marcus's on Monday night last, only a couple of hours before Vicky's body was found."

She recalled the comment Marcus had made about an email. Too much of a coincidence in her eyes. "Can you check if somebody else accessed my computer that night, please? Can you do that? I wasn't even in the office on Monday so I couldn't have sent it."

He ignored her request and her explanation, continuing instead with questions of his own.

"What would you say if I told you that Vicky saw you and Fintan together? That she shared that information with a close family member?"

This revelation shocked her, left her speechless. "But I was never with him. I don't even know the man. And how can you think I'd be capable of murder?"

"You had motive . . . get the wife out of the picture. Or maybe she called to tell you she knew and you didn't want your sordid secret getting out and ruining your reputation! A reputation that's already hanging on by a thread."

Ariel stared at him, the church bell tolling mournfully in the distance. "I was not having an affair with Fintan."

"Vicky saw you together in the club where he works. Now are you going to tell me the truth?"

This time she gripped the sides of the plastic chair she was sitting on. "What club does he work in?"

"The Manhattan. You know it?"

Ariel nodded. She'd been there once. A night she would never forget. What happened that night unfolded in her head. She remembered why Fintan had seemed familiar.

"I was there one night. And now I do remember seeing him there."

Her interviewer sat back in victory. "Convenient."

"The guy who's blackmailing me verbally assaulted me at the bar. I was really upset. I was scared. The barman – Vicky's husband – came out from behind the bar and moved him on, told him not to be annoying customers or he'd be chucked out."

"Chivalrous of him."

His sarcasm wasn't lost on Ariel.

"I was in bits by that time. Couldn't pull myself together. Fintan allowed me to spend some time in the office until I calmed down and that guy was long gone. He was really kind to me. After that I left and I've never set foot in there again. And never will."

"We'll check your story against CCTV. You wouldn't happen to know the date by any chance?"

"It was around a month ago."

"You've a good memory." The Guard was surprised. He'd expected her to deny it, brush his question away vaguely.

"The blackmailer was pestering me for a cash payment at the time. I ended up paying him a week later. I can get exact details from my bank account. That incident happened exactly a week before I withdrew the cash."

"Did you hand it over?"

She nodded. "I had no choice! At least it got him off my back for a while."

His tone changed at that point, his interviewing less aggressive.

"We'll get back to all that again. Do you want to tell me about the embezzlement case and why you're being blackmailed."

Ariel sighed and relented. At this point, she had everything to gain. It wasn't as if things could get much worse.

Putting her best foot forward, she gave as much detail as possible, leaving nothing out, not even the part about Ryan and her father, ending on as positive a note as she could muster.

"I didn't kill anybody. I don't know why Vicky was in my flat. I didn't even know she knew where I lived."

"Interview complete," the Guard recorded into his tape. "Ariel, don't go too far away. We may need to speak to you again. And I'll take the name and contact details of that guy who's been hassling you. It mightn't be any harm to have a word with him."

Ariel cried with relief once she was outside the Garda Station, the strong easterly gusts a welcome change from the airless room she'd been sitting in for the past forty-five minutes. She needed to talk to somebody. But who? Her parents were concerned enough as it was, so she didn't want to burden them. She stood on the side of the road, waiting for the funeral procession to pass her by, the details of her interview spinning round in her head, one ridiculous accusation coming to mind: Marcus. She'd have to talk to Marcus and find out what the hell they'd found on his computer. What the hell were they basing their assumptions on? Their notion that she was coming on to him?

A long trail of funeral cars made their way slowly from Malahide to Glasnevin crematorium, the route selected carefully to avoid passing by Military House. From Glasnevin, the funeral entourage would make their way to Deerpark Hotel in Howth to celebrate Vicky's memory.

Ben Ellis had approached Fintan with the suggestion. He had been on the verge of cancelling the reservation for the publicity event when the idea had dawned on him.

"Why don't you accept the hotel booking as a gesture from Ellis Enterprise, Fintan?"

"I couldn't, Ben. Honestly. Thanks anyway but you know how independent Vicky was. She hated taking anything without paying."

"She's earned this, Fintan. Please accept it. The location is perfect for your friends and family."

Rather than put up a fight, Fintan had shaken Ben's hand and accepted his offer. Little had he thought when he'd held Vicky's hand and cut the wedding cake in the main dining hall of the Deerpark Hotel six months before that he'd be back there on his 29th birthday to pay homage to his dead wife.

And while Fintan stared out the window of the funeral car, oblivious to the heavy afternoon traffic as he struggled to come to terms with shock and grief, he imagined Vicky's spirit floating high in the sky overhead, a wide beaming smile on her face, her soul filled with peace and contentment.

"You just caught me, Ariel. I was on my way out with Edel. What's up?"

"I really need to see you, Marcus. Can you spare me ten minutes?"

Marcus looked at Edel who was totally engrossed in the music channel. "I'm sure I can manage that," he said. "Why don't you call over here?"

"What's your address? I'll get a cab straight away."

While he was waiting for Ariel to arrive, he couldn't resist nipping into the bathroom and freshening himself up, spraying himself liberally with deodorant before putting on a fresh black tee shirt and jeans.

"Dad, you stink!" Edel commented. "I won't be able to taste my dinner with the smell of that stuff!"

"About that, do you mind if we wait a while. Ariel from work is calling for a few minutes."

"Ooh! Is that who's responsible for all that aftershave!"

He turned away from her to hide his red face, his heart rate picking up slightly when the doorbell rang.

"Want me to get it, Dad?" Edel sniggered but never moved from the armchair.

"Behave," he laughed, and went to let Ariel in.

"I'm so sorry about this, Marcus. But I have to ask you something."

"Come in at least," he offered.

When they were both sitting at the kitchen table and

394

he'd placed a cup of coffee in front of her, she finally got to the point.

"Karl Wilson – you know that Guard who's been interviewing us?"

Marcus nodded.

"Well, he seems to think I sent you a suggestive email." She sipped her coffee, refusing to meet his eye. Despite her embarrassment, she had to know what she was dealing with.

Marcus cleared his throat, pulling at the neck of his tee shirt, feeling very hot all of a sudden. "I did get an unusual email from you. It was in my account on Tuesday morning."

"But I wasn't anywhere near my email on Monday. What time was on it?"

"Around ten o'clock at night, I think. It's still on my system. I'll forward it to you."

Ariel inhaled and exhaled. "I didn't send that, Marcus. Somebody obviously has been accessing my computer. And I'm thinking that might also account for the stupid mistakes on my account."

"You think? But how? I don't get it."

"I have to ring Ben straight away. Oh shit," something else just dawned on her, "that's why my appointments were all mixed up too."

"Do you think there's some connection with Vicky and what happened? Do you think she was responsible?"

"Jeez, I don't know. Why would she?" She banged her cup on the table, a lot harder than she'd intended, milky coffee slopping on the black ash surface. She got

395

up from her seat, a rush of heat flooding through her. She stared at Marcus. Should she tell him what she thought? And if she did, would he believe her innocence?

"Ariel? What is it?"

"Karl Wilson told me that Vicky had got it into her head that . . ." she left it hanging for a moment, the idea absurd.

"What, Ariel?"

"That Fintan and I were having an affair!"

"What! Were you?" He couldn't hold back the question.

"Of course not! I don't even know the guy. But if Vicky thought that was true . . . Look, I have to go. I have to talk to Ben. There has to be some way of finding out if my suspicions are right. Thanks a million, Marcus. I'll give you a call later – let you know how I get on."

Marcus stared after her as she ran out the door, her energy remaining in the house long after she'd left.

One day, he thought. One day, I'll actually get to ask her out.

Chapter 49

"Slow down, Ariel. I can't follow one word you're saying." Ben sighed heavily. He'd had an emotional day, Vicky's ceremony really taking it out of him. And Ariel wasn't exactly top of his popularity list. But now that the funeral was over, he couldn't put off confronting her and the information she'd been withholding any longer. He tried to follow her ramblings on the other end of the line.

"Don't you see, Ben? It could have been Vicky at my files and stuff."

Ben couldn't believe what Ariel was suggesting. And he couldn't be sure he could trust her any more. He'd known Vicky for years. It didn't make sense. None of it did.

"I'll call Karl Wilson straight away. It's better if he deals with all this. I'll see you in my office first thing in the morning."

Karl Wilson went through the files he'd gathered, checking the pathologist report and trying to find a link, any link at this stage. But there were too many gaps. The only prints they'd found in the flat had been Ariel's and Vicky's.

Tracking down Ariel Satlow's blackmailer had proved fruitless where Vicky's death was concerned, the lack of evidence making it impossible to link him with the crime. The bullying tactics he'd used on Ariel quickly dissolved, however, when Karl read him his rights and brought him in for questioning on suspicion of blackmail.

He'd relented immediately, long before they'd even reached the Garda Station, his phone records giving Karl all the proof he needed.

"So you were nowhere near number 105 Military House on Monday night last?" Karl repeated, his dislike for the suspect increasing by the minute.

"I've told you already, I was at home with the wife all night. Just like I told that other Garda."

Karl frowned. Nobody else had spoken to him that he'd been aware of. "What other Garda?"

"Some old fella from Mountjoy Station. Brown, I think he said his name is."

Karl made a note of the name and took a written statement from his suspect, calling one of the other officers on duty to take him to a cell and organise a court hearing.

"Karl Wilson here, Detective Superintendent from Clontarf. Is Sergeant Brown on duty today?"

He chewed the end of his pencil while he waited, flicking through his notebook and trying to decide what avenue to follow next. "Ah, Sergeant Brown. You're on. Good stuff. I've a guy in here on a blackmail charge. He says you were talking to him already."

There was a loud cough from the other end. "Eh, blackmail? What's the name? You know yourself, the memory's not what it used to be."

Karl called out the details.

"Yeah, I might have had a word all right."

"And how did he come to your attention," Karl enquired.

"An old friend of mine asked me to give him a bit of a warning. He was giving a friend of his a bit of bother."

Karl wasn't sure he understood where Brown was going with this. He'd been to plenty of seminars advising against just that. "What friend would this be, Serge?"

"Ah, he's retired now. You'd hardly know him. Pete Scavo. He was one of the best. Helped out plenty of good ones in his time."

Pete Scavo. Karl Wilson listened to the name and stared at it circled in his notebook. He'd got the information he needed from Brown. "Thanks for your help, Serge. If I can repay the favour any time . . ."

He was due to go off duty any minute but decided he'd stick it out a bit longer. At least long enough to meet Pete Scavo.

His phone rang again.

"Ben? Perfect timing. I'm on my way up to the office now. Is Pete Scavo on this evening? He's the only one I haven't managed to catch up with yet."

Chapter 50

Pete pulled his cap over his eyes and leaned back in his chair, unable to concentrate on Aston Villa and Everton who were playing on the telly, his crossword lying open untouched.

He'd been over and over things in his head, each day that passed blurring the line between reality and imagination, sleep being his only reprieve from the haunting image of Monday night.

"Pete? Are you awake in there?"

Ben's voice startled Pete, his defence mechanism rising to the fore as he tried to think up an excuse for yet again being caught napping on the job.

"I was just eh ..." But he stopped short when he stepped out of the office and realised Ben was not alone.

"Pete, this is Detective Superintendent Karl Wilson. He's leading Vicky's case and wants a word."

Pete swallowed hard. He's young to be a Super was his first thought as he took in the other man's youthful

appearance – full head of hair, not a grey one in sight –
and lean physique. Suddenly, he felt old. And beyond
fighting.

"Why don't you use my office, Karl? I'll keep an eye
on things here."

Wordlessly, Pete led the way, his limp more
pronounced when he was tired.

Ariel pulled her feet up under her and for the first time
in months settled down to read a book. Glancing at her
mother – who was setting up stitches on knitting needles,
the beginning of a jumper for Ryan – and her father who
was supposed to be watching a movie but who had
actually fallen asleep, she couldn't help smiling.

The promise of seeing Ryan in a few short weeks had
instilled renewed energy into the house and her parents.
While they weren't forgetting about the court case and
all it involved, they were encouraged by the belief that
the truth would win out in the end.

And meanwhile, Ariel decided, she had some truths
of her own to deal with: Ben being top of her list.

"So Vicky was here on Monday night? Working on
Ariel's computer? Is that a usual occurrence?"

Pete shifted in the chair, resting his hands on his
knees and staring at the floor. "No. There's never anybody
here in the evenings."

He knew the way these interviews worked. Karl
Wilson would circle and circle until finally he'd catch him
out. He'd trip him up, sneak a few leading questions and

before Pete knew it, he'd have him admitting to things he hadn't even done. For his own sake, Pete decided it would be best if he led the case himself.

"Ariel, Karl, she's the one you should be concerned about. She's the one who had real problems. She asked me for help." He looked up for a moment, his eyes bleary with exhaustion.

Karl sat back and let him talk. There would be plenty time for questions later. "I'm listening, Pete."

The security man frowned, struggling to concentrate and remember the facts as they'd happened. Reaching into his pocket, he pulled out his bundle of paper cuttings and spread them out on the table, shuffling them around until he'd arranged them properly.

Karl leaned forward to take a look.

"It's not finished, Karl. I'm hoping you'll fill the last side for me. I've taken it as far as I can."

"I was talking to Sergeant Brown, Pete. He says ye worked together once upon a time?"

Pete nodded wistfully. "I remember when he started as a rookie. He was on my watch. I taught him everything I know. Clever young man he was too."

Karl couldn't help smiling, understanding only too well the admiration 'rookies' developed for their very first mentor. "He says you asked him for a favour?"

Pete moved his hands to the arms of the chair. "A favour? I s'pose you could call it that. But nothing illegal, mind. Just asked him to give a fellow a bit of a fright. A fellow who deserves a lot more than a fright if you ask me."

Karl watched him carefully, the lifelessness in his voice concerning. "Any harm in asking why you stuck your neck out for Ariel?"

"Would you mind if I stand up and walk around? I stiffen up when I'm sitting too long."

Karl nodded. "Once you don't mind talking and walking at the same time."

Pete fixed his cap on his head. "Ariel confided in me. She was being intimidated. It wasn't right. Too many bullies getting away with things nowadays."

"What time did Vicky leave? Was she driving?"

Pete shook his head. "Taxi. Can't say for sure. I'd say she left around ten."

Karl stood up too, finding it difficult to control the interview while Pete was over the far side of the room. And he found it useful to watch expressions.

"Two taxis came up here that night, Pete. Do you know who the second one was for?"

"That would be me."

"But weren't you working?"

"First time ever I took an hour or so off."

"Was it an emergency?"

Pete stopped walking for a minute, his eyes straying to the dark sky. There were no stars out tonight. Not like Monday night. The sky had been sprinkled with bright clusters on Monday.

"No emergency?"

Pete looked at him in surprise and shook his head.

"But you still left?"

"I did. I followed Vicky to find out why she was

going to Ariel's. I had a hunch she was up to something."

"Pete, how did you know where Vicky was going?" Karl leaned against the wall, crossing his legs at his ankles and putting one hand in his pocket.

"I checked with the taxi firm of course." He looked expectantly at Karl, almost as if he was waiting for praise.

"And what happened when you got there? Were the girls in the flat?"

Pete stared straight ahead, the blurring lines disappearing, the events of Monday night crystal clear.

"Even though I left some time after her, my taxi made good time and Vicky had just entered the hallway when I arrived. I watched her step into the lift."

"Did she see you?"

"No. She had her back to me. I've worked in that building many times and I don't trust that lift. The stairs takes me a while now with the arthritis in my knee so I had to do something to slow her down. You understand, don't you?"

Karl nodded and waited, not wanting to interrupt Pete's flow.

"I'm used to the electrics in that place – know my way around them if you know what I mean."

Again Karl remained silent.

"One flick of a switch and the lift was stopped."

"You halted the lift?" Karl didn't hide his surprise.

"For a while only."

"And then you called up to check on Ariel?"

"I got to the top of the stairs and heard her music playing. I didn't like to go in. So I waited."

"Waited for what?"

"Waited to see if she'd leave. I was only looking out for her safety. You understand that, don't you?"

Karl was getting impatient. "What about Vicky, Pete? How long was she stuck in the lift?"

Pete moved across the room, his hands crossed behind his back. "I'm coming to that, Karl. God, ye young fellows are always in such a hurry. Not like my day when interviews went on for days sometimes."

"Busy times, Pete." Karl scratched his face, thinking that he'd need a shave if Pete didn't increase his pace and bring his account of events to an end.

"As soon as Ariel left, I went back down and flicked the switch again." In his head, he could still hear the lift rattling its way to the top and, letting out a long deep sigh, he wondered how it could have been different.

"I presume Vicky knocked and got no reply? How did she get into Number 105, Pete?"

"I'm coming to that now. As I said, those flats are in poor repair – the cheapest of everything went into the building. Vicky was in a right state when she got out of the lift . . ."

"Where were you at this stage, Pete?"

"Keeping a close on eye on her from down the corridor. She should have left when Ariel didn't answer the door."

"But she didn't?"

Karl followed Pete to the window, moving to stand

beside him, noticing the perspiration on his brow, the peak of his cap obliterating it slightly.

Pete took a handkerchief from his pocket and dried his face. "She pushed the damn door and it opened."

Karl waited once more for an explanation.

"The clasp is loose and Ariel had a mop and bucket in her hand when she came out so she mustn't have closed it properly. She'd been washing the floors by the looks of things."

"Did you go in after Vicky, Pete? Is that what happened?"

Pete's breathing became slightly laboured, a heavy rattle in his throat. He brought a hand to rest on his chest. "No! That's not how it was."

"So how was it, Pete?" Karl licked his lips.

"She put on the light and went in. She had no right to trespass. She shouldn't have been there."

"Don't get agitated now, Pete. You're nearly there."

Pete nodded, his face very flushed, beads of perspiration on his brow again. In his head, he was back at the scene again, standing in an alcove on the landing with a perfect view.

"I watched her charging into the flat and flicking on the light. But she was barely inside the door when the light went out. The bloody fuse must have blown again. I only said to Ariel last week that they weren't strong enough."

Karl laid a hand on Pete's arm. "Did you go in to the flat at this point, Pete?"

Pete shook his head in denial, a faraway stare in his

eyes. "I could see her silhouette, the lighting in the hallway shining through the open door. The shriek she gave scared me half to death. One minute she was storming across the floor and the next she was crumpling to her knees, collapsing onto the wet floor."

"Surely you went in then, Pete?"

He wrung his cap nervously in his hands. "I froze. The silence was frightening, an awful deathly silence, the same as the night my Barbara collapsed."

Karl ignored Pete's tears. "I want you to think carefully, Pete. Did anybody else witness this?"

Pete looked at him blankly and nodded. "The man who hit her. He was already inside waiting. One fatal blow to the head with a golf club. He brought it down on the back of her skull. She couldn't have survived the blow he gave her. I reckon he knew exactly what he was doing. Judging by the strength he used, murdering that girl was no accident. I'd say 'twas that guy who'd been intimidating Ariel. I'd say he got the wrong woman."

Karl didn't allow the old man's ramblings to distract him from his line of questioning. "And then, Pete? Did you call for help? Did you try to stop him?"

Pete hung his head in shame, exhausted by now, his breathing laboured and uneven, his hand clutching his chest. "He walked out of that flat as if nothing had happened, leaving her lying there in a pathetic heap."

Karl stepped closer to Pete. "Did you see his face, Pete? This is important."

"Just his nose," Pete said, his mind flooding back to the moment the oversized youth had left Number 105, wearing a dark anorak-style jacket and his hood up. "His hood covered most of his face but his nose looked odd, like he'd broken it at some point."

"You didn't approach him, try to make him stop?"

"I'm too old now, Karl. When I was young like you, it was different. I was different. But on Monday, there was nothing I could do except wait."

"How long did you have to wait, Pete?" Karl jotted a few things down in his notebook. "Yer man was gone within minutes. He took the lift down. I went as far as the door, but she was on the floor, flipped over, not a stir out of her. I knew it was too late for her."

Karl was struggling to remain patient, knowing if he hurried the old man he'd get confused. "Did you call for help?"

Pete sighed. "I left the door of the flat open and made my way downstairs. I called the ambulance once I was outside. But then I left. I didn't wait for it to arrive. I didn't want to be involved. I didn't want to get the blame. You see, I shouldn't have stopped the lift. I went back to work and tried to forget."

Karl sighed. "You should have waited to speak to the emergency services, Pete."

The older man took off his cap, his hair damp underneath. "I can't save them all, Karl. I'm too tired. Ariel was my last. One day, you'll ..."

But Karl didn't get to hear Pete's words of wisdom, watching instead as his body wilted, the colour draining from his face as his legs buckled underneath him and he collapsed in a heap on the floor.

"Oh, shit!"

Karl ran to the door and shouted for Ben's help, getting to the phone as quickly as he could and dialling the emergency services.

Kneeling down beside Pete, he felt the side of his neck, relieved to get a pulse, however weak.

"Don't die on me, Pete," he said, loosening his tie and opening the top buttons of his shirt to free his airways. "You're the nearest I have to a witness."

In that instant, Karl got an unexpected and frightening flavour of the terror Pete must have felt when he'd watched Vicky Jones crumple to the floor and die instantly. Out like a light.

Chapter 51

Fintan sat at Vicky's piano, unable to play as much as a scale, yet needing to hear the distinct sound from the ebony and ivory keys.

"She played well, Fintan, didn't she?"

He looked at Joan in confusion. "Did she play for you?"

"She played 'Amazing Grace' and some other fancy stuff that night you took Olly and Callum. It was beautiful."

She was beautiful, Fintan sighed, staring at the keys and remembering the lightness of her fingers as she brought the piano to life.

"Are you sure you want to stay again tonight, Ma? What about himself? Won't he be giving out?" Fintan didn't want his mother to leave, dreading the thought of being in the house alone.

"He'll always be giving out. It's part of who he is, but believe it or not he wants me to take care of you now."

Fin nodded, accepting her words.

"Who was that on the phone, love?" she asked a few moments later.

Fintan continued tapping out random notes. "Detective Wilson. They've picked up their man. There's a special court sitting tonight. He's being charged with murder. Mistaken identity, Ma. She was murdered in place of somebody else. He'd been blackmailing Ariel Satlow, was lying in wait to take her out because she'd begun to defy him. It's so damned unfair." He brought his fist down on the piano keys, the tuneless thud vibrating through his body, vibrating through the whole house.

Joan went and put her arm around her son's shoulders, his weight loss visible, his grief palpable with every breath he took. "I have no words of comfort, son. What he did was animalistic. I hope he's locked up for a long, long time."

"But it won't bring her back, Ma. Nothing will ever bring her back." Tears coursed down his cheeks, plopping onto the piano as his fingers slowly made their way along the keyboard, gentler this time.

Joan's heart ached for her son's pain. "Shh, love. She's an angel now. Keep that in mind. It's the only way you'll get through this awful time. Now, will we see how Olly's getting on? He's been in the kitchen a long time making that surprise for you."

She held out a hand and Fintan grasped it tightly, tears in his eyes, a large gaping hole where his heart used to be.

Still, for the sake of the little boy in the kitchen, who'd insisted on doing something to cheer his uncle up, he went with his mother and pretended to enjoy broken crackers and hard lumps of cheese.

Chapter 52

A week later, Ariel placed a letter of resignation on Ben's desk. "I haven't been honest with you, Ben. I don't expect you to keep me on."

Ben swivelled gently in his chair, turning to look at Marcus before responding.

"Don't you think we should be the judges of that?"

She swallowed hard, her throat dry. "Yes, Ben. You should. And you too, Marcus, of course."

Marcus smiled across at her, still unable to believe that Ben had convinced him to disclose the vested interest he held in the business and play a more responsible role in the day-to-day running of the company.

"Karl Wilson's techno specialists have verified your files were tampered with so I guess you're a better consultant than we were giving you credit for."

Ariel shuffled her feet under her chair, wishing they'd stop stalling and put her out of her misery. And while she appreciated Marcus's comforting words, she knew Ben wouldn't let her off quite so lightly.

"I can't say I'm happy with the way you deceived me," said Ben. "And everybody else for that matter."

"I am very sorry, Ben," she said, clearly and distinctly. "And I'm not going to make any excuses. What I did was entirely out of order which is why I've written this letter of resignation."

He nodded, glancing at Marcus again.

"We've discussed it at length, Ariel, and feel you're certainly worth a second chance. I think this office has been through enough already. We're already down two staff. I don't really want to make that three."

"How is Pete?" Marcus cut in.

For the first time since she walked into the room, Ariel relaxed. "His heart operation went very well and the scars are healing. God love him. I know what he did was dreadful but coping with a heart condition as well as depression, you'd have to feel sorry for him. He has a very long road ahead."

"Give him our best next time you see him. Tell him I'll be up for a chat next week."

Ariel nodded. Despite the seriousness of what happened, she couldn't ignore the efforts Pete had made on her behalf and had been his first visitor after his operation.

Ben cleared his throat, bringing their attention back to the task at hand. He'd mulled over the situation for days and felt the decision he'd arrived at with Marcus was more than fair to all concerned.

"A year's probation, Ariel. It's up to you to prove we can trust you, that you're one of the team."

Ariel nodded gratefully, extending her hand and warmly shaking both of theirs in turn. She'd make sure they wouldn't regret it. Either of them. And now that a new investigation was underway about her embezzlement case and the prime suspect was up on a murder charge, she had a good feeling that things might work out a lot better than she'd ever have dreamed.

"Thanks so much. Both of you." She couldn't stop grinning.

"By the way, Marcus," she added, ripping her resignation in two, her eyes twinkling in merriment, "I'm still waiting for a response to that email I sent you. Maybe we could brainstorm our client lists together? You can let me know."

Epilogue

One year later

Fintan stood on the podium, shocked by the huge attendance and waiting for the applause to subside before delivering his opening speech.

Staring at the sea of people before him, he smiled at his mother who was squeezing her way up to the front to let him know she was there to support him. As she had been for the past twelve months.

"You may as well get started, Fin," Simon nudged him, "or we'll be here all day. And we'll never get that round of golf played!"

Fintan took a deep breath in and tapped the microphone gently. "Ladies and gentlemen, boys and girls," he began, "it gives me great pleasure to declare the Vicky Jones Play Centre open."

The thunderous applause that followed allowed him a moment to swallow the lump sticking in his throat.

"Losing Vicky left a huge void in my life, a void I

know I'll never fill. But thanks to the support of family," he found his mother's face in the crowd once more, visibly taken aback to see that his father was standing beside her, along with George, Suzi and their four children, "neighbours," this time he looked to Simon at his right-hand side, "and loyal friends, I haven't fallen apart." Again his eyes strayed through the crowd until he found his work colleagues as well as Ben Ellis and Marcus who'd worked diligently to bring this day to realisation.

Ariel had also played her part but to be sensitive and fair to Vicky's memory, she had remained firmly in the background, working diligently from behind the scenes.

Fintan glanced at the notes he'd prepared the night before, discarding them at the last minute and speaking from the heart instead.

"As well as playing the piano, Vicky's other passion in life was peace of mind and contentment, a state of mind she felt everybody – young and old – was entitled to. On the day she died, she asked Ben Ellis to become involved in a charity for under-privileged children. In Vicky's memory, Ellis Enterprise have become a proud and generous sponsor and this magnificent building behind me, as well as the huge adventure playground out back, is thanks in no small part to their huge donations."

"It was my idea, Uncle Fin!" a young voice shouted up at him from the crowd.

An uproar of laughter followed and Fintan beckoned Olly to join him on the podium, lifting him up in his arms so everybody could see him.

"This, ladies and gentleman, is my nephew, Olly. And the play centre was indeed his brainwave! Who better to ask what children need than children themselves? And now there's nothing left to say except – have fun!"

More applause followed by a huge rush of children scrambling to be first inside to play.

"I'll walk Scamp with you tomorrow, Uncle Fin," said Olly. "Deal?"

"Deal, Olly!" Fintan laughed, giving his nephew a 'high five' and smiling as the little boy rushed off to catch up with Callum. Olly had adopted Fin as his favourite uncle, only too happy to spend time with him, particularly since the arrival of Scamp into his back garden. Wearing a smile on his face for Vicky, Fintan made his way through the crowd to extend his heartfelt thanks for everybody's support, wishing as he'd been doing for the past twelve months that he'd listened to his wife's needs, convinced their relationship wouldn't have been torn apart if he had.

"Dad, Jenny's asked me to go for coffee."

"Want me to tag along?"

Edel smiled at Marcus but shook her head, reaching up to plant a kiss on his cheek. "I'll be okay. And she said she'll drop me home later so there's no need to worry."

He laughed and watched her go, reaching out to put an arm around Ariel who had joined him from the back of the crowd, her eyes red, her cheeks tear-stained.

One year on and she was still having difficulty

418

coming to terms with what happened. And not only the horrific murder in her flat and the fact that guy had been lying in wait for her. It still baffled her that she hadn't noticed something amiss with Vicky, hadn't noticed how much she despised her. Then, as her counsellor kept telling her, do we ever really know people? Do we ever know what's going on inside their heads?

"Looks like we've an afternoon to ourselves, Ms Satlow," Marcus whispered in her ear, bringing a smile to her face. "Any ideas on what we might do to pass the time?"

"Why don't we take a walk on Howth Head and remember Vicky before we go home and pack?"

"Good idea," he said, taking her hand in his and leading her through the crowd, more than ready to move on to the next chapter in their lives.

They were leaving for the Middle East the following morning – originally marked on Ariel's map by Vicky's red X. It would be their first trip together and Ariel's first journey abroad since she'd been granted the freedom to travel once more, her personal farewell to Vicky's troubled mind.

THE END